S. Bra
July 2

It Could Happen Again

OTHER BOOKS BY THIS AUTHOR

~

The Journey Home

The Stolen Years

The Lost Dreams

Silent Wishes

Southern Belle

Savannah Secrets

ISBN: 979-8-832371-65-8

Fiona Hood-Stewart

It Could Happen Again

A Novel

LELVR

It Could Happen Again

Published by Les Éditions la Voix Royale SA
Rue des Pilettes 3, 1700 Fribourg Switzerland

ISBN: 979-8-832371-65-8

~

To Sergio and Diego

Acknowledgements

Many thanks to Rose Chervet for La Maison des Anges, my editor Teresa Racekova, art designer Oleksii Zgola in Ukraine for his tireless work despite the shelling, and Gillian Cronson and Kim Paynter-Bryant for their insightful comments along the way.

"Sow a thought, reap an act;

sow an act, reap a habit;

sow a habit, reap a character;

sow a character, reap a destiny."

Chapter 1

Ephraim Wolf sat in his wheelchair at the dining room table of the Brooklyn apartment he'd lived in since he'd first arrived in New York in 1946. He was about to bite into a thin slice of buttered toast when the phone jangled.

"You take it, Mrs. Katz. It's the man about the heating. I complained to the building manager two days ago but they've still done nothing," he called in a querulous voice. Then he pulled his glasses out of the breast pocket of his velvet robe and peered at the selection of jams in the silver holder. Ah! Bavarian black cherry. Good. His favorite since childhood.

"I'm sorry, Mr. Wolf, but it's not the heating man, it's your great-nephew on the line. He says it's urgent."

"Oh, very well." Ephraim accepted the receiver of the 1970's house phone. "Hello, Carl. *Wat* are you ringing for at this hour?"

"Carolina Hampton just died. I'm at the penthouse waiting for Luna now. I thought you'd want to know."

"I see. When will the funeral take place?" Ephraim asked. The intonation of Carl's voice sounded exactly like his used to before old-age, tobacco and swallowing irritation altered it.

"Maria, the maid, says there's to be a wake first. According to her, Luna is insisting it be held here because she thinks the energies at the funeral parlor are contaminated. Don't ask. So, Fran E. Campbell will be bringing the casket over later this afternoon. I'll call you as soon as I know more."

"Very well. Thank you for calling, Carl." Ephraim handed the phone back to Mrs. Katz and sighed. "Old Mrs. Hampton just died," he remarked. "There won't be many of our generation left soon."

"How old was she?"

"Three or four years younger than I am, I believe."

"That's quite an age."

"Yes, I suppose it must seem so."

"The newspapers were sold out because of the election results," Mrs. Katz said, pouring more tea into Ephraim's cup. "I told the Strauss boy to see if he can get a copy at the deli."

"I doubt they'll have one. A divided country buys newspapers. And it was obvious to anyone with any sense that the man would win."

"It was?"

"The people can always be brought to the bidding of leaders. That is easy. All you have to do is tell them they are being attacked, and denounce the pacifists for lack of patriotism and for exposing the country to danger. It works the same everywhere."

"You say such clever things, Mr. Wolf."

"That wasn't me, Mrs. Katz. I was quoting Hermann Göring."

"Herman who?"

"Göring. The founder of the Gestapo and Hitler's greatest ally."

"Oh. Would you like some milk?" Mrs. Katz tilted the china jug. The right side of her auburn wig hung at an odd angle.

Ephraim replaced the morsel of toast on his plate. "Mrs. Katz, how many years have you worked in this house?"

"Fifteen next August, Sir."

"Fifteen next August. And you still ask if I take milk in my tea? Are you an amnesiac or just plain stupid?"

"I'm sorry, Sir."

"So you damned well should be. Milk in my tea, indeed. Lemon, my good woman, and thinly sliced. And make me another pot. This isn't Lapsang Souchong. It's Ceylon. And far too strong."

Mrs. Katz scuttled back to the kitchen.

Ephraim muttered under his breath. He pulled the cashmere throw testily up to his midriff and tucked the corners into the sides of the wheelchair.

Carolina Hampton gone. They were never close or even liked one another. Why should they? She was a Polish aristocrat and he was a Jew, and never the twain shall meet. Her death was not significant, but it brought home his mortality and all the unresolved issues still pending, and the memories of those long dead or disappeared from years ago. He also realized that while Carl had been the Hampton's family business manager for twelve years — thanks to *his* relationship with Henry Hampton to whom he'd sold several fine pieces during his career as an art dealer — he'd never actually visited the penthouse on Park Avenue, or seen the Hampton collection.

Ephraim rolled himself into the dimly lit living room and peered at its walls. He'd built up a reasonable collection himself over the years. Nothing compared to the Hampton one of course, nor his own family's back in Munich before WWII. His father, Aaron Wolf, had been one of the finest art dealers in Europe before he, and his twin brother Eli, were deported by the Nazis in 1938 and murdered in Dachau.

Ephraim stopped the wheelchair by the window and lowered the break. The leaves falling relentlessly onto the sidewalk reminded him of those peaceful days of his early youth in Munich, Germany, in the 1920s and 30s. Days he recalled clearly, despite the passage of time. It felt like only yesterday he and Eli — the bright one, the joker, who made everyone except him laugh — sat curled on the tapestried cushions, drawing faces on the frozen panes of the bay window in the salon at the Wolf-family home. There, Mademoiselle Celestine, their French governess, had filled them with a love of literature and all things foreign. Did the snow- covered gardens that glistened in his memory still exist?

He'd never gone back or sought to find out what happened to his childhood home. Maybe it had been bombed at the end of the war or converted into apartments. Baron von Heil, Papa's closest friend, had bought the property to avoid it being sold to an Aryan for a pittance. But the Baron had apparently been shot near the end of WWII, and his only son had entered the church. There were no known descendants. The state had likely robbed all their properties too. Whoever was fool enough to believe there were no Nazis left in Germany in the collective post-WWII-guilt-trip, was an idiot. Ephraim had thought of making a claim, but it would have required delving into other areas of the past he preferred to leave well alone.

He picked at the loose bit of leather dangling on the arm of the wheelchair. Should he tell Mrs. Katz to have it repaired or buy a new one? He might not live long enough to make it worthwhile. Stupid woman. Milk in his tea. The only sensible thing she'd said this morning was to name the month: November. That alone triggered memories. Who nowadays remembered Saint Hubertus and the official opening of the hunt?

In those far-off days, he and Eli had driven out to Schloss Heil, the Baron's family castle on Bavaria's most beautiful lake: the Tegernesee. Ephraim recalled the fall of 1933 and the murmured conversations among the adults about Hitler, the new Chancellor who'd declared the Third Reich. The name Göring surfaced. Despite a rising wave of anti-Semitism, the new Minister Without Portfolio declared Jews were not in danger, and everyone, including Papa, had wanted to believe him. Thus, the Baron and Papa and a Swiss banker friend, continued to hunt while the children played with their nursemaids, laughing and kicking the russet leaves that a few years on would turn dark with caked blood.

Faces and memories drifted with the leaves falling onto the Brooklyn street below; Eli beating him each time they'd raced to the lake … the Swiss banker's children whose names he couldn't recall … little Florian von Heil, trailing a one-eyed teddy bear behind Karina Lanzberg, a distant cousin, as she pushed her doll's pram along the gravel path. And then there was Rainer. Handsome and aloof, a moody teenager in his Hitler Youth uniform, his shoulder propped against the oak tree as he twiddled his swastika pin. All of them either dead now or disappeared.

"I brought the fresh tea, Mr. Wolf. Shall I bring you a cup?"

"Tea?" Ephraim looked up. "Ah, yes the tea. Pour it if it makes you happy. And make sure to give me lemon," he grumbled. "And Mrs. Katz, since you won't be in tomorrow, make sure my dark grey suit is brushed and one of my cream silk shirts with the embroidered initials properly ironed. I'm going to the wake."

Chapter 2

That morning, two unquantifiable events had crashed head-on into Luna Hampton's life: Donald Trump had won the presidential election, and Nana — whom she'd secretly believed would live forever — had stepped off the stage of life, leaving her orphaned for the second time. Forget Doctor Schultz and the emphysema and Nana being ninety-three. That wasn't how it was meant to be.

"She's gone."

"What?" Luna spun around.

Rachel, Nana's nurse of many years, was rescuing a drooping cigarette from between her fingers above a singed hole on the satin counterpane.

"Nana? Are you okay?" Luna grabbed the old lady's pulse beneath the cuff of the lace nightgown.

Nothing.

The flutter that was life had flown.

"I'm afraid she's dead, Luna," Rachel said.

"No she isn't! She can't be!" Luna shook her head. Surely Nana wouldn't disappear without warning?

They'd discussed the possibility of her death countless times, but never for real; only in a remote, abstract kind of way — the way you talk about something you don't believe would ever happen. They'd even set up a means for Nana to communicate with her from the other side; a security measure to ensure they could stay in touch.

Luna stared at Nana's palm lying in hers and followed the parallel life lines etched in the grooved skin curving upwards from between the thumb and index to her wrist. She raised it gently and stroked the veined inner forearm willing life to return.

"Please don't leave me," she begged.

The cuff of the nightgown slid back to the elbow. "Oh my God! What's that?" Luna cried.

"A bruise. We tried altering the needle of the drip from one arm to the other, but her skin was so fragile it was inevitable." Pushing Luna's hand aside, Rachel pulled the cuff back down abruptly.

"Wait. That's not a bruise, that's something else. Let me see." Ignoring Rachel's attempt to stop her, Luna dragged the cuff back up.

"Oh my God! It's a tattoo! Those blurred traces are numbers!" She gasped.

Her grip loosened. Rachel took advantage and dragged the sleeve brusquely back in place.

"I can't believe this," Luna whispered, unbelieving. "Nana was deported? But that's impossible, she never told me!"

"Leave her alone. She wanted no one to know. No one, do you understand? Now, let her go in peace." Rachel hissed.

Luna struggled for breath like a sparrow caught behind a window pane.

Propped against the pillows, past folds of damask in the center of the four-poster, lay a silver-haired doll draped in *dentelle de Bruges*, three rows of pearls clasped about her neck and watched over by filigree angels and a baroque Madonna peering from their perch above the headrest. Nana, Carolina Hampton III, born Countess Carolina Maria Orlowska, in a castle in Poland. Nana, who'd popped up in Luna's life like a Fairy Godmother, plucked her from the Colombian convent who'd discovered her — a days old baby in a trash can — and brought her to live with her and darling Henry, her husband, in their Park Avenue palace, thirty floors above the world when she was four years old.

And now, like Henry, Nana was gone. She'd opened their secret door and stepped through the magic mirror and left her. She'd disappeared among stitches of laughter, doe-eyed jealousies and hushed heartaches; a palette of memories spread across a century-old canvas; a work in progress embellished by Luna's own brushstrokes; an omniscient Velazquez in a background of *Meninas*, a vicarious witness, a co-creator of long lost souls, more real to her than the living.

"Luna, you must leave the room while I do what needs to be done," Rachel said.

"Why would they deport a Polish countess? It makes no sense," Luna whispered, ignoring her. "I have to know the truth."

"Luna dear, forget what you saw. Don't dwell on it. Remember her only as she wanted you to. And now please, you must step outside. It won't take long."

"What?" Luna blinked.

"I said you must leave the room a moment while I prepare her. It'll only take a few minutes."

Rachel's voice reached her like a distant accented murmur from another time. Her mohair cardigan smelled of washing powder and shadows, and her arm around Luna's shoulders weighed heavy with secrets. In all these years, the middle-aged spinster in the dipping tweed skirt had never touched her or called her dear.

Luna fixed her gaze on the sleeve that hid the truth. But Rachel had folded Nana's hands in a pose reminiscent of a Medieval saint: serene, bejeweled and stately.

"Please, Luna. This must be done before rigor mortis sets in." Rigor mortis. Death, rigid, implacable and final.

Luna hesitated, then leaned down and kissed the sunken cheek. Her hand shook as she gently lowered the paper-thin eyelids over the witnesses of those untold truths Nana had chosen not to share.

Now she looked asleep.

"I'll be right back darling," she whispered.

Retreating from the bed, Luna picked her way on tip-toe across the strips of daylight piercing the half-open slats of the electric blinds and followed the patterns on the carpet — a childhood habit like Hansel and Gretel's trail of stones in the forest — to ensure her safe return to Nana's side.

At the door, she stopped and glanced over her shoulder. Rachel had switched off the TV and was removing the sagging bag of morphine from the stand next to the bed. The throw Luna'd slept under for the past three months, as she and Nana followed the heated presidential campaign, lay strewn on the armchair in the same crumpled state as the country. Her laptop stood open. She'd left off writing as red spread across the electoral map like flames from a dragon's tongue and the Democratic headquarters had gone into silent shock.

Closing her eyes, she inhaled: stale cigarette smoke, fresh lilies and yesterday's present become today's past; a lifetime of truths jolted by the faded revelation on Nana's arm.

Alternative facts? Not lies exactly, just part of Nana's life she'd chosen not to reveal? But why? It made no sense. If only Nana would speak to her, send her some sort of signal or message, something she could interpret to dispel the shock.

Luna opened her eyes. Rachel stood expectantly next to the bed, her hands poised on the coverlet. Luna waited another split second for something to manifest.

Nothing.

But for a siren on Park Avenue thirty floors below, and the carriage clock ticking among the silver frames on the chest of drawers between the French windows, all was quiet.

Reluctantly, she turned the door handle, stepped out into the corridor and swallowed the emptiness.

Chapter 3

Luna stared at the bedroom door wishing she hadn't given into Rachel's insistence. But it was too late.

A few aimless steps led her to the foyer where she stood under the three-tier chandelier. She unclenched her fists and brushed away tears and unanswered questions. How could life in the penthouse continue so eerily undisturbed when her world was toppling on its axis? The lozenge marble floor gleamed, the crystal sconces reflected in the English mirrors and the wrought iron staircase with H.D.H. — Henry Durham Hampton III's initials entwined in gold leaf continued to preside from the landing as if nothing had altered. Even Juan, the butler, hummed a *vayanata* in the dining room as he polished the silver. The hoover purred in the study.

Past the drum table and the crystal vase with the twenty-four long-stemmed white roses was *The Girl in the Red Dress Under the Moon,* the Chagall painting Henry had gifted her on her twenty-first birthday. This was the designated tool via which she and Nana had decided to communicate if one day, God forbid, she passed over into the spirit world. They'd gone over it time and again: Luna would observe the painting, and if the goat flew higher or the violinist tipped further or there was any kind of change or movement, then she'd know they'd connected. Simple. But was it? If reality was not reality, how could she be sure of anything any longer?

Luna moved closer to the painting and stared hard at the girl in the red dress. She looked sadder than usual. But maybe that was just wishful thinking. She mustn't let her imagination run away with her. This was her only possible connection to Nana. And right now, she needed answers; there was no room for false illusions.

The colors blurred and her eyes hurt. Nothing had budged. The flying goat and the violinist and the synagogue whirling in cloud looked exactly as they always had. Luna drew her eyes away. Maybe it was too soon. Maybe Nana needed time to adjust to her new state.

But who was she? Rather, who had Nana been? A countess in a ball gown with a diamond broach, or a young girl in a sack dress embroidered with a yellow star? It had never occurred to Luna to question those impossibly romantic WWII stories. But what if Count Stanislav and Prince Carol — the heroes of her adolescent dreams — were merely figments of Nana's imagination? She'd lost count of the times she'd dreamed of them riding off in their braided uniforms, wielding their sabers as they led the cavalry charge to a glorious death. Or held the Count's wounded body strewn in the Polish mud and wiped blood from his wounds and sweat from his brow. Had she shed tears and prayed for a bunch of fictitious ghosts?

Propped against the tapestried wall, she dropped her face in her hands and let the tears flow. How could she have spent twenty-eight years in close proximity with Nana and never noticed the faded marks on her arm? No wonder she'd refused to wear sleeveless dresses. Of course she'd scorned older women who exposed their bare arms! The silent rule of never entering Nana's boudoir before she was fully dressed made sense now.

But why hide the truth? If Nana was Jewish, why keep it a secret? "Jesus, Nana. How the fuck could you?"

The clock on the landing chimed. Fifteen minutes had passed. She tried not to think what Rachel was doing to — oh my God — the body. She closed her eyes and shuddered and bit a loose piece of gel on her thumbnail and headed back down the corridor towards Naan's boudoir that connected to the bedroom. She must stay busy.

The connecting doors leading to the bedroom remained closed. She wished Rachel would hurry. But to interrupt the process would be disrespectful. She must find something useful to do until she'd finished. Of course! She'd choose Nana's clothes.

Luna spun around and faced the closet. Nana's outfit must be perfect. She'd make certain she travelled on her final journey the same way she'd gone to Europe: designer suit, a silk blouse, stockings and her favorite pumps. And an Hermès scarf. Nana would approve of that. In fact, she'd be seriously put out if it were otherwise. Forget Rachel in there and the rest for now. All that mattered was making sure Nana was as groomed and elegant in death as she had been in life.

She switched on the lights inside the walk-in closet; that unmistakable trace of Chanel No. 5 followed her like a paper trail as it had since age four. On the far wall, past rows of dresses and suits, floor to ceiling custom-designed shelves housed Nana's collection of Hermès bags. A *Sac à Dépèches* — a purse Nana said dated from before WWII — stood locked in a glass case at the very top. Luna stared up at it. How was it possible? How could Nana have held onto such a purse in a concentration camp? And what did this other silent witness have to tell?

She closed her eyes. Tattooed arms, barbed wire, men in jackboots and Chanel pumps swam past her.

"Luna."

She turned. Maria stood a few steps away. "She's dead," Luna whispered.

The tiny uniformed maid nodded. "I called Mister Carl. He's on his way over here."

Luna flung herself into her arms and sobbed. She sobbed as she used to sob when she was little and Maria was big. She sobbed until no sobs were left but those that could, or would not subside, and that she'd carry inside forever.

She drew back and swallowed.

Maria picked one of Nana's lavender scented handkerchiefs out of the drawer and handed it to her.

A dull, rhythmic thud beat in Luna's chest. She blew her nose and swiped the streak of wet hair stuck to her cheek.

"I must choose Nana's clothes," she gulped, blowing her nose again.

"*Muy bien*. The gentlemen from the funeral home can take them. They are waiting." "What men? What funeral home? Who told them?" Luna cried.

"*Senora* Rachel, she call them."

"But that's impossible. I don't understand!"

Luna burst out the walk-in-closet, hurried through the boudoir towards the connecting door and reached for the handle. She twisted it hard. Once. Twice. Then jiggled it until the door shook.

"Rachel?" She cried. "Open up at once!" But the door remained locked.

Chapter 4

"Rachel!" Luna screamed. She rammed the door twice with her shoulder, then kicked it until the key fell out on the other side and it burst open. Regaining her balance, she ran inside the bedroom. The bed was empty, the covers drawn back, and the pillows dented where Nana's head had rested.

"Oh my God!" she screamed, hands flying to her mouth. "Nana … NANA!" Maria gripped her right arm.

"Calma, Luna."

"She took her, Maria. Rachel robber her from me. She knows things that she doesn't want me to know," Luna cried, shaking her off.

"Stop!" Maria ordered. "*Señora* Rachel must have had the funeral home come and take Dona Carolina away to make things less painful for you. *Venga*."

"I don't believe that. She doesn't want me to know the truth about Nana."

"You're upset." Maria patted her hand. "You must be strong now for Dona Carolina. She no like to see you like this."

Luna withdrew her fingers from Maria's hold. She moved across the room and sat on the edge of the bed. Then laying her hand on the embroidered edge of the century-old Egyptian cotton sheet, she buried her face and stifled her pain in Nana's pillow. Those traces of tattoo: those hidden marks altered everything she'd held sacred. She's wished she'd never seen them, wished she could think of Nana as she always had. But it was too late. She had no choice now but to seek the ugly truth hidden under layers of lace and lies.

A dull indefinable pain spread through her heart, gnawed every inch of her gut and infested each particle of her soul like galloping leukemia. Déjà-vu. Somewhere deep in her psyche this feeling was not unfamiliar.

"... a complete earthquake. This was an earthquake unlike any earthquake I've seen since Ronald Reagan in 1980. It just came out of nowhere. Nobody expected it ... I mean Pennsylvania? Republicans haven't won it since '88 ... Wisconsin! I can tell you, as a Republican, we don't do well in Senate races in blue states in presidential election years. Something happened last night that will forever shake up the coalitions that make up the Republican and democratic parties ...

"Yes. There have been many historic astounding and shocking moments over the course of this campaign ..."

Luna sat up and searched frantically for the remote hidden under Nana's pillow that she'd inadvertently turned on. MSNBC and Morning Joe went silent. Luna sighed and placed the remote on the nightstand next to Nana's reading glasses. It was finished. Nana's race was over just like the presidential campaign: with a slew of unanswered questions.

"Luna, you can't stay there." Maria's voice reached her from beyond the drapes and cherubs.

"*Porfavor.*"

"*No*! Please Maria, I just want to be alone."

Alone. Alone with her memories: Henry holding her up to touch the angel on top of the Christmas tree... Nana in her beautiful ball dress and diamond tiara... pink laces dangling from a pair of pink sneakers way above a floor too far to reach.

"Luna, I hear the elevator bell. It must be Mr. Carl, and you must go and receive him." "Ok, ok... I'll go. Just give me a few minutes on my own. Take him to the drawing room and give him a coffee or something," she muttered. "And tell him to find Nana and get her back here. We'll have a proper wake right here at home."

Luna climbed onto the bed and sat curled under the tented swirls of fabric secured by the chubby cherubs ready to dive head-long into her ribs. It was here she'd always found refuge. Now with Nana gone, would it be the same?

"You think that is *correcto?*" Maria tilted her head and frowned.

"Of course it's right. I won't let Rachel dictate. Carl must get Nana back right away. I'll call Father Murphy and tomorrow we will have all of Nana's friends over at the penthouse. And I won't have Nana sending her last hours above earth in some dreadful funeral parlor, smelling of rose air-freshener and men in dark suits with folded hands and sad solicitous smiles, pretending they care. No way! Who knows who may have lain there in some gaudy casket. Nana wouldn't like it. If she refused to fly commercial, Maria, it is unlikely she'd hob-nob with any old spirit that might be lurking there."

"Bueno... I tell him." Maria shook her head, rolled her eyes, and moved towards the doors.

Luna picked up Nana's half-empty pack of cigarettes off the nightstand and sat silently twisting it as a plan took shape in her mind. Then she wiped her nose on the back of her sleeve, braced herself, slid off the bed and carefully smoothed the counterpane. She'd return here later and grieve, but now she must attend to business. Nana would expect her to be brave and dignified. Whoever else she may have been during those 93 years she'd spent on earth, one thing was certain, she'd been a stickler for good manners and doing one's duty.

Chapter 5

Carl Wolf first met Henry and Carolina Hampton's adopted daughter 12 years earlier when he'd come to work for them. At times over the years, he'd believed he and Luna had gotten closer. At others, she retreated into a shell as hard to pry open as a pearl in an oyster.

Now he observed her, curled among the cushions in the corner of the living room couch, shrouded in black from head to toe like a Sicilian widow. It was hard to believe they'd found her in a Colombian convent. She looked more Euro than Latino. Had the Hamptons put in an order for a blue-eyed, chestnut-haired child of European descent when they'd adopted? He wouldn't put it past them. One thing was sure, there was nothing remotely South American in her lineage. That Cinquecento face and the hair falling over her shoulders could have walked straight out of the Renaissance. Even with red eyes and blotched skin, and the damp handkerchief she twisted relentlessly between her manicured fingers, she looked more like a Botticelli Venus than J.Lo.

The Hampton blood might not run in her veins, but she was poised, educated and impeccably groomed. Everything you'd expect a Hampton First Daughter to be. Several generations worth of class had rubbed off on her, as well as the family fortune. Now, at thirty- two, and with Carolina gone, she had it all.

Carl liked Luna, but at times she irritated him with that absent, childlike and almost flaky manner, as though she lived on another planet. Granted, maybe she did. Living an entire existence closeted up here in the Penthouse with Carolina and Henry equated to living in another age.

Perhaps her Faye side was due to the strange manner in which Carolina and Henry had chosen to bring her up. He'd never understood why they'd opted to have her home-schooled. Surely attending school would have been an obvious choice for an only child? She certainly wasn't dumb. She'd graduated with a *Summa cum Laude* liberal arts degree from Vassar, and then went on to do a Masters in psychology and a PHD in something — he couldn't recall what — at Columbia. That's where she met Jeff, the mouse freak. The Hampton Trust had funded millions in projects for his science lab. Lucky bastard. He'd pinned Luna nicely to the wall like a butterfly in formaldehyde. Or had he? Maybe it was the other way around and *he'd* been selected as the fiancée? Luna didn't seem to mind having few or no friends of her own generation and appeared quite content living here with Carolina and Henry in their time warp. They formed a strange, tripartite nucleus sufficient unto themselves of which Jeff didn't form part.

He returned to what she was saying.

"… and Rachel asked me to leave the bedroom for a few minutes and the next thing I knew the door was locked and she wouldn't let me back inside. In the meantime, she'd called the funeral home and had Nana removed without so much as a by-your-leave. Who does she think she is?"

"Perhaps she removed the body to save you distress?"

"No! She didn't. She did it because of the ta—"

Carl waited for Luna to continue, but she'd obviously thought better of it. After all, he wasn't part of the family, was he? He just worked for them, and made sure their wealth was well looked after and increased each year to support their lavish lifestyle.

"You were saying?" He prompted.

"It's not important," Luna shook her head. "You're right. She's probably dealing with the shock of Nana's death too."

"We all have different ways of dealing with loss." Carl cleared his throat. "Fran E. Campbell said they'd bring Carolina back here by the end of the afternoon."

"Thanks for organizing that, Carl. I haven't told anyone except you and Father Murphy that she'll be here tonight. I want to have these last hours together alone. We'll share the waning moon together for the last time. A few days ago, Nana's astrological chart indicated a passage. I guess death and rebirth are that; a transition from one state of being to another," she sighed. "Do you believe in astrology?"

"Uh, I've never thought too much about it. When we were married, Amy used to read the horoscope in the paper, but that's about it." Carl glanced at his watch. "I'm afraid I have to run. Susan from the office is in charge of letting people know about the wake tomorrow afternoon, and I've dealt with most of the administrative details. I've talked to Jake Morton at the State Department and he's getting in touch with Arlington Cemetery about the burial details," he said, about to rise.

"Thanks Carl. I appreciate all you're doing. I haven't gotten to grips yet with the fact they're both gone. It feels so weird, so… so empty. It's really good to know you're here."

The sincerity in her voice plucked a string. Carl cleared his throat. "You know what? Don't think about any of that right now," he said gruffly. "Let's get you through the next few days. Now I'll be off and leave you to rest. You'll need it. It's going to be a long night."

Luna nodded. She unfurled her legs and slipped her right foot into the ballerina-styled slipper she'd shed on the Persian rug. She reminded him of the prince with the glass slipper in the movie *Cinderella*. Then she rose and the grieving Manhattanite was back.

In the foyer, next to the Chagall, Maria stood holding Carl's overcoat and gloves. "Thanks, Maria." He shrugged on the coat and turned towards Luna standing in front of the brushed metal elevator doors, her hands politely folded, waiting to see him off.

"My goodness. I almost forgot," he exclaimed. "My Great-Uncle Ephraim sent his condolences. He'll be coming to the wake tomorrow. He wants to pay his respects."

"Really? That is so awfully kind of him, but are you sure he should at his age?" Luna said.

"He's determined to make the effort."

"Then please tell him how deeply touched I am." Her eyes filled once more.

"I will. You take care, okay kiddo?" He squeezed her shoulder and pecked her left cheek. Technically she was his new boss but his role was one of consigliere. Henry had made that clear.

The elevator doors opened and Carl stepped inside. He pressed *ground*. Amy, his ex- wife, who never missed a chance to criticize, used to say it was easy to be gracious with that kind of money. That might be so. But there was something vulnerable and sincere about Luna, as though she needed to be shielded from the world. Which of course was ridiculous since she was more than protected for several lifetimes to come. Henry had seen to that.

The elevator doors opened and Carl stepped into the lobby. “Good evening, Sir.” The doorman touched his cap. “Evening, Manny.”

“We’re all sorry about the Countess,” the doorman sighed. “She was a fine lady. A real *senora*.”

“She was. Make sure no one from the press disturbs Miss Luna, okay?”

“You can count on me, Sir.” Manny drew himself up to his full 5’4”, and opened the entrance door with panache.

As Carl climbed inside the Uber, Luna and her future weighed on his mind. He was responsible for her finances, but what about the rest? What would she do now that she was on her own and with no other purpose other than consulting the stars? Would she finally marry Jeff, or was this her chance to get a life?

Not that it was any of his concern what she did, he just had to make sure the money was there to do it.

Chapter 6

It was nine in the evening by the time Luna halted before the double paneled doors of the dining-room-turned-funeral-parlor and braced herself for the ordeal she'd been dreading all afternoon. Incense and strains of Rachmaninov seeped into the foyer. She wished — oh how much she wished — these last hours above earth with Nana could be spent differently. But what choice was there? Either she ignored her misgivings and identified the tattoo on Nana's arm tonight or she'd forgo the opportunity of uncovering the only lead she had to Nana's truth.

Luna turned the door handle. The General, Henry's fifteen-year-old King Charles spaniel named after General Lee — followed her as she crossed the threshold into a *chiaroscuro* world. It took several seconds for her eyes to get accustomed. Little by little she distinguished the baskets of white roses and lilies — a gift from Nana's florist of 50 years to their oldest and most prized customer — perched like expectant flower girls on the buffet. The wreaths and bouquets that had poured in all afternoon lay dotted about and the moiré watermarks of the drapes she and Nana had replaced only three months earlier, shimmered in the Florentine mirrors on the walls.

Luna's gaze moved to the center of the room. Lying in state on the Georgian dining table Henry had inherited from his Great Aunt Emeline — a feisty lady who'd saved generations of family antiques from General Sherman's fiery descent on Atlanta — was Nana's casket, and kneeled on a cushion next to it was Maria, with her hands like small walnuts, bobbing to the count of her rosary beads and her bun, tightly scraped into the nape of her neck, swaying back and forth like a pendulum to the rhythm of her murmured prayers.

Luna swallowed and approached the casket. Four large wax candles in ornate silver holders stood poised like Knights in shining armor at each corner. She placed the sheaf of sage she'd brought to clear the energies carefully at the foot of the casket and peered at Nana. Her silver streaked hair resting on the white satin cushion was perfectly coiffed and her face — bathed in an aura of shimmering crystals that dripped like moonshine from the chandelier — looked strangely translucent; a fairy Queen on a funeral pyre of dreams ready to sail off to join the Gods.

The General grunted and went to lie in his favorite spot under the dining table. Scrambled eggs, roast beef, lobster Thermidor and half a century's worth of animated political debates raging across an aisle of silver cruets, fine English porcelain and wit had ceded their spot to the mistress of the house on the first lap of her final journey. There was no sign of Rachel. Perhaps Carl was right and she had the body removed to save Luna the pain of seeing her leave on a stretcher covered by a blanket.

She took a deep breath. She would not break down. Not now. Time was of the essence. She couldn't delay what had to be done. Mustering her courage, she stepped closer and laid her hands on the satin trimmed edge of the casket. Was it the hypnotic cadence of *Ave Marias,* or the candlelight playing tricks, or did Nana just smile? All at once their complicity was back and Luna experienced an urge to tickle her cheek as she used to years ago when she'd climb next to her in the Angel bed and Nana had kept her eyes firmly shut and pretended not to notice. Was she pretending now? Perhaps she'd open her eyes and rise from the bed of white satin, straighten the skirt of her designer suit and say, "Enough of this nonsense. Tell Juan to bring around the car, darling, and we'll dine at the Grill!

If only...

Luna bit back her tears and focused on the veined hands, folded over a single rose just below the midriff. Nana's golden wedding band glistened and cream-colored ruffles protruded from under the cuffs of her beige jacket sleeve. Identifying the tattoo by herself wasn't going to be easy. She glanced down at Maria then back at Nana. Outwardly everything looked perfect, yet below the layers of fine wool and silk, lurked the traces of a hidden past.

Maria! Why hadn't she thought it earlier? Of course, Nana couldn't have gotten by all these years without someone other than Rachel noticing the tattoo! Henry must have known and Maria had helped Nana wash and dress on Rachel's days off.

Luna peeked at the rosary beads gliding past the maid's fingers. There was still a way to go. She'd give it a couple more minutes, then seek her assistance. Reaching her hand out, Luna touched Nana's cheek and travelled back to their last conversation that morning. How was it possible that one minute she'd been smoking and discussing the election result and the fissure tearing the country apart that had finally split, leaving bits of melting iceberg floating in an ocean of unpredictability, and the next she was gone?

~

"Good morning, darling,"

"Good morning, Luna dearest. Have I overslept? What month is it?" Nana whispered. "It's November."

"November. Of course." Nana's eyes closed once more. "Did that man lose the election?"

"No. He won."

"I should have guessed. He's a man, and the world is afraid. That's a recipe for winning any election. *Plus ça change*... "

"Maybe it won't be so bad."

"That's what they said when Hitler came to power."

"But it was different back then, Nana. Now people have a voice. They protest. Half the country voted for Hilary. That *means* something in America. Not to mention, there's Congress and the Senate, and the executive and the judicial branches are all separate. The system works. Let's have a little faith."

A faint smile.

"November," Nana repeated. "It's so long ago, yet it all seems like yesterday." "What does?"

"The year it snowed in November."

She was wandering again. Luna glanced at the morphine bag on the metal stand to the right of the bed. Was the dosage too strong? She didn't like it when Nana drifted. Perhaps she was getting dehydrated. Luna reached for the plastic beaker and held it carefully to the old lady's parched lips. "Here, darling, have a little water," she coaxed.

"No, thank you."

"But you need to drink. Dr. Schultz said so." "I know darling, but not now."

"Rachel should be here any moment. Should I ring for Maria to bring your breakfast tray?"

"Very well. But I'm not hungry." "You must keep your strength up."

Luna pressed the button on the wall next to the headrest that signaled to Maria in the kitchen to bring in the tray. Nana likely wouldn't eat more than the tiniest spoonful of yogurt and brown sugar, but she must pretend things continued as normal.

"If we're in November, then it'll be your birthday soon," the old lady remarked.

"Not until February. And please, don't remind me! Thirty-two and not much to show for it. That's depressing."

"Don't underestimate yourself, Luna. How often do I have to tell you what a beautiful, intelligent, talented and sensitive young woman you are? What is it you keep writing on that machine of yours?"

"Nothing, really. Just notes. Thoughts for a novel that'll likely never leave my laptop," she muttered. Leaning across the bed she helped the old lady sit up comfortably against the pillows, then rearranged the folds of her robe.

"Why worry about writing a novel? Shouldn't you marry that nice science teacher?" Nana said.

"He's not a teacher, Nana. He's a Professor Emeritus at Cornell. And his name's Jeff," Luna rolled her eyes.

"Yes, yes. I know that. The one with the mice," Nana responded testily. "You've been engaged to him for far too long."

"Seven years. But Jeff would likely freak if I actually set a date," she murmured. "Anyway, he's been invited to spend a year at Oxford University to lead some department or other so it's not likely we'll marry any time soon. Still, apparently, the mice are doing very well. He even named one Carolina, in your honor."

"How very flattering." Nana's dry laugh turned into a cough, and Luna took her in her arms and eased her back down against the pillows, as the physiotherapist had taught her.

"Be an angel and light me a cigarette," Nana croaked.

"You're coughing. You know what the doctor said."

"*Ach*, leave the damn doctor out of it. He's an idiot. I want Dr. Feinstein back. He never talked nonsense like this one does. I'll only take a few puffs."

Luna reached for the cigarettes on the nightstand. Why protest? How could she deny Nana the single pleasure she had left? Plucking one out of the half-empty pack she lit it, leaned closer, then inserted it carefully between Nana's dry lips and held it while she took a long, satisfying drag. Forget second-hand smoke. Like her second-hand life, she was used to breathing her grandparents pack-a-day each, and Henry's *Romeo & Julieta* cigars were as much part of her existence as their past was her reality.

After a last puff, Nana leaned back and closed her eyes — the signal for Luna to stub out the cigarette in the ashtray on the nightstand. The stubs had gotten longer the past few days. But Dr. Schultz had said only to worry the day Nana *didn't* want to smoke anymore.

"Why don't you read me something from the newspaper?" The old lady murmured. "Only please, nothing more about this wretched election. It's over and done with now. I'm just sad I won't live to see a woman in the White House, but so be it."

"Of course you will! Hilary will run again in 2020 and you can vote for her then." "No, dear. I'm afraid it's over for the both of us."

Luna made no comment, simply sat on the chair next to the bed and unfolded *The New York Times.* "Let's see." She flipped the page. "Oh, here's something you'll enjoy: a fuchsia pink, alligator, Hermès Birkin with gold and diamond hardware, sold for $150,000 at an auction to a Russian oligarch."

"How very vulgar!"

"That's rich coming from the woman with the largest collection of Hermès purses in Manhattan!"

Silence.

Luna looked up. Nana had turned suddenly pale. Luna dropped the newspaper and grabbed her hands.

"Nana! What's happening?"

"Luna, there's something I must tell you." "Tell me what, darling?"

"It was in November of '38 that we first—"

An ethereal smile lit Nana's features. "Listen to me carefully, child." Her words were barely audible.

"I'm listening, Nana." Luna bent closer.

"I haven't got long to go," Nana said. "He's here, you see. He's come at last and he's waiting… And he's waited for so long."

"Who? Who is waiting? There's no one here, Nana. Just me," Luna reverted to her childish tone.

"I can feel him getting closer and closer. *Endlich bist du da mein Engel*—" Nana's right index twitched. She raised it abruptly. Then her eyelids drooped softly and the half-raised finger fell back on the sheet. "His *Romeo & Julieta*—it's in the Sa—"

"Please, please stay," Luna begged, choking on tears and squeezing her frail fingers. "Darling, answer me!"

But Nana's eyelids had dropped again and there was a subtle alteration.

~

The general grunted. Maria's prayers still echoed through the dining room and Luna returned to the now. Was she right to identify the tattoo and override Nana's wishes? One thing was certain: whatever her reason for hiding the truth, it must surely be a powerful one.

Ten minutes had passed and there was no more time to lose. Luna slid down onto the cushion next to Maria and nudged her. Maria broke off her prayer and turned.

"Maria, I need your help," Luna whispered. "Should I call *Senor* Carl?"

"No, no. Not that kind of help. I'm going to ask you a question and I want you to answer the truth. You know that Dona Carolina had a tattoo on the inside of her left arm, don't you?"

Silence. The maid hesitated.

"Maria, you have to tell me. It's *muy importante*."

"*Si*," she whispered reluctantly. "I see the blue marks. But *Senora* Rachel she tell me I must promise not to tell nobody nothing, never. She say it's Dona Carolina's *secreto*."

"Maria, I have to see that tattoo before they take Nana away." "But that's *imposible*. The marks they very, very faded.

"I have to try, and you must help me pull up her sleeve." "Luna, to touch the dead is *sacrilegio!*"

"But don't you see? I have to," Luna said in a loud whisper. "Nana tried to tell me something just before she died, and I'm certain it had to do with what's on her arm. Maria, pleeeeease," Luna begged as she used to years ago when she wanted something. *"Ayudame!"*

"*Hay Dios mio*," Maria crossed herself.

Luna rose and helped her to her feet.

"You stay on this side of the casket and I'll go to the other." She stepped around the dining table and poised her hands in readiness. "Okay, let's do it," she said taking a deep breath and closing her eyes a second. "I'll lift her arm and you hold it while I pull back her sleeve. Are you ready?"

Maria muttered. Luna touched Nana's hand gingerly, as though dipping a toe into freezing water. The skin felt taut and cold. She cringed, then told herself not to be silly. It was the same hand she'd held all her life, wasn't it?

Don't freak. You can do this.

She peeked at Nana's face. Her eyes seemed to flicker. Surely it was just a reflection caused by the candle.

"Her fingers are stiff," she whispered.

"Of course they is stiff. She is dead, *no*? And dead people is stiff. Dead people no want no one to disturb them, Luna."

"But I have to—"

"Stiff fingers is a sign *directo* from God what you're doing is wrong!" Maria hissed. "I don't give... I'm doing it anyway. I have to identify the number."

Their eyes locked across the corpse in a tug of wills. Then muttering under her breath, Maria shook her head and reluctantly raised Nana's wrist. Luna braced herself, then hesitated. Gas ovens and barbed wire flashed. She had no choice. She must draw back the sleeve of the jacket enough to uncover the forearm. Taking another deep breath, she folded back the left cuff of the jacket only to reveal the shirt ruffles hid a row of tightly closed buttons.

Luna fumbled with the buttonholes. Maria prayed.

At last they were undone. She closed her eyes and tried not to think of what she was doing. Her heart raced and her fingers trembled. Maria's worn fingers held Nana's frail wrist up, her lips pursed in disapproval.

Luna's mouth was dry as she prepared to roll up the sleeves. "Nana, please give me a sign, something to let me know it's okay," she whispered.

Nothing.

"Okay," She muttered leaning forward. As she reached for the sleeve the dining room door burst open.

"*Santa Madre ayudanos*!" Maria gasped. Nana's arm collapsed onto Luna's hand.

"Forgive me, child, I startled you whilst you were in prayer." Father Murphy said.

Luna gaped at Nana's priest approaching like a frigate in full sail and tried to free her hand.

Nana, for God's sake let go! She screamed silently.

As though adhering to her request, the arm loosened and she retrieved her fingers just in time to take Father Murphy's outstretched hands in hers. "I'm sorry I'm late. I came to watch over her with you, dearie. Good evening Maria."

Cold sweat trickled down Luna's back and between her breasts.

"Good evening, *Padre*. I am happy you are here. Now Dona Carolina can rest in peace," Maria said, sending a meaningful look across the casket at Luna. "I know for sure God will have a good place for her in the heaven."

"From your mouth to God's ear," Father Murphy nodded.

"Father, how kind of you to come," Luna managed, masking her dismay. "It's only natural that I would spend the last night here with her."

"But surely you shouldn't stay up all night? You'll be exhausted, what with the wake and the burial in Arlington the following day. I'll be perfectly fine here with Maria," she assured him.

This couldn't be happening. Father Murphy's arrival was the *last* sign she'd expected from Nana.

"No, no," the priest shook his head firmly. "I promised Carolina I'd look out for you as I do all my flock, and a promise is a promise," he said.

Letting go of Luna's hands he stood next to the casket and peered down at the corpse. "She was a fine woman, no doubt about it. She could be difficult at times, we both know that, but there we are. Now, do you have a glass of whisky for an old Irish priest, my dear?"

"Whisky?" Luna glanced at Maria slipping out the door. "And one for your good self, too."

"I don't drink whisky."

"Well then, maybe it's time you did. A dram never did anyone any harm, my dear. Call that good fellow Juan and ask him to bring a bottle of the Jameson Henry kept in the study. We've got the whole night ahead of us." He stooped over the casket again and muttered. "Let us drink to a smooth crossing, and may her soul rest in peace."

At four in the morning Father Murphy was as good as his word, snoring softly in one of the armchairs Juan had brought in earlier, ankles comfortably crossed on the ottoman and a bit of tartan sock peeking out from below his right trouser leg. The tumbler with his third dram lay loosely clasped between his hands on his portly belly.

There was no sign of him leaving before morning. Maria reentered shrouded in shadows and carrying fresh candles. She snuffed out the guttering ones and replaced them one by one, then joined Luna next to the casket, head bowed, and slipped to her knees.

"I must get to the tattoo. I have to try once more," Luna muttered. "No, Luna. You cannot."

"I must!"

The ormolu clock chimed.

"Jesus, Joseph and Mary!" Father Murphy exclaimed, heaving his bulk out of the armchair and straightening his jacket. "I fell asleep. What a disgrace. I'll never forgive myself.

Luna scrambled to her feet. "It was sweet of you to stay this long Father, and I'm sure Nana is grateful, but I think you should go home now and get some sleep. Tomorrow will be a long day. We all need to rest." Luna said.

"Nonsense! I've just had one dram too many. Two's my limit nowadays," Father Murphy said, regretfully.

"Think of the third one as Nana's."

"Ah, Luna," he sighed, smiling. "You're a fine lass. Even as a wee thing you were always kind and giving."

Luna watched helpless as Father Murphy's knees creaked onto the cushion she'd vacated and he took out his rosary. Could Nana have confided the truth to him under the seal of confession? She eyed the glowing tip of his red nose. Somehow she didn't think so.

She tapped Maria's shoulder and drew her towards the window. "He won't leave!" She whispered. "What do I do now?"

"*Nada*! Don't' you see? Dona Carolina bring him here so you no look for no tattoo, Luna. Now leave it alone. Let her go to her grave with her secret.

Was Maria right? Was this Nana's way of telling her not to pry?

Light trickled from the terrace lamps past the drapes and the potted palms. Nana had spoken. And as always she would obey.

Maria left the room. Father Murphy remained on his knees and Luna pulled one of the dining chairs up next to the casket and sat down. Maria had hidden the unbuttoned cuff and folded Nana's hands back over the rose. Luna stretched her arm over the edge of the casket and placed her fingers over them. These were the last moments she and Nana had to share on earth and for now she had no choice but to abandon her quest. But she wouldn't give up. No way! Somehow she would discover the truth. She'd make a request to the Universe and wait for an answer.

Father Murphy muttered and Luna's mind drifted. Nonentities crossed her mind: she'd cancel the General's vet appointment… she'd forgotten to call Jeff and tell him Nana had died. Strange. Shouldn't she have called her fiancé at once? The truth was, Nana and Henry — the only two people she'd ever loved — were gone and everything seemed insignificant.

A wave of loneliness swept over her. It felt oddly familiar, as though somewhere in the far reaches of her memory she recognized the sensation.

As dawn seeped into the dinning room Luna reached down and posed her lips on Nana's brow. And all at once Maria's words: *she will have a good place in the heaven* came back to her. Was it true? Would Nana have a front-row center seat next to Henry as she had at the Met, or was her place among the victims of a concentration camp?

"Travel safe, darling."

Then leaving Father Murphy to his prayers, she slipped away.

Chapter 7

Ephraim Wolf stepped out of the elevator and into the marble foyer of the Park Avenue penthouse, leaning on his silver-knobbed cane and his great nephew's right arm. Two men in dark suits conducted guests towards the dining room where presumably, Carolina Hampton was laid out.

Ephraim stopped under the chandelier and took stock of his surroundings. He should be living in a place like this, not a middle-class apartment in a building that stank of gefilte fish and matza bread at Yom Kippur. And he would have, if all had gone according to plan all those years ago, and Papa and Eli had cooperated and trusted him, instead of playing the heroes.

The Latino butler took his coat. "Shall wc go in?" Carl asked.

"Just a moment." Ephraim turned towards a gilt mirror and straightened his tie. Dealing in art might not have brought him the fortune he'd anticipated, but he hadn't lost his elegance.

Behind them the elevator doors opened, disgorging more guests. "I think we should go in," Carl said.

Ephraim cast a last glance in the mirror. As he flicked an imaginary speck of dust from his lapel, his hand stopped in mid-air. His eyes stayed glued to the painting reflected in the upper right-hand corner, and he caught his breath. Surely it must be a mirage?

Carl took his arm and nudged him, but Ephraim stood motionless, staring at the Chagall hanging above the console on the opposite wall.

"*Das ist unmöglich,*" he hissed.

"Is something the matter?" Carl asked.

Ephraim's head felt light. He swayed and his knees gave way. "Uncle Ephraim, what's wrong?" Carl grabbed his elbow.

But the old man didn't hear. He was back in Munich, on a misty October afternoon in 1938 stepping into another foyer...

~

Ephraim unlocked the front door of the turn-of-the-century mansion nestled in the secluded privacy of a lush garden in Borghausen-Herzogpark, Munich's most sought after neighborhood, and stepped inside the hall of what, for several generations, had been his family home.

Why was the foyer empty? Where were all the servants?

He stopped next to the table under the chandelier, sniffed the long stem roses and listened to the sound of voices drifting from the library.

He removed his coat and scarf, then dropped them carelessly on the chair under his grandfather's portrait, and glanced inside the dining room. Was he imagining things, or was some of the silver on the sideboard missing? At least the paintings were still all in place.

He stepped inside and peered at the picture hanging on the wall between the high, draped windows that looked out onto the well-tended gardens. Personally, *The Girl in the Red Dress Under the Moon* didn't appeal to him, but the Nazis couldn't get enough of Chagall, despite his works being officially labeled "Degenerate Art". No doubt one of these would satisfy Rainer's superiors. What a coup it would be if he could pull it off. But Papa and Eli would notice its disappearance. He'd have to find some excuse. If only they weren't narrow-minded and could see the bigger picture as he did. Sometimes, he thought them plain stupid.

Ephraim stepped back outside into the entrance hall.

The voices drifting from the library grew louder. It was Eli — the cocksucker — and Papa. Why had his twin always been Papa's favorite? Even as children when he'd tried so desperately to do well, Eli had invariably surpassed him be it at sports or in school. Not to mention the fucking riding trophies. He was the one who'd rode well until Eli decided to take up horseback riding and win one damn trophy after the other. Which wasn't fair after *he'd* gone to such pains to overcome his fear of horses, only to please Papa. And Eli drew; those silly, American cartoons everyone said were witty and satirical, but these days could get him into big trouble.

Of course, if Mama hadn't died, she wouldn't have allowed them to leave him out. He was only four years old when she'd left him, but even then, he knew that he, Ephraim David, was her *Bubelein*.

A glance at himself in the ornate mirror below the stairs, told him why. Who wouldn't like his light skin and eyes — so different from the rest of the family's — and his curling lashes. People said Eli had charm, but he looked dangerously Sephardic and Ephraim was pleased he'd taken after his mother's Ashkenazi ancestors.

Ephraim tip-toed towards the library and lurked in the shadows. Cigar smoke, worn leather and muted voices reached him through the door that remained ajar. As always, Papa and Eli were huddled in there together. How he hated their complicity, that bond of which he was not a part. He cocked an ear.

"… can be taped inside the back of the canvas of *The Girl with the Red Dress Under the Moon,* then covered," Papa was saying. "It's a small painting and easy to transport. But we must decide upon a code for the bank account. It should be something commonplace we can talk about publicly, if necessary."

"How about the—"

Ephraim frowned. He missed the last word of Eli's sentence.

"*Ach*! Good thinking, my boy. You're a bright one, Eli. A pity Ephi doesn't have your brains. I worry about him you know. He's so easily influenced and I don't know who his friends are these days. He could get into trouble. It's terrible to say this of one's own child, but I'm not sure he's trustworthy."

"He's not. In fact—"

Ephraim caught his breath. Did Eli know his secret? Was he going to give him away? More importantly, they were making plans, plans that apparently did not include him. His throat knotted. Tears burned his eye sockets. Should he burst in? Tell them what he'd just heard and have it out with them? Or would they feed him more smooth lies that would leave him wondering whether he was insane?

~

"Uncle Ephraim, drink this."

A voice reached him. Gradually, the images faded and he returned to Park Avenue, to Carolina

Hampton's wake, to Carl crouched next to him holding a snifter.

"Have a sip of this."

His hand shook as he lifted the cognac. Delamain. He'd recognize it anywhere. Trust Henry Hampton to only drink the best. He peered across the foyer at the Chagall. Could it be the one? Surely it couldn't have been here all these years without him knowing it?

Several mourners stood by solicitously.

Ephraim handed the snifter back to Carl. "I'm fine. Don't make a fuss, please. I'm so sorry. It's just a turn, nothing to worry about." He attempted to smile, then leaned back still staring at the Chagall through narrowed eyes. It was too far away to be certain.

"We'd better get you home," Carl said, rising. "But I should at least pay my respects."

"Never mind about that. I'll explain to Luna that you didn't feel well. She'll understand."

"I must see that painting," Ephraim muttered. But the butler was holding his overcoat, and Carl said the limo was downstairs.

Back in the car, Ephraim's mind was travelling thousands of miles across an ocean of memories.

"How do you feel?" Carl asked.

"I'm fine," he answered curtly. Leaning back, he stared out the window at the flow of afternoon traffic, thinking of the Chagall. How long had *The Girl in the Red Dress Under the Moon* been in the Hampton's foyer, only minutes away from him?

As the vehicle drew up to his building, Ephraim turned to his great-nephew. This was no time to blurt out something as important as what he believed he'd discovered. First, he must think out his strategy. Then Carl would come into play.

"I'm tired tonight. I think I'll turn in early. But once you've dealt with all the arrangements and you have some time, come over. There's something I'd like to discuss with you."

"Sure, Uncle Ephraim. If it's regarding your house insurance policy, I've dealt with that." "Thank you. No. This concerns another matter."

"Is it urgent? I could pop upstairs for a few minutes now if you like?" "No, no, my boy. It can wait. I see Mrs. Katz is waiting."

"Okay. Then, if you're sure you'll be alright, I'll go straight back to the wake."

"Of course."

The limo slowed. The chauffeur got out and helped him out of the car. Carl hovered solicitously and Mrs. Katz took his left arm. It irritated Ephraim to be treated like a mental deficient just because he was old. For although his body was weak, his mind was in good shape.

As they were all about to find out.

Chapter 8

Uncle Ephraim's building was like him: the sole survivor of an age when the neighborhood boasted well-heeled dwellers and still retained something of its former grandeur. As a child, Carl was proud that his great-uncle lived in a place with no cats on the stoop or kids lounging against the railings smoking pot and listening to Michael Jackson on their Walkmans, the front door always freshly painted and an intercom that worked.

It was mid-afternoon, three weeks after the wake, by the time Carl turned his key in the lock of his great-uncle's front door. Ephraim's endless calls had dogged him, but he'd been too busy to come over and visit sooner. The incident at the wake seemed to have destabilized him. He shouldn't have listened when he'd insisted on attending. It had obviously been too much for him. At times, Carl forgot his great uncle was ninety-six years old. His quick mind, dry wit and determination to remain independent, gave the impression of a younger man. That day he'd refused the wheelchair and appeared sprightly. What had happened to cause the malaise? It was as though he'd suffered a shock.

Carl was curious to know why the old boy was so anxious to speak to him so desperately, but years of mood swings had taught him to wait for the right moment before asking questions that would likely get his head snapped off.

He entered the hallway quietly, in case Uncle Ephraim was napping, and hung his coat next to several others in the oak armoire. That old-world scent he'd come across on several occasions when he'd visited Europe — a little musty, a little nostalgic, with hints of cologne and lingering memories — enveloped him.

He peered through the dining room doors. Mrs. Katz had left the tea tray ready: a lace cloth, a silver tea-pot and two English china cups with sliced lemon in them, a cake and a plate of finger cucumber sandwiches — like the ones Uncle Ephraim said he'd eaten at the Ritz in the 1920s. Carl didn't much like tea, but of course he'd be expected to partake of the spread.

He stepped inside the living room, surprised to see Uncle Ephraim up and seated in the wheelchair, close to the window overlooking the street. He appeared to be deep in thought.

"Hello, Uncle Ephraim."

Carl weaved among the fiddly bits of 18th century French furniture. Amandine, the Persian cat, sidled up and rubbed herself against his Brioni trouser leg. He wished she wouldn't do that. The hairs were hard to remove.

"Hello, my boy, hello. I'm glad to see you at last."

"I'm sorry it's taken so long. There was so much to do after the funeral."

The two men shook hands and Carl sat down on a tasseled cushion on the window seat. "How was the funeral?"

"There was quite a turnout at the cathedral — friends, dignitaries, you name it. The burial was just family and the usual Arlington pomp and ceremony."

"I don't doubt it. How's Luna bearing up?"

"I'm not sure. She puts on a good front but I sense she's very lost. Like she's wandering in a world of her own."

"Don't worry, she won't wander long with that kind of money," Ephraim answered dryly.

"I guess. How are you feeling?"

"I'm well. That is, I'm still a bit shaky."

"What do you think happened?" Carl frowned. "You seemed so well that day and then you turned around and the next thing I knew you were falling. Was it your blood pressure?"

"Perhaps. But let's not worry about that. Why don't you get the tea tray?"

"Sure." Carl headed towards the dining room. Uncle Ephraim seemed mellow today. He picked up the tray and returned with it to the living room.

"Put it here on the table between us. Ah! *Stollen kuchen*. A favorite of my mother's." "You remember that far back?"

"I'm not sure. Maybe one of the servants told me later on. They talked about her all the time. She was French you know."

"Yes, you told me." He didn't add *several times* not to appear rude. Uncle Ephraim liked to remind people that his mother had been a minor aristocrat whose father, a French civil engineer, was knighted at the end of the 19th century.

Carl poured the tea. Uncle Ephraim talked about the weather and the election and what he believed the future administration were capable of. Carl glanced surreptitiously at his watch wondering when he would get to the point. He hadn't been summoned here today for no reason. But Uncle Ephraim seemed to be in no hurry. He ate another piece of cake and sipped a second cup of tea.

"I'm sorry to appear impatient," Carl said at last, "but you said you wanted to speak to me about something in particular."

"I do, my boy, I do." The old man laid his cup back in the saucer and paused. "It's regarding the Chagall in the foyer at the Hampton's."

"What about it? Did you sell it to Henry?"

"No, I did not. In fact, that brings me straight to the point. Do you think you could find out where he acquired it?"

"I can ask Luna," Carl said, doubtfully. "The paining is actually hers. Henry gave it to her as a twenty-first birthday gift."

"I see. So, it's been there a while." The old man's fingers drummed the arm of the wheelchair.

"Yeah. About eleven years." "Hmm."

Carl waited. Where was all this leading?

"Any particular reason why you want to know where Henry got it?" He asked, casually. "Yes as a matter of fact."

"May I ask what that is?"

"Certainly, since it concerns you directly." "Me?" Carl frowned.

"Yes. I believe that Chagall belonged to my father." "Are you kidding?" Carl sat up straighter.

"I'd have to take a closer look to be certain, but I'm confident it's *The Girl in the Red Dress Under the Moon* that hung on the dining room wall at the villa. The one I told you was stolen by a Nazi officer."

"You mean the son of family friends and who turned out to be a traitor?"

"Precisely," Uncle Ephraim said in a clipped voice. "Neither the gallery paintings nor any of the ones from our family collection have appeared on the open market since WWII. Who knows where they may have ended up."

"It might just be a similar Chagall," Carl murmured. "Hel must have painted others in the same genre."

"No doubt. But if it is the original, you might want to consider how to get it back." "I'd have to look into it. What proof of ownership do you have?"

"What I believe to be hidden in the back of the canvas." "And what was that?" Carl's pulse skipped a beat.

"Information regarding funds he'd managed to get out of Germany." "Jesus Christ! Is this for real?"

"If the painting is the original, then yes. I'm counting on you, Carl. It's time we got some of what was stolen returned to us. But we must act quickly, there is no time to waste."

"This is unbelievable," Carl muttered.

Naturally, Uncle Ephraim was impatient. He'd spent three quarters of a century searching for his family's fortune. But they couldn't act rashly. What were the chances of the painting being the one? He was an old man. His memory and wishful thinking could be playing tricks on him.

Carl remained silent. He couldn't bring himself to voice his doubts. For now he'd play along.

"I'll talk to Luna." He said finally.

"Don't be ridiculous. She mustn't know a thing." Ephraim snapped.

"Why not? It's the obvious thing to do. I'm sure she'd be the first to cooperate."

"What faith you have in humanity, Carl. Sadly, life destroyed mine and I'm less sanguine about people's reactions when it comes to being divested of their patrimony. You think she'll hand over a valuable Chagall just like that?"

"But if, as you say, your father placed information in the back of the canvas, then that in and of itself would prove ownership."

"Ach! you are a *Dumbkopf*! You understand nothing of these things. Stop arguing and listen to me. I know what I'm saying. If she decides to take lawyers and go the legal route this could take years to resolve. And I don't have years," he said deliberately.

"I'll see what I can do. If it's true, it would be the most amazing coincidence."

"Coincidence? Synchronicity my boy. Don't you read Jung?"

Uncle Ephraim stubbed out the cigarette in the ashtray next to him and inserted another one carefully between his lips.

Carl peered at his great uncle out of the corner of his eye. He was staring out the window likely far into the past. Could this be the beginning of dementia? Should he call Dr. Frankel and have him tested? There was about as much chance of the story being true as there was for a meteor to land in Times Square.

"Very well, I'll look into it. I have a meeting set up with Luna for tomorrow night anyway. I'll see what I can find out, without giving anything away. And now I'm afraid I have to go."

"Go, dear boy. And Carl," Ephraim said reaching out a shaky hand, "I understand how implausible this must seem. But you're the only one I can trust. I'm relying on you to help right the wrongs that our family suffered."

Chapter 9

The crackle of logs, an Adam fireplace brought over from an English manor, and the sense of timelessness. How comfortable and secure Henry's study felt. What must it be like to grow up taking all this for granted? While Henry's ancestors lived in Palladian mansions in the Old South, his were escaping Pogroms in Odessa and more recently, Nazi persecution.

Upon his arrival earlier, Carl had stood before the Chagall and experienced a new sense of connection with his bloodline. He'd let his index glide over the ornate frame and looked at the synagogue in the Chagall's clouds and felt ashamed for distancing himself from his roots. Tales of Russian villages and ghettos and *Pitchipoi* had been a big part of his early childhood, but at eleven years old he'd chosen to step away from being a Jewish-American and opted to be simply "American."

It was that summer when he'd walked the three blocks from his parent's apartment one Friday at sundown with Mama complaining and Papa pretending to listen. They'd stopped in front of the *sheitel* shop to greet Mrs. Wasserstein and congratulate her on her daughter's acceptance to an Ivy League university. Mrs. Wasserstein wore a crisp white dress and a straw hat over her wavy hair. Her teeth glistened when she smiled. Apparently, she'd been to school with Mama, but you'd never have known it. She'd looked cool and fresh and expensive, and made Mama's flowered cotton print, the damp rings under her arms and the heavy flat shoes, seem dowdy. That day, as Papa asked polite questions and dabbed the sweat trickling onto his brow from under the beaver rim of his shtreimel, Carl vowed he would never wear outdated, Central-European clothes designed for sub-zero temperatures that would mark him out as different. He'd be like Great-Uncle Ephraim and wear smart suits and silk ties. He'd travel to Europe and see the larger-than-life world that his great-uncle described in such detail. And if he ever married, his wife wouldn't be frumpy and fat. Her hips would be boyishly slim like a model, she'd be classy and elegant, educated and a little distant. She'd carry a fine leather purse with a gold clasp like Mrs. Wasserstein's, and wear hand-made, calf-leather shoes.

Now, seated opposite Luna at Henry's desk, Carl removed his glasses and leaned back and observed her. She looked drawn and even skinnier than her usual slender self. "First world worries," a friend of his from Zambia once said; worries that touched 10% of the world's population, whilst the other 90% struggled to stay alive. To give Luna her due, she was neither spoiled nor arrogant. And it wasn't surprising that she was distraught. Carolina, Henry and she were a unit that functioned in a world unto themselves. It would take time for her to find her way; right now, she was like an astronaut floundering in space and searching for gravity. On the flip side, it was hard to feel sorry for someone lucky enough to be adopted into such wealth. If she chose, the world could be her oyster.

"These are the Hampton Trust quarterly reports," he said, sliding the last file across the worn leather desktop. "That's pretty much it for now. Unless there's something else you'd like to address?"

"No, that's fine. Is everything running smoothly with Nana's will?"

"Carolina's and Henry's was a joint will so foundation goes on just as before with you as sole beneficiary."

"Good. Then let's call it a night." Luna pushed her chair back. "Shall we sit at the bar and have a glass of wine?"

"Good idea."

Luna came out from behind the desk. Even in a pair of old leggings, an oversized sweater and her hair scooped on top of her head, the woman looked like a world-class model on her day off.

Carl loved elegance. Real elegance. The old-world kind that couldn't be bought and that came from generations of good genes and fine breeding. Where had Luna's originated? In his own case, he had no doubt that Great-Great-Grandfather Aaron exuded it. Uncle Ephraim certainly did. Carl took it as a compliment when his great-uncle said he reminded him of himself back in the day. Nevertheless, the old boy could be embarrassingly closed-minded, and his occasional moodiness tempered his good manners and spoiled the effect.

He had always gotten along well with Uncle Ephraim. It was he who'd understood that working for the high-pressure law firm Carl had joined straight out of Harvard Law was not his niche, and gotten him the job as Henry Hampton's business manager. At the time, it had seemed like a dream come true. Henry was a real southern gent. He never got flustered, never raised his voice and never gave a crass order. Always a polite request. That said, Carl had learned early on that *perhaps we should consider…* or *don't you think?* Meant make damn sure X Y or Z was dealt with as soon as possible. Which was fine. He'd admired the man with his Saville Row suits, designer ties and handmade English shoes, his Purple Heart and the influence he wielded. Carl had overheard several jovial, subtly-veiled phone calls with members on

The Hill, and whoever happened to be in residence at 1600 Pennsylvania Avenue.

Carl rose and joined Luna at the bar. He watched her study the labels on the bottles and leaned against a leather barstool. He pondered how to best broach the subject of the Chagall with her. Despite his insistence, Uncle Ephraim had categorically refused to let him tell Luna the truth. He understood his paranoia given all he lived through, but it was a setback that would require going behind Luna's back. And that notion disturbed Carl profoundly.

Carolina's diamonds on Luna's right hand gleamed as she placed cheese sticks in a crystal dish,

then reached for a bottle of Pouilly Fumé.

"How's your great-uncle doing?" She asked, handing him the bottle and the corkscrew. "I felt terrible when Maria told me he'd had a turn. If I'd known, I would have come to the foyer and made sure he was okay," she said placing the wine glasses on the bar.

"He's fine, thanks, but upset about the election. It reminded him of the rise of fascism in Germany in the 1930s. He's worried"

"Aren't we all! Apparently, the president-elect is even in denial about climate change and thinks the Paris Climate accord is bullshit!"

"Maybe temperatures in Palm Beach don't rise like in other places," Carl said, tongue in cheek.

"Yeah right. Or the temperature of the stock market makes it worthwhile ignoring," she riposted.

"Let's hope this isn't the harbinger of worse to come."

"Seriously. Already, people are voicing racist opinions they never would have a month ago. And the wall with Mexico... How crazy is that?

"Totally."

"Anyway," she said, raising her glass. "Go on telling me about your great-uncle and what happened at the wake. What do you think triggered his malaise?"

"It was the shock of seeing your Chagall," Carl said. This was the opening he'd been seeking.

"How come?" Luna frowned.

"Uncle Ephraim's father was a famous art dealer in Munich up until the time the Nazis arrested him in 1938, and deported him and Great-Uncle Eli — Ephraim's twin brother — to Dachau. Apparently, he owned an almost identical Chagall to yours that disappeared along with the rest of the family's collection. He's been searching for it ever since," he said, twisting the corkscrew.

He was tempted to tell her the truth, but habit — doing Uncle Ephraim's bidding — won. "Oh my God! No wonder he had a dizzy spell. I can't begin to imagine..." Luna's voice trailed off. She turned suddenly pale. "Are you okay?"

"Yes. I'm fine. For some reason, I find that period of history harrowing. Maybe it's Henry having been in WWII with the British Army, and in the second tank that entered Belsen, that makes it seem close to home. I was watching a programme last night—" She cut off and shook her head. "Poor Mr. Wolf. How terrible for him."

"Lately, Uncle Ephraim seems to go more and more back into the past. He talks a lot about politics in the 1930s. He says people should be made to remember just how fast a populist politician can alter the status quo and things can go south very quickly. The rhetoric he's hearing on the news reminds him of Nazi propaganda. An exaggeration, of course, but I guess when you've been through what he has, it's not surprising. Uncle Ephraim has never gotten over what happened to his family."

"I don't suppose anyone would," she muttered. "Does he ever talk about what actually occurred?" She asked, her expression thoughtful.

Carl poured the wine and handed her a glass.

"Not really. He used to tell me all sorts of wonderful stories about his childhood and going to visit his father's best friend, a Baron with a castle by a lake and their German friends, and how he and his brother were brought up with English and French governesses and all that, but he rarely speaks about the period after the arrest."

"How come he wasn't arrested too?"

"Luck. Destiny. Call it what you will. He was on his way home when he saw a truck of SS men and a staff car in front of his house. He slipped into the garden of the villa opposite and watched through the railings. He saw it all: his brother being dragged unconscious down the steps, and his father being thrown in the back of the truck like a piece of trash. He said it was the worst moment of his life. He wanted to rush in and try to save them, but he knew he'd suffer the same fate and be of no use to anyone. At least if he stayed free, he might have a chance of freeing them."

"And naturally seeing the Chagall brought it all back," Luna murmured.

"Yes. It did. I remember when Henry gave it to you," Carl reminisced, swirling the wine in his glass. "I'd only been working here for about a year and I remember thinking how amazing it was to be given a Chagall as a twenty-first birthday present, as though it was a box of candy. When I turned twenty-one, both my parents were gone. Uncle Ephraim remembered and gave me a tie. Otherwise, it was a day like any other."

"Oh! I'm sorry, Carl. I never knew your parents had passed." "I guess there's a lot we don't know about each other." "Weird, isn't it? Twelve years, and we've never really talked."

"Yeah," he smiled. "Why did Henry choose to give you that particular painting?" "He said the girl in it reminded him of me. Maria calls it the *Moon Girl* painting." "Luna. Of course. I wonder where he discovered it."

"I'm not certain. I believe it was bought from a private collector, but other than that," she raised her palms and shrugged.

"I see. An American collector?"

"I really don't know. I'm so sorry it upset Mr. Wolf. I guess if any little thing can trigger stuff, imagine something as significant as that—" She cut off abruptly and her eyes filled.

"Are you okay?" Carl laid his glass down and reached for her hand. *Where was the fiancé for Christ's sake? Fixing the mice's fucking cage?* It wasn't his job to be the boyfriend. Uncle Ephraim had hinted that he should consider dating Luna after he'd divorced Amy, but he didn't want to get into a relationship that could only end unsatisfactorily. He squeezed her hand in a friendly manner.

"Are you okay?" He asked again.

"I'm fine. Just your great-uncle's reaction to the painting reminded me of something that triggered a shock in me too and I—" She shook her head and drew her hand away. "I'm sorry. I'm being totally stupid. Let's drink to something positive. Like my trip!" She raised her glass. "Trip? What trip?" Carl feigned interest. Right now, he needed a valid excuse to retrieve the Chagall and get it to Uncle Ephraim. "My trip to Poland."

"Poland? Why Poland?" He frowned.

"I thought I'd visit Nana's birthplace. She talked so much about it and it might help bring closure. I feel useless here now that I'm alone. And with the holidays around the corner and everyone I meet depressed about the incoming administration, I thought..." She shrugged and took a sip.

"I see. What about Jeff? Is he going with you?" "No. It's over. Jeff and I broke up."

"Excuse me?" Carl brought his glass down on the bar, goggle-eyed. "You broke up with Jeff?"

"Actually, I did," she demurred.

"You're kidding, right? When did this happen?"

"Just before Thanksgiving. We had dinner in here on the card table. Maria prepared his favorite roast pork with *frijoles* and *patacones.* I didn't feel ready to share the dining table with Nana's casket."

"I can understand that," Carl muttered. The entire notion of Carolina lying on the dining room table had struck him as morbid and grotesque, but since Luna was determined to have it that way, he hadn't voiced an opinion.

"So what happened?"

"I'm not exactly sure. It was kind of weird. Like one of those surreal moments you see in a movie. I asked him how the mice were doing and…"

~

"The mice are doing fine. They're reacting positively to the new formula," Jeff said. He cleared his throat. "How are you feeling?"

"Ok, I guess. I've written so many thank you notes my hand's ready to drop. But it's hard being without Nana. Without her and Henry. At least I was with her right up to the end."

"It was a totally unhealthy existence. You never left the penthouse. Never went out."

"I know," Luna sighed. "Not even to vote. I felt terrible about that. By the way, Maria made these especially for you," she said, passing the *tamales*.

"Thanks."

"So, did you vote?" Luna asked.

"Yes, I took a few days off and went home to Birmingham." "Well, I'm glad at least one of us supported her up to the end." "Her?" Jeff frowned.

"Hillary." Luna laid down her fork and looked at him across the table. "Jeff, you're not seriously telling me you voted for Trump, are you?"

"Actually, yes. "

"Oh my God! How could you?"

"Well, the family are all supporters and I didn't see why not. We feel he'll do great things for America. The country's in a mess. Someone must put a stop to this hemorrhaging. Look how far it's gone."

"I can't believe I'm hearing this. You voted for Donald Trump?"

"It's my democratic privilege to vote for whomever I choose," he bristled.

"But you're a scientist, an intellectual, an educated human being. How could you give your vote to someone whose vocabulary is limited to 140 characters and thinks women should be punished for having an abortion?" She cried.

"Hey, don't get upset. It's over now and you'll see, he'll run a good show. Surely you didn't think an old lady who didn't have the stamina to get through the campaign on her own two feet could run the country?"

"Jeff, those are, quite literally, trumped up lies. Nobody is saying Hillary is perfect, but she's certainly one of the most accomplished, clever, and prepared politicians in this country, maybe even the world." Luna shook her head and threw her napkin down next to her plate.

"Maybe, but those emails... I dunno... and Comey coming out at the last minute... It's obvious there must be some sort of cover up," he said, reaching for more *tamales.*

"Oh, and Russia interfering with our elections doesn't bother you? And another thing, in all these years, you never told me you voted Republican."

"We never talked about it."

"No, I guess we didn't. Perhaps we should have."

"Luna, don't you think you're making a mountain out of a molehill? After all, Henry was a Republican."

"Henry, along with all the brave men and women, Republican *and* Democrat, buried in Arlington Cemetery — not to mention the Founding Fathers — must be turning in their graves seeing their country split down the middle, riots in the streets and their values shredded and destroyed," she threw. "Henry would never have voted for someone whose ideals are so far from the GOP's."

"For God's sake, Luna. Does this have to be such a big deal? Politics was never an issue before, why now?" Jeff sighed.

"Because it just became a big deal. There are people whose lives may be deeply affected by the decisions of the incoming administration. Many may be left with no health insurance, or even funding for research like yours could be scrapped."

"Now that you mention it, I wanted to speak to you about the project funding." Jeff wiped his mouth on the linen napkin and peered at her through thick lenses. "It's a bit awkward."

"Don't worry. I'll tell Carl and the trust will wire the money directly. He's a trustee and the rest of the board will agree."

"Thanks. I'm grateful."

"Good. But I think we should talk about us, Jeff," Luna said. "What about us? Nothing's changed, has it?"

"Actually, it has."

"Surely you're not going to let something as insignificant as a presidential election come between us?" He laughed.

"Jeff, I don't think I could spend the rest of my life with someone who believes in a man who says if he stood up and shot someone on Fifth Avenue, he wouldn't lose any voters, or calls Senator McCain — one of our country's great war heroes who spent years in a Vietcong jail being tortured — a loser."

"You're being ridiculous. He didn't mean it."

"Oh no? Then perhaps you'd like to explain exactly what he did mean?"

"This is absurd. I'm not getting dragged into an argument with someone as poorly prepared to discuss politics as you."

"Excuse me?"

"Let's face it, what views, if any, do you hold that weren't spoon-fed to you by Carolina and Henry? I don't think you're in a position to bandy opinions about."

"I have every right," Luna exclaimed. "Might I remind you that while you're attending to your mice, I actually follow current affairs and take notes."

"Notes? What for?" Jeff snickered. "Are you planning to write a treatise or something?" "No. A novel."

"You're joking, right?" Jeff shook his head, shifted his long legs out from under the small table, and rubbed his beard with the back of his hand. "Look, I've had enough of this discussion, let's talk about real life. I'm seriously thinking about that fellowship at Oxford next year. Being married would likely help advance my cause," he frowned.

"Excuse me? Am I hearing you correctly? That's the reason you want to marry me?" "Well, now that you've no more oldies to look after," he shrugged.

Luna placed her fork down and peered across the empty plates and *tamales* into his magnified eyes.

"Then you'd better find another fiancée Jeff, because after what I've just heard, I won't be marrying you any time soon."

"What?" He spluttered. Jeff's fork clinked on the plate. "Luna you're being ridiculous. This is a serious matter."

"A very serious matter. Which is why you should listen carefully."

Jeff sucked his cheeks in and looked her over as he might a newt under a microscope. "You know something? For years, my friends and family have been telling me you're a spoiled, selfish princess. But I wouldn't listen. I stood up for you. Even when the question of your gene pool and being adopted in Colombia from God only knows what kind of people arose, I never flinched. Who knows what may be lurking in your genes. Your birth parents may have been criminals. And genes can jump several generations. As my mother pointed out, what if there were blacks or Indians or even Jews in your past? Breeding is a risky business. But I'm not prejudiced."

"How magnanimous of you Jeff. Your solicitude and concern for your bloodline is touching. But you know what? You don't have to work that shift anymore. As of now, I'm returning your ring," she said, pulling the ugly ruby that belonged to his great-grandmother off her ring finger and placing it on his bread plate and rising. "Now, if you'll excuse me, I think we're done here. Oh, and before you ask, you'll still get your money for the project. Consider it severance pay for the seven years you apparently wasted blotting your pristine copybook with me in it. Good luck."

~

"Well I'll be damned." Carl said. "You seem to be taking it pretty well."

"Actually, I feel liberated. Do you realize I might have married a man who I'd never actually talked to about the things that matter? That's scary."

"You should be proud of yourself. Honestly Luna? I never imagined you were this gutsy. And a novel? I never knew you wrote."

"It's nothing, really. Just an idea."

"One you could pursue on your trip to Europe. When exactly do you plan to leave?" He asked.

"As soon as I can. There's still letters to write and people to thank."

"I see," Carl pondered as an idea occurred to him. The means to remove the Chagall legitimately from the penthouse had just fallen into his lap like a piece of ripe fruit. "I'll need you to sign a power of attorney so I can attend to matters while you're away. Did I mention that Sotheby's needs to do a new appraisal of several of the paintings?" He added, clearing his throat. He hoped his cheeks weren't as flushed as they felt.

"I don't recall you mentioning it, but I seem to forget everything these days," she apologized.

"It's for insurance purposes. Some of the policies need to be renewed. They date back at least ten years. I'll take care of it while you're away."

"Thank you." Luna held her glass in mid-air, then placed it carefully back on the counter. "Does the Chagall need to go, too?"

"Honestly? I don't know. I'll have to check the inventory to see which of the policies need updating."

"Okay."

Carl drained his glass and poured himself more wine. Having to lie to achieve his objective made him feel like a schmuck. Luna didn't deserve to be tricked, much less by her consigliere and business manager, but his loyalties were split. He owed it to Uncle Ephraim to at least try. The likelihood of the Chagall being the original was infinitesimal. But whatever the outcome, at least his great uncle would be appeased. As for the painting, it would be back in place within a few days, and Luna none the wiser. Right now was not the time to speculate. He'd crossed the Rubicon; it was too late turn back.

Chapter 10

Nowhere does the sun concede and evening possess with the audacity and grace as New York City.

Luna leaned on the icy balustrade of the West-facing terrace outside her bedroom wrapped in Nana's favorite mink and watched blood-orange strips sink across the West side. At this time tomorrow, she'd be on her first commercial flight to Europe. Henry and Nana had disapproved of her using public transport. The hazards spanned from flight delays to germs to possible "unsuitable" fellow passengers. But this time, Luna dug her heels in. Lately she'd surprised herself. Despite her grief and three weeks of sleepless nights spent watching documentaries of Auschwitz, Belsen and Treblinka and trying to piece together bits of Nana's hidden past, she'd sent her fiancée packing and felt nothing but relief. If she could do that, then surely she could deal with Susan, Henry's secretary of forty years? And so it was. After Susan exhausted her arguments in favor of booking a private jet, Luna calmly instructed her to book a commercial flight to Warsaw via Frankfurt.

Asserting herself for the first time was easier than she'd imagined and although the motive for her trip was a sad one, Luna was excited. She'd never been allowed to travel alone. Ever. Not even on a bus or the subway. Whenever she'd hinted she might "pop on a plane" Carolina brought up the dangers befalling young women foolish enough to mix with the masses.

Now, she wondered what had triggered Nana's obsession. Had she been arrested by the Nazi's in Poland on a bus during WWII?

Luna understood Nana and Henry's fear of losing her as they had Charlotte, the daughter who was never talked about. Aside from a small photograph on Henry's desk, she'd faded into oblivion. Luna did her best to live up to their expectations and never give them cause for worry or disappointment. They deserved her total gratitude. Thanks to Tia Bella, her godmother, they'd chosen her, a Colombian orphan, as Charlotte's replacement and she owed them everything. But it hadn't always been easy. Getting them to allow her to take her driver's license was a mission, and Tia Bella had to intervene when it came to attending college. According to Henry, every decent establishment in the country was riddled with handsome, horny left-wing anarchists whose sole aim in life was to seduce and entice vulnerable young women into abandoning their Upper East Side existences and join communes, or worse… look at Jim Jones. Luna had never discovered why Henry coupled the victims of a mass suicide decades earlier with Vassar or Bryn Mawr, but the pregnant silences and meaningful looks exchanged between him and Nana across the dining table warned her *not* to ask the question burning her tongue: had Charlotte died while she was in college? Or been corrupted by a communist? Had she gotten into a drunk car crash? And were Nana and Henry afraid she'd follow in her footsteps?

Dusk faltered on the skyline. Lights flickered in the buildings across the city and the Big Apple readied for its evening show. What would it feel like alone in Warsaw or Paris during the holidays? The Upper East Side with its palatial buildings and brownstones was her home. The daily strolls on Henry's arm, lunch at Cipriani, Nana's dry comments about Mrs. Hodgson and her Russian billionaire and her diamond collared pug and nights at the Met of which they were patrons… Did memories stay locked in the heart forever, or would they sink into the purple flow of the Hudson and leave her in a starless vacuum?

But lately, she'd felt a subtle change in New York. An indefinable heaviness weighed like rain clouds on a hot windless day. The vibe on the streets had altered, and when she went out, all she wanted to do was to get back inside as fast as she could. She wished she was less sensitive to the divisive tension she picked up. Even people's body language had altered, as though everyone was armed and ready to defend their political stand.

"Luna. *Dios mio*! Are you *loca?* You've just had bronchitis!" She sighed at Maria's voice. It was time to go in and pack. "I'll be there in just a minute."

"Come in the *casa* right now. What would Dona Carolina say?" "Maria, please. I need a few minutes."

Maria grumbled but gave in. Across the street the elderly lady who lived in the penthouse opposite, drew the living room curtains. Over the years, Luna'd conjectured about her. The apartment seemed lively. Who were the shadows who came and went? Did she have a large family? What must that be like? They'd smiled at each other from time to time in spring and summer when the old lady directed her gardener and snipped herbs from the terracotta pots on her terrace. Luna never told Nana, but occasionally, she and the lady waved to one another; a deliciously warm, politically incorrect gesture in a square mile of top-dollar refinement. There'd been times when she'd thought of crossing the street and asking the doorman to announce her.

But of course she hadn't dared. Now she'd likely never know who the old lady was. She might die before she returned.

Luna closed her eyes, placed her hands on the

icy balustrade and aligned her hips. She breathed in the wind picking up in the east, the choppers overhead, honking horns and the rumble of traffic thirty floors below. She pictured roots reaching down from her feet through the steel and concrete structure of the building, past layers of bedrock and the metamorphosed sediment left by the glaciers, on and on until they reached the earth's epicenter. Once she'd connected, she drew the core energy back up until it flooded her entire being.

A last look at the New York skyline and Luna turned. Her fingers and her ears tingled as she stepped back inside the warmth of the bedroom. The chintz shaded lamps and the fireplace were lit. Clothes lay strewn across the bed and the loveseat. She dropped Nana's mink in the back of the armchair and stared at sweaters and underwear, jeans and shirts. She and Nana used to discuss what they'd pack for a trip several days ahead of time. It was part of the ritual. But there was no Nana to consult with any longer. Or so it seemed. She'd spent hours each day glued to the Chagall seeking a sign until her eyes ached, but she'd seen no movement. They'd been certain they could communicate, but each day Luna's anxiety increased. What if Nana never showed up? She must take a picture of the painting with her phone. You never know when she might decide to appear.

Luna stepped inside the walk-in closet. Her luggage stood open on the counter. Next to it lay the leather document holder with her passport and airline ticket.

She should place it directly inside the purse she'd be taking on the trip.

Choosing a purse from among the collection of Hermès bags kept on the glass shelves in Nana's walk-in closet meant going back into her room, and except for locking the doors to make sure Rachel stayed out, she hadn't been back there since the day Nana died. Was she ready? She'd wanted to leave that hurdle for after her trip to Europe, but she needed a purse, so there wasn't much choice.

Luna stepped into the corridor and moved reluctantly towards Nana's bedroom. She turned the handle. Stale smoke lingered as she stepped inside the darkened room and listened. If only Nana would come. She flipped on the light switch. The wall sconces glistened and the electric blinds buzzed and shuddered, then groaned and light from the terrace filtered past the slats.

Nana's world looked exactly as it always had;. the four-poster with its baroque drapes and silk counterpane, the flower paintings and prints on the tapestried walls and the silver framed photographs of Henry's sepia-faced ancestors peering stiffly into a turn-of-the-century camera lens, continued to crowd the top of the Louis XV commode between the French Windows. Behind the glass doors of the eighteenth-century English bookcase on the opposite wall were the hand-painted enamel boxes she'd collected, Teddy Roosevelt's monogramed silver hairbrush and letters written by Eleanor addressed to

Henry's mother, from 1600 Pennsylvania Avenue.

The room felt more like a shrine than a bedroom. To dismantle it would be tantamount to stripping an ancient chapel of its treasures. Surely Nana must be close by? Her presence was impregnated everywhere, even in the chintz drapes and brocade wall covering and the tattered copy of *All Quiet on the Western Front* and her reading glasses still lying on the nightstand.

Luna's eyes filled. She turned and moved quickly towards the boudoir. She'd come for a purse; not fall back down the hole of emotions she was slowly climbing out of.

Wiping her eyes on the back of her sleeve, she turned the light on in the walk-in closet and surveyed the rows of designer suits and silk dresses. Each item carried a memory; a shopping spree on Bond Street, the Via Candiotti and Avenue Montaigne. What should she do with these carefully chosen clothes worn with such elegance and grace? She refused to have them end up in cartons at Father Murphy's Catholic Mission. She'd find a use for them nonetheless.

And all at once she wept. Loud, unrestrained wails shred her chest and her heart. The document holder fell on the counter as she tugged open one drawer after another, caressing the silk scarves opera gloves, and worn leather jewelry boxes; a life time's accoutrements held in custody like refugees with no power to determine their future.

Enough. She must pull herself together and focus

on the purse for the trip. Nana wouldn't like her to be out of control like this. After all, she was stepping out into the future wasn't she? Even if it was in search of the past.

She moved towards the glass shelves and studied the collection of Hermès bags that spanned nearly eighty years. Luna's first Birkin that Nana had gifted her on her 17th birthday — the year she'd studied in Switzerland — was among them. She drew it off the third shelf and opened and placed the purse on the island. Of course this was the one she'd take on her trip into the past. Seeing it brought back memories. Tia Bella, her godmother and Nana's best friend since they'd met on a ship going to Colombia after the war, had come to Gstaad with them to celebrate that weekend. Luna still hadn't figured out what the two old ladies had quarreled about ten years ago. Nana said Tia Bella had treated her unacceptably, but would not go into any details. And she'd made it clear Luna was not to communicate with her godmother any more either.

Luna was upset. She'd thought of staying secretly in touch with her godmother, then dropped the idea. It would be wrong to disobey. Instead she'd done her best to persuade Nana to climb off her high-horse and get back in touch with her old friend. Surely life was too short to quarrel at this stage? But Nana'd refused. Still, Luna had made a point of writing a note to advise Tia Bella of Nana's passing.

Surely that couldn't be considered disloyal?

On the top shelf, like a museum piece, stood the *Sac à Dépèches* that was gifted to Nana back in 1937, and never removed from its glass case. Luna had never seen it up close. But now she felt compelled to look at it. How, if Nana had been in a camp, could she have kept it? Surely it too was a survivor? Had Nana left it up there and out of reach so the past couldn't touch her present?

Curiosity and something more got the better of her. She pulled a stool out from inside the shoe closet, kicked off her ballerina slippers, climbed up and pulled open the double glass doors. The purse's vibe was so strong her fingers shook. A familiar scent of tobacco filled her nostrils.

She drew the trapezium tan leather purse closer and traced the grooves in the creased leather. It must be one of the first of its kind. The design — created in the late 1920's based on a saddle-bag — became fashionable in the mid-1930s and was the precursor to the Kelly made popular by Grace, Princess of Monaco, and later, the coveted Birkin designed for the actress Jane Birkin, which had turned into every fashionista's dream.

Removing the purse from the shelf Luna held it to her breast and closed her eyes and pictured a young Nana on the brink of womanhood. Who had given her the purse? Her father? Surely she'd have been too young for it to be a husband or a lover? It vibrated with yearning and longing. Luna's breath caught in her chest as a feeling of pure love too deep and intense to describe wrenched her heart; an impossible love, the kind you read about… like Romeo and Juliet.

"Romeo & Julieta," she gasped.

Nana's last whispered words! And when she'd said *"In the Sa—"* she must have meant the *Sac à Dépèches*. Oh my God! A saddle bag; a bag designed to carry dispatches and messages!

Clutching the purse Luna stepped off the stool and placed it gently on the counter next to the Birkin. They were identical in color. The purses stood side by side highlighted under the halogen lamps. Was Nana's true story hidden inside three-quarters of a century's worth of scars and scuffed leather? Luna trembled as she studied the lateral straps and gold hardware drawn across the front of the flaps and the padlocks. A miniature pouch dangled from the stiff round handle of the *Sac à Dépèches*. She shuddered. Her fingers shook as she removed the key from inside it and inserted it into the tiny padlock. It turned and the lock gave way.

Luna withdrew the padlock and slipped off the gold clasps. The leather straps drooped. Again, she hesitated: she felt like a voyeur.

But it was too late for scruples.

She pulled the leather wide open and again caught a whiff of stale tobacco. At first the bag appeared empty. Then, she felt inside it and slipped her hand into the inner pocket and withdrew a stale cigar between her thumb and index. It disintegrated immediately, shedding tobacco inside the purse and on the counter, leaving her holding a burgundy and gold *Romeo & Julieta* label.

"This can't be real!" She gasped. Surely the cigar couldn't have been here since before WWII?

A toothpick-sized tube rolled among the leaves on the counter caught her eye. Luna scooped it up carefully and held it in her palm then hurried out into the boudoir and perched on the edge of the stool at Nana's dressing table. She switched on the lamp and held the tiny tobacco-stained scroll under it. It was thicker than it first appeared. Her heart raced. If she tried to unravel it, would it suffer the same fate as the cigar? She touched it gently with the tip of her right index then inserted her thumbnail gingerly under the miniature edge. Reluctantly, the stiff paper unfurled, crackled then bounced back. She made a second attempt, coaxing it millimeter by millimeter but each time she pried it open, it curled back inwards, as though unwilling to divulge its contents. She tried again. This time traces of ink appeared. Finally, the minute piece of torn vellum, no larger than a centimeter wide lay flat on the glass dressing table. On it in scrawled black slanted letters were written the words:

Banque Lourriel, Freiburg Chagall

Chapter 11

On his way up to the penthouse in the elevator, Carl checked the flight departures on his Smartphone. Luna was airborne. The coast was clear.

Carl had never felt so divided.

The realization that Uncle Ephraim might be right about the Chagall, came as a shock. And a dizzying prospect. Any amount of money stashed in a bank or a safe for nigh on eighty years was bound to be worth a fortune. And he, Carl, was his great-uncle's sole heir.

But to find out, he'd had to lie to Luna. And Carl was not a good liar. Truth and transparency were high on his agenda. At least they were, up until now. She'd left town less than an hour ago and already he was betraying her trust. He'd told himself over and over that he had no choice. Short of coming clean and explaining Uncle Ephraim's misgivings, he could see no other way of going forward.

The doors of the elevator opened and he stepped inside the foyer. Juan stood to attention. "*Buenas noches, Senor* Carl."

"Hello Juan. I won't bother removing my coat. I only came to pick up the painting," he said pointing at the Chagall.

Juna inclined his head, his face impassive. Carl never knew what he and Maria thought of him. They were invariably polite, but their faces like Egyptian tomb paintings, were neither friendly nor hostile.

In all the years he'd worked here, Carl had never given the Chagall more than a cursory glance. It was one more painting among many in the Hampton collection. He liked English landscapes, Turner, Constable — art that he understood. That is until the other evening, when he'd come face to face with his heritage; both real and symbolic.

He stood now before *The Girl in the Red Dress Under the Moon*. Henry was right, the girl did look like Luna. She had that same detached look, as if flying goats and violinists floating in a starry sky and synagogues whirling in a cloud, were par for the course. It made the notion that a clue might be hidden in the back of the frame, even more preposterous.

He hesitated. He was about to commit a felony. The mere idea triggered heartburn. "Do you need help, Sir?"

"No, thanks, Juan. That's fine."

The butler's eyes bored into his back. He raised his hands and touched the frame. It took all his willpower to stop his fingers from trembling. He eased the wire off the hook and removed the painting carefully from the wall.

He carried the picture over to the table and placed it face down on the surface. Twisted wires were attached to two hooks screwed into the scarred back of the wooden frame and cardboard. It was clearly old; bits of grubby labels and a sticker stuck sideways on the lower left hand corner.

He studied the back of the frame. There was no way they could open it without causing some damage. He'd be obliged to tell Luna that the Sotheby's expert had insisted on verifying the authenticity of the back of the painting. She'd likely buy it; she trusted him. Which only made it worse.

His armpits stuck to his shirt. He must get going. Uncle Ephraim was likely chain smoking in the wheelchair by the living room window scanning the street, wondering if this was the moment he'd been waiting for most of his adult life.

Maria stood impassively at the entrance to the dining room.

"Maria, do you have a bag I could put this painting in? It has to go to be expertise tomorrow morning." He hoped he sounded casual.

"*Si Senor.* I bring you a bag."

The maid scuttled off down the passage. A minute later, she returned with a large Bergdorf shopping bag and held it open for Carl to slide the painting in.

"Perfect. Thank you." He held the bag by the handles and smiled. "I'll be off then." "You want Juan drive you?" Maria asked.

"No, thanks. I have an Uber waiting for me downstairs. Did Luna get off alright?"

"Yes. She go to Switzerland." Maria stepped across the foyer and pressed the elevator button.

"Switzerland?" Carl frowned. "Wasn't she flying to Poland via Frankfurt?"

"*Si Senor*. But she change. Maybe a better connection?" Maria raised her palms and shrugged.

"Perhaps she found a better connection through Zurich," he said. But the change left him disconcerted. Why hadn't she told him?

The elevator took a while to arrive. The clock on the landing ticked. His palms sweated.

Get a grip. It might all turn out to be nothing more than an old man's delusions.

The ping of the elevator.

"Good night, Maria. Good night, Juan. Thanks for the bag. I'll bring the painting back once the experts are done with it."

"*Buenas noches. Vaya con Dios.*"

Inside the elevator, Carl peeked at the Bergdorf bag dangling in his right hand. Even if it led to nothing, surely it would help his great-uncle let go of the past and find some peace at the end of his life?

The blind trust in Maria and Juan's eyes had gotten to him. Luna's too. That trust had not been bestowed on him lightly. If any of what he'd done tonight came out, it would be over. Unless... But he didn't dare to think what the next step would be if Uncle Ephraim turned out to be right.

The elevator reached the ground floor. Carl stepped into the lobby. His throat was dry to the point he could hardly answer the night porter. He never would have imagined he'd be disappearing like a thief in the night with a masterpiece in a shopping bag.

Chapter 12

Ephraim Wolf shifted in his wheelchair. His bones hurt. He'd dozed off as he awaited Carl's arrival, but his were troubled dreams. He raised his wrist closer to the light bulb and peered at the Roman dials of his flat gold watch. Almost 8pm. Carl had rung an hour ago to say that Luna had left on her trip and he was on his way to the penthouse. *Mein Gott,* doesn't the boy realize that he's an old man and has waited nearly eighty years for this moment?

Every day since Carolina Hampton's wake, he'd become more convinced that the Chagall was indeed *the* one. Surely it must be? Fate could not be so cruel as to place it in his path only to taunt him with a fake.

Mrs. Katz had left him his supper tray with a bowl of soup, apple compote and a pot of tea, but it lay on the table untouched. Ephraim reached inside the left-hand breast pocket of his velvet robe and pulled out a pack of cigarettes. He held a gold lighter to the tip, shielded the flame and inhaled. He'd smoked since he was twelve years old when Madame Rushkina, the piano teacher, gave him his first cigarette after a perfect rendition of Czerny's piano exercises. Today she'd likely be in jail. Idiots.

What a strange world filled with prohibitions they lived in. They proned democracy, but to Ephraim, the arbitrary attitudes of today seemed frighteningly similar to those of 1930's Germany.

People had lost their common sense. Take that stupid Liebfreund woman who lived with her children and their runny noses on the third floor. One day he'd pointed out to her that if she stopped allowing them to run around barefoot on the cold floor and dried their hair after they'd showered, they'd stop catching colds. Three days later she'd come to him in raptures. The children's noses had stopped running and he was a miracle worker. How dumb could you get?

Ephraim inhaled deeply. Surely Carl must have the painting in his possession by now? He glanced down the street, but there was no sign of a car. He took another drag. Smoking was the only real pleasure remaining these days. He stared at the smoke caught in the lamplight and blew a smoke ring. He and Rainer used to do that. They'd talked and laughed and drank champagne. And made plans.

He pushed the wheelchair away from the window and stared into darkness.

At the sound of the key turning and the grinding of locks, he sat up straighter and turned the wheels to face the door. Carl was in the hall. He could see his shadow as he removed his coat. He restrained himself from calling out. He must remain calm. The boy was too American by far, and must be managed with care.

"Hi, Uncle Ephraim."

"Good evening, Carl." He eyed the large shopping bag in Carl's right hand. His fingers shook as he stubbed out the cigarette in the metal ashtray that he carried on his knee.

"This is it," Carl said raising the bag. "Take it into the dining room."

Ephraim's mouth twitched as he pushed the wheels of his chair across the rugs and through the mirrored doors.

"Close the drapes, and turn on the lights," he ordered.

Carl followed instructions, switched on the chandelier and placed the bag carefully on the dining room table.

"We can only keep it here tonight," he said. "I have to get it to Sotheby's tomorrow morning before anyone suspects. I'm not certain if the insurance policy covers any damage or, God help us, theft."

But Ephraim wasn't listening. Three-quarters of a century's worth of expectation had deafened him to anything but the task at hand.

He removed his gold framed glasses from his breast pocket and placed them on his nose. His right index shook as he touched the frame and his excitement grew. He'd recognize old Levi Blum's work anywhere. He was the best picture framer in Germany. He scanned the swirling brush strokes, the clouds, the violinist and the texture of the paint; remembering the last time he'd seen them, lying on Rainer's lap in the back of the SS staff car on that fateful day that changed the course of all their lives and had haunted him ever since. Even now, the sound of a rumbling truck engine sufficed to remind him…

~

"You're certain that nothing bad will happen to them, right?" He'd said between nervous puffs.

"*Naturlich*. Just a few routine questions down at headquarters, and then they'll be released — on the condition that your father sells me the paintings at a fair price, for old times' sake."

"He will. Once I've explained it clearly."

"Fine." Rainer pulled his leather gloves over his long fingers. "Stay here in the car. I won't be long. I just want to make sure everything goes according to plan. The men can get out of hand if I'm not there to supervise. Now remind me, which painting was it you particularly wanted?"

"The Chagall above the buffet in the dining room. A girl in a red dress staring up at the moon. You can't miss it. It's not very valuable, but... errr... it was my mother's favorite."

"*Sehr gut.*"

The chauffeur opened the door and stood to attention. Rainer stepped out of the car and straightened his uniform.

"*Wartensie hier,*" he ordered curtly.

"*Yawohl, Herr Oberst.*" A click of heels and a salute, and the door closed once more.

Ephraim lit another cigarette and took a long drag. From time to time he peered out the rear window. The car was parked only a few hundred yards from the gates of his family home. The soldiers had descended from the truck and entered the grounds. All at once, the full implication of what he'd set in motion sunk in and he retched.

He'd acted on impulse. In anger.

On that evening, after he'd overheard the conversation in the library, he'd walked through the dusk consumed by rejection and a desire for revenge. How dare they cut him out? How dare they hide funds and information that was rightfully his as well?

It had seemed such a good idea at the time: Rainer would pretend to arrest Papa and Eli. He would give them a little fright — just enough to scare some sense into them — then release them. And after that, they'd include him in everything. It would teach them not to hide codes in the back of paintings and not leave him on the sidelines. It's wasn't fair. Never had been. Now, they'd be obliged to respect him. Plus, Papa and Eli would finally understand that to survive in this increasingly dangerous environment, they must cooperate and understand that the friendship with Rainer was their one chance. What choice did he have but to act in their interest, since they refused to help themselves?

~

"Are you okay, Uncle Ephraim?" Carl asked.

The furrows between the old man's brows and around his mouth had deepened, his cheeks were drained of color and his breathing was labored. For the first time, he looked his age.

Carl held the painting, uncertain what to do. He should have realized that the emotion of seeing it might cause a shock. Particularly in his present weakened state. Ephraim dabbed his mouth with his handkerchief.

"Lay it face down on the table so I can look at the back," he croaked.

Carl turned the painting upside down. He pulled a folded cloth closer and placed it beneath the Chagall. Ephraim's lips twitched. His eyes narrowed and he pointed to the remains of a torn label on the upper right hand corner.

"That was a Wolf Gallery label."

"Are you certain?" Carl dropped into the chair next to him. "Of course, I'm sure." Ephraim snapped.

"The one down on the left," Carl pointed. "BA. That could be Buenos Aires. And if those numbers represent January of 2005, the date would fit with Luna's birthday."

Ephraim didn't respond. Carl watched him, taken aback when the old man removed a switchblade from the pocket of his robe, and flipped it open.

"Be careful with that," he exclaimed. "You could hurt yourself. And we mustn't damage the back of the frame."

Uncle Ephraim paid no attention. "Push it closer," he muttered. Carl obeyed.

Once the painting was within reach, the old man leaned forward and in three clean, swift movements, sliced the top and sides of the back of the frame. Then he slipped the knife back inside his pocket and eased the frame off with both hands. Carl watched bits of cardboard and wood crumble; a faint smell of dust just like that of his late mother's apartment the week after she died. He secured the sides of the frame. Ephraim eased the back and it gave way.

"Holy shit!" Carl exclaimed.

A thick vellum envelope had been taped to the back of the canvas exactly as Uncle Ephraim had predicted.

The old man stared at it. Then he laid the back of the frame to his right. His shoulders shook. Tears coursed down his craggy cheeks. And all at once he laughed and pointed to the envelope, and coughed and clutched the arms of the wheelchair. “Get it out of there,” he spluttered.

Carl eased his right index nail carefully under the edge of the tape and the tack that secured it, afraid the envelope might tear. He pictured his great-great-grandfather placing it there, and in a flash, his life made sense. He experienced a hitherto unknown sense of belonging. His earlier doubts dissipated. It was clear to him that his job, working for Henry Hampton, had but one objective: being in the right place at the right time to recover the family’s rightful heritage.

Forget scruples and loyalty. He, Carl, was the link to this sacred bond that reached beyond space and time. For the first time, as he removed the envelope from the back of the frame, Carl understood what it meant to be reborn.

Uncle Ephraim snatched it from his hands and turned it over. The envelope was sealed. The crest glistened under the light of the chandelier. The old man slipped his thumb nail under the red wax seal. It cracked. Bits of dry wax rolled off onto the floor.

Carl sat on the edge of his chair and watched Uncle Ephraim pull out a single piece of cream-colored writing paper and unfold eighty years of expectations. Was this for real? It felt like a movie, not real life. Not his life.

Uncle Ephraim’s hand trembled and the piece of paper fluttered to the floor. Carl reached down and grabbed it. A smiley face. And next to it, in stark black ink, the words *Viel Glück!*

“Is that the code?” He asked.

The old man’s face turned ashen. He hissed a single word. “Eli!”

Chapter 13

The first-class carriage of the InterCity train Luna boarded at Zurich airport was half empty. It was as clean and comfortable as she remembered the Swiss railways from years ago. She stowed her carry-on case, which held Nana's *Sac à Dépèches,* in the luggage compartment and sat in a window seat close to the entrance. She placed the Birkin carefully on her knee. In it, safely sealed in one of Nana's embossed envelopes, were with the note and the remains of the cigar she'd discovered in the *Sac à Dépèches.*

"Départ du train InterCity pour Bern, Fribourg Lausanne..." Said the voice on the loudspeaker. The train jogged as it moved slowly out of the station.

Was she nuts racing off to Fribourg with a scrap of tobacco stained paper and bits of an old cigar?

A few clicks online had been sufficient to discover the Banque Lourriel was a small private bank in Fribourg, Switzerland which had opened its doors 150 years ago. The directors were named on the website. Luna'd studied the photographs and wondered how to present her case. She opted to call *Monsieur* Henchoz who looked young, had a nice smile and might be more understanding of a crazy woman popping out of nowhere with an implausible story. After some deliberation, she used a ploy Henry would have approved of: bankers, he'd told her, were always available for potential new clients hinting they'd like to investment in their establishment. And it worked. Monsieur Henchoz said he'd be delighted to receive *Madame* Hampton at 3pm in his *bureau* this afternoon. Oh God! What would he say when she told him the reason for her visit? Have her kicked off the premises? And would this bring her any closer to Nana's truth? Had Count Orlowksy, Nana's father opened a Swiss account? Nana had spoken of foreign travel, concerts in Salzburg and Vienna and ski trips to Kitzbühl and Lech when she was small. There were one or two faded black and white photographs of a couple and a little girl in old-fashioned ski clothes. But why choose a hard to reach spot like Fribourg rather than one of the big financial centers like Zurich or Geneva? And what had the Chagall to do with it?

Luna pulled out her Smartphone. She'd been tempted to stow the Chagall in her luggage but she didn't want to deal with customs at the airport, so she'd opted to make *The Girl in the Red Dress Under the Moon* her screensaver instead. Not that Nana had manifested at all since her passing, which was worrying. Still, since her discovery inside the *Sac à Dépèches* and the Chagall reference, Luna's hopes soared: surely it was clear Nana had chosen the Chagall as their means of communication for a reason? Maybe she was one step closer to finding out what that reason was.

So many questions and so few answers.

Swiss banks were reputed for their discretion and reliability. Many fortunes had been secretly stashed in Switzerland before WWII, some of them still unclaimed. Perhaps hers was not as crazy a story as it first appeared, but what if there was a fortune lying hidden in the Banque Lourriel to whom would it belong? She had no clue if Nana had any real descendants — blood relations — and not just an adopted child from a Colombian orphanage.

Who was the woman behind the tattoo?

At times avoiding the well-intentioned individuals who suggested it was time she "got out there and lived," or hinted that Nana's death was a "blessed deliverance" overtook her grief.

But what did anyone know of Nana? She'd lost the person she loved most in the world. People didn't understand that. It affected her deeply. She'd barely touched the *frijoles* Maria insisted were good for grief. Occasionally she nibbled sushi Juan fetched from the take-out restaurant or the Mars bar she kept with her at all times as she wiled away the hours alternating between bouts of tears, staring at the Chagall, hoping Nana would manifest and thinking she'd heard Nana's bell echoing down the empty corridor where she wandered, holding onto memories for fear they might fade.

In the end, she'd fallen sick and had lain in bed for a week with a temperature of 103.

To her amazement Rachel, who'd disappeared since the day Nana died, reappeared and looked after her as though nothing out of the ordinary had occurred.

~

"I can't be sick I have to leave to Poland," Luna croaked.

"Why Poland?" Rachel said, lifting the remains of Luna's untouched lunch tray.

"You know perfectly well *why Poland*," she threw. "Don't pretend, Rachel. I'm going to find out about Nana's past whether you want me to or not."

"It'll be a waste of time," Rachel sighed, carrying the tray to the door.

"Why? Why is it a waste of time? As soon as I'm well I'm going and that's that." Luna'd muttered.

Rachel's attitude left her more frustrated than she already was. Short of tying her down and extracting information from her under duress, she saw no way of obliging the woman to tell her what she knew. But why prevaricate? Nana was dead. Why the hell couldn't she know the truth?

Rachel looked grayer and more shadowy still since Nana died. As though she too had mutated into another state of being. A rush of anger gripped her. Rachel had been here forever hovering in the wings until the final act. Now she'd appeared on stage and refused to say her lines.

"Why do you pretend to know nothing? You saw that tattoo on Nana's arm every day for years. It's obvious she must have been in a concentration camp. So why don't you just tell me which one? I'm going to find out anyway," Luna cried, hoisting herself up and reaching for Dr. Schultz' medication on the nightstand.

"It was very faded. I never tried to identify the tattoo. I don't know any more about Countess Carolina's story than you do."

"You're a bad liar, Rachel. I'll bet you know exactly which camp she was in." "What point is there in raking up the past? It's done and finished."

"There's every point. I've been fed a pack of lies and I am determined to discover why. I must know the truth. How else can I give closure to any of this?"

Rachel said nothing and opened the door silently. As she closed it behind her, Luna grabbed her one-eared teddy bear and threw it across the room after her.

"Fuck you Rachel."

Then she fell back and buried her head in the pillows. It wasn't fair. Everybody, even Henry, had deceived her. Her entire existence was based on lies. Knowing nothing of her own real origins hadn't mattered until now since she'd claimed Nana's and Henry's. Jeff's words at their break up meeting rang loud and clear: *"You don't look Latin and you have no idea what may be lurking in your genes."* Oh God. She must know the truth if she was to get a life. Any kind of life. As for Rachel, why hadn't she fired her right away after what she'd done, like any normal person in their right mind would have? But how do you fire an elderly woman who'd devoted her life to someone you loved?

For the next two days Luna said and did everything short of bullying Rachel into vouchsafing all she knew. In the end, she railed against herself for never having questioned what she'd been told and having lapped up Nana's tales like a dumb puppy licks its bowl.

~

Luna pressed her brow against the rattling train window. Fields emptied of cows tucked away in their stalls for the winter, post-card perfect villages and snow capped mountains flew past. How distant this neat, centuries-old world seemed from the chaos she'd just entered. Up until the day Nana died and America voted for Trump, she hadn't questioned the order of play. Now, nobody knew what would happen. It was as though her little world and the big world out there reflected one another; what was real and what wasn't? Hard to tell. She'd heard people talking at the airport as she was about to board the flight — as many opinions as there were voices. A man with a booming voice and an alligator briefcase said, "Give him a chance. He'll be fine, once he's in office he'll tow the line. That was just campaign stuff…" Two women in stilettoes and jeans on her left spoke in nasal whines: "Oh my Gawd… I just love *her* clothes. She'll look so totally great in the White House. What do you think Ivanka will wear to the inauguration?" Someone else muttered that the GOP had prostituted itself and how it would pay the price, but no one listened. Luna had boarded the plane and stuffed her earplugs into her ears and blanked out the entire electoral process. Surely she had enough to contend without politics to add to her list? Right now, all she had was a possible clue and a meeting at a Swiss bank. But it was more than she had forty-eight hours earlier. At least it was a place to begin.

An hour and a half later the train drew into Fribourg station. Luna tugged at her carry-on and clunked it onto the platform. She'd never pulled a case before. Should she have gotten a limo? What would she do with her luggage while she went to the bank?

She headed into the main hallway of the station and went in search of a locke. Her hasty departure had left her no time to withdraw Swiss Francs, but she'd come across an envelope of small change in one of the drawers in Henry's desk where he'd placed currencies left over from various trips abroad. She slipped the coins into the slot, proud that she was managing well on her own steam. Who said it was that hard? No doubt she'd come across an ATM machine later. Plus, she had a bunch of credit cards.

With her luggage locked up, Luna ventured out the main entrance of the station. It was two-thirty in the afternoon. That gave her half an hour to get to the bank for her meeting. She glanced at directions on her Smartphone. It was only a ten-minute walk away.

She'd thought about calling Carl, then changed her mind. She'd bring him up to speed after her meeting.

Snow fell thicker as she wandered past the taxi rank and the station car park. She pulled her hood over her head as she crossed the main road, glad she'd opted for the shorn mink three- quarter-length jacket Nana gave her last Christmas. She reached a roundabout. On the corner opposite was a large department store. She headed past the entrance and down a pedestrian street called the Rue du Midi. There was a Christmas atmosphere to the street:

lights, decorations and an old man playing violin outside a store. She stopped and dropped a coin in the cap lying on the cobbles at his feet. He nodded and smiled.

Fribourg had a good feel to it Luna decided. She reached a square called Place Python, crossed it and headed right. Should she have a coffee? No. She was antsy enough without caffeine to add to it.

She reached the Rue des Alps and stood at the traffic lights next to a Buddhist monk. Bits of orange robe peeked from below his army surplus jacket. When the pedestrian light turned green, she crossed. On the opposite pavement, she went to the balustrade overlooking the *Vieille Ville* and glanced at an explanatory panel. She was glad she spoke fluent French and Nana had insisted on her being multilingual. She read that the river running through the medieval Old Town below was called La Sarine. It divided the German and French speaking parts of the city. Luna leaned on the railing and gazed south at a row of staggered tiled roofs hanging over the steep incline towards the river. A few rays of sunshine pierced the cloud highlighting church spires and the Alps rising on the horizon. At any other time, she would have found the scene enchanting, but right now all she could think of was the growing knot in her gut as the visit to the Banque Lourriel and the thousand questions inside the Birkin loomed.

Snow piled on the cuffs of her coat sleeves. She shook it off and peered down the street to the east at several architectural gems. A street sign pointed to the *Chemin de Saint Jacques*, a pilgrimage famous thanks Paulo Coelho and Shirley Maclane's books. It had several departure points in Europe and ended up in Santiago de Compostella in Northwestern Spain. The blurb on the sign said Fribourg was a main stop for pilgrims who'd begun their pilgrimage in Southern Germany and Austria.

Cold seeped through the soles of her designer leather boots as she walked in the direction of the bank. She might as well get there on time and wait in the reception before she caught her death out here.

A pilgrimage. Was that what she was undertaking? A pilgrimage into the past to seek truth in the present?

Chapter 14

A discreet brass plaque to the right of a smart double-paneled entrance door read *Banque Lourriel SA*. The establishment clearly catered to high-end private clients.

Luna took a deep breath and grounded herself. There was no use feeling nervous, she was here now. She pressed her right index on the doorbell. A ring echoed. Fifteen seconds later a middle-aged man in a dark suit ushered her into the reception. A blond secretary in her mid- thirties smiled and rose from behind a desk. She reminded her of Miss Clemens, her nursery school teacher from when she'd arrived in New York before they'd gotten her the governess and had her home-schooled.

Luna stated her name. The secretary took her coat and Luna followed the man down a corridor dotted with mountain landscapes. She felt increasingly uncomfortable. What the hell was she going to say? *Actually, I have no intention of investing any money in your bank it was just a ploy to get you to see me?*" She should have thought it all out first before jumping on a plane and coming here impulsively.

The man opened the door and Luna stepped inside the conference room. She sat down in one of ten leather chairs.

"*Monsieur Henchoz vous rejoindra tout de suite. Un café, Madame?*"

"*Non merci.*"

Luna smiled briefly. She felt queasy. She peered up at the domed ceiling. A kaleidoscope of filtered dust particles exploded through a prism of stained glass forming a multitude of colored swirls, polygons and circles like the thoughts in her jumbled mind. What was it Descartes said in the Sixth Meditation? *You can see the three lines of a triangle but you can only imagine those of a chiliogon because a thousand lines is only possible to...*

She closed her eyes, straightened her back and connected with her root chakra. A moment later she opened them and pulled a coffee table book from the middle of the long table and flipped through it distractedly. It told the Banque Lourriel's history. Founded in 1866 by Solomon Lourrie, the bank remained in family hands to date. She poured over the list of directors and board members. Uh oh. Hubert Henchoz, the managing director and CEO was not a shapeless middle aged man in glasses and an anonymous grey suit as she'd imagined him, but a well-built designer clad forty-year-old. Couldn't she at least have chosen an underling to address her queries to? On the other hand, as Henry always said: it was better to go downstream than up.

She continued down the names. Nikolaj de Lourriel, board member and legal advisor. He looked intelligent. The list went on with the bank's capital and revenues, the mission statement and philosophy.

She snapped the book shut and studied the Aubusson rug and two fine landscape paintings. The only concession to modernity was a coffee machine with a colorful selection of capsules placed on the console next to the long, multi-paned window overlooking the snow- covered grounds. The wood paneled room oozed time-tested trust and solidity.

She pulled out her Smartphone and peeked at the Chagall on her screensaver. "Please," she whispered. "Give me a clue."

Luna jumped at the knock on the door and looked up as *Monsieur* Henchoz stepped inside, followed by another man. A warm smile and a firm handshake.

"I'm sorry we kept you waiting. This is Nikolaj de Lourriel my fellow director and board member as well as our legal counsel. As you are American, we thought it better he joins our discussion. The new laws about investment for American citizens being what it is and all." He said in fluent English and raised his palms.

"Enchanté Madame."

Both men sat opposite her and placed pads in front of them. "To what do we owe the honor of your *visite, Madame?"*

Luna paused wondering where to begin. It was worse than she'd thought. She swallowed, then looked up and folded her hands on the table.

"I'm not quite sure where to start. You see, I wasn't entirely truthful when I said I wanted to invest money in your bank."

"How so? You do not wish to invest because of the difficulties with the IRS? I assure you, as long as the money is properly declared, there is no problem, *Madame.* Only undeclared accounts can cause grave problems with your tax authorities." Nikolaj de Lourriel assured her.

"Well, that's just the thing, you see—" She cut off again and shook her head. "I'm sorry. I don't know where to start."

"How about the beginning," Monsieur Henchoz said, pulling a pen from his inner breast pocket. "Do you mind if I jot down some notes?"

"Not at all."

"Then go ahead. I'm listening."

Both men were only a few years her elder but they projected confidence and reliability. A bit like Carl did. She sighed and bit the bullet.

"A month ago, Nana — I mean, Carolina Hampton — my, well my mother, actually," she said fumbling for the right words, "died in New York."

"My condolences, *Madame*."

Monsieur Henchoz looked genuinely concerned and Nikolaj de Lourriel frowned behind his glasses. Luna hesitated, unsure how to continue. She caught the two men exchanging a brief glance, but she was by no means ready to share the tattoo. Not yet anyway.

"I'm sorry, I'm not doing a great job at explaining. The thing is, after her death, I was looking through an old purse she'd owed from before WWII, and I discovered this." She opened the Birkin and pulled out the embossed envelope, laid it on the table, then opened the flap and took out the tiny tube of tobacco-stained paper and unfurled it carefully on the table.

The two men leaned forward.

"The cigar was in the inside pocket. It disintegrated when I touched it which led me to believe it must be very old and stale, and inside I found this." She pointed to the tiny roll of paper.

Monsieur Henchoz put on his glasses and Nikolaj de Lourriel's brows met over the bridge of his nose. "May I?" He asked.

"Please."

The banker lifted the note between his thumb and right index. He unrolled it carefully and studied it. "This is *extraordinaire*," he said. "*Tiens*, Hubert, take a look."

"This is the remains of the cigar." Luna said, opening the envelope further and showing them the bits of tobacco leaves. "It's a *Romeo & Julieta*. This is the label."

"Incroyable!" Monsieur Henchoz nodded. "And the code name for the account is obviously *Chagall.* Does that mean anything to you, Nikolaj?"

"Non. But we shall make *des recherches." "Madame* Hampton, do you know who wrote this?"

"I have no idea. It's neither of my parent's handwriting. But, as she was dying, Nana whispered the words *Romeo & Julieta* to me. She seemed to think that someone had come for her." Luna stopped and shook her head. She pulled a paper handkerchief out from next to the half-eaten Mars bar in her purse and blew her nose as Nana's death flew back at her like an inside curve ball out of left field.

"*Désolée* it was not my *intention* to upset you, *Madame*," an embarrassed *Monsieur*

Henchoz murmured.

"Don't be. I'm sorry. It's just all been a bit of a shock."

"*Excusez-moi, chère Madame*, but you said your mother owned the purse from before WWII. How old was she at the time of her death?" Nikolaj de Lourriel inquired.

"Ninety-three."

The two men exchanged another astonished glance.

"Oh, yes, I see," Luna nodded. "That would be impossible, wouldn't it? Henry and Carolina Hampton weren't my birth parents, they adopted me."

"*Ah, je comprends.* It would indeed have been an event of biblical proportion," he answered, with a touch of humor.

"It would indeed," Luna smiled. "Though knowing Nana it wouldn't have surprised anyone if she'd managed to wangle even something as extraordinary as that."

"She sounds like a *Grande Dame*," *Monsieur* Henchoz said. "*De caractère*," Nikolaj de Lourriel added.

"She certainly was a character," Luna sighed.

"And she never spoke to you of an account in our bank?" "Never. I don't' think she knew about it."

"And do you have any idea who she might have been referring to when she uttered these last words to you?"

Luna shook her head. "I was hoping you might be able to tell me."

"We shall begin making enquiries *immédiatement*. Nikolaj, you're the historian, you have the best knowledge of what went on at the bank in the 1930s. Our Great-Grandfather, Jean de Lourriel was the chairman back then," *Monsieur* Henchoz added.

"The first thing is to look at the records. Would you object if we keep the note and have it analyzed by a specialist? We will of course furnish you with a receipt."

"Certainly. I—I'm very interested in discovering anything you can find out. I have the impression there may have been things Nana never spoke about."

"It may take us several days to identify the account." "So you think an account really exists?"

"*Naturellement*! We have many long-standing accounts that were opened before WWII. It was common practice for the holder of the account and a bank officer to agree on a code name. Obviously in this case, it's *Chagall.* We will do everything we can to find it, and unless it was closed at some point, there should be a record of that too. We'll start checking right away but it may take a few days."

"I see. Well, I guess that's fine." "Where can we get in touch with you?"

"Uh—" Luna closed her mouth and thought. She hadn't planned for this. "I have nowhere else to go for now so I might as well stay here in Fribourg while you look into it. Can you recommend a hotel?"

"*Avec plaisir.* Sylvie at reception will do all the *nécéssaire.*"

"Just one thing," Nikolaj de Lourriel said, rubbing the lenses of his glasses. "You are a US citizen, *nest-ce pas, Madame*?"

"Yes. I am."

"As I mentioned, Switzerland and the US have new treaties. If the account still exists and you are established as a beneficiary, we must proceed with caution."

"But I haven't made a claim." Luna said taken aback. "Of course not, *Madame.* It was merely a *reflextion.*"

"We'll do our best to clarify the situation a soon as possible. Unfortunately, the bank closes early today since we have a holiday weekend here in Fribourg." *Monsieur* Henchoz said. "Bu I assure you, Nikolaj and I will do our utmost, and hopefully by

Tuesday or Wednesday of next week we'll have news for you."

"Okay." Luna wondered whether she should go to Paris for the weekend and return on Monday, but she was tired and didn't feel up to another journey. She gave Monsieur Henchoz her phone number.

"We will be in touch as soon as we know something," he said as they parted at the bank's front door.

She shook hands with Nikolaj de Lourriel whose shirt tail protruded from the back of his pants. Both men seemed frank and ready to help. She appreciated their attitude. They could easily have taken her for a fraud, but they'd accepted her story. She was no closer to knowing about Nana's past than she had been yesterday, but at least it was a start.

The door closed behind them and Luna pulled out her Smartphone and tapped in Carl's number. He'd be mighty surprised to learn she was in Switzerland and not in Poland.

She'd even surprised herself. She wasn't used to acting spontaneously. Maybe it wasn't so bad?

Chapter 15

It was past 9am when Carl tip-toed across the creaking wooden floor to Uncle Ephraim's kitchen, opened the refrigerator door and removed the milk. His uncle's revelations and the lumpy mattress had rendered sleep impossible.

He reached up and removed a glass from the cupboard. What a night it had turned out. Uncle Eli's smiley face swam before him with all its implications.

He poured the milk.

He used to draw himself, before he'd channeled all his energy into working for the Hamptons. He'd been proud that he'd inherited Uncle Eli's talent. All these years he'd been described to Carl as a vibrant, smart, talented young man who sketched on paper napkins and liked fast cars; a boy on the verge of manhood, deported and murdered in the name of prejudice and bigotry. His eyes filled. It was crazy, but he was having a hard time accepting that the young man he'd been taught to revere and admire since childhood was a product of Uncle Ephraim's imagination. The bitterness with which he'd spoken of the twin brother whom he'd professed to love were disconcerting. He himself had no siblings, but what kind of brother would do such a thing and at such a time? When so much was at stake?

Clearly reality had been too painful and Uncle Ephraim had lived all these years in denial, preferring to rewrite the past. Yet only a few noxious words coupled with the cartoon had sufficed to expose the depth of loathing and rivalry that existed between Ephraim and his twin. Eli the hero, the holocaust victim, the young man herded into a cattle pen, his dreams destroyed and cast into hell, his body emaciated, his soul ground to rubble, his gold fillings picked from a pile of bones and ashes to be distributed among men who'd lost all semblance of humanity, had turned into a bully, a manipulator who'd persuaded their father to give him the codes of a hidden fortune, then left a false trail in their place for his brother to find.

Still, the cartoon discovered in the back of the Chagall frame established some proof of ownership. He'd thought about it half the night and arrived at the conclusion that for now, the best way to go forward was to return the painting to the Hampton penthouse foyer as soon as possible and address the matter with Luna once she returned from her trip, despite Uncle Ephraim's reticence. He did not believe it would come to a legal battle. He sure hoped not. It would be a serious loss for Luna, but he didn't think she'd refuse to return the painting. But before mentioning anything to her, he'd look into the legal ramifications.

He drained the glass.

Mrs. Katz would arrive soon and Uncle Ephraim would be up. He'd shower and wait to have breakfast with him and explain his plan. He placed the glass in the sink. His phone vibrated. It was Luna.

"Hi, did you have a good flight? Maria said you flew via Zurich." "Yes. I—look Carl, there's something I need to speak to you about."

He straightened. "Shoot."

Mrs. Katz bustled around in the kitchen singing a Ladino love song off key. Carl tucked his smartphone into his pants pocket, entered the dining-room and stopped in the doorway. Uncle Ephraim sat in the wheelchair. His hair was disheveled, there was stubble on his chin and his shoulders slumped. It was as if overnight he'd turned into a little old man staring at the past through a cartoon designed to send him on a false scent. Carl had never seen him like this.

"Good morning Uncle Ephraim," he said sitting in the chair to the old man's right. "I just got off the phone with Luna. Could you remind me where your father studied in Switzerland?"

"Fribourg."

"That's where Luna is."

"What's she doing in Fribourg?"

"She's visiting a bank. She found a note inside an Hermès *Sac à* something — a purse that belonged to Carolina since before WWII with some account information. All this seems like too much of a coincidence. Don't you find it odd that we discover a cartoon in a Chagall you believed contained the information about your father's money, the same Chagall that's hung for years in the Hampton's foyer, and simultaneously Luna *happens* to come across a note stuck in a *Romeo & Julieta* cigar in a purse that belonged to Carolina Hampton? And get this, the account code is *Chagall.*"

Ephraim's face paled. The teacup in his hand shook.

Chagall. So, that was the code Papa and Eli had chosen the day he'd overheard them in the library…

~

Ephraim backed away from the library door. Eli and Papa had gone silent. He swallowed the unshed tears and moved into the hall shaking with pent-up rage, nearly toppling a bronze statue in the process. In the hall, he stood perfectly still, heart racing and his breath short. What were they referring to? What were they planning to hide in the back of the Chagall? And what secret code was it they'd just come up with that they didn't plan to make him privy to? Something in the library no doubt. He must think what his next step should be. There was not a moment to waste.

Seconds later, Ephraim grabbed his coat and scarf from the back of the needle point chair. The eighteenth-century gnomes that had haunted him since childhood jeered at him.

But not for long. Not anymore.

It was cold as Ephraim stepped through the front door into the October dusk and pulled the brass handle closed. The house felt so safe. But for how long? Papa and Eli hadn't a clue just how dangerous things were. They thought the Nazis respected their status, that being friends with Baron von Heil and other aristocratic Germans would help. But he knew better. He knew the only way was to be in with men at the top. Men like Rainer Lanzberg. It was said that the Führer was a frequent visitor of the neighbors down the street. Rainer had mentioned the exclusive location of the Wolf-family villa on several occasions. He knew it wasn't merely a comment. It would be only too easy for him to get hold of the villa now that the new laws obliged Jews to sell their assets to Germans for a pittance.

Up until then, the Wolfs had been left alone, but that's because mother was French. A generation ago nobody minded a beautiful and impoverished German aristocrat marrying a wealthy Jew. But not anymore.

Ephraim pulled on his leather gloves and hurried down the street. What if he arranged for Rainer to buy the house at a good price? The Lanzbergs lived in the well-to-do bourgeois neighborhood of Sollin, but he knew that Rainer, a rising star in the SS, had other aspirations. The young man and childhood friend was involved in all sorts of areas that Ephraim sensed would make him increasingly vital to his own personal survival. He must stay on Rainer's good side. For his sake and the family's. Not that they'd appreciate it if they knew what he was doing. Still, if Rainer came to live in the house, not only would that make their situation with the authorities less risky, but he himself would know all that was going on. It would look to be a safe guard. Papa and Eli would just have to bear it, but in the end, they'd be thankful.

~

"Uncle Ephraim, are you alright?" Carl said.

"What's the name of the bank Luna's at in Fribourg?" Ephraim asked, placing a cigarette between his lips.

"Banque Lourriel."

The corner of Ephraim's left eye twitched. "And you say Luna discovered this note in Carolina Hampton's old purse?"

"Yes, as I said, an Hermès purse she'd owned from before WWII. What are you getting at, Uncle Ephraim?"

The old man reached for the lighter in the pocket of his robe and slowly lit the cigarette, his eyes narrowed into bleary slits.

"Carl, go to the chest of drawers in my bedroom and bring me the buff file that's behind the socks in the second drawer."

The chair scraped as Carl rose. He sighed and went down the corridor wishing he hadn't mentionedhe Swiss bank or the note. But what choice did he have? In the bedroom he tugged open the stiff drawer and came face to face with rows of socks like colored balls in a lottery machine. He pulled it open further, pushed the socks to one side and saw a file. Several bits of paper and newspaper clippings protruded from it. Carefully he carried it back to the dining room. Uncle Ephraim obviously had a bee in his bonnet. But what did he seek to find?

Carl turned the chandelier on as he re-entered the dining room. His uncle reached out his hand for the file. The cigarette hung loosely between his lips as he flipped it open and withdrew a faded newspaper clipping. He stared at it a moment, then handed it to Carl.

The clipping: a grainy photograph of a good-looking young couple mounting the steps of a mansion was dated 1942 and came from a copy of the *Völkishe Beobachter*, a popular Nazi propaganda newspaper published in Munich. The man was dressed in a fancy black uniform. The woman on his arm wore a suit with a fur stole around her shoulders and carried a handbag.

Both looked straight into the camera. The man was smiling. The woman's gaze seemed cold and haughty, as though being photographed was an intrusion. Carl's German was by no means perfect, but he read aloud:

"*SS Oberst Sturmführer Lanzberg und seine hübsche Schwester Karina, treffen im Göbels Palais ein* — SS Colonel Storm Leader Lanzberg and his lovely sister Karina arrive at the Goebbels *Palais…*"

Carl frowned. "Who are they?"

"I'll explain in a minute. Tell me, does that woman remind you of anyone?" Uncle Ephraim asked.

Carl stared at the young woman in the picture.

"Not really. This picture's really old, it's hard to tell. She could be anybody."

"Look closer. Imagine that same woman with a stole like that around her, with lines on her face and white hair."

Carl peered closer. There was something familiar in the woman's features and the way she held herself but he couldn't place her.

"I've been a total fool, Carl. I never saw what was under my nose." "What do you mean?"

"It was she, yet I never recognized her," Uncle Ephraim spoke as though to himself. "*Was für ein Dumbkopf ich bin.*"

"Recognized who?" Carl cried impatiently. "Who are you talking about?"

The old man inhaled. Ash fell on the tablecloth as he placed the cigarette in the ashtray to right of his plate.

"That woman was Carolina Hampton." "What?"

"Karina Lanzberg back in those days. All these years I've been fooled," he said with a bitter laugh. "No wonder she avoided me, never let me get close to her husband and rarely let him buy any art from me. The risk of recognition was too great."

"Are you suggesting this Nazi Lanzberg woman in the picture paraded as a Manhattan socialite for over half a century and nobody recognized her?" Carl dropped onto the nearest chair. "That's pretty far-fetched. You'll have to explain."

"Very well. You remember me telling you about Schloss Heil?"

"Baron von Heil — your father's best friend's castle, on the Tegernsee whom you visited each year for the St. Hubertus. Sure, I remember."

"Very well. Karina Lanzberg's mother, Frau Lanzberg, was a distant relation of Baron von Heil and the family. Herr and Frau Lanzberg, Karina and her older brother Rainer were also invited, as were the Lourriels—"

"Lourriel? The bank in Fribourg?" Carl exclaimed.

"Exactly. It is not a common name. The Lourriel family joined us from Switzerland each year too. Father and Jean de Lourriel and Baron von Heil had studied together at Fribourg University just after the 14-18 war. I've told you this several times, Carl," he added irritated. "I don't remember much about Karina back in those days. Four years is a big difference in age when you're growing up. Rainer, the man in the picture," he said pointing with his cigarette," was my age. He and I had struck up a friendship even though he was a Nazi and had joined the Hitler Youth. Strange how at first none of that seemed to matter. It was only as the years went by things got tricky. But we remained friends. Or so I believed."

"Oh my God! He was the officer who arrested your father and Eli!" "Carl, I wish you wouldn't interrupt," Ephraim said testily.

"I'm sorry." Carl muttered. "But how can this Karina have been Carolina Hampton? It would take a hell of a lot of chutzpah to carry that off and get away with it."

"To you it may seem so, but you've never known a real Nazi. They're cunning and devious." He took another long drag and his eyes wandered. "I should have known the moment you mentioned that purse," he said, shaking his head back and forth. "I should have realized it was she on the day Eli and Papa were arrested when I saw her from the car."

"But you told me you were in the neighbor's garden, and you saw all that happened through the iron railings."

"*Ach*, I may be mistaken. It must be my memory. One forgets the exact circumstances after a while."

"Even something as significant as that?" Carl frowned.

"What does it matter to you where I was?" Ephraim snapped. "Isn't it enough that the last time I saw my father alive was with a rifle in his back, being pushed like a common criminal into an SS truck, and Eli dragged out of our home by his heels, his head bumping on the pavement and blood everywhere? I wanted to rush in and help them, but I knew if I did they'd arrest me too and I'd be of no use to anyone."

Uncle Ephraim sighed, his features distorted behind a spiral of smoke.

"I have carried the guilt ever since. Why them? Why not me? It will go with me to my grave. Of course I did my best to save them. I went straight to see Baron von Heil. I asked him to use his contacts, anything to get them released. But he wouldn't budge. At the end of the day they were all Nazis and we were Jews, and the so-called friendship simply frittered away. I found out soon enough why. Baron von Heil had bought our house. I never learned whether he paid a fair price for it."

"I see," Carl said gently. "But let's come back to Karina Lanzberg. You said she was outside your home on the day of the arrest?"

The old man paused and sighed. "After they took Papa and Eli away, I saw a woman at the top of the steps with Rainer."

"So he was the Nazi officer who betrayed your family?" Carl insisted. "Yes he was. Carl, you sound like a parrot."

"But why? You said he was your friend."

"There were no *friends* for us Jews in Germany in 1938. When I realized that Rainer was the officer in charge of the arrest, I was paralyzed. A man who'd called my father "uncle" all his life, a dear friend since childhood. A man I—" his voice broke and he took several fast puffs before continuing. "I saw a woman talk to Rainer, then come down the steps and out the gate. She passed by my car and—"

"So you were in the car."

"*Verdammt noch mal*! One more interruption and I shall stop talking! Yes, she passed my car," Ephraim snapped. "Then she walked down the damn street, as though she was in a hurry. She wore a headscarf and a baggy English raincoat and you know what she was carrying?" He plucked the cutting from Carl's hand and pointed. "That handbag."

"How can you be so sure it was this *Sac à* something Luna discovered in Carolina's closet?" Carl frowned taken aback. "You can't see it properly in the photograph. Maybe you're confused."

"Not about that," Ephraim shook his head firmly. "It was a distinctive purse, different to the bags girls carried in those days. Likely she'd purloined it from some poor Jewish woman she'd had deported."

"And you think—".

"I don't *think*, I'm certain. Carl, you must get it back. The purse is our ticket."

"But what about the Chagall? It's proof." He glanced at the painting lying discarded at the end of the dining room table.

"You can take down the Picasso print in my room and hang it there instead."

"But it can't stay here Uncle Ephraim, I must take it back to the Penthouse. Luna could come back any day and discover it missing."

"*Ach*, leave her alone. And make sure you keep her there in Fribourg until you can get there and sort this out."

"You want me to go to Fribourg, Switzerland? To do what? Claim Carolina Hampton was Karina Lanzberg with no proof to back it up?" Carl exclaimed. "Things aren't that simple, Uncle Ephraim. The woman had an excellent reputation. Who would believe a man like Henry Hampton had married an escaped Nazi? He was an officer and a gentleman. The man had a Purple Heart. He's buried in Arlington Cemetery, for Christ sakes. Plus it doesn't explain how the cigar and the bank info got inside the purse. And another thing," he added, "surely if Carolina had known the was an account, she would have gone after it herself?"

"And risked being exposed and spending the rest of her life in jail? That would hardly have been a wise decision."

Ephraim laughed bitterly and leaned back. His eyelids closed. His breathing was labored and his hands clasped the arms of the wheelchair like talons. Carl wondered if the dementia Dr. Frankel had mentioned might be more advanced than they'd thought.

Uncle Ephraim revived and reached automatically in his pocket for another cigarette. He seemed off in a world of his own unaware.

Carl peered at the photograph and imagined Gestapo officers, prisoners with bruised faces tied to chairs and blood everywhere...Luna and Carolina shopping at Barneys and dollar bills floating like green clouds in a sky filled with human skeletons and striped pajamas. He rose and paced the room. In the kitchen Mrs. Katz hummed off-key. He turned back and faced the table. The cat jumped up and settled in Uncle Ephraim's lap.

"Let's regroup," he said. "Assuming Karina Lanzberg escaped Germany and got away with the Carolina Hampton disguise, it still doesn't explain why Eli drew that cartoon. You were certain there was something in the back of the Chagall, Uncle Ephraim. And there was. But not what you expected. I always thought you two got along well. But that seems a pretty twisted thing for a twin brother to do to the other."

"Carl, Carl, it doesn't matter. Stop reasoning like a lawyer. Time is of the essence. Surely it's obvious my father would have entrusted any money he'd gotten out of Germany to Jean de Lourriel, a Swiss banker and his trusted friend? Any possible money is ours. I know it. I feel it. You must go there at once and explain to the bankers before Luna claims it."

Carl got up, shook his head and stepped over to the window. Some of what Uncle Ephraim said made sense. He'd been partially right about the back of the Chagall and his reaction to the cartoon was a clear indication Eli had drawn it. A link between the purse and it's contents, the painting and the Banque Lourriel seemed reasonable. Oh God. Was it possible he'd worked all these years for a man whose wife had helped murder his family?

"I'm not sure what to do." He muttered, dragging his hand through his hair. "You're the lawyer. You should know."

"There's a legal protocol that needs to be followed."

"No Carl! There's no time to waste."

"Short of freezing Luna's assets based on a claim that Carolina was a war criminal, I really don't see —"

"There you go! She gave you an unlimited power of attorney, didn't she?" "Yes, she did."

"Then use it, damn it!"

Chapter 16

Luna took a wrong turn at the top of the hill and ended several blocks north of the Fribourg train station. By the time she'd found her way back and retrieved her carry-on case and trundled it back down the street to the roundabout, she was ready to drop.

She crossed the road. A few hundred feet down to her left was the garage entrance to a shopping mall. She walked past an Italian restaurant and into the *Grande Place*, a large square dotted with tour buses and parked vehicles. Behind these was a nondescript concrete high-rise she assumed was the hotel.

At the entrance, a group of Japanese tourists was about to board their bus. Luna stepped inside the lobby and heading over to the reception, waited for a sullen-faced girl behind the counter to look up from her screen.

"Bonjour," Luna smiled, and placed her Birkin on the counter to attract her attention. *"J'aimerais une chambre pour une nuit, s'il-vous-plait."*

"Vous avez reservé?"

"Non."

"A single?" She cast a look behind her as if expecting a man to pop out of the faceless

decor.

"Yes, a single. Unless—is it very small?" "A bit."

"Then make it a double." All she needed was a bed, a Wi-Fi connection that worked and hopefully a bathtub. She might as well be as comfortable as possible. "Do you have a Spa?"

"No."

"Never mind." She watched as the young woman consulted her screen.

"I can give you a double with bath and view over the Old Town, on the fourth floor." "I'll take it."

"That'll be 380 CHF, breakfast included."

"Perfect." Luna pulled out her wallet and retrieved a credit card from among a row of platinum plastic and slid it across the counter.

"I'll leave my bag here and go and have a drink once I'm registered," she said. "You can't leave it here. There's no one to take it," the girl said.

Luna was not used to unhelpful receptionists who acted as though she was a nuisance and they were doing her a favor.

"Is the mall next door still open?" She inquired.

"Yes," the girl answered grudgingly, swiping the card.

"Good!" She wasn't sure why she'd asked. Right now, she felt brain-dead and all she wanted was to go to her room and crash. She stifled a yawn and waited for the receptionist to finish checking her in.

"I'm sorry, *Madame*, but your credit card has been refused.

"Refused? But that's impossible. Can you try it again, please?" She wasn't sure what the limit on any of her cards was, or if there even was one. They'd just always worked.

"I've tried twice already, and it's being refused again."

"There must be a mistake. Perhaps your machine has a problem?"

"The machine is fine." The girl shrugged and handed Luna back the card. "Do you have another one?"

"Sure." She pulled out another card and handed it to her. "It's asking for your code."

"Of course." The receptionist swiveled the credit card machine on the counter. Luna's stomach lurched as she tapped in the numbers.

"I'm sorry, but this one has been refused as well."

"But that's simply not possible!"

"It happens." The hazel eyes across the counter altered from sullen to sympathetic. "I hate it when it does. I wanted to buy my mom — who's in the hospital with terminal cancer — a gift, and my card didn't go through." Her eyes filled. "I apologize," she mumbled. "That was unprofessional of me. I don't know why I said it. My manager would be furious if he knew." She wiped her eyes and glanced over her shoulder.

Instinctively, Luna placed a hand on the young woman's and squeezed her fingers. Then a man's shadow appeared in the doorway behind her and she let go. "Perhaps I can pay in cash," she said, fumbling in her wallet, "but I'll have to withdraw some more money. Can you hold the room for me?"

"I'm sorry, *Madame*, not without an authorized card on file. The hotel policy forbids it. There's a cash machine around the corner, to your right," she pointed.

"I'll be right back".

A middle-aged couple waiting behind her to check in watched in tandem as she retreated, trundling her carry-on. Their eyes bored into her back as, cheeks flaming, she hurried out of the lobby.

It was cold and already dusk lurked. Luna hastened to the corner, turned right, and made her way to the ATM machine in the wall of a building.

"Pleeease, pleeease work," she begged. She pulled out a cash card and waited impatiently for the woman in front of her to finish her transaction, before stepping up to the machine and slipping her card inside the slot. She'd never experienced tension like this, not to mention embarrassment. She waited impatiently for the screen to alter and tapped in her code.

Pas de transaction possible en ce moment.

"Oh no! Not again?" What is wrong!" She exclaimed. "*Excusez-moi, vous avez fini?*"

She glanced over her shoulder at a young man with a toddler waiting expectantly behind her.

"*Pardon.*" She smiled apologetically, then turned around to retrieve her card. Nothing.

She tapped harder. Then desperately. But her card had been gobbled up and the screen read:

Your card has been retained. Please contact your bank.

Luna's hands shook as she stepped away. This had to be a nightmare. At the corner of the slippery pavement she stopped to catch her breath. The wheels of the carry-on caught her ankle.

"Ouch!"

She must phone Candice, her bank manager. Perhaps she'd blocked her cards as a security measure to avoid fraud?

She dialed Candice's direct line.

A cold north-easterly wind had picked up. Luna trod the pavement to keep warm, then walked with one hand clutching her phone and the other her case, past the drivers at the taxi rank standing in a huddle next to their cabs, waiting for fares.

She stopped in the outer entrance of a building and listened to the phone ring in Candice's office.

"Hello. Loretta, assistant to Candice Leroy, speaking."

"Hi Loretta, is Candice there? It's Luna Hampton speaking."

"I'm afraid that Candice is in a meeting right now, Mrs. Hampton. Can I help you?"

"Probably. I'm in Switzerland and for some reason my cash and credit cards are being refused, most likely as a security measure. It's my fault. I should have advised that I was going to travel outside the US." She experienced relief now that she'd identified the reason for her cards being blocked.

"Just one moment, Mrs. Hampton, I'll get right back to you."

Bumper-to-bumper traffic at the round-a-bout. Barbara Streisand crooning about one less bell to answer in her left ear. She peered across the parking lot at the hotel. Within minutes, the card problem would be sorted and she'd walk back inside the lobby, head high, smile graciously across the counter and hand that poor young receptionist her card. How quick we are to judge.

"Sorry to keep you on hold, Mrs. Hampton." "No problem."

"Candice said to tell you that she's very sorry but that all your cards, both cash and credit, have been blocked until further notice."

"What?" Luna squealed. "But that's crazy. Did she tell you the reason?"

"I'm sorry, but I'm not at liberty to discuss the reasons for which your cards were blocked at this time, Mrs. Hampton. All Candice said to tell you was," she adds, lowering her voice, "that there is nothing she can do about it personally, since the order came from the top."

"But that's crazy. There has to be a mistake!"

"That's all I'm authorized to say, Mrs. Hampton. Good bye."

The phone went dead. In the distance, the cathedral clock struck six times. The moon rose behind the clouds. Surely this had to be unreal? She was the sole beneficiary to the Hampton fortune yet unable to afford to stay at a hotel, that minutes earlier, she'd turned her nose up at and which right now felt like heaven compared with nowhere.

Carl would sort it. She punched in his number but his phone went straight to voicemail. She left a frantic message. Oh, my God! What if he didn't listen to his voicemail for several hours? She' be stranded. Never in her entire life has Luna been without money, or worst case, the ability to access some immediately.

Her hands were frozen and her teeth chattered. Was it cold or fear? She stepped out into the parking lot, unsure of where to go. A warped reflection stared back at her from the darkened windscreen of an SUV. She should have gotten the bank director's cell phone numbers. The Bank was closed now. Unless Carl got back to her, she'd have nowhere to stay and be left trailing her case around the streets all night.

American heiress freezes to death on the streets of Fribourg… In the early hours, this morning a corpse was discovered…

Up until she'd stepped off the train that morning, Luna's life was protected and predictable, and now she was stranded.

To the left of the parking lot, pumpkin-colored lights flickered in the windows of a run- down two-story house with squiggly blue and white painted shutters. A sign over the entrance door read: *Paddy O'Reilly's Irish Tavern.* It might not be the Grill at the Four Seasons, but at least it'd be warm while she figured out her next step.

Chapter 17

Luna hastened across the lot and sidled up to a wooden door plastered with flyers. As she pushed it open, she was met with the pungent odor of fish and chips.

The fake-beamed interior fulfilled the pub's outward expectations. An excited voice commented a horse race on the flat screen TV. Luna held the door and hesitated. Seventies pop music, stale cigarette smoke, deep fried food and beer stains. She hadn't stepped inside a place like this since college, and even then, never alone. But what choice was there? It was this or freeze.

She entered the tavern. The barman with tattooed biceps pumping under a skimpy tank top as he polished a glass with a checkered dishcloth, sent an appreciative glance her way. Forty-eight hours ago, she could have texted Juan to pick her up on the curb, or signaled a waiter who'd understand what she wanted without being told. Instead, three men perched on leather stools and sipped pints. One of them grinned at her. Part of a chewed French fry deliberately fell on his unshaven chin. The other two appeared to be engaged in a serious conversation. Luna hadn't eaten since her first-class breakfast mimosa on the plane that morning, but any hunger just died. The good news was that it was warm, and most of the booths appeared empty.

Pretending not to notice the grinning French fry chewer, she marched inside the tavern and headed past a smooching couple towards the furthest booth where she squeezed as far along the wooden bench as she could, and sat under a tipping Guinness poster and a wilting felt shamrock.

Her case stood beside the table. Luna placed her purse next to her on the bench, leaned back and ignoring the stench of moldy carpet, closed her eyes to catch her breath. Surely, this was just a nightmare from which she'd wake up?

Images jostled and the years lost their boundaries: Nana, in a twin set and pearls reading *Pride and Prejudice* to her in the Park Avenue drawing room while she played with the cord of the drapes… Her Barbie dolls vying for space among china ornaments on the Louis XV commode that resembled the one in Nana's bedroom, and her soft lilting voice as she'd recounted fairy tales of princes and wolves and children lost in the forest. And more recently, seated in her tapestried chair in the dining room beneath the Murano sconces, where she'd lain in her casket, her fine hands peeking from beneath the cuffs that she'd been unable to raise sufficiently to identify the only real clue to Nana's past.

The candle-lit pumpkins in the window embrasures grimaced at her. All at once she remembered Alice, a girl from her boarding school right here in Switzerland. Alice had married an Indian prince. The last time they'd lunched together in Paris, she'd told her that she was afraid to get divorced for fear she wouldn't know how to pack a suitcase by herself any more. Which begged the question: had she lived thirty floors above reality, cut off from the world for so long, that she didn't know how to function in the real world either?

"*Bonsoir.*" A waitress in a bright mini skirt threw her a bright smile, stretched across her to wipe the table with a damp cloth, then planted a plastic menu with garish photographed dishes onto the scratched wooden surface.

She must order *something* if she was to stay in the warmth. She'd consumed enough coffee at the bank to keep her wired for a month. A row of whisky bottles on the shelves above a fake Irish antique sideboard, caught her eye.

"*Un whisky, s'il vous plait.*"

"*Lequel?*" The girl pushed the gum she'd been chewing inside her cheek and rolled off two-dozen names of whiskies that meant little or nothing to Luna. At last she pronounced Glenlivet, one of Henry's favorites.

"Un Glenlivet s'il-vous-plait." "Rien à manger?"

Luna peered at the plastic menu.

"Rien, merci."

In the next booth, the smooching couple were lost to the world as were the three girls giggling and drinking pints in the far corner.

Minutes later, a glass of amber liquid appeared. Her first whisky. Neither Nana or Henry would approve. But they weren't here to approve or disapprove. In fact, they'd left her high and dry. She took a sip and welcomed the warm sensation that crept up inside her. Perhaps she'd turn to alcohol.

Carl hadn't called back. She dialed him once more but to no avail. She left another message.

After a second sip, Luna tipped the contents of the Birkin onto the table and stared at her strewn belongings; she had seventy bucks in her wallet, a bunch of useless plastic, crumpled receipts, a lipstick-smeared Kleenex, yesterday's boarding pass, a half-eaten Mars bar and an empty Evian bottle.

Why the rush of tears? It is pointless to panic.

Since the night of her wake, Nana was silent despite Luna's efforts to establish communication. The truth was, she was alone. All alone. Was this how Nana had felt when she stood at the gates of the concentration camp, her *Sac à Dépèches* clutched in her young girl hands, uncertain of what the future held in store?

She needed a miracle. Luna opened her phone. *The Girl in the Red Dress Under the Moon* stared back at her. "Please Nana," she whispered, "If you're out there, could you please give me a sign?"

But nothing moved in the painting and no Rolls Royce burst through the fake-beamed ceiling to swoop her up and carry her to safety, as Nana had when she was four. Instead, the waitress slipped the reality check under the ketchup holder: she was 4000 miles from home, she had no working credit cards and little ready cash. Carl hadn't rung her back, and worst of all, she had no accommodation for the night.

Chapter 18

A seventy-five-year-old newspaper clipping was not enough evidence to stand up in court. He needed concrete proof to build his case. Blocking Luna's funds impulsively was a rash move, but he'd done it anyway. Plus, she had the envelope he'd had couriered over to the penthouse before her departure with five thousand euros in cash. It was unlikely she'd need to use her credit cards.

He'd turned off his phone to focus on obliging Uncle Ephraim to go over the details of the past again and again. The old boy's altered version of the arrest was troubling. He'd always said he'd been hiding in the neighbor's garden when it happened. Now he claimed he was in a car parked down the street. Carl was having a hard time accepting this alternative version of Uncle Ephraim's past.

The passage of time had obviously played a role. And the idea that Carolina was the woman in the grainy photograph disguised for over half a century as a Polish Countess and Manhattan socialite, not to mention Luna's discovery of the purse and its contents and the cartoon in the back of the Chagall, was as far-fetched as it gets. Still, what if Uncle Ephraim's theory was less crazy than it at first appeared? One thing he'd learned at Harvard Law, was to step out of the box and compartmentalize.

Carl had given up trying to remove the Chagall from Uncle Ephraim for now and left it hanging on the wall opposite his bed. He slipped the 1942 newspaper clipping inside his pocket to make copies and stepped out into the cold. He turned right and ambled slowly up the street and thought about what to do next.

The wind had picked up and Carl pulled his scarf over his mouth, tramped up the pavement to the brightly lit restaurant on the corner and pushed open the glass door with the chipped slanted red letters that read: *Avi's Diner.* He'd last stepped foot in it at the age of ten when Mama was giving birth to Leah, his baby sister. He'd been sent to stay with Uncle Ephraim and had been given five dollars — which he'd spent on a vanilla milkshake and a burger, here at Avi's. He invested the rest on Sonny, a goldfish he'd bought at the pet shop down the road, and kept in his room in a bowl, just as Uncle Ephraim had told him he and Eli had kept their goldfish back in the old country. Those days spent in Uncle Ephraim's exotic universe and the realization that the old man in the velvet robe had once been a ten-year-old too, bonded them. From that day forward, Carl became his great-uncle's disciple. He begged for stories. He pictured people and locations. Uncle Ephraim's rich storytelling abilities linked him to a long-lost world that had little in common with his middle-class upbringing. Even as an adult, Carl had never stopped to wonder or question how real the anecdotes that had embellished his youth and separated him the most common of mortals, actually were.

Now, seated on the same red stool as the one he'd sat on the day he'd acquired the goldfish, Carl swallowed a lump in his throat.

"What can I get you, hon?"

He ordered. The diner was cheery. Avi's grandson flipped burgers on a sizzling range. French fries sizzled in deep fat. Coffee filtered in large glass pots. A pot-bellied middle aged man, two stools to his left, was sharing his views on the recent election with the waitress pouring his coffee.

"What's done is done and they should give the guy a chance," he said. "You never know, it may turn out for the best. Never hurt to have a tough guy at the helm. Who else would tell those motherfuckers over there to get lost? We've pussy-footed around for long enough. It's time to get tough. And the markets are on the rise..."

Carl sipped his root beer and stared into the bowl of chicken soup. He picked up the spoon and stirred, reminded of the Nobel Laureate, Elie Weisel and the fish head and how he tried to find something positive even in the disgusting gruel that had kept him barely alive in Auschwitz. But all Carl saw floating just below the surface were alternative versions of the past…

~

He'd been to Bavaria and done the twenty-minute trip from the Marien Platz to the picture-perfect village of Dachau, on a stop-over on his way to a conference in Salzburg. He'd joined a tour with a middle-aged Chilean music professor and his Canadian wife, who'd both lost family members during the Holocaust and had lived their own experiences of torture and terror during the Pinochet era, and an Israeli girl of nineteen in hiking boots and a backpack almost as big as her. It was her fifth visit to Dachau. She'd told them proudly it was her third vacation touring the camps. She'd been to Auschwitz and Treblinka too. She talked endlessly, rolling out statistics in a Brooklyn twang. Carl felt sorry for her, so young yet trapped in a time warp. She'd confided that she was on a dating site with a settler, and her dream was to marry him and go live in the Golan Heights.

Carl had mixed views on the matter of appropriation of Palestinian land. The legal basis struck him as tenuous, at best. But he kept his mouth shut. He'd distanced himself from all that years ago, and learned early on in life that arguing with fanatics was a waste of breath.

The guide was a Latvian history student. They'd chatted on their way. Carl had tried to imagine what Eli and his father must have felt when they made the same trajectory, the moment they'd stepped through the wrought iron gates with *"Arbeit macht Frei"* written above them, and their first glimpses of skeletal inmates, and the realization of the horror they faced.

The cabins seemed sterile. No smells, no lice, none of the human anguish, just neat wooden bunks a bit like a student hostel. The German government had made a point of preserving the camp as an historical landmark; a reminder of this dark period of the country's history. But life goes on. Rows of inhabited houses bordered the barbed wire fence. How, he'd wondered, could people live here?

The communal showers. He'd imagined lines of naked men standing right here where he stood. Their screams, their despair. The panic. Fingernails clawing the tiled walls. His breath became short. All at once he could smell the scent rising from the nearby chimneys. Mirja, the guide, had been told by an elderly inhabitant of the village, that there was no mistaking the acrid scent of burning flesh.

He'd gazed up at the pipes, imagined the lethal gas emerging… then wondered where Eli and his father had fallen, and what their last thoughts were before they'd succumbed.

Carl had hesitated before entering the red brick building that housed the ovens. Which one were Aaron and Eli's bodies burned in? Finally, he'd stepped inside and came face to face with the unimaginable: a small child from another tour group, who'd escaped its father's hand, ran towards one of the ovens and climbed inside. The mother laughed and snapped a picture on her phone. Carl wanted to hit her, drag the bitch outside and throttle her. Stick her fucking head inside the oven and turn on the Goddamn mains and see how funny she thought that was! Instead, he'd exited the building and hurried behind it and retched. Mirja was waiting for him when he returned, wiping his mouth with a tissue that he chucked inside a pristine trash can.

"Are you okay?" He nodded.

"I do this tour because my great-grandmother died here. She was fifteen. It's my way of keeping her memory alive. As for them," Mirja said, following the couple with the child wandering off in the opposite direction, "it's just something that happened a long time ago. They have no idea."

They'd joined the others. On the train, back to Munich, a loud-mouthed Aussie harped on about how history should be looked at in perspective. Maybe the Jews were in part responsible for what had happened to them. After all, everyone knew that they'd run the German economy. Maybe they'd gotten too big for their boots and needed to be taught a lesson.

Carl rose. "Excuse me, but I overheard what you said."

"Yeah? What's the matter, mate?" The truculent red-faced man challenged. "My family was murdered in Dachau. I don't appreciate your comments."

"I'm sorry about that, but facts are facts, mate, and everyone has a right to their opinion."

"Sure. But I'd just like to advise you that I'm an attorney, and one more comment like the ones you just made, and I'll fucking sue you from here to the Great Barrier Reef."

The rest of the carriage stared at him, amazed. He was amazed. He'd never reacted like that before in his life.

~

"Aren't you gonna' eat that, hon?"

"No, thanks. I'm not hungry. I'll have the check, please." Carl blinked at the middle- aged waitress. Her red lipstick and caked makeup emphasized the grooves surrounding her mouth. He got off the stool and pulled a twenty-dollar bill out of his wallet and placcd it on thc countcr.

"Keep the change," he muttered.

Back on the street, he glanced at his watch. It was almost 6pm. It was obvious that his duty right now was to try and dig up all and any proof he could. For all their sakes. But how would he go about it? The only place he could think of was the Hampton's penthouse.

He took a few more steps, stopped on the corner and thought for a moment, then hailed a cruising cab. It came to a crunching halt and he climbed in.

"Drop me off on the corner of Park Avenue and East 56th, please."

If he was going to be a sleuth, he might as well get on with it.

Chapter 19

The whisky had left Luna light-headed. The soles of her high-heeled boots skidded like ice skates on the skating rink of the *Palace Hotel* in Saint Moritz where in her cherry-red skirt and white tights, she had performed figure-eights under Fraulein Traut, with the skating teacher's critical gaze, while Nana and Henry watched from the sidelines wrapped in fur and smiles. She was eight. They'd stayed for a month. They'd ridden in horse-drawn sleighs and sipped hot chocolate. And Henry's team had won the curling championship.

Luna tottered across the empty street. It was midnight and the city felt like a ghost town. The waitress had recommended a small cheap hotel in the Rue de Lausanne, a few hundred yards away. Why, oh why hadn't Carl answered her messages? This was all his fault. If something was wrong at the bank, then it was his job to fix it, damn it! And fast. It was outrageous that she should find herself halfway across the world, in a strange city with no means of sustenance. If Henry knew, he'd fire him on the spot. Not that she wanted Carl fired. He'd proved he was much more than just a business manager. He was a friend. And she had so few.

Clutching her Birkin in one hand, and pulling the carry-on with the other, Luna slithered across *Place Python.* Her teeth chattered. Several youths lounging in a doorway smoked and laughed as she passed as she tried not to trip on the cobbled street. Snowflakes settled on the shoulders of her shorn mink. Thank God it was not ostentatious. It could even pass as a fake among the illiterati.

At last, she saw a dingy glass door surrounded by tacky colored Christmas lights and *Cabaret* lit above it in neon light. The hotel entrance looked like something out of a 1960's B movie. Luna paused, then shrugged and headed inside. A base box thumped presumably in the cabaret next door. She pushed open the door and entered. Her fingers and cheeks tingled at the sudden warmth. She walked down a corridor leading to a neon lit reception desk. Her nose and eyes were running. She let go of the carry-on and fumbled in the Birkin for a Kleenex while a churlish, middle-aged man, sitting slouched in a plastic chair, looked up and gave her the once-over.

"*Quel est le prix d'une chambre simple*?" She asked, cheeks flaming. She'd never inquired the price of anything in her entire life, let alone a hotel room in an establishment of this category.

"*Ca depend*," he replied. "Are you alone or expecting someone?" "Alone."

"Then it's 80 francs."

A side door burst open and music blared. A girl in fishnet stockings and a skirt as short as the waitress' at the pub, a leather jacket, heavy eyeliner and an expanse of bare breast weaved in.

A fake diamond disappeared between her bosom. She leaned on the arm of an older man with silver-streaked hair. Another man wandered in behind them dressed in a dark suit and an open-neck shirt. His jet-black hair was slicked back with large quantities of gel. The minute he spied Luna, he ogled her, then let out a low whistle.

She froze. The ogler sidled closer. She took a step back. He touched her arm and she cringed. A voice inside her head screamed, but her mouth remained shut.

"Classy," he murmured, stroking the fur. "Looking for company, *ma belle*?" His right index finger glided over the fur suggestively. She drew further back until she was plastered up against the wall. "Shy are you, *chérie*?" The man laughed. "Surely not? Somebody must have been damn pleased with your performance to have given you this coat. *Allez, viens*. Let's go up. The room's on me," he added turning to his cohort behind the desk. The girl and the man snickered.

Luna was back on the street unsure of how she'd gotten there. Her legs trembled, but she trudged on, anxious to put as much distance as she could between her and the man's fetid breath and sickly aftershave.

Christmas lights arched above her. Four brightly clad youths were making merry. Otherwise, the street was empty. Her boots squelched. Her feet were soaked. But she kept going, up the *Rue de Romont*, past the closed banks and stores and restaurants, hopping towards the only familiar spot: the train station.

She reached the main entrance. Surely there was somewhere she could sit and figure out a solution?

The main station hallway was not warm, but it was a darn sight less cold than outside. One coffee shop remained open and Luna hurried towards it, collapsed on a bench and ordered a hot chocolate. She unzipped her boots. Her stockings stuck to her soles. She massaged her frozen toes. When the waitress placed the steaming cup before her, she clasped it in both her palms, thankful for the warmth. It reminded her of the vets she'd seen living under bridges. She licked the froth off the top of the hot chocolate. Nana always said it was vulgar to do that. But tonight, the last thing that mattered was etiquette. She needed every ounce of warmth she could get her hands on. The frothy, hot liquid tasted delicious. And familiar. And brought tears to her eyes; Vienna and the Sacher Hotel... *Papagino Papagino*... Mozart's Magic Flute. Her first opera at the age of seven. It was still her favorite. And *Papagino* still enchanted.

A train rumbled above her. Late night commuters' briefcases swung past their calves — intent on getting home. Three hoodies lounged against the wall. Two girls in black leather and pierced ears and noses approached them. A package exchanged hands. Oh God! Drug dealers!

She checked her phone. What was the matter with Carl? Surely he must have picked up her messages by now? In all the years she'd known him, he's never not picked up. Wasn't being available at all times part of his job? But what if Carl's silence wasn't voluntary? What if, at this very moment, he lay sprawled on the tarmac, run over by a bus or a car? He could have been mugged running in the park, or victim of a terrorist attack and fighting for his life in the hospital, hanging on by a thread, while she thought of money and her own present needs.

Surreptitiously, Luna counted the coins in her wallet. Sixty-three francs and a few cents left from the envelope.

She'd never had nowhere to sleep. Would she be obliged to spend the night here in the hallway of the train station like a homeless person? Shit, her battery was about to die and her charger won't fit in the Swiss socket. If she'd remembered correctly, her international adaptor was in the bottom of her case. Luna switched her phone off and thought about who in the world, except Carl, she could call upon to help her. It wouldn't be fair to worry Maria and Susan was in Maine visiting her mother.

Surely there must be someone? Henry and Nana's few remaining friends were too old and wouldn't understand. Jeff? No. She'd lost touch with everyone she knew in college. In truth, she'd lived vicariously in Nana and Henry's world for so long that she was alone outside of it. The real world was a place she'd only dipped her toe into periodically.

She depleted her meager funds and ordered another hot chocolate. Luna was the only client left in the cafe. The waitress behind the counter was removing trays of sandwiches and doughnuts while another pushed a mop in her direction.

"On ferme en dix minutes, madame."

Luna zipped up her damp boots. She placed the Birkin on her carry-on and pulled them both with one hand and held her cup of hot chocolate in the other. Then, exiting the cafe, she walked across the empty station hallway to the nearest bench and sat down. The hoodies watched. Luna held her Birkin tightly on her knee and crossed one arm over it. Trains rumbled overhead like grumbling monsters and a cold draft blew from the direction of the station entrance. She sipped the hot chocolate but it did not transmit the same reassurance as the previous one had.

The trash can next to her stank of motley sandwich remains and cigarette butts. Luna slid along the bench as far removed from it as possible. The hoodies and the girls let out raucous laughs and chugged beer. There was little room left on the girls' faces for any more studs, or on their bodies for more tattoos.

The word *tattoo* conjured up images of Nana's arm and the endless testimonies she'd read and watched; the horror of the cabins, dysentery, feces dropping from upper bunks onto the person below. Flees and diphtheria. The horror and degradation that the soldiers, like Henry, who'd liberated the camps, had discovered. The stench. Piles of corpses lying by the wayside, rotting. Guards fleeing and mass graves. Every time Luna's anger surged at Nana for not telling her the truth, the thought of what she must have witnessed, doused it. Would she have wanted such an experience to be the single most marking moment of her life? That which she'll be remembered for? Or would she too, have left it behind and sought to make a new life with no baggage and a clean slate?

But Rachel knew. Rachel knows everything. She could call her now, but there was something about that woman she didn't trust. Not after what she'd done.

Nana had wanted to preserve Luna. That she understood. She'd done it with almost everything; the flowers, seating arrangements at dinner parties, house parties and plane trips. Nana had always gotten her own way; not aggressively but subtly. Henry once said that Carolina was the iron hand in the velvet glove. Perhaps he was right. She ignored what she didn't want to talk about, including the subject of her daughter Charlotte.

Who was Nana?

A month spent analyzing the universal truths that had dictated her life up until Nana's death were no longer etched in stone.

It was scary.

No less scary were the hoodies and their empty beer cans lining the floor next to them. One of them looked at her, then whispered something to the other.

Luna clung to the Birkin. The hoodies might know its true value. Birkin's are coveted items these days.

And, would God hear her prayers? She never went to church except to Christmas midnight mass with Henry and Nana and weddings and christenings. And funerals, of which lately there had been too many. Can mediation be counted as prayer? Not the *God, who art in heaven* kind of prayer, but more a conversation with the angels that happen to be around, and a connection to a higher power she's always known existed. Maybe. Still, both Einstein and Max Planck deduced it must exist, since beyond the beyond there was still a beyond that couldn't be identified.

Luna fixed her eyes firmly on the closed shutters of the newspaper stand. She read the billboard next to the door.

Trump menace l'aboliton d'Obamacare!

Oh God. If Obamacare was repealed and her funds remained frozen who would pay for Maria's blood pressure medication and Mrs. Rudge dialysis? She sent up a silent prayer and did a quick recap of her life. She'd never consciously done harm to anyone. She'd cared for both Henry and Nana and tried her best to make everyone happy. Even after Henry died, she continued to have old Buddy Sinclair over every Wednesday evening for a whisky and listened to the same WWII parachute stories again and again — pretending she hadn't heard them before and filling in the bits he'd forgotten. Buddy was 98 years old.

The hoodies were getting more rambunctious by the minute. This had to be a nightmare from which she'd wake up, stretching in 1000 count sheets with Maria pulling back the drapes and the scent of freshly ground coffee and gluten-free croissants wafting from her breakfast tray.

No coffee. No croissants.

The hoodies leered at her. She better keep her eyes down. She imagined a golden bubble of light surrounding her. Protection. She'd pray and hope Nana and her guardian angel would not abandon her.

Maybe this was a test of faith.

Chapter 20

Avoiding Carl's continual questions proved tiring, and after he left, Ephraim fell asleep. He woke, trapped in troubled dreams of the Chagall hanging on the wall opposite his bed. The last time he'd been this close to it was in the back of the staff car waiting for Rainer to return from inside the villa on that fateful day in 1938…

~

Ephraim lit another cigarette, smoked it down to the filter, then stubbed it out and lit another.

Why the hell was Rainer taking so long? Surely he should have called him to come inside the house by now? They had agreed *he* would be the one to explain to Papa and Eli how things stood, make them understand how lucky they were that he'd managed matters so skillfully, and that all would be well as long they cooperated.

Shouts from the villa had him scrambling on the back seat and plastering his face to the glass of the rear window.

"Oh mein Gott!" He gasped. Papa was being pushed into the truck with a rifle in his back. And what is that they were dragging? *Um Gottes will!* It was Eli. This wasn't how it was meant to be!

Ephraim gagged. What had he done? He was about to jump out of the car, but thought better of it. This must be part of Rainer's persuasion tactics, and he'd do better not to interfere.

He sagged into the depths of the leather seat and retched. His hands trembled badly. He could barely light another cigarette. What was Rainer doing? Why were things turning out differently to what was planned?

The chauffeur stood next to the vehicle. Ephraim leaned forward and peered in the rearview mirror. Two SS men were closing the doors of the back of the truck. He could see Rainer standing on the front porch talking to a young woman. He watched her descend the steps and exit the gates. She wore a headscarf and carried a brown leather handbag. The sleeves of her raincoat drooped over her hands. He watched her step onto the pavement and turn in his direction. When she was almost parallel with the car, Ephraim slithered down as she glanced over her shoulder. She looked familiar, but he couldn't place her. Seconds later, she was gone and Rainer came marching out the gate carrying something under his arm.

The chauffeur stood to attention. The door flew open and Rainer climbed back inside. "What happened? What have you done? This wasn't what we agreed!" Ephraim cried, restraining himself from grabbing his arm. "Why were they pushing Papa like that?"

"It's nothing." Rainer soothed. "It got a little out of hand, that's all. Everything will be fine."

"Were they dragging Eli unconscious?" He said, his lips trembling. "He acted up and had to be subdued. That's all. He'll be fine."

"You're sure that nothing bad will happen to them?" Ephraim peered out the rearview window again but the truck had gone. His hand shook as he reached for yet another cigarette. What had he done? What wheel had he set in motion?

Rainer pulled the glass partition closed and leaned towards him.

"Don't worry, *Mein Lieber*. It's just a little scare. They'll be taken to Gestapo headquarters and there they'll make sure they don't try anything stupid," Rainer studied the nails of his right hand. "There were pictures stacked against the wall ready to be moved. They were obviously planning to flee."

"Without me," Ephraim muttered. His shoulders slumped. He should have guessed how little they cared about him.

"Now, tell me, is this the right painting?" Rainer turned the picture he'd propped against the seat between them around and placed the Chagall on his knees as the car began to move."

"That's it. Thank you, Rainer." Ephraim reached for the painting. But Rainer whisked it out of his reach. "Not so fast, Ephi. I'm sending someone back in there to take some more pictures but I can't be greedy or take more than a few pieces without raising suspicion. So, which ones should I keep?"

"You mean *we*?"

Their eyes met. Rainer's lips curled. *"Naturlich!"*

Ephraim hesitated. A voice inside his head screamed, *beware*. For the first time, he didn't trust Rainer. But it was too late and he was in too deep. The die was cast and all he could do was play along. "Everything in there is valuable," he said at last. "Go for the small Breughel and the other Dutch masters. Now, can I have my painting?"

"All in good time." Rainer placed his leather gloves in the pocket of his overcoat and smoothed his manicured hand over the frame.

"Rainer, you promised me nothing would happen to Papa and Eli."

"Stop whining, *Mein Lieber*. Everything's fine. Just trust me and let things take their course." Rainer placed his right hand on Ephraim's knee and squeezed it. "You'll feel better after some champagne."

~

Chapter 21

Numb feet, stiff limbs, followed by pins and needles.

Luna stretched. The Fribourg station bench was hard. Oh my God, she'd dozed off! Was her case still next to her? She peered under her knees. Ouf! The Birkin still sat on her lap. She huddled it closer and searched for her phone. No battery left and nowhere to charge it. She wasn't used to sleeping in train stations or being left dangling like a spider on the end of a cobweb. She felt anxious and insecure.

At least the hoodies had left but the stores and cafes were still closed. Was she dreaming or was she lost and alone in an empty train station hallway with no money and nowhere to go? She felt like the bag ladies she'd seen in Hong Kong — women with fine features ravaged by life and unforeseen destinies.

Steps echoed. Two policeman passed by. One looked her way, but they didn't stop.

She pulled her jacket closer and the hood over her head. Did she look like a hoodie now too?

She'd never felt this stiff or this cold. Across the hallway a figure lay huddled asleep on a piece of cardboard, next to several plastic bags. The sum of their possessions? She thought of the time she and Henry returned from the White house to the Hay Adams through Lafayette Park…

~

It was nearly past 5pm on a grey December afternoon by the time she and Henry finished tea with the President and the First Lady and exited the White House. Henry had dismissed the limo saying he needed a walk. Nana was waiting for them back at the Hay Adams, still weak after a bout of flu.

They crossed Pennsylvania Avenue. On the corner of the street, a group of hearty, brightly clad carol singers sung *Deck the Halls.* Headlights and Christmas lights fused as afternoon turned to dusk.

They headed into Lafayette Park where a group of protestors was packing up for the night, then walked briskly on. Henry liked to walk at a good clip. He prided himself on keeping up a regular exercise regimen.

Up ahead, a pair of scruffy, bearded vets sat huddled on a bench lighting cigarette stubs. Henry slowed and touched Luna's arm.

"Look at that," he muttered. "It makes all those subsidies we talked about today sound like hubris when poverty, hunger, job loss and tottering health care lurk within a few hundred yards of the White House." He shook his head and Luna nodded. Henry's America had always been a haven of privilege and plenty. He'd fought a war in the name of the democratic values his ancestors had helped found. But sights like these sullied the hope-and-glory image of his country. She knew it disgusted him that the nation's capital — the center of world power that by the same token possessed the simple charm and grace of a small southern town — ignored the consequences of that might.

"Let's give them something," she said. "Do you have any change?"

"No, but I have a hundred-dollar bill," he muttered, feeling inside his coat pocket.

Luna stood next to Henry as he struck up a conversation with the two men. She loved him for the genuine interest he took in those less fortunate and the time and dedication he put into the causes he espoused. He pressed the bill in the palm of one of the surprised veterans and continued across the park.

"Its' not good enough," he said. "It's just not right. I'm having lunch tomorrow with Senator Byrd. I'll make sure he knows what's going on."

On the far side of the park they'd slowed; raw, pungent dampness even at this distance, drifted in from the Potomac.

"Luna. Always remember. Those men gave their lives to defend this country. When I'm gone, make sure you keep up our work with the vets. I'm counting on you."

~

Once she'd gotten a hold of Carl and he'd reinstated her cards and all this was sorted, she'd make sure all the Christmas donations had been taken care of. Having nowhere to go and nowhere to sleep for one night was bad enough. Just Imagine living like this 24/7?

It was 4am. Everything was still closed. She'd wished she'd invested in a bottle of water instead of the second cup of hot chocolate — now clotted dregs stuck to the side of the paper cup next to her on the bench.

Luna picked up the cup. Each time she threw something in the trash she experienced a connection with the rotting items abandoned there as she had been. Surely the angels who'd blessed her back in Medeelin would not have brought her this far to then desert her? She placed the Birkin in her lap and prayed. If they'd seen fit to give her an Hermes purse worth thousands of dollars, then surely they'd find a place for her to stay?

Something on the bench caught her eye: a business card. She picked it up, certain it hadn't been there before.

La Maison des Anges. B&B. Chambres 50 CHF.

"The Angel House?"

She turned the card over. On the back was a sketch of a small château. It looked perfect and was doable within her present budget. She'd go there at once.

It suddenly occurred to her she'd taken more decisions in the last 24 hours than she'd had in the past 28 years.

Luna rose and grabbed her case. Her prayers had been answered after all. And Nana was closer than she'd thought, and had come to her rescue. Of that she was certain.

Chapter 22

The clock on the wall above the desk in Henry Hampton's study struck twice. Carl stretched. It was 10:30pm and he'd sifted through files for the better part of the evening.

Upon his arrival at the penthouse, he'd explained to Juan and Maria that this was the only time he had available to sort Henry's papers.

"I'll likely be here a while, so don't stay up," he'd said to Juan.

"Maria says if you work until *muy tarde* you should sleep over. She prepared the Blue guest room for you, *Senor.*"

Carl had pretended to hesitate. Juan had insisted as he'd entered the study and removed his jacket and placed it on the armchair, then stepped behind the desk and sat in Andrew Jackson's swivel chair and raised his hands in mock resignation. "It's very thoughtful of her. I might just do that."

On the desk was an unopened envelope, written in his hand and addressed to Luna; the money he'd sent over.

"Damn," he muttered. She must've missed it. Perhaps she'd already left by the time it arrived. Oh, well. No doubt she'd taken a stash of dollars with her that she could exchange for local currency.

He stepped over to the cabinet beneath the sailing prints and studied rows of color-coded files. They were all in perfect order. He searched for anything remotely connected to Carolina: *Jewelry Inventory, Personal Documents*, etc. He flipped through them. Nothing.

He searched further until he reached *Art.*

Carl withdrew the file and sat down at the desk once more and sifted through several receipts pertaining to minor artwork Henry had acquired at galleries and art shows. A nameless bill handwritten in Spanish caught his eye:

Marc Chagall

La chica en en el traje rojo mirando la luna.

$4,320,0000

On the bottom, left-hand side, Henry had written R. Monteflecha. Buneos Aires, 12/12/04.

Carl's pulse quickened. So, Henry had acquired *The Girl in the Red Dress Under the Moon* in Buenos Aires. Had he bought it from a fugitive Nazi? Some contact of Carolina's whom she'd kept in touch with?

Carl pocketed the receipt. He'd ask his old college friend, Rick Marchese, to investigate. His law firm had an office in Buenos Aires. Maybe they could find something out.

As he'd predicted, Maria returned with a lace-decked tray: lobster bisque served in an English porcelain bowl, French rolls and tiny swirls of butter in a cooled butter dish with a miniature silver cloche and brightly polished cutlery.

He sat on the leather couch next to the fireplace and sipped the 20-year-old Château Margaux that, despite his protests, Juan insisted on bringing up from Henry's cellar. He hated snooping. Juan and Maria's trust and solicitude reminded him only too clearly of the confidence that Henry and the family had bestowed upon him. Now he knew how Brutus felt before he'd stabbed Caesar. But he had no choice. He was duty-bound to at least look for *some* tangible evidence, but aside from the receipt for the Chagall, he'd discovered nothing that could back up Uncle Ephraim's claim.

The only option now was to investigate further. He'd wait until all was quiet, then pretend to go to bed. After that he'd begin his search. But where? Luna had discovered the purse in Carolina's walk-in closet. If the old lady was living a lie, then she'd have made damn sure she left nothing incriminating lying around. But if there was any proof to be found, surely it would be in her room or boudoir?

He picked up the photocopies of the *Beobachter* newspaper clipping and slipped the original in the right-hand pocket of his jacket. The General snored, undisturbed in his basket by the fireplace. His groomed coat shone in the dying embers.

All seemed quiet.

Carl stepped into the foyer. The dimmed lights gave forth an ethereal glow. White roses glistened in the Baccarat vase. Henry's initials reigned at the top of the staircase. A Monet hung on the landing wall. It didn't get any more kosher than this. He could distinguish the patch on the wall where the Chagall usually hung. He must return it tomorrow without fail. Was he mad to imagine that generations of legitimacy could hide a secret of such horrifying proportions?

Carl padded down the corridor. He looked up at the ceiling cameras. The alarm he'd had installed flashed at regular intervals.

In the Blue room the bed was turned down and a pair of Henry's made-to-measure blue and white striped pajamas and a robe, lay folded on the bed. A bottle of Evian stood on the nightstand.

Carl placed the photocopies on the dressing table and dropped his jacket onto the flowered chintz armchair. He peeked inside the bathroom. A toothbrush, toothpaste, and a shaving kit.

He took off his shirt and pants and hung them on a hanger in the closet and stared at Henry's striped pajamas. It felt weird stepping into a dead man's clothes, especially when he was about to go snooping for evidence that might posthumously convict the man's late wife and alter his adopted daughter's. But Eli's and his great-grandfather's pajamas in Dachau had been striped too. Striped and numbered. And that's what this was all about: seeking the truth and establishing whether Uncle Ephraim's story was real, or just years of mistaken belief and distorted memory.

Carl pulled the robe on over the pajamas, tied the sash and glimpsed at himself in the long gilded mirror. Dead man walking? This was weird. It sent chills down his spine. He chugged some Evian and braced himself. Time to rock n' roll.

Carl slipped his reading glasses into the pocket of the robe and softly opened the door. In the passage, all was silent.

He trod lightly down the passage guided by the picture lamps. Carolina's rooms were at the far end of the corridor, off an alcove. Halfway down, he stopped next to a Picasso etching and listened. Maria and Juan were likely fast asleep in the service area off the kitchen on the other side of the building by now, but he must be careful. The timeless serenity was the same he'd experienced when he'd accompanied Henry to the White House; a reassuring state of equanimity conferred by tradition and the passage of time. Security, he realized — not for the first time — had a particular scent. Like the judge said about pornography: you couldn't define it, but you sure knew it when you saw it.

To his right was a door. Luna's door. He'd never been inside her room. He hesitated, curious. You could tell a lot about a person by the space they occupied; their books, the way they arranged things. Was it trespassing? At this point, surely that was a non-starter? And let's face it, if Uncle Ephraim's theory proved to be true, he'd likely have to negotiate with Luna. In which case, the more he knew about her, the better. In fact, it would be foolish — even unprofessional — to forgo what likely could be the only chance he'd ever get to visit her inner sanctum.

The first thing that hit him, as he stepped inside the room, was the scent. Jasmin. His little sister Leah's favorite flowers. He'd brought a bouquet home to her on his way back from work on the eve of her death...

~

Mama stood in the kitchen trying to keep busy. She looked up, her eyes red and rimmed from crying and lack of sleep. In the three weeks since they'd learned of Leah's racing leukemia, her hair had turned gray. Her hands shook as she removed a vase from the cupboard, then placed it in the kitchen sink and turned on the tap and let the water run, chattering all the while in a strangled voice.

"I don't think she's got long to go, Carl. She keeps asking for you," she said, placing the flowers in the vase. "You take them to her," she said handing them to him. "Papa will be home soon. He's having a hard time dealing with all this," she murmured. Her shoulders slumped, her eyes filled once more and her hands fell limply to her sides as though they served no useful purpose.

Carl hugged her, then carried the vase to Leah's room. A young girl's room filled with posters and the remains of a childhood ebbing away like the red globules from her adolescent veins. Leah was fourteen, ten years his junior.

He'd stayed with her and Mama and Papa all night, holding Leah's hand and caressing her cheek. Just before dawn she opened her eyes and smiled. Then, she'd left in the same sweet, gentle way she'd come; an angel whose presence had blessed them for a while, then disappeared to wherever it was angels come from.

~

Carl's eyes filled. Fourteen years later he never thought of Leah without a lump in his throat. Despite their age difference, he and Leah had been close. She'd looked up to him and he'd looked after her. He was down to earth and she was ethereal, but they were imbued with a common understanding and acceptance of their differences. No one had ever loved him as Leah had. And he had never loved anyone again as he had her. Despite her youth, she'd understood his differences without him having to explain and never judged him.

A year after her death he'd met Amy Feinstein and married her. He still wasn't sure how it happened. She bored him, she interrupted him, she whined. Five years later — which felt like fifty — they'd divorced with, thank God, no kids and no baggage to weigh him down.

Carl placed his fingers on the door handle of Luna's room and twisted it open and Luna's world sprung from the shadows: a small four-poster with white lace, ruffles and dolls and a loveseat stacked with teddy bears and chintz cushions. He reached for the light switch and played with the dimmer.

Was this for real? In the far corner was a dollhouse, and to his right, a life-size rocking horse. The only testimony to adulthood were the desk and chair he spied through the archway that led into, what he assumed, was her den.

Carl removed his Smartphone from the right-hand pocket of Henry's robe, activated the torch and switched off the light. He stepped across the thick pile carpet and stood before the dressing table. Its bombazine skirt flared stiffly between the French windows opposite the bed, the glass surface crowded with cloisonné hairbrushes, miniature china boxes, silver-framed photographs and an oval mirror on a stand; a 19th century virgin's boudoir, not a 21th century thirty-two-year-old's room. It was no secret

Luna lived in Henry and Carolina's time warp, but still, this was downright freaky.

He moved into the den. The light in his right hand hopped like a laser beam. What a contrast: floor to ceiling bookshelves, a simple scholastic desk, a chrome lamp and a wooden schoolroom chair. Two candles in glass holders. And in a niche to the left of the desk, a Buddha in prayer. He browsed the books: Descartes, Spinoza, Socrates and Aristotle shared shelf space with Danielle Steel, Nora Roberts and Paulo Coelho. There were volumes in French, Greek, Spanish and Portuguese, first editions of Goethe and Schiller in German, and an entire wall dedicated to poetry ranging from Baudelaire and Tennyson, to Pablo Neruda. Another shelf was dedicated to the tarot, books and several decks of cards. Then angels and angel cards. And spirituality, and Montaigne's essays, and historical biographies, fine arts, politics and fairy tales, all jostling for space on the shelves.

The den looked like the office of a distracted professor. Holding the phone up, he glanced through the curtained arch at the bedroom. Could the same woman inhabit two such contrasting universes?

Carl stepped back inside the bedroom troubled. The dichotomy implied by these contiguous, yet disparate rooms, disturbed him. It was as if Luna was two entirely different people. And then some. What about the Luna he knew, who resembled neither of the two he'd discovered here?

Carl stopped once more before the dressing table and flashed the phone on the knick- knacks and baubles, then pinpointed the photographs in the silver frames; Luna with Henry and Carolina arm-in-arm with the Eiffel Tower in the background. The three of them at Royal Ascot, Henry in top hat and tails and she and Carolina decked out in extravagant hats. He reached for the frame closest to the mirror and tilted it seeking a resemblance between the elderly woman waving next to Henry at the stern of their yacht, with the Panama flag unfurling in the breeze, and the young woman in the 1942 newspaper clipping. He didn't see it.

Why did people give their yachts such weird names, he wondered? *IRKANA III* sounds like a province in Turkistan.

"*I—R—K—A—N—A,*" he spelled out. "Wait! It's an anagram! Karina!"

He stared at the letters painted in gold lettering on the stern of the yacht. The thudding inside his chest as he pocketed the photograph, hurt. He exited Luna's room and headed down the half-lit corridor, uncertain of his next move. He'd come in search of proof and he'd found it.

He'd loved and admired Henry like a surrogate father. He'd enjoyed Carolina's wit and personality. Both of them fakes, cheats. To think he'd eaten and laughed and enjoyed the company of the woman who'd assisted in eliminating his own flesh and blood. And Henry had condoned it.

To date, Carl had never allowed prejudice or bigotry to influence him. He'd deplored vengeance, and exacting retribution had struck him as primitive and uncivilized. Yet, the raw anger and hatred was such as he'd never experienced before.

Which of the two was guiltier? Carolina, for God knows how many war crimes and the destruction of innocent lives? Or Henry for condoning them by aiding and abetting her to escape justice and live a fake luxurious life, while in her purse lay the secret vestiges of her crimes that like her, had escaped unscathed. Henry, a man who'd espoused the same democratic values as him, who'd pruned tolerance, liberalism and lobbied for abolishing the death penalty. He felt like the figures he'd seen on a tarot card in Luna's room just now, toppling from a crumbling tower and flying through the air as though a bomb had been set under it and causing it to implode from within — the hidden schisms that he'd tried so hard to escape, exposed.

Carl stood before the door of Carolina — no, Karina's — boudoir, and turned the handle. He turned on the light and stared at the photograph. He didn't care if he was caught. The bubble was about to burst anyway. The layers of dissimulation and conniving had lasted long enough. Uncle Ephraim was right. Why shouldn't they retake possession of the Chagall? And why should he pussy-foot around Luna afraid of hurting her feelings? Nobody'd cared about Eli or Aaron's feelings when they'd thrown them into the back of a truck and shipped them to hell. She'd been the beneficiary of all this luxury and pampering her entire life. Look at her dollhouse and her childish bedroom. She even kept the purse that Carolina likely stole from a Jewish woman and paraded on her arm when she consorted with her SS brother Rainer and Hitler and Goebbels and the other high-ranking Nazi elite. She'd sipped champagne robbed from French cellars and laughed and flirted, while Eli and his great-grandfather stood naked, choking to death on gas spewed from shower heads — their dreams and souls collapsed in a heap of skin and bones on a tiled floor and peered at through a peephole by a guard stifling a yawn. Did he have time for a fag before they sent in the capos to shovel the dead into the ovens and clean up for the next lot?

Carl's hands trembled. He thought of the protests on the streets that had erupted since the presidential election. Yesterday they'd seemed no more than a nuisance causing traffic delays. Now they made sense. If the half of America that had voted against having its unalienable rights trodden on and was not heard, it could happen all over again in the blink of an eye. Jews wouldn't be the main target this time around — though anti-Semitism was on the rise with graffiti visible on train carriages in Chicago and swastikas painted on walls. But others would be. People like his journalist friend and editor of one of the country's finest weekly news magazines, might find himself denied entry to the US because he happened to be Muslim by birth. Just as the Wolfs — if German for several generations — had been stripped of their citizenship so might others.

Carl felt guilty for having played golf on election day instead of going to vote. *Every vote counts* made sense now.

He stepped across the room to the walk-in closet. He switched on the halogen lights and stared at the rows of designer suits, silk dresses and fur coats. He passed his fingers over the soft sensuous textures, then stopped before a blue mink stole. It resembled the one in the newspaper clipping. He snatched the edge and dragged it off the hanger, then spat on it. The photo frame dropped to the ground. A strangled cry escaped him as he tore at the fur in desperation. The silk lining ripped and he dragged the lining apart.

He didn't stop until shreds and silver tufts carpeted the Nazi bitch's closet and all that remained of that perverse symbol was the filling and whatever shit they stuffed into their stoles. Maybe this was the original one. Maybe she'd managed to escape with that too.

Carl's hands drooped to his sides, exhausted. He stared at the destruction, then turned to the glass shelves littered with Hermès purses that altogether amounted to the value of a house. He approached them slowly, his palms sore from shredding the fur.

He looked at the time on the Pateck Phillipe watch Henry and Carolina had given him on his fortieth birthday. He'd always wanted one and had worn it with pride. He'd never thought of buying one himself. Like the ad suggested, a Pateck was an heirloom. It was Carolina who suggested the present. The old bitch had read him like a refrigerator manual. Press here. Pull there. She'd pin-pointed his weaknesses and manipulated him from the first day he'd walked in the door. Had she manipulated Luna too? Was Luna a victim or an ostrich burying her head so far up her ass to not see? It was hard to believe that an intelligent woman wouldn't pick up some sort of sign.

One by one Carl removed the purses from the shelves and placed them on the island in the center of the vast walk-in closet. He opened a dust bag randomly and withdrew a grape- colored Kelly. The rich scent of leather, the fine silver hardware; a purse that breathed status and class and all the things he'd believed working for the Hampton's in his privileged capacity of trusted counsellor, would rub off on him. In fact, giving him the job could have been Karina's way of keeping an eye on him and Uncle Ephraim. My God, how naive he had been.

Carl abandoned the purses on the island. He needed air. He wished he smoked. He walked through the connecting doors to the bedroom. The bed was made. All was silent and tidy. He moved towards the armchair and ottoman where Luna had spent the better part of her nights for the past months. What was he going to do about her? What if he'd been completely wrong? What if she was not what she appeared to be at all?

He flopped in the chair and hoisted his legs up on the ottoman. You have to give it to Carolina Hampton: the Polish Countess story was a great cover. Though the fact that she never frequented other Poles and was not part of the Polish club should have been a red flag. She'd brushed it off saying she had no time for a bunch of nostalgic old ladies living in the past. He'd admired her for it. Carolina was a woman of the present.

Karina.

When would he get used to calling her by her real name? And what about Arlington? Should he blow Henry's cover posthumously and have them dug up and thrown out of the cemetery? How would that affect Luna? And did he care?

Several hours later, Carl woke, startled, to a purring sound and light drifting inside the room. He jumped up. Holy fuck! It was ten in the morning.

He tip-toed to the door and opened it, enough to peek into the corridor. A hoover hummed in the distance. He had to get out of there — and fast. He thought of the shredded fur and the purses strewn throughout the walk-in closet.

Too late for regrets. The dice were thrown.

Chapter 23

Luna held the business card she'd discovered on the Fribourg station bench between her thumb and index. Only thirty francs a night for a room? Incredible! And the place looked nice.

She scrambled to her feet, collected her things and pulling her carry-on, headed towards the station entrance. A blast of wind met her as she stepped outside. A woman was opening the newspaper stand opposite. To her left was a taxi stand.

Should she be extravagant and take a cab with so little money in her pocket? What the hell? Luna hurried towards first cab in the line. The warm interior of the vehicle made her eyes water and her hands tingle. Her driver's name was Djoko. His nametag dangled from a red tasseled banner attached to the dashboard and he hummed to the rhythm of Shakira.

"Vous allez ou?" He asked, twisting his head around. Luna handed him the card.

"Ah, La Maison des Anges," he nodded.

"Vous connaisez?" She asked.

"Bien sur. It's *Madame* Rose's place.*"*

"Is it too early to arrive there?" Luna asked.

"*Non, non. Madame* is always up with the cows."

Luna sank back and stared out the rear window. It was still night but early morning traffic was already beginning. Then she stopped thinking and let go, rocked by the car's movement.

The taxi drove west out of the city. Luna peeked anxiously at the counter. Eighteen francs. Surely it couldn't be much further? She could distinguish a forest followed by moonlit fields.

Then the vehicle slowed and made a sharp right turn and ambled along a country lane. Luna lowered the window. A blast of cold air brought tears to her eyes as she peered at a château in moonlight, surrounded by ancient trees.

The car turned inside the gates. She could hear the crunch of gravel as the cab rode up the driveway. A man in robes and an anorak was walking down the gravel path towards the gate.

A priest? And at this hour?

The cab came to a halt at the foot of a wide flight of stone steps.

She stepped out of the car. Despite her troubles, the place felt enchanted. It smclled of fall and burned leaves and reminded her of Maine and the cottage. A candle flickered through the wide glass and iron front door at the top of the steps. She took out her wallet and drew out one of her three remaining bills. Parting with it felt like losing an old friend.

Don't worry. In a few hours, Carl will be in touch and all will be well. Everything'll be sorted. It's just a mistake.

A minute later the rear lights of the cab disappeared down the lane. Luna stood at the foot of the shallow stone steps. She ran her fingers through her hair and stood up straight. What would the proprietor think when she saw the state she was in?

Placing one damp boot on the bottom step, Luna blinked back tears and focused on being thankful. She was here and not leeched over by a creep! Surely that was a huge plus?

The front door opened and a woman appeared flanked by two stone cherubs. "*Bonjour*," she said.

Luna pulled her carry-on up the steps. "I'm *désolé* to arrive so early," she apologized. "*Pas un problem.* I was up early to give Father Florian, our resident priest, his breakfast.

He goes out early to tend to his refugees. *Bienvenue à la Maison des Anges.* I am Rose Chervet."

The two women shook hands. Luna's fingers tingled.

"*Mon Dieu*, your hands are freezing!" *Madame* exclaimed. "Come inside *immédiatement* and get warm. Have you had a long journey?"

Uncritical and warm, there was something frank and earthy about plump *Madame*; something motherly that brought tears to Luna's eyes. She swallowed and returned the woman's friendly smile with a watery one.

Madame helped her pull her carry-on inside the hall. Luna sighed, relieved. The place was lovely. A chandelier hung from the stucco ceiling and an apricot candle glowed in a bronze holder. She sank gratefully into the chair *Madame* offered. How good it felt to have a roof over her head once more, even if it was only for one night.

Through the door of *Madame's* office, a chubby-fingered, gold-flecked cherub reminded her of the ones above Nana's four-poster. They too reached out precariously above the pool of papers, pencils, highlighters and objects on *Madame's* desk. Had Nana answered her prayer? The Château was enchanting and it felt like heaven. Next to the candle, on the hall table, were brochures and business cards advertising a variety of spiritual seminars, Ayurvedic treatments, kinesiology, acupuncture and vegan retreats; a reminder of the thousands of dollars she'd spent in search of inner peace.

"How many nights will you be staying?" *Madame* asked. "Just the one. Maybe two," she hesitated.

"Will you be paying cash or by credit card?"

"Uh—cash," Luna stuttered. "I seem to have a problem with my credit card. It happens sometimes when one travels outside the United States—" Why was she giving explanations? She was paying. Surely that was all that mattered?

Luna extracted her passport and the last francs from her wallet, leaving only chump- change, a couple of creased receipts and a bunch of frozen plastic.

Madame jotted down the details, then handed the document back to her with a receipt.

"Voilà!"

"Merci."

"You speak perfect French," *Madame* remarked unhooking a key from a board behind her.

"I went to school in Rolle for a year and I had a French—" She cut off. Telling her she'd had a governess sounded like something out of a 19th century novel. Instead, she followed *Madame* through a door leading into the dining room. The lights came on; ironed table cloths and flowered china announced breakfast that would be served shortly. In the hallway of the opposite wing, she smelled incense.

"Here, let me help with that," Madame said, hoisting Luna's carry-on onto the first step of a steep stone staircase, "I know you asked for a single room, but I'm putting you in the loft under the eaves. You'll be more comfortable there."

"That's very kind, but I assure you, a room will be fine," Luna murmured. After the night's experiences, even an old couch would seem heavenly.

"The loft is empty so you might as well enjoy it." Madame threw a smile over her shoulder. "I won't charge you more for it."

"*Merci*. That's very kind of you."

Their steps echoed as they climbed the stairs. A blazing light popped on. The walls were painted pale green. It smelled clean and monastic. By the time they reached the second landing, Madame was out of breath and Luna was ready to drop. *Madame* unlocked a door to her right and stepped aside for her to enter.

"The loft runs from north to south and links both wings of the château," she explained. "The priests used to cure ham here."

"The priests?"

"The château used to be a seminary." She switched on a lamp light and Luna step inside the living room. Through the dormer window, a full moon filtered through the bare branches of the trees, highlighting two heavy beams that sustained the apex of the château's slanting roof. A couch and an ottoman, and a pile of leather-bound volumes and a vase filled with lilies, completed the decor.

"It's enchanting," she said. "How kind of you to put me up here."

"C'est un plaisir. I'll leave the keys here." *Madame* placed the keys in a pewter dish on the pine commode to the right of the entrance. Above it hung the sketch of a young girl seated under a tree.

"It's so peaceful here," Luna said, laying her Birkin on the couch. The station, the ogler and the French fry chewer all seemed a world away. "*Merci*, Madame."

"Please call me Rose. *Madame* makes me feel like I'm a hundred!" "Okay. Rose then. I'm Luna."

Rose's phone rang. "*Oh lala*! Who can be ringing this early?" She muttered. "I have to take this, I'm afraid. Take a bath and get some sleep. You look as though you need it!"

The front door of the loft creaked shut behind her. Luna leaned against it and closed her eyes. Switzerland, Fribourg, Nana, the *Sac à Dépèches*, the cigar and the note, her blocked credit cards, and Carl not answering her calls. Anything else? What did it all mean?

Outside, day flirted with the dipping moon. An owl hooted. In the distance a dog barked. Soon daylight would break.

She took the few steps across the living room and stepped inside the bedroom and switched on the light. The crisp white pillows and plump duvet brought tears to her eyes. She wanted to drop straight into bed. But she needed a shower first. At least for now she was safe and dry.

She rose and went to fetch her case. She unzipped it and extracted a sponge bag and a pair of pajamas. She placed the silver framed photograph of Nana and Henry on the chest of drawers opposite the bed. She was too tired to unpack, and for one night it was hardly worth it. She would take Rose's advice and hop in the tub squeezed under the eaves between a tiled ledge and a wicker basket filled with bath salts and heart shaped soaps. She thought of the homeless guy she'd seen at the station lying on a piece of cardboard and felt humbled. And grateful. As she turned on the taps she sent up a prayer of thanks. To Nana. To her angels and the Universe.

She tested the water. Steam rose filling the tiny bathroom. She added lavender salts, then sank in the water and closed her eyes. Never had a bath felt this good.

Minutes later, she was tucked under the feather duvet and pinching herself to make sure she wasn't hallucinating. Was all that had happened to her in the past twenty-four hours real?

She turned off the light and stared past a crack in the curtains at the bare branches etched in the dawn light. How many miracles had happened in Nana's life for her to have survived the camp with her *Sac à Dépèches* intact? Had Nana worked a miracle? She always said there were angels on earth as well as those up above. Had she brought Luna to this sanctuary; a House of Angels? *Madame* Rose sure felt like an Earth angel and this place a sanctuary.

Luna curled up in a fetal ball on her side. Her eyelids drooped. Nana always took care of everything. Was she an angel in heaven now too?

It took several seconds upon waking for Luna to remember she was in Fribourg, Switzerland, tucked in bed at The Angel House — the B&B she was certain she'd been guided to and not on a station bench as she'd first thought. She must have slept all day. Outside, darkness had fallen.

Luna swung her legs out of bed and stepped onto the carpet and did a yoga stretch. She drew the drapes back and opened the window. A gust of wind... a flurry of leaves fluttered onto the gravel. A bright yellow van turned into the gates and crawled up the snow-covered driveway. It came to a halt at the foot of the front steps and the postman got out. She could see the crown of Rose's head bidding farewell to a pilgrim. She pin-pointed the embroidered scallop on the pilgrim's backpack as he began his descent through the park towards the fields and the next leg of his journey and followed him until he disappeared into the forest. Surely he'd get far enough before nightfall? What leg of her journey was she on? She wondered. All she'd wanted was to discover why Nana had been deported and why the note and the cigar were in her purse; but now she was stranded penniless and alone halfway across the world.

She must find Carl and sort out this mess.

Must this. Must that. Her entire life was made up of a long list of "musts."

Another wave of exhaustion hit and Luna climbed back into bed and pulled the duvet up under her chin. She shut her eyes tight and pretended none of this was happening. And why was it? She'd never broken the mold, never tried to get out there and conquer the world, never pushed the boundaries or stretched the limits imposed upon her; never rebelled. She was happy in her cocoon with Nana and Henry.

The world out there did not entice her, it scared her. And up until yesterday, it had never struck her as strange that someone, somewhere, made sure her credit cards were paid and that cash was readily available. Money had never been an issue, it was just something that, like sex, was never openly discussed.

Luna rarely withdrew cash. Why would she? Juan drove her wherever she needed to go, then brought her home. When she shopped at Bergdorf's or Barneys or lunched at the Grill at the Four Seasons, it went on the bill, which in turn went to Susan at the office, who no doubt sent it to the bank. Yet right now, all she had left to her name were a few bucks in change and a first-class ticket home. The privileged existence she'd taken for granted was crumbling about her like shortcake.

She linked and stared at Nana and Henry smiling at her from the silver framed photograph on the pine dresser. If only they'd trusted her enough to tell her the truth.

A loud knock echoed through her room. She jumped out of bed to answer the door. A glance in the mirror sufficed to make her groan. What a wreck. She hadn't been to a hairdresser or beautician in months, and it was unlikely that in her present financial debacle, she'd be visiting the salon any time soon.

She reached the door and opened it.

"Bonsoir," Rose stood on the threshold smiling. "I came to see if you're alright and if you'd like to join a friend of mine and I for fondue?"

"Really? That would be lovely. *Merci.*"

"Then I'll see you in the kitchen in half an hour," Rose said.

Luna closed the door. A star glistened through the clouds and the dormer window. Her stomach growled. She hadn't eaten since getting off the plane yesterday. It occurred to her that she was not used to the gratuitous kindness from strangers. People were usually helpful because they knew who she was. She was always under the impression she needed to pay. People thought she had it all. And up until yesterday, she supposed she had. At least she'd been able to buy pretty much anything she wanted. But how about the rest?

Rose's didn't know Luna from Adam.

I'm just another pilgrim passing through, she reflected, pulling on her jeans. And sent a prayer of thanks up to the universe.

Nana was surely watching over her from somewhere.

Chapter 24

Carl sat at the Old King Cole bar and ordered a fourth Bloody Mary with Henry's pajamas still on under his clothes.

What a Goddamn mess. Ephraim was right. To think he'd worked twelve years for a treacherous piece of shit who'd married the woman who'd assisted her brother in sending his family to the gas chamber for fuck's sake! How sick is that? He felt sick of everything. Of the Holocaust. Of Luna. Of himself. Old Ephraim was right. He'd get his shit together and go to Switzerland.

He drained his glass and asked for the check. He'd go over to Ephraim's and get the painting back. He couldn't afford loopholes. It was game time and he needed his ducks in a row.

He drained his glass and pushed his credit card across the bar. He must move fast so the incident in Carolina's closet didn't catch up with him. Maria didn't necessarily go in there every day. She likely only opened the blinds in the boudoir and bedroom from time to time. If he got lucky, it'd take days before she discovered the mess and the shit hit the fan. But by that time, he'd be in Switzerland and *Mademoiselle* Luna would have already learned who exactly her darling Nana really was.

The doorman hailed him a cab. He gave Ephraim's address, covered his mouth and breathed. Yuk! His breath smelled fetid. No more fetid than Henry and Carolina lying buried with honors next to the bravest and finest in the land. He'd have them exhumed and chucked into a cesspool where they deserved to be!

He pulled his phone out. The voicemail notifications from Luna flashed. He couldn't bring himself to answer nor unblock her accounts. Acting unlawfully went against every fiber of his being. But that was before. And this was now. What a fucking mess.

At times, he wished he'd never taken Uncle Ephraim to that damned wake that had woken the dead, or removed the Chagall from the penthouse. If only all this could be dealt with in a civilized, mature, non-emotional manner. It would be neat and tidy as opposed to the past reaching its sinewy tentacles, wrapping them all into an ever-tighter vice, and choking the air out of their lives.

Carl swallowed. He'd built his world block by block, effort by effort. Now it lay tattered and shredded like Carolina's fur stole on the floor of the walk-in closet.

Carl let himself into his great-uncle's apartment. Even as he entered the front door, he could tell the old boy had been smoking more than usual. Mrs. Katz was out and Ephraim appeared to be asleep.

He removed his fur lined boots, hung his coat in the closet and moved across the wooden floor boards on tip-toe to Ephraim's room.

"At last. I've been waiting for you." Ephraim was seated propped up in bed smoking.

"Hello, Uncle Ephraim." "Did you find anything?"

"I sure did." Carl removed the photograph frame from his pocket and approached the bed. Ephraim reached out a bony hand, picked up his reading glasses off the nightstand, and placed them on his nose.

"*Wat* is it?"Carl held the frame closer. Ephraim frowned. "A photograph of the two of them on their yacht. So what? Why do I want to see this?" He pushed the frame aside, irritated.

"Look carefully."

"*Ach* Carl, I am tired. I have no time for guessing games," the old man muttered, crossly. "Read the name of the yacht," Carl insisted.

Muttering, Ephraim peered at the photograph once more. He shook his head. "ARKANI III. A stupid name — all the rich name their yachts silly things with no sense." he said, dropping the frame on the duvet.

"Don't' you get it? I—R—K—A—N—A. Flip the letters and what do you get?" "*Mein Gott*... Karina!"

The old man grabbed the frame once more and stared at the letters. "So it was she. I knew it. I've remembered so many things this night. Carl, you *must* go to Switzerland."

"I know. I'm going as soon as possible."

"Do it fast, Carl. The time for niceties is over. I must die with this resolved. If it's the last thing I do, I want to see justice done."

Ephraim fell back against the pillows, pale and exhausted.

Carl stood at the foot of his great-uncle's bed. He heard Mrs. Katz enter, then shuffle around in the kitchen. The cat jumped onto the end of the bed and curled next to the bump where Ephraim's toes lay under the duvet.

"I'll get what's ours, Uncle Ephraim. I promise. But I must take the Chagall back to the penthouse first."

"No."

"I must. "No."

"You don't understand, right now having it here is a crime. It's stolen property."

"Are you stupid?" Ephraim asked, opening his eyes. "Didn't they teach you anything in those fancy schools I paid for? How can it be stolen when it's mine?"

It was useless arguing with anyone this obtuse. Uncle Ephraim saw the world through a one-dimensional lens. Everything began and ended with him. Would he ever stop reminding Carl what he owed? Of course he was grateful for school fees that allowed him to study without having to work. Grateful too, for the times the old man had come to his rescue. But did he have to be permanently reminded of it?

Carl glanced at the Chagall and hesitated: he should return it. On the other hand, possession was 9 /10ths of the law. Maybe he'd leave it here for now and deal with it later. Things might look different after his trip.

"I'll be off then," he said.

"Go, go." Ephraim waved a dismissive hand and closed his eyes.

Carl swallowed. It was silly, but as always he felt swept aside like an empty beer can kicked in the gutter.

Chapter 25

The emotions of the past days had left Ephraim tired and anxious and he'd stayed in bed dozing off, drifting between the present and the past, trying to recall the other time he'd seen the woman with the distinctive purse.

Of course! It was in the Maximilian Strasse in 1944! How could he have forgotten?...

~

That morning Ephraim had touched up the roots of his hair with more blond. It enhanced his hazel eyes and made him look more Aryan. Or so Rainer said. Still, Ephraim rarely looked anyone in the eye in those days. A Jew, hoping to pass unobserved in a society of snitches and traitors could never be too careful.

He wiped the dye from the enamel basin in his room in case Frau Schenker, the landlady, should enter. There was little danger she'd suspect his alias Herr Rudolf Hafner — a good burger from a small village near Rosenheim, a Nazi card holder who worked as a clerk in the government department who spoke with a heavy Bavarian accent and paid his rent on time. Still, one error sufficed. He blessed his talent for mimicking and languages. And from time to time — not too often to not overdo it — he brought Frau Schenker little gifts and paid her gallant compliments that sent ripples quivering through her heavily creased jowls, and caused her non-existent eye lashes to flap flirtatiously.

That day — the 23rd of February, 1943 to be exact — he'd walked towards the Kaufingerstaraasse, then onto the Marienplatz. He remembered the date well because the previous day he'd seen Rainer in the small room nearby where they sometimes met. Rainer was in a jovial mood chortling with delight at the summary execution of the young White Rose anti- Nazi resistants — the siblings Sophie and Hans Scholl and several other members of the movement that had taken place after a summary fifteen-minute trial by the *Sondegericht* the day before.

"Good riddance," Rainer had said as he removed his SS uniform and flopped on the bed. The White Rose group, born at the University some time earlier had, according to him, pestered society with subversive inflammatory pamphlets and triggered the birth of other subversive groups wanting to undermine the *Fuhrer*, people, he said, face turning dark, who were closer to home than he'd imagined.

"You wait and see," he'd boasted. "I'll get the lot of them in the end." "I'm sure you will, Rainer. You always do," Ephraim fawned.

Things between them were back to normal. In fact, they'd been on smooth footing for a while. The Chagall was still an issue, but Ephraim felt he was close to regaining possession of the painting, confident that in the end, he'd win. He tried not to think of Papa and Eli or denouncing the Blumenthal's who'd been hiding for three years in their cellar. In the end, self- preservation and common sense prevailed. Of course he'd made Rainer promise that nothing would happen to them. But even as he uttered the words he knew he was paying lip-service to his conscience with which he'd long since parted company. The pills helped. The magic pills produced a tonic effect. Thank God Rainer kept him well supplied, and would continue to for as long as Ephraim produced the goods. It was all in a good cause, he reminded himself. Some had to be sacrificed for the common good, for example, him. And art of course. Art had to be preserved at all costs. Men and women came and went, their lives were but a trivial passage in the bigger scheme of things when compared with the temporal. Art survived it all. He was certain even Papa would agree, perhaps even welcome being sacrificed for its survival.

~

The room was dark and Ephraim switched on the bedside lamp and stared at *The Girl in the Red Dress Under the Moon* through the shadows. His mind wandered a lot these days. Sometimes he found himself walking down streets that he knew but couldn't name. Were they in New York or in Lisbon where he'd managed to escape to, or in Munich? Maybe even Berlin. Time and faces and places merged. Visions of Rainer lying in his underwear on the bed, his ankles crossed, proudly showing him the Mauser pistol that the *Führer* had given him as a reward for the part he'd played in catching the White Rose dissidents. The following day, there was something that had happened too, but it eluded him, like the shadows on the flagstones playing hopscotch as a child.

Ephraim glanced at the alarm clock he'd owned since 1950 and wound religiously each day. It read 4am. Time dragged these days. He wondered where Carl was and what he was up to. He reached for the cigarettes on the nightstand and lit one still thinking of that day Rainer showed him the Mauser. The Gestapo were everywhere; vulgar and commonplace men who'd soared to power, and exercised it with glee. Some swaggered in black leather coats, while others enjoyed the hunt and mingled unobserved among a *Volk* that had embraced the nationalist populist agenda of the Third Reich — their psyches imbued with simplistic slogans that rang true in the ears of young and old alike. Society was embedded with suspicion and treachery. An environment of fear reigned. Children who denounced their parents were touted as loyal. And he'd embraced it in an effort to survive.

All at once Ephraim remembered where he'd seen the woman with the purse once again. He'd recognized her, for she wore the same oversized raincoat as she had the day she'd descended the steps of the Villa five years earlier…

~

That day he'd walked purposefully — he always walked as if he knew exactly where he was going — past the Hofbrauhaus. At once he'd stopped, made a show of glancing at his watch and shaking his head — as though having forgotten an engagement — and altered course. He'd ·followed her discreetly along the pavement until she reached the tram station where she'd stopped and cast a fleeting glance left and right as though she was expecting someone. That was when he'd recognized her as Rainer's sister, Karina.

His pulse raced as he stepped back into the shadow of a doorway and waited, his hat lowered. He lit a cigarette. Soon, another young woman dressed in a plain brown coat and hat stopped a few feet away. The two women exchanged a brief glance as the tram rumbled to a stop. They boarded it separately and sat in different rows. Ephraim hopped on the tram as it was about to leave and stood near the door next to two SS men. One of them asked him for a light. He smiled and kept his hand from shaking as he lit the man's cigarette. They made comments about the weather.

The tram was headed in the direction of Hauptbanhof, the city's main train station where the two girls got off. Ephraim hesitated. The Hauptbanhoff, with its busy traffic and security checks, constituted a danger. But he knew he must follow them. Karina Lanzberg was up to something and God knows he needed every bit of leverage he could get his hands on these days. He had no news of Papa or Eli since the day of their arrest, neither had Rainer returned the painting. If Rainer's sister was in any fishy business, it could be the joker in the pack that he's been waiting for.

Ephraim hopped off the tram and followed the girls as they headed separately inside the main station building. He stopped at a kiosk and bought a copy of the *Beobachter* and slipped it prominently under his arm, then made his way into the main hallway mingling with troops and SS men and soldiers parading up and down with German shepherds. He must not be afraid. They said the dogs were trained to pick up the scent of a Jew. But he knew that to be rubbish. Thanks to Rainer, his ID papers were in perfect order. The others, the real ones, were hidden in the heel of the sole of his shoes.

He had nothing to fear but fear itself.

The words of Franklin D Roosevelt, the American president that Eli had so admired, burst upon him like a volley of bullets causing a wave of nausea. But he pulled himself together and stood in line several paces behind the girls queuing at the ticket office. He must find out their destination. He was willing to bet they were headed in the same direction. To get nearer to them, he pretended to trip, then excused himself profusely to the elderly lady in front of him. This allowed him to lean close enough to overhear the second girl ask for her ticket.

Tegernsee.

Why would they be going there? Perhaps he was wasting his time and they were just off for a day's outing or to meet their boyfriends.

He bought a return ticket to Tegernsee regardless, followed the girls through the dank and busy station to the platform and stood several paces behind them. He helped an old lady and gentleman climb onto the train. Inside the carriage, the two young women sat opposite one another in the same compartment. Karina Lanzberg hid behind a newspaper. The other girl in an Austrian feathered hat and glasses had her nose in a book. She looked like a student and seemed familiar too.

Aside from the elderly couple and a young mother with three children, the carriage was empty. Ephraim sat in a window seat several feet away where he could observe the girls without being noticed. Karina's purse was on her knees. That's when he'd noticed how different it was from any other he'd seen before. Classy. Refined. Expensive. Where had she gotten it? The fine leather and gleaming hardware were unusual and reminded him of a picture he'd seen in a fashion magazine lying around at the Villa, in a world only minutes away, but a universe apart and now inhabited by Nazis.

The girls continued to act as strangers, neither acknowledging the other's presence. That in and of itself felt suspicious. Wouldn't two young women — even strangers — chat to one another? Perhaps not. These days no one was at ease. The simple, ordinary interactions of everyday life were a thing of the past. People pretended to be gracious of course, but no one knew who was who, or what lay behind a smile.

The train chugged out of the station. Ephraim watched the troops lining up on the platform. More cannon fodder for a war that was going nowhere. He didn't believe Rainer's bluster and Goebbels's propaganda. Not since he'd managed to sneak a radio into his attic room and install an antenna on the roof of Frau Schenker's home. It was dangerous, of course, and required staying up until the landlady or anyone else who might be around went to bed. Then he'd push up the trap door in the ceiling and squeeze his way past trunks, broken toys and unused furniture into the dusty attic where he'd installed the radio and got decent reception. Crouched under the open dormer window and extending the antenna to catch a good signal, he thanked Miss Hitchin and *Mademoiselle* Morel who'd made sure that he and Eli spoke fluent English and allowed him to tune into the BBC news and the coded messages of free French radio. Thus, he knew before the government admitted it publicly, that Stalingrad had fallen, and followed the uprising in the Warsaw Ghetto — God help their poor souls — and knew that US forces were advancing in the Pacific. Despite all Rainer's bluster, it was obvious that Germany was losing ground. Allied troops had now liberated North Africa and the Soviets were advancing on the eastern front and lately British bombers were hammering Berlin every night. The question was how to escape? He had no plans of leaving until he had the Chagall back in his possession. It was the key to his future. If a future there was.

Soon they'd left the city behind, replaced by the fairytale countryside, snow-covered fields, and picture-perfect Bavarian villages. The Allied bombs hit the city itself. But out here all seemed as it was long ago. Ephraim leaned his brow on the cold train window. For a while he forgot the reason for the trip caught up in memories of Papa and Eli and *Mademoiselle* Morel driving this same route to Schloss Heil, to Baron von Heil's castle, on the shores of the Tegernsee. He hadn't seen Baron von Heil or any of their old friends since the arrest. Many believed that Ephraim had been arrested with his father and brother. And it suited him fine that way. No one knew, or wanted to know, where people who'd suddenly disappeared actually were. He had no wish to consort with other Jewish families who might ask him for favors. He had his own skin to look out for. In fact, he'd gone straight into hiding and remained incognito, protected by the shock of dyed blond hair, a pair of round glasses and the typical Bavarian clothes he'd adopted. He even squinted and had convinced himself he had an eye problem. It helped to believe in his own persona. At times, he lost track of which was which. Surely that was a good thing?

The ride to the Tegernsee took just over an hour in which time the girls had still not communicated. As the train slowed, Ephraim snapped back from his reverie and peered out at the Tegernsee station coming into view. Then the train shuddered to a halt, the whistles sounded, and the two girls rose, still feigning not to know one another. The other passengers in their coats and felt hats waited for the guard on the platform to open the doors. Ephraim graciously allowed them all to go first. Then, all at once, Karina turned. Her eyes rested on him for a moment. Ephraim's heart stood still. He kept his eyes lowered, relieved when the door finally opened and the girls, the elderly couple and the nuns moved smilingly past him and stepped down onto the platform.

Ephraim waited a few seconds before climbing down the steps. The hissing and puffing of the engine sounded like a tired dragon returned to its lair. Tegernsee was the end of the line so he had no choice but to exit the station. He scanned the entrances and exits. Good. No check- point. Why would there be? It's freezing cold and the Tegernsee is a Nazi enclave. The *Fuührer* himself comes here regularly to visit his publisher. Why would anyone be crazy enough to stick their head in a noose?

He walked through the main building. As he stepped outside onto the icy station front Ephraim's efforts were rewarded. For there, on the curb, was a gleaming Mercedes that he knew all too well and standing next to it was Franz — Baron von Heil's uniformed chauffeur. Ephraim stopped in his tracks, then retreated a few steps and pretended to consult the train timetable while keeping a trained eye on the girls and the car. The nuns and the couple had hurried off. There was no one left but them. Then the moment he'd been waiting for: Karina nodded to the other girl and they walked over to the car and climbed inside. Franz shut the doors and got into the driver's seat. As the Mercedes pulled out of the station, Ephraim caught sight of the other girl's face through the rear window. Of course! It was that Jewish friend of Karina's who used to come to

Schloss Heil with her for St Hubertus. What was her name? Ella? Something along those lines. Never mind. The burning question was: what were they doing getting into the Baron's car?

Ephraim watched the vehicle disappear. For the first time since Eli and Papa's arrest, he felt elated. Leverage at last! Whatever Karina Lanzberg was up to with that Jewish friend of hers, her brother wasn't going to like it. And what, he wondered, did Baron von Heil have to do with it? Rainer was already furious with the Baron for having bought the Villa from Papa several months before he was arrested. He'd counted on moving in there himself. Papa had trusted his old university friend. But was he right to do so? In the end, when it came down to it, and despite the liberal views he may have held, weren't they all cut from the same cloth?

~

Ephraim stared at the fallen ash sprinkled on the duvet cover. He brushed it off and sank back among the pillows. He switched the light off and shifted. His old bones ached and the memories weighed despite his ability to banish them. Soon he and most of them would be forgotten. Yet among them lay the key that could unlock the padlock and turn the tide of history in his favor.

Everything hung on that purse. He was certain of it.

Chapter 26

Bubbling cheese, white wine and laughter.

Luna's stomach growled as she peered inside the kitchen of the Angel House where Rose presided over a large stove and chopped herbs into a pot and a woman sat at the long pine table under bunches of dried flowers. Another chandelier with the signature angels dangled from a wide-knotted beam, and above, a copper oil burner and fondue bubbled in a red enamel pot.

In the book that never left her laptop, Luna'd written of such a kitchen; a vortex where friends gathered, exchanged laughter and confidences over a glass of wine and picked each other up when they were down. But she'd only imagined it. The penthouse kitchen was a modern, functional space with granite counters, two freezers and two dishwashers designed to entertain. She could count the times she'd been inside it.

Rose looked up from her chopping. "*Ah! Luna. Entrez.* Come in and sit wherever you like. I've set four places since Father Florian said he might join us." She extended a welcoming gesture. "*Voici* Luna de *New York*." She announced. "And this is Lizzie."

An attractive woman in her mid-forties with short chestnut hair and wide blue eyes looked up and smiled.

"Nice to meet you. Here, have some wine," She picked up the bottle and filled Luna's glass.

"Hi." Luna smiled and sat down opposite. "Father Florian. Would that be the priest I saw coming down the path this morning when I arrived here?"

"Yes. He's been here since the Château was a seminary bought by the *Verba Divina di Roma* in the late 1930s to house priests fleeing Nazi Germany."

"Wow! And who stays here in your B&B now? It's such a beautiful space," Luna asked, curious.

"Mostly pilgrims on the *Camino* to Santiago de Compostella. Though in truth, all my guests are pilgrims. Some stay a night, others a few months. Each has a reason for passing through the Angel House. Now, you must be hungry. We won't wait for Father Florian to begin. He's usually late."

Rose sat down and passed her the bread basket. "*Merci.* You've been so kind to me," Luna said.

"How long are you staying?" Lizzie asked, spiking a bread cube on her fondue fork and placing it inside the pot.

"I'm not sure," Luna murmured.

Oh God... she mustn't think. Hopefully Carl would call any minute and all would be sorted. Unless she got her cards back to working order, she couldn't stay here. What was the matter with him? Surely he'd gotten her voicemails and talked to the bank by now?

Luna nibbled a gherkin and tried not to think.

Rain slashed. The old windows of the chateau rattled. She remembered the bench at the station and shivered. What if the weather was like this tomorrow night and she had no money and nowhere to go?

"What a night." Rose leaned across the table. She lit a match and held it to the wick of a candle until the flame took hold, then she bustled back to the range, lifted a pan of potatoes, drained them in the sink, then tipped them into a padded basket and covered it with a checkered warmer.

Outside a dog barked. The handle of the kitchen door turned and the same robed figure Luna had encountered that morning, stepped inside. He stopped, rubbed the soles of a pair of sturdy boots on the mat, closed a large, dripping black umbrella and placed it in the stand next to the wall. A racking cough followed.

"Father Florian," Rose hurried over and kissed him on both cheeks. "You must take care of that cough.

You should have it looked at. Have you got *sirop?* I'll give you some of my herbal cough mixture. May I introduce Luna? She's here from New York."

"*Bienvenue* to the Angel House, *Mademoiselle.*" He took Luna's hand, and raised it to his lips in a courtly gesture that reminded her of Henry and brought tears to her eyes. If he were alive, none of her troubles would be happening.

"Come. Sit at the head of the table," Rose said.

"Ah, *la fondue*. Hello Lizzie," Father Florian smiled rubbing his hands and sat down. Rose poured him wine.

"*Santé*."

Luna raised her glass and they toasted. Rose's eyes held understanding and compassion. Lizzie's seemed thoughtful and full of practical wisdom; Father Florian's defied his age, for they shone with the ardor of youth.

After another bout of coughing the priest spiked a piece of bread and plunged it into the fondue. Two days ago, she wouldn't have touched gluten, but right now allergies and intolerances were the least of her concerns. She must eat. Keep her strength up for what might be ahead. Plus, it was free.

"*Quel temps*! It's miserable outside," Father Florian said. "I would have come earlier but my refugees went to their French class, otherwise I would have brought them with me. They're making great progress. I find it hard to believe it's only been four months since they escaped the bombs and horrors of Aleppo. Which reminds me, I may have to leave in the middle of dinner to attend to the others who are trudging through the Balkans at the present, not to mention those in the Mediterranean. They have no shelter and I'm liaising with local parishes and the Vatican to see what we can do to help. It's terrible what's going on. I'm ashamed to be European. We're supposed to be a union, yet we are only when it comes to receiving subsidies for all sorts of unnecessary gimmicks, and when it comes to humans, everyone aside from Germany is closing their doors."

Luna, are you all right? You look pale," Rose frowned.

"I'll be fine." Father Florian's words had just highlighted her own plight: if Carl didn't call and do whatever it took to unfreeze her funds in a few hours she'd be back on the station bench with no roof left over her head either.

"Tells us about America and the election," Lizzie said.

"It's a mess. You mentioned Europe and the refugees, Father, but I'm afraid it's not looking much better there. Maybe even worse if the president-elect actually goes ahead and implements half the plans he's campaigned including a Muslim ban. God only knows where our country will end up."

"You mean he wants to ban all Muslims from entering the country? Surely that's impossible nowadays?" Lizzie said, sipping more wine.

"There's that and the wall with Mexico."

"Is that a joke?" Rose said, sitting next to Father Florian. "Sadly I'm not sure that it is."

"It reminds me of what happened back in 1938 when the Nazis rose to power and nobody wanted to allow the German Jews in," Father Florian murmured. "And look what happened then. I sometimes wonder what they teach in schools these days and if anyone bothers to look back at history." He shook his head and accepted the wine Rose poured him. "I was disappointed with the US election results. I'd hoped people would see through the masquerade." "So did I," Luna, said with feeling. "It's been a shock to everyone. Well, to half of the country at least. The other half seems too drunk on populist fervor right now. We'll see how long it actually lasts. I never got the *Make America Great Again* slogan. I thought we were great already."

"It seems unbelievable," Lizzie said, passing the potatoes. "Surely he doesn't believe half the things he says? And what about his wife?"

"She seems a nice lady," Luna said. "I don't know her personally."

"*En tout cas* she and the daughter are beautifully dressed," Rose said laughing. "You have to give them that."

Everyone laughed. Luna relaxed for the first time that day and dipped her fondue fork back in the pot. Despite her inner turmoil, she felt at ease and participated in the conversation. She wasn't used to being among strangers. But neither Rose not Lizzie nor Father Florian seemed like strangers. She'd been here only a few hours yet she felt among friends. Luna thought of the hotel in the Rue de Lausanne and the leering man with the greased black hair fondling her jacket and shuddered. Surely an angel guided her here?

"… and if you plan to remain on a few more days, you're welcome to stay in the loft. I have no reservations any time soon," Rose was saying.

"*Merci.* That's very kind. Unfortunately, I'm not sure if—."

Father Florian's cell phone played a loud, jolly tune and saved her from having to answer. He pulled it out of his robe pocket.

"*Je m'excuse,*" he said rising and stepping into the hall.

"That'll be him off," Rose sighed and shook her head. "He's not well but he never stops working and helping those poor souls."

Father Florian returned and took his anorak off the hook. *"Je suis désolée,"* he said to the room at large, "but I must be off. We have an ongoing situation and I need to get on Skype, and that requires me going back to the cottage to use my laptop. Thank you, *chère* Rose, for the fondue."

"But you've hardly eaten a bite," she protested.

"You are *trop gentille."* The priest slipped his arms inside the sleeves of the anorak, hoisted the hood over his head and lifted his dripping umbrella from the stand. He took Rose's hands in his. "Good night, *ma chère*. Many thanks to you all."

A quick wave and a gust of wind blew in when he opened the door. Rose held it. The dog scrambled inside and shook itself and moved towards the table, tail wagging, leaving a trail of muddy paws.

Rose gave Chichi a dog biscuit. "I'll keep you inside tonight," she promised. The dog settled under the table.

Luna lifted her fondue fork and spiked a piece of bread when her phone vibrated. Carl! At last!

She dropped her fork and fumbled in her pocket, swamped with relief.

"*Pardon,* but I really must take this," she apologized. Her chair scraped as she pushed it back and hurried out into the hall.

"Hello," she said breathlessly. "Luna, it is me, Maria."

Luna's shoulders slumped. She stared out the double-glazed door at the bare branches of the trees battered by the storm and swallowed her disappointment.

"Hi Maria, *como estas*?" She said, rallying. "Bad. *Muy mal.*"

"Bad? Why? What happened?" Luna's heart skipped a beat. "It's Meester Carl."

"What about him?"

"I am very *preocupada.*" "*Porque*?"

"The night you leave, Meester Carl he come here," Maria's voice took a stealthy tone. Luna closed her eyes and curbed her impatience. Long experience had taught her that Maria never got straight to the point.

"He come and he say he need to take the *Moon* Girl picture to go to—" She hesitated. "Sotheby's. Yes, I know. It's for an appraisal. Go on."

"Then, next evening, yesterday, he come back. He go to Meester Henry study. He say he must go through the files. The weather it is very bad so I say to Meester Carl if he stay too late it better to sleep over. And he say yes, okay, fine." Maria stopped.

"Go on," Luna urged.

"This morning I go to open Dona Carolina's boudoir." A pregnant silence.

"And?" Luna groaned.

"I open the blinds."

Luna rolled her eyes and paced the hall. "Yes, okay *and*?"

"I go in Dona Carolina's walk-in closet."

"Maria *porfa*vor! Just tell me what the hell's going on?" Luna cried.

"The purses they are all opened, the coats they are thrown everywhere and Dona Carolina's favorite fur wrap, the silver *zorro,* he is torn, shredded into little *pedazos* all over the floor and—"

"Oh my God!" Luna stiffened.

"Meester Carl he already left. He say nothing to me. And he still no bring back the *Moon Girl.*"

"That's normal. The appraisal may take a few days, but the other... Are you sure a cat or something didn't get inside the closet?"

Her phone pinged. Luna opened the pictures Maria was sending.

"Oh my God!" Her hand flew to her mouth. Every Hermès bag lay open on the counter, ransacked and the floor was strewn with fur and dust bags.

"No one else was inside there, Luna. I know it was Meester Carl. After I say to Juan did he notice any strange thing? He say to me yes. Meester Carl he was *nervioso*."

"But why? What would he do such a thing for?"

"Luna, you be careful. After I see this, I call Jairo, Juan's brother, the shaman back in our *pueblo*. He say Meester Carl is a *traidor*. How you say in English?"

"A traitor," Luna whispered.

"*Exactamente*. A rat. Like the ones Meeses Rudge she put the poison to kill them up at the cottage."

Luna swallowed. She must keep things in perspective. Jairo the Shaman's predictions had been accurate in the past, but Maria often dramatized. Still, the pictures spoke for themselves. What on earth had come over Carl? It made no sense. There had to be an explanation.

"I should come home immediately and sort all this out," she muttered more to herself. "*No, no, no*, Luna! *Por Dios*! The shaman say me *Moon Girl* she must not come home.

It *is muy muy* dangerous for her."

Her head spun. She felt dizzy and leaned against the wall next to the doorjamb and closed her eyes. "Maria, I'll call you back. Things here are a bit complicated. Don't let anyone inside the penthouse and take more pictures of everything in the walk-in closet exactly as it is and send them on through. Are you sure you're okay?"

"You no worry about us, Luna. You worry about you. *Vaya con Dios*" "*Gracias,* Maria." Luna's voice broke as she hung up.

Her last link to home just went dead.

Chapter 27

Maria. Dear Maria.

Maria who prayed for Henry and Nana's souls, the souls of her children and her nephews, nieces and her cousins as she polished and ironed...Maria who for thirty years had said *si Senora* and *no Senora* to Nana, and who saved every penny she earned to send back home; Maria, whom she'd had to insist accept the money to pay the *coyotes* to help her son Pancho cross the border to a better life. The first one pocketed the funds. The second time the border guards got him and sent him back. But she kept on praying and hoping. Would the new administration indict her for trying to reunite a family?

"Luna.'"

She looked up. Rose stood in the hall doorway. "*Tout va bien*?" "I'm fine."

"You don't look fine."

"Oh! It's nothing," she muttered, surprised. How could Rose tell?

"*Ma chère*, I know we only just met but that doesn't matter. You are among friends and we girls stick together when we have troubles. Now come back in the kitchen. Sylvie popped by. Come and meet her." She drew her by the arm.

Reluctantly, Luna returned. She had no desire to meet anyone else this evening but after Rose's kindness it would be ungracious to refuse. Good manners won and she accompanied Rose back inside the kitchen.

"Luna, this is Sylvie."

Luna smiled perfunctorily at a slim woman in a snazzy short dress, high-heeled boots and a pink streak in her hair, and sat down next to Lizzie.

"Ca va?" Lizzie frowned. "You look terrible." "I feel terrible."

Luna hesitated. She wasn't used to opening up. She drained her glass in one gulp and Rose poured her another.

"There's no use beating about the bush," she said at last. "I'm in deep *merde*. That was my maid Maria, on the phone."

"You have a maid?" Sylvie goggled. "Sylvie!" Rose sent Luna an apologetic look.

"Maria is part of the family. She's been with us forever. My mother—well, my adoptive mother who died a month ago, brought her from Colombia with me years ago."

"So what brought you to Fribourg?" Sylvie asked, ignoring Rose's frown and dipping her fork in the hot cheese.

"It's a long story. I won't bore you with it, but it seems my business manager might have gone bezerk."

"Wow!" Sylvie's eyes widened.

"What can you do about it?" Lizzie asked. "Right now, not much."

"That's *la merde alors*. Here, have a gherkin. I always feel better when I eat gherkins." "Sylvie!" Rose and Lizzie said in tandem.

"Please. That's fine," Luna said. "She's right. If all Maria just told me turns out to be true, then I am, as Sylvie rightly pointed, totally fucked."

"*Alors* that settles it. You must stay here until you get it all sorted." Rose poured more wine all around.

"I wish I could, but sadly that's not possible," Luna sighed. "Why not?" Rose frowned.

"Because I'm unable pay you for even your cheapest room."

"Never mind. It's not a *problème.*" Rose shrugged.

"But it *is* a *problème*. A huge one. Oh *mon Dieu* that sounded terrible. What I meant was, I'm so appreciative of all your kindness, Rose, but I'd feel like a parasite staying here for free. I couldn't live with myself."

"Then what do you plan to do?" Sylvie asked, placing anther bread cube in the fondue pot.

"Something will come up, I'm sure," Luna muttered. "Like what?" Sylvie cocked her head.

"I don't know. Something."

"What are your options. Could you get a job?"

"Not unless you need a dishwasher," Luna muttered.

"Honestly? I don't think that washing up is your *spécialité,*" Sylvie shook her head. "Surely everyone knows how to stack a dishwasher? Or how about housework?" Luna asked.

The three women exchanged looks. "I don't think so," Sylvie reiterated.

"Okay. Not housework. But maybe I could help out with your foreign guests?" She turned to Rose. "I speak seven languages fluently."

The china clinked as Lizzie picked up the plates and laid them on the counter. She turned and leaned against it. "What did you bring with you on the trip?" She asked.

"Nothing much. Just the usual stuff: jeans, sweaters, a couple of shirts and dresses and an evening bag just in case. I didn't even bring much jewelry. I was planning on shopping in Paris and Rome after I—" Her voice trailed off. She didn't want to get into the reasons she'd intended to go to Poland.

"That purse," Lizzie pointed at the Birkin standing on the counter beneath the china cupboard.

"Is it real?" Sylvie asked

"Real?" Luna queried, taken aback.

"She means is it an original or a fake," Rose supplied.

"Oh! Real, of course. I mean I'm sure it must be. Nana gave it to me for my 17th birthday and she bought it at Hermès, in Paris, in the *Faubourg Saint Honoré.* I doubt they'd sell anything that wasn't one hundred percent kosher!"

"How much do you think it's worth?" Lizzie crossed the kitchen and assessed the purse. "I really couldn't say," Luna murmured, digesting her words. She'd never thought of her personal items in terms of their monetary worth. It was their sentimental value she'd taken into consideration.

Until now…

"Purses like that have good market value. You could get a good price for it." "*Sell* my Birkin?" Luna gasped. "But where?"

"On eBay, of course!" Sylvie said.

"Are you serious? You mean people actually *buy* other people's purses on the net?" The notion was intriguing.

"All the time" Sylvie nodded and poured the last of the wine.

"It's true," Lizzie corroborated. "Let's take a look at what's being auctioned right now," she said, scrolling through her phone.

"I'll bet your purse cost a fortune," Sylvie said, eyeing the Birkin and tilting her like a funky sparrow.

Her purse worth a fortune. A novel concept indeed. The Birkin had likely cost a good 15k or so. Yesterday 15K had seemed like pocket change to Luna, but right now it sure felt like a fortune. She thought of all the Birkins and Kellys she'd bought over the years. She'd never dreamed of asking their price. She'd simply handed her credit card over to the sales lady and signed the slip, waited for a dark suited security guard to open the door and follow her out and hand the bags to Juan, waiting for her on the curb…

~

"Where to now *Senora*?"

"I've a charity luncheon at the Grill, Juan. Why is traffic so slow?"

"A fender-bender two blocks down, *Senora*, but it's only here on Madison."

~

"*Oh lala, regardez*!" Lizzie exclaimed.

Luna snapped out of her daze.

"A 40-centimeter gold, caramel, calfskin Birkin with palladium hardware… and it's almost identical to yours, Luna. Here, take a look." Lizzie skirted the kitchen table and crouched between Rose and her, extending the phone for them to see.

"That's amazing!"

"It's bidding at 9,650 CHF!" Lizzie said.

"You paid all *that* for a purse?" Sylvie peered over Lizzie's shoulder at the phone. "It's worth much more new," Rose said

"May I look at it?" Sylvie asked.

"Sure." Luna reached for the Birkin and handed it to her. Nine-thousand Swiss francs was almost the same amount in US dollars. How did that fit into the stuff people calculate their lives on such as rent and food? She glanced at the screen once more. Why was the owner of that Birkin selling *her* purse? Had her life fallen apart too? Or was it a gift from an old boyfriend she wanted to get rid of? Perhaps the color was too "last year" and she wanted a change.

Sylvie carried out a thorough inspection of the Birkin, then placed it on the kitchen table next to the bread basket. "This bag," she declared, "is a rip off."

"It's a mess," Luna agreed, embarrassed at the jumble sliding around the bottom as Sylvie tilted the purse towards her. "But why do you say it's a rip off?"

"Where are the pockets for your phone or your lipstick?" Sylvie queried, then picked up a pink plastic tote from the floor and placed the purses side by side. "Take a look at that," she announced, unzipping it and displaying the purse's interior.

In the depths of the made-in-Taiwan tote, phone, sunglasses, lipstick and wallet lay neatly stowed in individual pockets; a far cry from the sticky Mars bar wrappers, the remains of her boarding pass and her wallet filled with useless plastic. It was sad to say, but right now her purse was the reflection of herself: outer gloss and inner chaos.

Sylvie continued to extol the benefits of her tote. "I bought this one in a two-for-the- price-of-one deal at the market in Bern for just 99 francs. I say sell this over-rated piece of leather and buy a couple of these instead."

"Sylvie, you don't understand. A Birkin isn't just a purse," Lizzie said. "It's an heirloom. "Princesses, people like Beyoncé and Kim Kardashian, all the celebs have one. The Birkin was designed specifically for Jane Birkin, the actress. It's a status symbol."

"You're exactly right," Luna nodded." It isn't just a purse, it's a negotiable asset. You've had a fantastic idea, Lizzie. Could we put my Birkin online?"

"Are you serious? A purse like that is an heirloom," Rose said, uncorking a new bottle of

wine

"Will the buyer pay cash?" Luna asked.

"It's up to you how you want to get paid. You can decide different forms of payment. The risk is theirs if you don't deliver the goods," Lizzie said.

"Who would do a thing like that?"

"You'd be surprised at the number of scams," Sylvie's bright pink nails flashed as she reached for the potato dish.

"Adly the world is full of dishonest individuals who profit from others' ingenuity, *ma chère.*" Rose agreed.

"As I've discovered to my cost," Luna muttered, still registering the growing possibility of Carl's defection. A traitor. What a horrible word. She closed her eyes a second, then took the purse off the table and placed it gently on her knee. Was she right to sell it? Nana had held on to the *Sac à Dépèches* through much worse times than these? All at once ,she pictured her, a young girl stepping inside the gates of hell clutching the Hermès purse. This was nothing by comparison.

"I'd like to go ahead and sell it, if you'll help me," she said at last. "Are you sure?" Lizzie looked at her, then at the others.

"Why not? It's all I've got to sell right now."

"There'll still be time to change your mind if you get cold feet," Rose said, squeezing her hand. It was as if they all understood how much more lay behind her decision to sell her purse.

"And I can lend you my other tote," Sylvie offered. "You'll like it. It's purple. It goes with everything."

"Thanks, that's very kind," Luna murmured. She took a gulp of wine. "Let's do it now."

"Très bien. You'd better empty it so we can take pics."

Luna drained her glass and watched Sylvie hold the Birkin at impossible angles while Lizzie photographed. It felt almost promiscuous. At one point, she almost grabbed it back. But soon they'd finished and the Birkin popped up on the screen.

Lizzie held out her Smartphone. "Ready?" The girls crowded around her.

"*Vas-y.*" Sylvie encouraged her.

Luna raised her right index. Already the Birkin felt less hers.

The kitchen turned silent. An owl hooted and the wind rustled in the trees in the park. Should she?

Luna's pulse raced. She tapped *ENTER*..

"We're on," Lizzie said.

"YES!" Sylvie cried, giving Luna a high five.

"Shush Sylvie! You'll wake up the Pilgrims," Rose admonished.

"*Merde les* pilgrims!" Sylvie split the dregs of the second bottle between them and raised her glass. "*Santé, les filles.* To Luna and her *courage*! Bravo!"

"It's not *courage*, its common sense," Luna demurred. But as the enormity of what she'd just done sank in, so did a rush of exhilaration. She, Luna Arabella — named after Henry's mother — Hampton, had just broken the mold.

"You'll see, it'll go fast," Lizzie assured her.

"That," Luna answered with a wry smile, "is exactly what I'm afraid of."

Chapter 28

Once he'd arrived at JFK's Terminal 4, Carl checked in and headed straight to the First-Class lounge. The front of the lounge was busy with passengers heading to Europe and South America, but his flight to Zurich was scheduled to leave on time. He wouldn't have long to wait.

He opted for the back where he found an isolated seat. Lately people irritated him. His patience felt as stretched as a rubber band about to crack. Even dealing with minor issues like listening to Mrs. Katz complain about the weather annoyed him to an unbearable degree. Carl prided himself on his good manners and patience, but since the night at the penthouse, his nerves were as shredded and tattered as Carolina Hampton's fur stole.

He laid his carry-on luggage next to the seat and went to pour himself a scotch. A woman stood at the counter. She picked up a wine bottle and studied it, then replaced it and reached for another. Carl fidgeted. Her blond hair scooped in a knot at the back of her neck irritated him. She looked German. She was likely a Nazi. Or maybe her grandmother was. Whatever. He needed a drink.

He poured himself a single-malt, straight, and returned to his seat. A young man sat down one seat away. He spoke on his phone in German. Why had he elected to sit that close? There were other free places weren't there? Carl eyed him suspiciously. Years ago, when he was a child, Uncle Ephraim had warned him about secret Gestapo members gone into hiding after the war. They lurked undercover, biding their time, waiting for the tide to change to crawl from under stones and out their burrows and permeate society with their venom. No one was safe. Not anymore. Not now that the tide *had* changed. Since the election he'd reminded himself over and over that this was America and there existed a Constitution, a Bill of Rights making all men equal and drafted by men determined to ensure they and their descendants never suffered the same persecution and religious intolerance their ancestors had known. He'd read the Magna Carta. Thank God for the Barons. A rhyme came to his mind from one of Leah's books — dearest Leah, how he missed her:

King john was not a nice man He had his little ways…

Maybe not, but at least he'd signed the damn document and altered the course of history.

The young man laughed. Carl listened and experienced a twinge of attraction. My God he was handsome: that hair, that lightly bronzed skin, the elegant gestures. And his clothes. He'd recognize Ermegnildo Zegna's cut anywhere.

As though sensing his gaze the young man looked up and smiled. "... '*na schön, wir sehen uns dann Morgen am...*"

He hung up. To his horror Carl returned the smile.

Nazis were wily. They got through the tightest of loopholes.

He drained his glass and rose to get a refill. By the time his flight was called his second glass was empty and Carl stumbled on his carry-on luggage. The young man glanced in his direction and reached out to help him.

"Gehst es ihnen ok?" He asked.

"I don't' speak German," Carl muttered.

"That's fine. I'm Norwegian. Are you flying to Zurich too?" "Yes."

They walked together out the lounge and headed for the gate. Norwegian. Not an enemy. He must beware though. He could be an agent in disguise.

The young man chatted. He'd been marlin fishing in Key Largo and was on his way back to Oslo. He had business to attend to in Zurich. By the time they boarded they'd introduced themselves.

The First Class cabin was half-empty. Carl and Gunnar's seats were in the same row. They smiled. Carl's pulse quickened as he read the inflight magazine. Should he suggest they dine together?

In the end, he was saved the trouble since the easy-going Norwegian popped the question himself and came across to join him. Soon they were air born and sipping champagne. It was years since Carl had indulged in pleasure. Overt pleasure. The occasional ambiguous encounters he'd allowed himself from time to time, glancing over his shoulder to make sure he wasn't followed, didn't count. It felt oddly natural. Unlike anything he'd experienced before. And Uncle Ephraim's life-long dream of recovering the family fortune, the unreturned Chagall and the meeting he planned to surprise the Banque Lourriel with on the morrow, faded into tiny specks thirty-thousand feet below as Carl loosened his tie and settled among the clouds.

Chapter 29

All night she'd tossed and dreamed: Nana in a sack-like dress, her head shorn and clutching the *Sac a Dépèches*; Carl's face split down the middle, the right side dark and grinning, the left pasty white, a clown's cheek with big black tear drops painted on it. Dreams and reality overlapped. Nothing was clear but time, running like a Kenyan sprinter to the finish line.

6:50am and only minutes left to go before the auction ended. What if the Birkin didn't sell? Her immediate financial future hung on the whim of an index wavering over the *ENTER* button of a keyboard out there in the virtual world. What would she do if the sale closed and there was no offer?

Luna pulled herself up among the pillows and fumbled for the switch of the bedside lamp.

Moonlight shifted across the dawn sky, filtered by the window and highlighting the living room beams. Through the crack in the curtain the branches of the chestnut tree looked as barren as she felt. Aureoles of light spilled out across the duvet. Her jeans, t-shirt and a pair of laddered pantyhose lay strewn on the floor where she'd discarded them last night. A dog barked in the farmyard next door. On the chest of drawers, the Birkin and the *Sac à Dépèches* stood side by side etched in chiaroscuro. Why had she chosen to bring her oldest and dearest Birkin along for this trip?

Still, it had to go.

Until she could straighten this entire mess out and find out why Carl had acted in this crazy manner, she was stuck, halfway across the world, with no money and no way of getting any. But she must find a way to stay and see what the Banque Lourriel had to tell her. Oh God. What if Nikolaj de Lourriel and Hubert Henchoz confirmed the account existed? What if there were funds in it? Would the IRS think she was trying to evade tax? Would they arrest her? What then? Handcuffs, perp walk, flashbulbs and ritual humiliation? Surely she'd be considered innocent until proven guilty? Maybe. But maybe not. Maybe they'd book her and spend thousands of dollars of tax payer funds on lawyers and keeping her in jail for a crime she hadn't committed; money that would certainly be better spent on healthcare or education than her shuffling around in a jumpsuit.

Horrifying scenarios presented themselves. In the meantime, she had to eat. She had to pay rent. Selling the Birkin was the only way she could do what most people did the better part of their lives: provide for themselves.

Two purses. Two sets of memories. The Birkin had its own tales to tell; the yapping pug at Delmonico's taking the handle for a dog biscuit and the day she and Nana waited for Henry's test results at Sloane Kettering. It was hard to pretend it wouldn't break her heart to part with it. Her first Birkin would always be special to her...

~

"Happy birthday, Luna." Nana wafted across the room and placed the large orange box tied with brown cotton ribbon on the bed, then enveloped Luna in *Joy de Patou* and the scent of 50,000 Hungarian rose petals.

Luna sat up, cross-legged among the pillows. The orange box was identical to several on the glass shelves in Nana's walk-in closet. Could it contain what she'd been dreaming of for the past months?

"May I open it?" she asked.

"But of course. Bella's ordered breakfast but we've a few minutes before it arrives." Nana perched on the edge of the bed. Tia Bella sat in the armchair near the window.

Luna saw them exchange a complicit glance as she pulled the box towards her and undid the ribbon.

"Go on, open it," Nana urged.

Luna removed the ribbon and lifted the lid with the coveted Hermès name and chariot logo. Inside was a brown dust bag. She stood it up and untied the strings. The tip of two leather handles peeked. She peeled the dust bag off and the Birkin rose like Botticelli's Venus from the shell.

"Oh my God!" She'd shrieked. "I don't believe it!"

"You like it?"

"Like it? I love it. Oh, Nana!" She threw herself about her neck. "Thank you. Thank you so, so much! I'll keep this Birkin all my life!" She exclaimed.

Tia Bella rose and padded across the room, her carpet slippers flapping. She looked like the bronze Kokoschka frogs in Henry's study, but with a sweet smile. Luna loved her godmother dearly. She must really love her too to have left her beloved Jung institute snd come all the way to spend her birthday weekend.

"I thought caramel was a good color to start with," Nana said. "It goes with everything."

Tia Bella sent her a quizzical look. Nana frowned. Something was going on between them Luna couldn't capture. But she was too enamored with her new purse to care. Then she looked up and saw great sadness in Nana's eyes.

"What is it, Nana?" She reached out her hand and touched her sleeve.

"Nothing dear!" She tweaked Luna's cheek and rose. "Come along now and tidy that hair. You'll have all the time in the world to look at the Birkin later. And put on your robe. You mustn't catch cold."

Nana moved across the wood paneled room and pulled the drapes back further. "It's snowing hard. Don't the mountains look magical, Bella?"

"They do indeed." The two women stood at the window in silence. Then Tia Bella turned and schlepped back towards the living room of the suite.

Luna swung her feet to the floor and laid the Birkin tenderly in the center of the bed. The girls at school would be green with envy. She walked across the room and leaned her head on Nana's shoulder.

Outside the world was white; the gardens, the tennis courts and the pine trees.

"I'll never be separated from my Birkin ever, for as long as I live," she said, slipping her hand in Nana's.

"I said that once about a bag." "And what happened?"

"My words came true." "You still have it?"

Nana turned away from the window. She let go of Luna's arm and stared silently at the Birkin. Luna held her breath. It was as though the purse had turned into a mirror of memories reflecting something only she could see.

"Now come along and get your dressing gown on and have breakfast," Nana said.

The moment passed as fast as it came. All returned to normal and Luna reveled in her joy at her first Birkin.

~

One minute to go. Fears, tears and laughter wrapped in togo leather and silver palladium exposed now for the world to see; memories that, should she be so lucky as to receive an offer on in the next forty seconds, would be replaced by someone else's.

The countdown continued.

Fifteen seconds left. Luna swallowed and raised a hand, about to close the laptop.

Ping!

She jolted. "Oh God! Someone just made an offer!"

Her finger hovered over the keyboard. She was thrilled. Of course she was! She'd done it, hadn't she? She'd found an answer to her immediate crisis. No panicked phone calls or pleas for assistance.

If she pressed *ENTER,* for a while at least, she could take care of herself entirely on her own. She'd no longer be destitute. Fears of the station bench would disappear and Carl could go fuck himself for not taking her calls and leaving her in this situation.

Last night before going to sleep she'd emptied out the contents on her bed: lipstick, her wallet, the photos of Nana and Henry and the protections that Jairo, the shaman had sent her years ago. It was for the best. Forget the memories in each scuff and crease and questioning if the Birkin might have a soul. It was a purse; bits of leather sewn together to carry stuff in. Nothing more.

Luna looked at the Birkin, then at the screen. She closed her eyes and held her breath. "I'm sorry," she said.

And pressed *ENTER*.

Chapter 30

At 3pm, Luna stood at the kitchen sink and washed her coffee cup. Rose had gone to visit a friend. On the table next to a poinsettia in a silver pot, was the wicker basket that she'd asked her to take over to Father Florian's cottage.

Luna slipped the handle over her left arm and stepped outside. *La Bise*, the biting east wind blowing in from the Russian Steppes whipped the snow off the ground. Father Florian's cottage stood at the edge of the park overlooking the fields that led to the forest and the *Camino*. Sharp icicles hung from the spout of a copper pipe under the roof; a perfect weapon to impale or stab Carl with. A sharp icicle straight through the heart would do the trick nicely. By the time the police arrived, it would have melted leaving no trace. Maybe she should study criminology instead of battling with writing her romance novel, a subject she knew little about. The few trysts with Jeff under the Led Zeppelin poster in his room in the student dorm, were hardly a reference.

Luna stepped under the porch. A wooden bench piled with sheepskins and checkered cushions stood before a wood-burning stove. A wreath of leaves and berries hung above the bronze knocker on the front door. Luna banged it once and waited.

Except for Chichi barking, all was silent.

She knocked again a little louder. Nothing. Perhaps Father Florian was a little deaf. At last she tried the door handle. It gave and she gently opened the door.

It was mid-afternoon, but it was dark inside the cottage. It took a second or two for Luna to accustom her eyes. Then she gasped as a shadow formed. She grappled for the light switch. A dim lamp came on.

"Oh my God!" She cried.

Dropping the basket, she ran towards Father Florian — his grey face and watery eyes barely recognizable, his dressing gown untied and a woolen shawl falling from his shoulders like a shroud.

"Excusez-moi," he whispered. A racking cough followed. "I'm not very steady. I shall return to bed."

Luna grabbed the priest's arm and together they shuffled across the room. His cane echoing on the floor boards between the threadbare rugs, sounded just like Henry's.

"Lean on me, *mon Père*," she insisted, shocked at the swift transformation. She slipped her upper arm around his back to give him support.

"*Merci*."

They progressed slowly past the fireplace and on towards a beam of light that shone through an open door she assumed was his bedroom.

The room was like a monk's cell: a single bed, a wooden nightstand, a simple chair and a cupboard. She helped him sink onto the side of the bed and automatically set in motion the familiar gestures she'd performed for years.

"Would you like to take off your dressing gown?" She took his cane and placed it within easy distance of the bed, then bent down to remove his slippers. The soles were coming off. He could trip and fall and break a hip. She'd check his shoe size. Rose likely knew where they could find an identical pair. If Father Florian was anything like Henry, he'd hate to change them.

Luna straightened the sheet and plumped the pillows and the duvet before easing Father Florian back against them. Carefully, she raised his legs and made sure his hips were aligned. Then she pulled the duvet up over his chest — not too high, in case it irritated him. Then, perching on the edge of the bed, she placed her hand on his brow. It was feverish as she'd suspected. She placed her right index and middle finger on the fine skin of his left wrist and checked her watch.

A slight arrhythmia. She glanced at the nightstand. Next to a rickety lamp with a burnt shade, was an empty box of paper handkerchiefs and his medications on a plastic tray; blood pressure, vitamin drops, eye drops, cough mixture, syrup of figs, and the usual over-the-counter flu remedies and pain killers. She'd be willing to bet that glass of water hadn't been changed in days.

Father Florian's labored breath concerned her. She lay his hand carefully back on the cotton duvet, then picked up the glass and reached for the waste paper basket, crammed with used tissues, and carried them through to the kitchen. The sink was piled with dirty dishes.

As soon as she was out of earshot, she called Rose. The phone rang several times but she didn't pick up. She hurried back to the bedroom. Father Florian's breathing seemed worse. There was no thermometer in sight but she didn't need one to tell he was running a high fever.

Rose's phone kept ringing. "Pleases pick up," she begged.

Slipping the phone between her right ear and shoulder, she hurried across the room to close the window and check the radiator below it.

"Oh my God it's freezing!" She muttered. No wonder the poor man was sick. Why hadn't he said something?

She hurried back to the bed. Father Florian's mouth hung open. His lips were dry. Dehydration.

She must get him to the hospital fast.

An old Nokia phone vibrated on the nightstand. Should she pick up? Maybe it was someone who knew Father Florian and could help. She answered.

"Hello."

"*Padre—*"

A man's voice broke off. "Hello?"

Static. Crackling sounds.

"*SOS. Aidez-nous.* Help us, please, *Padre*. We're drifting off the Libyan coast. The boat she sinking. Woman have baby. Children on board. For the sake of the God help us *padre—*"

"Hello, Hello?" Luna shook the phone but the line went dead. It must be one of Father Florian's refugees he'd talked about. Oh God! What should she do? The screen read *number unknown*.

"Father Florian," Luna crouched by the bed and gently touched his arm. "*S'il-vous-plaît,* there are refugees stranded off the Libyan coast. Their boat is capsizing. You said you warned the Italian coast guard."

Flickering eyelids opened, then closed.

"Oh God, please!" Luna placed her hand on his brow. The fever had worsened. She sent Rose a quick text message telling her to get an ambulance as soon as possible, then waited for Father Florian's phone to ring again. Who should she prioritize? A ninety-three-year-old with possible pneumonia, or those men, women and children stranded in the Mediterranean?

She grabbed his phone and raced through contacts. If Father Florian was regularly in touch with the Italian Coast Guard, surely their number must be here? *Guardia*-something. She knew the name. She'd seen it on the boats patrolling the coast the last time Nana, Henry and she were in Portofino.

"*Guardia Costiera*! That's it!" She cried and punched in the number. Several seconds of crackly rings.

"Pronto, Capitano Troncini parlando. Havete la posizione SAT de'lla nave, Padre?" "*La nave esta posizionatta cerca la costa della Libya.*" Thank God she'd learned Italian. *"Aspetta perfavore."*

Hundreds of miles away down a cackling line, engines revved and voices shouted.

She glanced at Father Florian, still as a mummy. The nails of her left hand dug into her palm. Had she given the right SAT position? What if she'd understood wrong? Would she be personally responsible for the drowning of dozens of men, women and children?"

Snowflakes drifted past the window panes. It was getting dark. She imagined the panic- stricken refugees; the boat swaying, the screams and terror. Seconds felt like hours. Imagine being tortured this long?

Father Florian's breathing was barely perceptible now. If he died, she'd be to blame.

"Pronto. Abbiamo identificato la posizione della barca e stiamo andando lì adesso. Stiamo cerca. Grazie per la chiamata."

"Thank you. *Grazie.* Oh God, thank you."

Her hands shook. She brushed away the tears. Now what? She held the two phones wondering what to do next. Father Florian's phone buzzed once more.

"Hello."

"Alo alo."

The refugee's voice was desperate.

"The *Guardia Costiera* are on their way to you now," she cried. "Are you alright?"

"The crew, they have abandon us. The boat she's adrift. I try stop the panic. We pray. We pray to the God."

"Tell them the *Guardia Costiera* is arriving immediately and—" She caught sight of the crucifix, the Buddha and copies of the bible, the Talmud and the Coran on the shelves opposite

Father Florian's bed. "Tell them we're praying to every God there is to pray to out there. Stay calm. Hang in there. God is with you. I promise you'll be safe."

"*Inch Allah. Chukran.* Thank you. Bless you. You're an angel. Please pray with me now together to the God," his voice cracked up again.

Luna dropped to her knees at Father Florian's bedside and began to pray. Her voice and that of a desperate stranger on a sinking boat thousands of miles away, resonated in a single vibration down the line.

"Our father who art in heaven, Hallowed be thy name…"

Beyond their voices joined in prayer and words muttered with conviction, came wails and screams, fear at its most pungent and raw. She reached for Father Florian's limp fingers and closed her eyes.

"Please God, my Angels and Spirit guides, Nana, Henry and whoever the heck is out there, do not allow any more souls to die in a sea turned graveyard of dashed hopes."

Luna's prayers tumbled down the line. The power of prayer *could* work miracles. Hadn't she experienced it herself? She begged for the refugees to make it safely to a European shore and that once there, they would be met with kindness and humanity, not barbed wire and rejection. Surely after all they'd lived through, they deserved that human decency that the West pronged?

The line went dead. The link was severed.

"Oh my God!" Had the boat capsized? Father Florian's face was replaced by bodies flailing in the water. Until minutes ago, the tide of human suffering fleeing razed homes, barrel bombs and persecution, were a parenthesis, a paragraph amidst her personal issues; issues that now seemed about as significant as a flea on a rat's ass.

The phone remained silent. All she could do now was entrust them to the Universe. She must stay in the now and get help for Father Florian. She laid the old Nokia back on the nightstand. How many lives had it saved?

Her own phone vibrated. Rose, at last.

"L'ambulance arrive."

She raised her eyes to heaven and whispered: "Thank you!"

A blaring siren announced the arrival of the ambulance. Luna opened the door and Navy blue uniforms filled the tiny cottage. The medics lifted the frail figure from the monastic bed and placed him on a gurney. The apparatus beeped and vital signs, a drip, oxygen has all been put in place in a matter of seconds.

"*Je peux l'accompagner*?" Luna asked.

"*Oui. Venez*," the young medic flashed her a warm smile as they lifted the gurney and passed into the living room. Luna popped Father Florian's bible and rosary and the old Nokia that linked him to the refugees into a plastic shopping bag. Oh God, had they made it?

She opened a drawer and grabbed underwear and a pair of socks and a pair of fresh pajamas, then hurried through to the living room where she waited for the gurney to pass through the front door. The lights were on and for the first time, she looked up at the walls plastered with photographs, paintings and mementos.

It was as the gurney was wheeled out the door that she heard the plaintive strains of a violin. A shudder convulsed her and her eyes flew to the painting above the fireplace. She gasped. *The Girl in the Red Dress Under the Moon*. Was she seeing double? She stepped closer. Even the frame looked identical. She could swear the girl's head was turned as though peering over her shoulder. The violinist and the goat whirled in cloud. The violin grew louder. Luna's head swam and she closed her eyes. Elliptical flashes. Chanel No. 5… .Dusty flecks floating beyond her grasp caught on the edge of her memory and her soul lost in translation. She reached out and touched the frame. The goat's distorted face popped out at her like a freak on a ghost train ride, then a Swastika grew between the eyes and the goat's features transformed into those of an old man.

"*Madame*?"

Luna jumped and turned.

The young medic's head peeked around the door. "*On est prêt à partir*," he said.

She glanced back at the painting. The sound of the violin faded. She hurried out the cottage. The front door closed behind her and she scrambled into the back of the ambulance.

Father Florian lay hooked up to a drip. She pressed his fingers. The last strains of violin gave way to those of the siren as the ambulance veered around the bend.

Chapter 31

The ambulance came to a halt and the hospital and the medics opened the doors. Father Florian's eyes opened for a second. Luna smiled and squeezed his hand, then let go as the ground staff pulled out the gurney.

She hurried through the swing doors afraid if she let Father Florian out of her sight he might die like Nana had and leave her with another enigma to solve.

She stopped breathless before the elevator. One of the aids held the closing door with his foot.

"Can I come with you?" She asked him.

"*Désolé Madame,* but I'm afraid not. We're taking him straight to the intensive care unit."

"But I must stay with him," Luna insisted. "Are you a relation?"

"*Oui,*" she lied. "I'm his—his great-niece." There. She'd said it! "Then we'll keep you advised of his progress."

The elevator doors closed like metal jaws. She could hear her heart thump.

Should she dash back to the cottage? No. She couldn't risk leaving Father Florian. If he didn't make it, she'd never learn about the Chagall she'd just seen above his fireplace. Oh God. How selfish was that? Was her only reason for wanting him to live to satisfy her curiosity about a painting?

Maybe she was hallucinating? She'd spent hours since Nana's passing standing in the foyer staring at *The Girl in the Red Dress Under the Moon* until her eye sockets burned. It had gotten to the point where she'd begun to believe their system didn't work and that Nana was lost to her forever. Yet, the second she'd set eyes on the painting in the cottage, it had come alive. Had Nana come back to her?

Luna called the elevator and pulled out her phone. The girl in the red dress stared back at her. She could swear the painting in Father Florian's cottage was identical. Still, the lighting in the cottage was poor. Perhaps in the rush of the departure and the aftermath of rescuing a boat full of refugees she'd imagined it? Crazy. All of it. She could scream with frustration at more unanswered questions.

But answered questions were her lot in life. In her teens she'd been haunted by them. She'd grasped at elliptical memories. They hovered just out of reach like flecks of dust in sunlight; flashes that grazed the edge of her mind, clear one second, melting and hazy the next as though reality and illusion had fused, leaving her lost. In fact, she'd never addressed the subject of her own past for it upset Nana and Henry to go back to the time of their daughter's death. And anyway, the past mattered. She must have done something good in a past life and that's why the Universe had blessed her and guided the Colombian nuns who'd discovered her. She'd realized too that her purpose in life was to bring joy to the people who'd given her so much and do her best to pay back their kindness and generosity with good behavior and companionship.

The elevator docked. Luna stepped out glad to leave the smell of disinfectant behind; it reminded her of Sloane Kettering. She glanced at her phone. A text message from Rose blocked the violinist on the screensaver; she and Lizzie were on their way to the hospital. Would Rose think she lost her mind if she confided her doubts about the Chagall in the cottage when perhaps it was only an illusion?

At 1am the doctors still hadn't brought news of Father Florian.

In the dimly lit waiting room next to the IC unit, time lagged. Lizzie had gone to fetch more coffee, Rose dozed and Luna's mind was back at the cottage. As far as she was concerned, the only magical powers the painting possessed were those attributed to it by Nana. But how had it gotten there? She didn't even know where her painting actually was. After the phone call with Maria, she'd rung Sotheby's, but no expertise for any of the Hampton paintings had been solicited. The only explanation for Carl removing the Chagall from the penthouse was if he'd taken it to show old Mr. Wolf. If so, why hadn't he just asked her?

But it still didn't explain how the painting had arrived above Father Florian's fireplace.

Did you put the Chagall in that cottage, Nana? If you did you'd better make darn sure Father Florian doesn't disappear with his secrets like you did. I've had enough! I want answers!

Luna sat up straight and blinked. She'd never spoken to Nana like that before. But she had to. Father Florian couldn't die and leave her hanging on the end of a thread of suppositions.

She touched the handles of the *Sac à Dépèches* on the chair next to her. Rose — dear Rose who thought of everything — had brought it with her. It seemed natural to replace her beloved Birkin with this silent witness of Nana's past; the scarred protector of hidden truths that for nigh on a century had courageously guarded a message, wrapped in folds of tobacco named after a tale of love and woe, to its destination.

Rose touched her arm as Lizzie entered carrying paper cups of coffee. "The doctors are coming," she said, handing them each a cup.

The three women hurried into the corridor as the two men approached.

"I'm afraid the news is not good. Father Florian is *très faible*," Dr. Schlago, the elder of the two, said. "It's a serious case of pneumonia. At his age, it will be a miracle if he survives the night."

"Then we must pray," Rose said. "*Merci docteur.*"

One by one their voices joined in prayer for Father Florian. Luna drank in the words; French, English. Same words. Different Sounds. Same intention and most importantly an identical vibration: that of the ecstatic evolutionary impulse of the Universe.

The prayer ended.

"I wish I could stay here the night but I have to get breakfast for twenty pilgrims and Lizzie you must be at work at 7am," Rose said worried. "We shall pray for him and return in the morning."

"I'm staying," Luna said. "Are you sure?"

"*Oui.*"

"That's kind of you, Luna. Call me in the morning. I'll pick you up once we know if—if he's still with us," Rose said, her eyes wet.

"He will be."

"Luna, you heard what the doctors said. There's no use trying to gild the lily. He's very old and the truth is, he doesn't stand much of a chance," Lizzie pressed Luna's hand. "Don't get too tired."

"I'll be fine. *Merci.*"

Rose leaned towards her and they kissed on the cheek. Luna thought a second. As Rose turned to leave, she grabbed her arm.

"Can I ask you a favor?" Luna said. "Of course."

"You know the painting that's above Father Florian's fireplace?" "The Chagall? *Oui, bien sûr.*"

"So, it really is a Chagall?"

"Yes, it's an original."

"Could I go see it when I get back to the Angel House tomorrow morning? I'll explain later why."

"Tu viens, Rose?" Lizzie asked from the doorway. "I'll explain later." Luna said to Rose.

"Ok, see you tomorrow. *Courage."* Rose said as she followed Lizzie out the door.

The lights were dimmed. Luna sat alone in the waiting room. No emergencies had been brought in, and aside from the occasional murmur of nurses in the corridor and the opening and closing of doors, the place was strangely silent. At times during the night Luna drifted back to Sloane Kettering, holding Henry's hand; to those final moments before Nana died and she'd whispered those last words: *Romeo & Julieta. Mein Engel.* Why had she spoken in German?

Luna stood up, stretched and stepped noiselessly into the corridor. The lights were low. Through a glass divider, a night nurse filled reports on the computer. She looked up, bright and friendly despite the late hour, and smiled at Luna through designer lenses.

"*Comment va le père Florian*?" Luna asked. "Has there been any change?" "I'm about to go and check on him."

"May I come with you?"

"I suppose. You're his great-niece, it might bring him comfort." Luna smiled weakly and didn't answer.

She accompanied the nurse down the passage to the wide door leading inside the emergency unit. A glimpse of her reflection in the small oblong pane showed a haggard face and dark ringed eyes.

Inside the unit were five empty beds and at the end, a figure lying motionless, hooked to life support. An oxygen mask covered his face.

Luna stepped up to the bed. The nurse checked the mask and the drip. Luna reached out and touched the frail veined hand lying loosely on the flat coverlet. She squeezed the fingers gently and connected down to the roots of the earth, then up, beyond the building to the energy above, seeking the impulse of the Universe of which they were all a part. After several seconds, the nerve ends of her fingers tingled. She swayed back and forth slightly to capture the frequency. She opened her eyes. The nurse was frowning and checking Father Florina's vital signs a second time, then she took his pulse and the temperature again.

"It's *incroyable*," she said, "but I could swear that since you took hold of his hand his pulse has picked up and his breathing is less labored. His blood pressure is almost regular again."

"Really?"

"Yes, you seem to be doing him good. Would you like to stay with him?" "If you'll let me."

"*Ma chère*, Father Florian is a dying man. Right now, he may not survive the next few hours. If your presence can help him, whatever the outcome, I assure you Dr. Schlago would be the first to agree." She drew up a chair and placed it next to the bed, then poured a glass of mineral water from the bottle on the table next to it.

Luna sat down and took both Father Florian's hands between her palms. Moonbeams streamed through the slats of the half-closed blinds creating an aura around the crown of the priest's head and pale, boney face. How different he looked to that of the man who'd marched into the kitchen only days earlier.

"Please don't go," Luna whispered. "Stay and tell me how you came by *The Girl in the Red Dress Under the Moon.*" Had Chagall painted more than one version of the dreamy- eyed girl lost in another world?

She pressed Father Florian's fingers tighter, then placed her right index and middle finger on the inside of the priest's wrist and pulsed every ounce of energy in her until their hearts throbbed in a single beat and Father Florian's soul rose with hers into the moonlit sky.

The scent of Chanel No. 5… the same strains of the violin she'd heard earlier in the cottage…

A trolley rattled and voices echoed from the corridor. Luna loosened her hold of Father Florian's fingers. It was morning already. She must have fallen asleep.

Dr. Schlago entered, accompanied by two orderlies. Machines were checked and clipboards discussed in low professional tones. Then the doctor came over to her.

"*Bravo, Mademoiselle*. I don't know what you've done but I think you've saved Father Florian's life.

There are times when the body alone cannot survive unless the soul decides to remain. It appears this was one of those times." He smiled and squeezed Luna's shoulder. "You should go home now. We'll keep him in until he's fully recovered. Let us give thanks for a *miracle.*"

"No, thank you. But if it's ok, I will stay with him a little longer."

"Comme vous-voulez, Madame."

Chapter 32

At 10am, Father Florian was sleeping peacefully behind the oxygen mask. Despite her exhaustion, she needed to return to the cottage and make sure the Chagall was real and not a figment of her imagination.

Luna stretched and prepared to leave the room still adrift in her altered state. The scent of Nana's Chanel No. 5 still lingered. She slipped her jacket on, touched Father Florian's brow gently, then stepped out into the corridor.

She stepped into the corridor and collided with a trolley.

"Pardon Mademoiselle," a young orderly apologized. *"Vous êtes okay?" "Oui, merci."* She must be more tired than she realized.

She mounted the flight of stairs. The phone rang. Unknown number. "Hello."

"*Bonjour Madame Hampton, Nikolaj de Lourriel à l'appareil.*"

"Bonjour. Do you have news regarding the account?" Luna said excitedly as she stopped near the cafeteria where patients in dressing gowns read newspapers and sipped morning coffee. *"Oui, Madame.* We have identified the account. There is just a situation that has occurred. Could you come over to the bank *immédiatement?"*

"Of course. I'll call a cab and be there in a few minutes," she said.

The Chagall will have to wait. Was she on the verge of learning Nana's secrets?

She hung up, hurried to the reception and asked the girl behind the desk to call a taxi.

"Le taxi sera là en 5 minutes, Madame." "Merci."

Luna headed out the main entrance. She could barely contain her excitement.

At last she would get answers; answers to help her discover Nana's truth and what lay behind the tattoo.

Chapter 33

Ephraim woke and dozed intermittently. He walked down a street in Munich, or was it New York? He'd lost count of time. Snippets — wisps of thoughts that he couldn't quite grasp — hopped back and forth like the dancers in a Nutcracker suite he'd been taken to at Christmas long ago. Ducks on the pond… swans… bags of dry bread to feed the sheep and laughter… Karina pushing her doll's pram with little Florian following, dragging his mottled one-eyed teddy bear. And Rainer. Always Rainer. Handsome, edgy and exciting.

Why hadn't Carl called? Surely he'd landed in Switzerland by now? It was always the same and it wasn't fair. All his life he'd been left out when *he* should be the first to be informed.

Ephraim opened his eyes. His back was stiff. He reached for the handle that allowed him to pull himself up, switched on the lights and stared hard at the Chagall.

"Mrs. Katz," he called.

"It's me, Debra, Mr. Wolf," A plump, pale, young woman in horn-rimmed glasses, a shapeless dress and baggy blouse came bustling in. "Mrs. Katz will be in later."

Ephraim shook his head. "What time is it?" "It's past 4am, Sir."

"Turn on the TV and bring me a whisky. Didn't the Katz woman tell you I always have a whisky at 6pm?"

"But it's four in the morning, Sir."

"Ach! Stop arguing and get it for me"

The woman hesitated, then shrugged. "Very well."

"Two fingers mind, and in a long glass. And water. Cold. No ice. Understood?" "Yes Mr. Wolf."

"And hand me those TV controls," he said testily. "I'll do it myself. You'll likely mess them up."

Debra passed him the TV controls and scuttled off in search of the whisky.

Ephraim fiddled with the buttons. Damned technology. Why did they complicate it instead of making it easier? Some *dumbkopf* had invented more and more buttons to do what you used to with one. And who needs hundreds of programs? Weren't two good enough? No wonder they'd dumbed down the population. What could you expect when all they did was watch nonsense and eat rubbish?

He flipped through cartoons and a couple of soaps until he found CNN where a replay of Christiane Amanpour's programme was on. He liked her. She and Wolf Blitzer and Fareed Zakaria were the only ones who talked sense. He augmented the volume and laid the control down on the duvet and reached for the glass of water on the nightstand.

"*... And finally, tonight a story that must give hope to all those seeking a better life across the Mediterranean. Three hundred refugees were saved off the Libyan coast thanks to a call from an old Nokia phone, owned by an elderly priest in Fribourg Switzerland...*

... this incredible story has been confirmed by Swiss journalists in Fribourg who tried to interview Father Florian. Sadly, the priest is now in a local hospital with pneumonia. Here at CNN we send him our prayers and good wishes for a swift recovery. Thank you and good night from New York."

Ephraim pressed the mute button. Florian. Fribourg. It rang a bell. Florian von Heil had entered into the church. But could it be? It would be a hell of a coincidence, but he'd heard a rumor just after Eli and Papa's arrest that the Baron had sent him to Switzerland. Fribourg was an obvious choice, what with de Lourriel connection.

Ephraim pulled a cigarette from the pack in his pajama pocket. What an unexpected stroke of luck it would be if it really was the Florian he once knew. Florian was likely the only person alive today who could vouch that he was Aaron Wolf's heir. Plus,

Florian knew nothing of the circumstances of Papa and Eli's arrest. He must get Carl on the phone — if he'd ever bothered to call — and ask him to investigate. Imagine a long-lost reencounter? The news anchor mentioned he was sick and in hospital. Life couldn't be so cruel as to tend him this perch only to withdraw it. There was only one possible glitch that could put a spanner in this gently revolving wheel, if Florian remembered that day at dawn, back at Schloss Heil, when he'd stepped out of Rainer's room…

~

The ancient Schloss Heil floor boards creaked as he tied the sash of his dressing gown and stepped out into the dark corridor. The servants weren't up yet. Ephraim peered right and left before tip-toeing down the passage. He hated the damned suits of armor looming over him; Teutonic Knights sending accusatory glances at him through their visors from another age.

He was about to creep up the next flight of stairs when he glanced back and saw a shadow. He couldn't distinguish it clearly in the dark. Surely that was Florian's door creaking open and a figure emerging?

Ephraim backed into the shadows and the figure disappeared down the main stairway. He let out a sigh, then scampered up the stairs and back to his room. He'd likely not been observed. It was just Florian going to the chapel for morning prayers. That was okay. Florian was naïve. An innocent. He wouldn't cause any trouble.

~

Ephraim filled his lungs with another long, comforting dose of nicotine and twiddled the ring on his pinky. As soon as Carl got in touch, he'd put him on it.

Ephraim's mind began to wander.

But there was a lot at stake. Of course Florian would need to be managed right, and Carl was too wishy-washy.

Matters were starting to reach a climax far too risky to let others handle them.

Ephraim grew anxious. He must take charge. He couldn't leave it only to Carl. It was too sensitive of a situation.

Debra returned with the whisky and placed it next to him on the nightstand.

He grunted.

"What time does Mrs. Katz arrive?" "She'll be here at eight, sir."

"Good. When she gets in, tell her to go straight down to the cellar and bring my green suitcase up. I'm going on a trip."

Chapter 34

It took fifteen minutes in traffic for Luna to reach the bank. The snow had stopped and the sun was out as she hurried up the slippery steps. At last she was about to learn something concrete that might set her on Nana's trail.

In the lobby, the receptionist called through to announce her arrival. Luna glanced at herself in the mirror. She looked a mess. She hadn't slept or showered since yesterday. Smudged mascara rings under her eyes gave her an owlish look. Never mind. She was there to hear what Hubert and Nikolaj had to tell her, not pose for a photoshoot.

The same man who'd received her last time appeared and offered to take her jacket. "I'll just keep it, *merci*."

She followed him down the corridor.

The bank officer stopped at the door, knocked, then opened it and held it for her to pass through.

Luna stepped inside a small conference room. Nikolaj rose from behind an oval table and came hurrying towards her, his tie askew and his shirt tail peeking from the back of his pants, just like the first time she'd met him. Hubert followed, his face flustered. A third man sat with his back to the door. He turned and Luna stopped dead in her tracks.

Carl.

He'd aged light years since the day she'd blithely signed the power of attorney. There was gray at his temples and new lines furrowed his brow. What was he doing here?

"*Merci* for coming so promptly," Nikolaj said. "Why is he here?" She said.

"It's my fault. Luna, I'm sorry." Carl rose. "I thought if you knew, you wouldn't come," he said stepping out from behind the table and moving towards her.

"Why haven't you called me back? I've left all tons of messages. You have no idea what I've been going through. None of my cards are working. I had no money!"

"I'm sorry. I never should've blocked your cards."

"You blocked my cards?" Luna's eyes widened. "Why?" "It's a long story. I acted on impulse. I'm sorry."

"You're sorry? What the fuck is going on?"

"Luna, *s'il-vous-plait, restez calme,"* Nikolaj begged.

"We have a situation. The bank has never been in such a position before. Luna, *je vous en prie.* Please sit down and allow us to explain," Hubert implored.

"Non! There is something wrong here. Why are you talking to him? What does Carl got to do with all of this?" Luna's breath felt strangled in her throat.

She must get air. She burst out the door and into the corridor and ran towards the bathroom.

Distance. She must distance herself. She didn't trust Carl anymore or Nikolaj de Lourriel or Hubert Henchoz. They were clearly in league. But why? Had Carl come to do her harm? If so, he had no bed to hide under.

Luna entered the bathroom, slammed the door behind her and locked it. The lights came on automatically. She coughed and leaned over the basin, shaking. Her breath was short and fast.

She looked up. The face staring back at her from the mirror wasn't hers: it was a child's face; blank eyes, hair sticking to her cheeks as it had when she'd heard their steps on the creaking stairs...

~

They'd told her they'd be back soon but they hadn't returned. And he was here.

She pulled the sheet down the side of the bed and crawled under it and lay motionless under it not daring to breathe. Motes of dust caught in her throat. She mustn't cough or he'd find her. Could his arm reach this far?

She heard the door open. She closed her eyes tight. An empty beer can crashed into the waste basket. *Pop!* Another one opened. The floor creaked as he roamed the room.

"Luna? Little Luna? Where are you little Luna? Big Daddy's here." She bit her hands not to scream.

"Come on out from wherever you're hiding. You know I don't like this game."

He sat on the bed. The springs of the mattress came down on top of her, digging into her back as she pressed herself flat on the ground and buried her face in the moldy carpet.

All was dark. He snored. Had he fallen asleep?

A little later he snorted and rose, and the springs gave. Shudders gripped her. She breathed again.

"Come on, stop trying to fool me, I know you're here. You can't fool me."

The gramophone needle scratched. Music blared. Words filtered... It was Mama's song, the moon song... her song... Mama said the moon was sometimes light and sometimes dark.

... Round and round and round.

A loud burp. Muttered words. She heard him spit and clear his throat. Pee ran down her legs. She was a bad girl. They'd be angry with her. Maybe they'd spank her if they found out and she'd be sent to bed with nothing to eat and her tummy'd hurt.

Voices.

The door burst open. “Where’s the bitch’s kid?”

“Dunno. She’s not here. I looked.”

“Fuck. They said social services are coming to see about her. Someone ratted. And the damned hurricane’s about to hit.”

“Then let’s get the fuck out.” “What about the kid?” “Leave her. Fuck it.”

The song ended. Silence. Outside sirens blared. Then all went dark.

~

Luna drew herself up. She grabbed a paper towel and wiped her face. Why were these flashes back and popping out of nowhere? She mustn’t let them. She mustn’t feel sorry for herself. She was lucky. *So* lucky. She had Nana and Henry to protect her.

HAD.

Now she was alone. She must pull herself together and handle it. She bent down and drank from the tap. Why had Carl come and what were they conniving about in there? She must get a grip. She wasn’t little anymore. And this time she’d come out from under the bed and stand up for herself. She’d sold her beloved Birkin and felt empowered, hadn’t she? If she could part with her most prized item, then surely she could deal with Carl? She’d be brave and they couldn’t get her. She just mustn’t trust them. Not even Nana. That tattoo told a whole other story to what shed' been told. And now she'd popped up in the wrong Chagall!

Lies, lies, lies. All fucking make believe. Make *her* believe.

She wiped the smudges from under her eyes and off her face. She dragged her fingers through her hair. She'd go back and hear what it was Carl had come to tell her. If she was to defend herself, she must know where she stood.

Luna unlocked the bathroom door and stared down the corridor. She closed her eyes and grounded herself. Carl's presence had sent warning signals flashing, but she refused to be afraid. There were too many shades of unknown and it was up to her to wipe the blurred lens. Old Mr. Wolf's face flashed. Then Nana's and Henry's. How had she not remembered that incident?

Nana and Henry quarreling at lunch over Carl's great-uncle and Nana stalking out of the dining room. Was there more to it than just a temper tantrum?

Luna opened her eyes and loosened her clenched fists. She rubbed her damp palms on her thighs. She dragged her fingers through her hair and pulled herself up to her full height. Shoulders back, Nana'd said. She took the remaining steps down the corridor.

Chapter 35

Luna reentered the conference room holding her head high.

The only available chair was next to Carl. He stood up and pulled it out for her. Hypocrite. He needn't think good manners would stop her from asking the questions she intended to throw at him.

Luna sat down reluctantly, wishing she could distance herself. What was his game and why had he come here? At times, she rued the day she'd opened the *Sac à Dépèches* and what was turning into a supersized Pandora's box. Anger — a different kind of anger to any she'd previously experienced — rose within her like lava about to spew from the mouth of a crater. She understood now what it meant to see red.

Carl sat down again and Nikolaj resumed his seat. Hubert shuffled papers between nervous smiles.

"I am happy to tell you we have now identified the Chagall account but not the account holder. Which makes the situation *compliqué*," Nikolaj de Lourriel said, clearing his throat. "You see, *Monsieur* Wolf claims that he and his Great-Uncle Ephraim Wolf are the beneficiaries to the account."

"What?" Luna spun around and faced Carl. "Have you no decency left? Isn't blocking my funds and stealing my Chagall enough?"

"Luna, please, it's not what you think." "No? Then just how is it?"

"Luna, *Monsieur* Wolf brought this with him. Please, take a look." Nikolaj slid a piece of paper across the table.

Luna frowned. "So? It's a cartoon with *viel glück* written next to it. Good luck. Is this some kind of joke?"

"*Monsieur* Wolf believes it was drawn by his great-uncle, *Monsieur* Eli Wolf." "In 1938," Hubert supplied.

"Eli was Uncle Ephraim's twin who was deported and murdered in Dachau," Carl broke in. "I must be honest, Luna. We found the cartoon hidden in the back of *The Girl in the Red Dress Under the Moon*."

"Which you removed from *my* home *without* my authorization!" "I had your POA so technically I—"

"Technically? How dare you use lawyer's jargon on me? I trusted you, Carl. Henry trusted you. You've betrayed us and—"

"Luna please," Carl begged, his features strained. "You have every right to be pissed. I apologize for what happened and I promise I'll explain everything, but bear with me for now."

Luna opened her mouth to respond then closed it. Nana always said never air dirty laundry in public.

Nikolaj pushed two more pieces of paper towards her and aligned them side by side next to the cartoon. "Please, *Madame.* This is the note we discovered in the files relating to the Chagall account. Compare the writing with that on the cartoon and the note you discovered in *Madame* Carolina Hampton's purse. I don't think it needs a graphologist to see these were written in the same hand and on similarly grained paper."

Luna peered at the page and the embossed coat of arms on the heading.

November 5th, 1938

Cher Oncle Jean

Below are instructions for the Chagall account.

If I am unable to claim the funds myself, consider the beneficiary to be the person who presents the note with the account code, Chagall, *written in my hand. Papa agrees and thanks you for your help.*

A squiggle served as a signature.

Luna reached out and touched both notes with the tips of her index fingers. A current. A tingle. She closed her eyes. A hand. A strong, young masculine hand… A thick-nibbed fountain pen and a slanted scrawl. A scent. Was it *Creed?* Henry used that eau de cologne.

"Are you alright, *Madame*?" Both men glanced at her, then at each other. "You look pale. Would you like a glass of water? Hubert open the window there's no air in this place," Nikolaj said.

"*Pardon. Excusez-moi.* I'm fine. I—" she broke off embarrassed and flushed under the intensity of Nikolaj's gaze.

"Are you *certaine*? For a second there you seemed to be somewhere else," he said reaching for an Evian bottle.

Luna glanced at the bits of paper spread before her, then studied them one after the other. It was true. It needed only a cursory look to realize that the writing on the cream-colored vellum addressed to the bank in November of 1938, the scrawl on the tobacco stained snippet she'd removed from the cigar, and the two words circled next to the smiley face on a piece of sketching paper, were written in the same hand.

"This is totally far-fetched, but no more than the rest of this Mad Hatter's tea party you've set up," she exclaimed bitterly. "You really think I'll believe your great-uncle wrote all three notes one of which was in Nana's purse?" She said, turning to Carl. "What proof do you have? A squiggled, unrecognizable signature?"

"Uncle Ephraim will be able to recognize if the signature is his twin brother's."

"No doubt he will. And how convenient since he's the only person alive who can claim to know."

"You can't disprove it," Carl threw. "And as Nikolaj and Hubert here will confirm, their Great-Grandfather, Jean de Lourriel and Aaron Wolf — Eli and Ephraim's father — studied here in Fribourg together. Hence the *Oncle Jean* in the letter. He was a family friend. Naturally they would have turned to him when they wanted to get money out of Germany."

Enough tension reigned in the conference room to ignite a powder keg. Luna regrouped. Maybe she was missing the point here: this was all about money.

"*Monsieur* de Lourriel, *Monsieur* Henchoz, let me ask the million-dollar question. Just how much money is in the account?" Luna said.

"Would you like the balance in Swiss francs or US dollars?" *Monsieur* Henchoz opened his laptop.

"US dollars," Carl and she responded in tandem.

"By today's rate of exchange the balance is one hundred million, seven hundred and eighty-two dollars and twenty-three cents."

"Excuse me?" Carl sat up straighter.

"I shall repeat the figures, One hundred mil—"

"But surely that's impossible!" Luna stared across the desk flabbergasted. "There must be a mistake!"

"*Madame,* our bank does not make accounting mistakes," Monsieur Henchoz bristled. "No. I'm sorry. I didn't mean it like that. But one hundred million dollars—"

"Seven hundred and eighty-two dollars and twenty-three cents." Monsieur Henchoz raised his right index to emphasize the precise calculation.

"Right. What I'm saying is how did that happen without anyone being aware? It's ridiculous!"

"I assure you, *Madame*, our bank is renowned for its *sérieux*."

"Of course it is, but you've been managing whoever this account belongs to for eighty years."

"Exactly. And I believe the account holder would be satisfied with the results. Despite the low interest rates of the past few years."

"But how can the account holder be pleased when he's most likely dead?" "*Is* dead. My great uncle died in Dachau as I said." Carl reiterated.

"Okay. Assuming he wrote the notes, how did this one get into Nana's purse?" Luna said pointing to the stained scrap of paper. "She didn't even live in the same country as your great- uncle for Christ sakes."

"Luna, stay calm, okay?" Carl said.

"No. It's not fucking okay. It'll only be okay when everyone including you and Nikolaj and Hubert stop acting as though my head is so far up my ass I'd believe this nonsense. And why did you rip up Nana's fur stole?"

"Because—look, I wanted to break this to you gently but you're making it impossible." "I don't know what you're talking about."

"Luna, what I'm about to tell you will be a shock, but I must. You see, there's stuff— things you need to know about the past."

"What things?"

"Please, trust me," Carl begged.

"Trust you?" Luna let out a bitter laugh. "Why on earth would I trust you, Carl? You've cheated and lied to me. You think I'm dumb? I bet you took the Chagall because your great- uncle thought it might be his family's one. You think I haven't figured that out?"

"Luna, what I have to tell you isn't about any of that. It's about Carolina." "What about Nana?"

"We've found out something about her past that changes everything." "So you know." Luna's shoulders sagged and she let out a sigh. "Yes."

"I only found out after she died. Was it Rachel who told you?"

"No. I figured it out. It was the letters of the name on the yacht in the photograph of Henry and Carolina in your room."

"What? You were in my room?" She exploded.

"Luna shut up and listen, will you? The name A R K I N A. It's an anagram." "An anagram? I don't get it," she shook her head.

"Carolina's real name was Karina. Karina Lanzberg. She was a Nazi from Munich Germany. Henry knew. That's why he named the yacht—"

"That's absurd," Luna cried. "Nana was Carolina Maria Orlowska, born in Poland."

"No, she wasn't." Carl snapped open his briefcase, pulled out a newspaper clipping and slapped it on the table before her. "I thought you said you knew. Here, take a look at this." He rose and pushed the newspaper clipping under her nose. "*That* is who your precious Nana really was," he pointed his right index at the woman in the photograph, "and that's her brother, Rainer Lanzberg, a high-ranking Nazi SS officer who murdered my family. *Now* do you get it?"

Luna stared at the faded newspaper clipping. She grabbed it off the table and stared hard at the photograph.

"Oh my God!" Her heart leaped to her throat. Her left hand flew over her mouth. The picture reminded her of another photograph: Henry and Nana at the Kennedy Inaugural Ball. The hair, the profile and the angle of Nana's shoulders peeking from under her fur stole. She gestured and shook her head unbelieving. "This can't be. There must be some terrible mistake." Luna looked at her purse, then back at the photograph. She gasped. The woman held an identical *Sac à Dépèches.*

"But Nana couldn't have been a Nazi," she shook her head vigorously.

"Luna, for once will you stop trying to make-believe? Is your head *really* so far up your ass, as you said, that you can't see what's in front of you? Carolina was a Nazi. A war- criminal. She sent people like my family to the gas chamber. Rainer Lanzberg, her fucking brother, deported and murdered my Great-Great-Grandfather Aaron and my Great-Uncle Eli. And by the looks of it, Carolina was part of it too."

"But that's impossible!"

"Then where did she get the purse? Uncle Ephraim remembers her with the purse the day his father and brother were arrested. He was hiding in a car down the street and he saw her walk by with it. She'd stolen it from inside the house."

Luna stared at the *Sac à Dépèches* next to her. If this was true, what other secrets did it carry?

"No," she cried. "When you asked me before if I *knew*, I thought you were referring to the tattoo."

"Tattoo? What tattoo?"

"The one I discovered on Nana's arm moments after she died. It was faded and it all happened so quickly I wasn't able to identify it."

"That's a lie."

"I swear it's true. Nana was a victim, not a perpetrator. I don't know why she's in that photograph but she wasn't a Nazi. Not Nana. Never. She must have taken Carolina Orlowska's identity for a reason."

Carl sat down heavily in the chair opposite her.

Luna stared at the picture in the clipping. Her fingers shook and tears rolled down her cheek.

"She wasn't a Nazi. I'm certain of it."

"Luna, don't you know *anything*? When the Nazis realized they'd lost the war, and it was only a question of time before the Allies invaded Germany, they went to the craziest extremes not to be caught. Having herself tattooed and hiding in a camp is not as outrageous as it sounds. In the chaos at the liberation, she likely took another woman's identity, gave herself a title, got herself shipped out to Colombia and from there made it to the US and married the Zion of a Brahman American family. What better cover up than that?"

"I don't believe it."

"Then don't! Be in denial if that makes you happy, but look, you're even carrying her purse! Oh, and by the way, take this as a memento," he said pulling a copy of the clipping out of his briefcase and slamming it on the table. "You can frame it and add it to the rest of your family pics."

"I don't believe one word of this. You're using this picture as an excuse to find ways to cheat me more than you already have."

"Cheat you? A Colombian chiksa out of a trash can in Medellin who got lucky? It's time for a fucking reality check!"

"How dare you! I don't believe a word of your shit. Or your uncle's. Nikolaj and Hubert, are you just going to sit there and let him make these absurd claims?" Luna cried.

"I am very sorry I—we—" Hubert cut off and looked at Nikolaj for help.

"I'm not listening to any more of your insults and lies." Luna rose and grabbed her jacket off the back of the chair. "You think I'm weak and stupid; that I'd cave in and grovel the minute you turned off the taps and left me high and dry with no money. Well, think again because I can do perfectly well on my own. And since according to your Great-Uncle Eli's supposed letter, the beneficiary of the account is the holder of the note," she added scooping the note off the table, "I think I'll just take this with me until all this is sorted."

"Give it back" Carl lunged.

"No way!" She said stuffing it past her shirt and inside her bra.

"S'il vous plait," Hubert protested. Nikolaj rose unsure what to do.

Carl's right hand flew out and slapped Luna's left cheek.

Her hand flew to her face. She turned and ran to the door. "That's it. It's over, Carl I'm revoking your power of attorney. You're fired!" She said choking back tears.

The door reverberated behind her.

Luna burst into the bank reception, past the man in the dark suit and on towards the front door. She yanked it open and hurried down the icy path towards the steps and the wrought iron gate. Tears poured down her face. It was all lies. It had to be.

Her cheek stung.

Luna stepped onto the pavement tarred by the brush of doubt and the growing horror triggered by the newspaper clipping, and Carl's words spreading like red wine spilled on silk, disfiguring the past, staining the present and muddying the future.

Chapter 36

"This case is very heavy, Mr. Wolf."

Ephraim sat propped up in bed and watched Mrs. Katz haul the dusty case up onto the luggage rack she'd discovered in the cellar. How long was it since he'd last used it?

"Are you sure it's a good idea to go on a trip?" She asked, doubtfully. "Of course it's a good idea." He snapped.

"But you can't walk properly."

"What do you mean I can't walk? Of course I can walk." Ephraim said. "Stupid woman," he muttered under his breath. Was it his lot in life to be surrounded by humans of inferior intelligence?

"Mrs. Katz. I have no intention of altering my plans. Now please open my case."

With a sigh, Mrs. Katz undid the worn leather straps and tugged the stiff brass zippers, until finally they opened. She flipped the canvas top back. "There's all this inside," she said, lifting a pile of tissue paper and a pair of wooden shoe-trees. "Should I throw it all out?"

"Are you *meshugene*? That's my tissue paper to fold my suits with, you silly woman. Don't they teach you anything nowadays? Now go fetch my grey pinstripe, the navy-blue blazer and the Prince de Galles."

"The what?"

"The checkered one." Ephraim rolled his eyes. In a better world, he'd have a valet. Maybe after his visit to Switzerland he could afford one. And a change of address. Not that he minded the apartment. It was home and a move was always an upheaval.

Florian being alive was a stroke of luck, a sign things were finally moving Ephraim's way. About time too. A real live witness. Imagine that.

He hadn't mentioned his forthcoming trip to Carl since Carl hadn't bothered to phone him yet. So selfish. But as far as he was concerned, it was all on track. He'd book a flight, fly directly to Zurich, Carl would pick him up at the airport and drive him to Fribourg, where he'd go straight to the bank and sort them all out. Then he'd visit Florian in the hospital. He had to make sure he fell in line too.

Ephraim sighed and closed his eyes. He ignored the pain in his back and the fact that he'd been unable to sit comfortably in the wheel chair these past few days. Instead, he stared hard at the Chagall on the wall opposite and thought about who else might still be alive.

Rainer?

The nervous twitch at the left corner of his mouth returned. It happened each time Rainer's name floated to the surface. Ephraim loathed and relished their memories; love and hate, a game of Russian Roulette, guilt and justification enveloped in denial. He'd tried hard to escape them, but they pursued him to this day. It was impossible to imagine Rainer as weak and old, older than Ephraim himself, a shadow of the blond man lying among the rumpled sheets who'd reached out to stroke his hair…

~

"You promised you'd get me the paintings by the end of last week."

Rainer switched on the lamp on the nightstand and propped himself up against the pillows to light a cigarette.

"I know. But it's not easy. I can't simply barge in there and rip masterpieces off the wall, Rainer."

"My superiors won't wait much longer, you know. If you're not careful they'll have your balls sliced off and sautéed for dinner. I've heard that Himmler enjoys exotic dishes."

"Are you threatening me?"

"Not threatening, just warning. After all, it's largely thanks to me that you and your family can remain in Munich unmolested."

"I don't know. A lot of other Jewish families are being left alone," Ephraim shrugged. Rainer's hand dropped. He rose abruptly and pulled the sheet about his hips.

"How long is it since you've seen the Rosenbaums?" He asked, casually placing a cigarette between his lips.

"A while."

"That's because they've been arrested and deported," Rainer carefully lit the cigarette, inhaled and turned. "To a camp for dissidents."

"Does that include homosexuals? You should be more careful, Rainer. A whiff of what goes on in here and it won't be just me they'll ship off. I doubt they'd appreciate a homosexual SS officer sleeping with a Jew."

"That depends on the Jew. As long as I'm sleeping with one who facilitates the acquisition of beautiful pictures to hang on their walls, greed and good taste will outweigh any other considerations. After that…" He shrugged.

The sheet dropped to the floor. Rainer moved across the room and studied his naked body in the full-length gilt mirror. Then, stepping over to the arm-chair where his clothes lay, he reached for his underwear.

Ephraim watched as he pulled his pants and shirt on as well as the black SS jacket. Better to remain silent. Rainer can be mercurial.

"Just make sure you get me those paintings by next week. I'd hate for something to happen to you," Rainer said, sitting down in the chair to pull on his jack boots.

"Nothing will happen to me," Ephraim responded. "How can you be so sure?"

"Because you won't denounce me. Not while you enjoy this so much." Ephraim lifted a riding crop from among the sheets and swiped it playfully." "Give me that," Rainer lunged towards him.

"Promise me I'll be safe?" Ephraim taunted.

"You drive me nuts," Rainer's voice thickened. His cheeks suffused. A high-pitched giggle followed. "Tuesday at three?"

"Maybe." Ephraim leaned back against the pillows. He crossed his ankles, gazed up at the acanthus scrolls on the plaster ceiling and continued to twiddle the riding crop.

"Give it to me," Rainer ordered.

"Yes Rainer." Ephraim smothered a smile and tended the crop. Rainer grabbed the opposite end.

"Until Tuesday, then. If you're still around," he added with a titter. "What do you mean?"

"I shouldn't be telling you this." It was now Rainer's turn to play with the crop. "But the Gestapo are planning on rounding up more Jews like your friends the Rosenbaums and sending them to camps for people suspected of being unwilling to work."

"Don't worry. I'll work on getting those pictures if that's what you're implying." "*Wunderbar*!" His teeth flashed and he leaned over the bed and dropped a kiss on

Ephraim's lips.

"*Bis dienstag*!"

~

Ephraim brought his attention back to the bedroom. Mrs. Katz was folding the jacket of his grey suit.

"*Nein*, Mrs. Katz, not like that," he exclaimed shaking his head. "And don't forget to put in my Sea Island cotton underwear and fresh handkerchiefs. I'll choose the ties once you've finished the rest."

Chapter 37

It took a few moments for Carl to register where he was: in bed on the first floor of the de Lourriel rambling turn-of-the-century family home. Nikolaj had insisted on bringing him here after yesterday's meltdown with Luna at the bank. In fact, it was the very room his Great-Great-Grandfather, Aaron had slept in as a guest a century before.

Carl propped the plump feather pillows against the carved wooden headrest of the small old-fashioned bed and let the previous day's events unfold.

"Oh Jesus," he muttered. What had gotten into him? He'd lost control, seen red. Was he possessed? It had felt like someone else had gotten inside his body and lashed out.

He closed his eyes. How could he have treated Luna like that? The awful things he'd said left him queasy. It was horrible.

He must apologize immediately. Oh my God! That's right, she'd fired him. And with good cause. What a mess. Ever since Uncle Ephraim fainted at Carolina — Karina — whatever her real name was — wake, aside from his meeting with Gunnar on the flight over here, nothing but shit had come down.

Carl lifted his phone off the nightstand. Two text messages:

... Come for Scandinavian Christmas in Norway!...

... Freezing here but my house has good central heating and a great fireplace. My neighbors have a reindeer! LOL!

How light and joyful and simple it sounded. What would a life without the past looming over him be like? A life free of fear. A life where he could be himself, walk arm in arm down the street with whoever he chose without worrying someone might snitch on him to Uncle Ephraim or the Hamptons. Maybe even consider a real relationship?

But all that mattered right now was Luna. He must think what to do.

Carl's thoughts were interrupted by a concert of church bells flooding the stucco ceilinged room through the half-open window. Faded brocade drapes hung from brass curtain rails, flower-themed watercolors dotted the walls, and a whiff of lemon and beeswax filtered through the room. How peaceful and timeless it was. He doubted it had altered much since Aaron slept in this same bed.

He reached for the pack of meds in the nightstand and popped a Xanax. The face-off with Luna at the bank and her dramatic exit had upset him badly. He was grateful to Nikolaj and Hubert for their hospitality and understanding. Anyone else would have called the cops.

The past seemed incredibly present here in this medieval city. Was Luna experiencing it too? How could he have broken the truth of Carolina's real identity to her so cruelly? But he couldn't help it. A levy inside him had burst and unleashed an unstoppable barrage of secrets sweeping everything in its path and drowning all reason in a flood of anger and vindictive regret. He must find a way to remedy the situation. It was crazy, the both of them, half-way across the world, their lives put on hold, high-jacked by ghosts. Surely they should be pooling their resources and talking, not building barriers?

He climbed out of bed. He'd asked Nikolaj to take him to the Angel place Luna was staying at. Better that than text. He must see her in person and ask her forgiveness. He'd felt bad in his life before, but hell, never as bad as this. What was happening to the world and to him? Had someone rubbed the proverbial lamp and an evil genie emerged and unleashed across the planet from Pyong Peng to Washington to Fribourg fucking Switzerland?

He opened his case and pulled out a sweater. He'd go at once and get it over with. Luna didn't deserve any of this.

He needed to phone Uncle Ephraim, but not now. He wasn't up for grievances and whining. He'd call him later on once — he hoped — he'd sorted things with Luna. Somehow he must right this wrong and hope for her forgiveness.

Chapter 38

Through the dormer window of the loft, stray rays of sunlight cast aureoles on the half-packed suitcase lying on the floor next to the couch. Yesterday she refused to think or talk about it. She'd not answered Rose's calls or eaten. She'd come straight up to the loft and opened her laptop. Twenty pages of raw anger later, she'd pulled her case out the closet and flung clothes in it. When adrenaline turned to exhaustion, she'd dropped into bed and slept for twelve hours.

She drew back the curtain. A grey day with the promise of snow hanging low in the clouds. She'd tell Rose she was leaving, finish packing, book her ticket and go to the airport as soon as possible.

On the pine dresser, Nana and Henry's photograph and the newspaper clipping stood reflected in the mirror next to one another. She crawled to the end of the bed, reached out, grabbed them both and chucked them into the wastebasket. Finished. Over. *They* were not part of her baggage. Not anymore. Once she was home she'd decide what to do. She wanted out. Out of here, out of the penthouse, out of her whole farce of a life.

Luna climbed off the bed and moved through the loft to the coffee machine. Clothes lay strewn on the floor below. She stopped in her tracks and starred at *The Girl in the Red Dress Under the Moon* lying propped against the cushions on the couch. She couldn't believe her eyes.

What was it doing here? A yellow post-it stuck to the upper right-hand corner of the frame offered a sanguine explanation:

Know you wanted to see it. Brought it over but you were asleep. Call me in the morning.

Big hug, Rose

She scrunched the post-it and turned her back on the girl, the goat and the violinist. Another troop of tricksters ready to perform at Nana — the puppet master's — bidding. What was wrong with her head? How had she believed all of Nana's bullshit? Who did Nana think she was? An avatar? Now wonder she'd liked Wagner; Nazis were crazy about him. Maybe she'd believed *she* was the Queen of the Night.

Luna perched on the bar stool careful not to bang her head on the eaves, slammed a capsule into the coffee machine and watched it rumble and spurt frothy brown liquid into the white espresso cup, then took a long sip. The night, fraught with strange dreams and bouts of wakefulness, had not brought her the rest she'd hoped for.

A knock on the door.

Luna laid the cup down on the counter and climbed off the stool. She padded barefoot to the door, stifled a yawn and opened it.

"*Bonjour*—Holy fuck!"

Her heart leaped and she pushed the door back as hard as she could. A foot blocked it.

"Luna, please don't shut me out, Carl said. "I came to apologize. What I did was awful. I never wanted to hurt you. I don't know what came over me. It was rash and impulsive to block your accounts, but I've reversed that now. I'm so sorry. And I feel terrible I broke the truth to you about Carolina in such a crass and unfeeling manner. I realize what a shock it must've been. It was totally insensitive."

Luna pushed. Carl shoved. She closed her eyes and blocked her ears and placed her full weight back against the door. Her phone lay next to the coffee cup just out of reach. She'd scream. The pilgrims would hear her cry out and come to her rescue.

"Luna, I beg you. We must talk. Like it or not we're in this together. You, me, Carolina, Uncle Ephraim, the bank and even the Chagall. None of it makes sense. But unless we're to spend the rest of our lives in the grip of whatever force has been unleashed, we have to fight it. Together. We can't let their past control us."

Carl's desperate words reached past the toe of the boot wedged in the open crack. Words. She was sick and tired of words; tricky tools, the craftsmen of make-believe worlds.

... *We can't let their past control us...*

But that's exactly what it had done all her life. The boot lifted. The door gave and she stumbled.

"I can't oblige you to hear me out but I'd appreciate it if you did. I don't know how to persuade you other than repeat how terribly sorry I am."

He sounded contrite. But that meant nothing. She touched her cheek and hesitated. That same sensation she'd experienced when she ran out the bank was back. A step into shadows she couldn't quite grasp.

"Luna, please."

The shadows faded. She starred at the Chagall and her half-opened case. "Wait for me downstairs," she muttered.

"Okay. Thanks. You forgot your purse at the bank, I'll leave it in front of the door. And Luna, for what it's worth, I really am sorry," Carl said. "I hope that someday you'll forgive me."

The door closed. She leaned against it, shuddered and waited until Carl's footsteps died on the stone stairs, then opened it a few inches. The *Sac à Dépèches*, the cherished relic of days earlier, now an enemy's courier satchel. She picked it up by the handles like contaminated trash, kicked the door shut and pitched it hard across the room where it landed next to the bookshelf. Her passport, wallet, lipstick and airline ticket spilled out and coins rolled across the uneven floorboards like 30 pieces of silver. Her nails bit into her palms. She must remain calm, not let her emotions get the better of her. Carl was right about one thing: they were in the eye of this hurricane together. She must think like a mature adult and not let Nana's warped fantasies get in the way. Likely Hitler believed he communicated with Germanic divinities too.

She returned to the counter, sipped cold coffee and eyed the Chagall. Unless it had flown to Fribourg on a magic carpet it was clear there existed two identical paintings, one in New York the other in a Swiss cottage. *Doppelgangers* like Nana; one dark, one light, one good, one evil.

One real, one fake?

Luna moved across the room and turned the painting over. The back of the frame was held loosely together with peeling tape. It had obviously been tampered with at some point. She thought of Carl waiting for her downstairs and placed the painting face-up against the cushions, then reached for a pair of jeans and sweater from the suitcase. She'd finish packing after they'd talked, then get going. In a way, it wasn't surprising he'd lost control. Imagine if she was in his shoes and had learned Nana's story as he had? It wasn't her he'd slapped but Nana and her Nazi brother, and the blinkered world that had fawned and applauded under Swastika banners at the 1936 Olympics, and Chamberlain, kicking the can down the road, waving a worthless agreement: *peace in our time.*

But while the world bent over backwards to appease, the beast laughed harder, ate more bratwurst, drank more beer in Munich's beer gardens and planned the Final Solution, while the land of Schiller and Goethe stepped into darkness.

Millions of dead souls later, the same world said *oops!*

What a colossal miscalculation.

Chapter 39

Voices filtered from the Angel House kitchen. Luna sighed with relief. Coming face to face with Carl would be easier with Rose present.

"*Ah, voilà* Luna." Rose sat opposite Carl at the kitchen table. "I was telling your friend about Father Florian's return here today. He says their families knew one another back in Germany before WWII. What a small world. Father Florian will be delighted to learn that you're here," she added turning back to Carl. "Perhaps we can arrange a meeting if he's well enough. According to the nurse, he's being impossible and driving the hospital staff mad. I suppose it's a good sign, but I confess I'm dreading the extra work," she said rising.

"I'll help you," Luna said. "And thanks for the delivery," she smiled.

"De rien." Rose smiled back.

"Shall we go for a walk? I could use some fresh air." Luna suggested to Carl. "Good idea."

"Have a nice *promenade*," Rose said. "Take Chichi if you want. He needs a walk and I don't have the time to take him out this morning. I have an appointment in town. Why don't you and Carl have lunch here after you get back? There's a quiche ready to pop in the oven and salad in the fridge."

"Thanks," Luna muttered. Why didn't Rose just shut up? The last thing she wanted was more time with Carl than necessary. "Shall we go?"

"Of course."

"I'll go fetch a jacket then." She turned back into the inner hallway and selected a weather-beaten wool-lined Barbour from among an array of anoraks and jackets hanging on the coat stand. Carl was making an effort to ease the atmosphere between them, but she wasn't ready to lower her guard. Or get too close. Taking the dog along was a good idea. Chichi's presence would act as a buffer if emotions ran too high again. Worse case, she'd tell him to bite.

She wished Rose hadn't suggested lunch, but likely Carl would want to make the meeting as brief as possible too and leave.

Outside the kitchen Chichi greeted her with yelps and a wagging tail. She crouched to pat the dog between the ears.

"Tu viens?"

She removed the leash from the side of the kennel and hooked it to his collar. The dog barked. A sharp tug on the leash and Luna skidded down the gravel driveway.

"*Attends* Chichi! I'll fall if you pull that hard," she cried.

The dog helped diffuse the bomb ticking between them since yesterday. It was reasonable to assume Carl had come to apologize but didn't know how.

They continued in silence towards the stile gate that opened onto the *Camino*. She held it open for Carl to pass through, then closed it carefully before unhooking the leash. Chichi trotted obediently beside her, then scampered off into the snow-covered fields in search of rabbits as she and Carl stepped onto the bumpy path. Luna looked up at the sky. A falcon circled. "We shouldn't be too long; it may snow again. By the way, this is a leg of the *Camino*, the famous pilgrimage to Santiago de Compostella." It was something to say.

"I read the book by Paulo Coelho," Carl nodded. "It was enlightening. Maybe *I* should do a pilgrimage."

"Perhaps we all need to do a pilgrimage of sorts at some point in our lives."

"I guess. Luna, about yesterday, I—" He cut off and shook his head. "I don't know what to say except apologize again and ask you to forgive me if you can. Also for breaking my fiduciary duty to you and blocking your funds and ripping the furs in the closet. It was abominable. All of it. And you were right to fire me. I'll help you find someone to replace me."

"Let's not talk about that now."

"We can't sweep what happened under the carpet, Luna. When you left the bank yesterday I realized just how far this situation has driven us. You: rushing off to Europe to follow the trail of a scrap of paper and the tattoo you saw on Carolina's arm. Me: stealing your Chagall for Uncle Ephraim and finding a cartoon in the back. It's as though we've been caught up in a time twister and dropped into a past that's not ours but we're obliged to deal with the consequences. We must take back control of our lives."

"Did either of us ever have it?"

"I guess maybe not. You've been a captive of Carolina and Henry's past and I've spent most of my life trying to live up to Uncle Ephraim's standards."

"Being what they wanted."

"But not ourselves."

"Do you know who you are Carl? 'Cos right now I have no idea who I am. What you said yesterday was true, I'm a—"

"Please. Don't remind me!" He cringed. "I'd do anything to unsay those unjust and cruel words. Don't take anything I said to heart, I beg you. I was mad. I don't know what the hell came over me."

"But those words were true. And I got really, really lucky. Too lucky it seems. It was all too perfect. And now it's over. I don't know anything about myself beyond what I've become, thanks to Nana and Henry. And now I'm not sure who they were." She stared across the field at the dog burrowing in the snow. "Carl, we need to talk about the account," she said, changing the subject. "I don't know how the note got into Nana's purse but I have an idea how the money may have been brought here from Germany."

"Really?"

They came to a clearing and stopped walking. Luna kicked off wet leaves and snow sticking to the soles of her boots and sat down on a log. "It's about Father Florian, the priest who you were talking to Rose about who knew your uncle's family back in Germany. He came here in the late 1930s. You're not going to believe this but he brought an identical Chagall to the one in New York with him."

"Are you serious?" Carl stopped dead and stared at her.

"And the back of the frame has obviously been opened up at some point." "Now, wait a minute. How do you know all this?"

"Because I saw it in Father Florian's cottage when he got sick and now it's in the loft. I can show you the painting when we get back to the Angel House."

Carl sat down next to her on the log. He shook his head and let out a huff. The cold air made his breath white like smoke.

They stared at one another.

"Let's go back now. I have to see this." He said. "Okay. We'll go back across the field, it's quicker."

Luna called Chichi to heel and hooked the leash back on and they walked in the snow. The bells in the village church up the road struck twelve and the sun peeped through the clouds, highlighting the copper rain pipes below the Château's *mansarde* roof.

At the top of the hill they stopped for breath. Luna threw Carl a glance. He looked better now that his cheeks were flushed from the trek. The fresh air had done him good.

They descended the slope. Once inside, they reentered the boundaries of the property, she let Chichi off the leash and he scampered towards the kitchen.

A siren sounded and an ambulance turned off the main road and into the lane.

"That must be Father Florian coming home." She said. "He'll be exhausted after the trip from the hospital but as soon as he's better, we should try to talk to him and ask him to tell us everything he knows about the Chagall."

"Yes, and if that's how the money was brought here, then Nikolaj and Hubert should be there too."

"You're right, they should be a part of it. Come on, we'll go inside the back so as not to get in the way."

They entered via the cellar and felt their way through the dark to the back stairs. "I can wait down here and you can bring the painting if you'd rather," he said. Luna hesitated.

"No. It's fine."

On the second landing, Luna unlocked the door. The floorboards creaked as they stepped inside the loft.

"There." Luna pointed to the Chagall on the couch.

"This is unbelievable," Carl muttered, moving closer.

"I told you. Even the frame is identical. Turn it over."

Carefully, he lifted the painting and looked hard at the back of the frame, then at her. "One of them must be fake," he said at last. The question is which one?"

"I thought about that. Either they made a fake one for the priest to bring the money or valuables in—"

"*Or* Great-Uncle Eli had a copy done to put the cartoon in as a decoy to fool Uncle Ephraim."

"But why? Who would do such a thing? Did he hate his brother?"

"On the contrary. Uncle Ephraim always said they were close, but after he discovered the cartoon, he told me a different story."

"It seems there are endless versions of all their stories. Let's pray Father Florian can shed some light on all this."

"Absolutely. Wouldn't it be great to get him and Uncle Ephraim on the phone together? Can you imagine? I doubt they know the other one is still alive."

"That would really be something." Luna said. "Let's go back downstairs and have lunch." "Thanks, but I should get going. We both need time on our own to process all of this.

Thanks for letting me come and hearing me out."

"You know what Carl, let's move on."

Luna stood on the front steps and watched Carl's taxi head off down the drive, then turned back inside.

"Luna, there you are. I need your help while I settle Father Florian in," Rose said, unlocking the office. Could you stay here and receive the pilgrims I'm expecting?"

"Of course." Luna peered inside the office remembering her arrival here, days earlier. Right now, the Angel House felt more like home than the penthouse, a haven cut off from the past and future, a sanctuary of light on her darkening horizon.

"Oh and with all the kerfuffle with Father Florian, I forgot to give you this. Your package. DHL dropped it off while you were out this morning."

"Merci." Luna took the parcel from her and reached for the paper knife on Rose's desk. "I'm going back up." Rose bustled out.

Luna sat down and tore open the top and withdrew several letters. Three invitations to Christmas charity bazaars, a Saks catalogue and a hand-written, cream-colored vellum envelope with a Swiss postmark. She turned it over:

Dr. Prof. Isabella de la Vega Baur du Lac

Zurich, Switzerland

"Oh my God, Tia Bella!" She murmured. "She must have received my note advising her of Nana's death."

Luna tore open the flap and pulled out a flowered card.

My dearest Luna,

Thank you for taking the trouble to write me so quickly. Learning of my dear Ina's death was a shock. We shared so much during our lives and I regret that in the end we became estranged, but we must retain the precious memories and not linger on the sadness.

If you're ever in Switzerland, please come and visit me.

Thank you again for remembering me.

Your loving godmother,
Tia Bella

"Ina?"

Chapter 40

The taxi from Zurich station to the Baur au Lac Hotel was a seven-minute ride full of memories: walks arm in arm with Nana to Grieder department store and Sprüngli — Zurich's famous chocolatier — while Henry met with his bankers in the *Paradeplatz.* How could Nana have paraded blithely down the *Banhofstrasse* with its trams and smart boutiques when her kid- gloved hands were smeared with guilt?

Was she right, Luna wondered, to have followed her impulse and rushed here to see her godmother — the last man standing on the littered battlefield of her lost world? Should she not have stayed at the Angel House and attended the meeting scheduled with Father Florian, Carl, Nikolaj and Hubert? Perhaps it was cowardly, but she couldn't vouch for her reactions to any more revelations. Plus, Tia Bella might know something, though that was unlikely since Nana and she met after WWII and by then Nana had shed Karina Lanzberg — the ugly Nazi duckling — and emerged an aristocratic swan.

The doorman welcomed her and Luna stepped through the revolving doors and into the Baur au Lac Hotel lobby.

Thanks to the fortune of the late Camillo de la Vega — the Colombian coffee planter

whom she'd married after WWII, Tia Bella — who'd retired after a long career as a Jungian analyst — lived in a luxurious two-bedroom suite on the first floor. Was it a coincidence that Chagall had lived at the hotel too when he worked on the stained-glass windows for Zurich's Frauen Kirche?

After leaving her coat and carry-on at the cloakroom, Luna headed straight to the hotel's *Pavillon* restaurant. The head waiter greeted her with a smile. Crisp white cloths, velvet upholstery and tranquil elegance; neither the décor nor the guests had altered since she last dined here with Nana and Henry.

At the far end of the room next to the circular windows overlooking the frost bathed gardens and lake, she saw the back of a wheelchair. Luna's heart leaped. It was the first time she was seeing her godmother since she and Nana quarreled seven years earlier. Right now, the wisps of white hair sprouting from beneath a velvet beret, tilted in the manner of a French artist felt as confronting as a lighthouse in a stormy sea. As though sensing her approach, the old lady turned and looked up. Her face broke into a creased smile. She reached out her hands. Luna clasped them tight. How good it felt.

"*Ach*! Dearest child. What an unexpected pleasure."

"How kind of you to receive me so quickly." She kissed the old lady's wrinkled cheek. "The pleasure is all mine. Come. Sit down here on my left. That's my good ear. And

Pierre," Tia Bella said, turning to the headwaiter, "we'll have two glasses of champagne. This is a celebration."

"*Très* bien, Madame."

Luna sat down. The waiter glanced at Sylvie's purple tote as he placed it in the empty chair next to her. It was totally out of place in the sophisticated environment of the Baur au Lac. Tough. At least she knew it's provenance: the Bern market and what it contained. She was done with carrying other people's past around.

The sommelier appeared with champagne and poured. Tia Bella raised her glass. Luna followed suit with a knot in her throat; they'd performed this same gesture many times over the years with Nana.

"I know we ended in strife, but I would like make a toast. To my dearest Ina," Tia Bella said.

"Why Ina? You always called her Carolina."

"That was Carolina's nickname when we were little."

"What do you mean? I always thought you and Nana had met on the ship on your way to Colombia after the war." Luna cried. "Please don't tell me you lied to me too."

"I was afraid this would happen one day," Tia Bella sighed. "I told Ina over and over she must tell you the truth, but she refused. That was the reason we ended up estranged. Ina and I were best friends since we were six years old," Tia Bella began. "We went to school together. We played at one another's homes as children do. We were inseparable. She loved my grandfather Levi, dearly. He played the violin with the National Philharmonic orchestra until he was banned for being a Jew. Our house was fun and a bit of a mess. Ina loved it. We spoke in Yiddish. We laughed and told jokes. Intellectuals, journalists, writers and musicians came in and out and my mother cooked and our home was an open house. I liked Ina's house too, though of course it was very different; rather bourgeois and always impeccably tidy. I had to take off my shoes and wear large felt slippers not to spoil the parquet floor. One day, the headmistress of our school called me into her office. She told me that because I was Jewish she could no longer risk keeping me in school. It was a terrible shock. We were stripped of our German nationality even though we'd been Germans for generations, and suddenly my brothers and I could no longer be educated. Ina was revolted. She brought me the schoolwork so I could follow the syllabus from home. You see, she and I had dreams," Tia Bella sighed. "I wanted to become a doctor and she a journalist and a writer."

"A writer?" Luna said. "She never told me that. In fact, when I told her I wanted to be a writer she dismissed the idea. She said I'd never be one of the Brönte sisters."

"Perhaps she was afraid your dreams would be smashed as hers were. You see, Hitler had other ideas. According to Göring and the Führer, a woman's world was smaller than a man's and her only ambition should be *Kinder Kuche Kirche* — children, church and home. But Ina didn't care, she went on writing. Perhaps she was afraid for you, Luna. She was very protective. Too protective. I used to tell her so, but she never listened. I kept insisting she tell you the truth because I knew one day the truth would come to light. But that was Ina. *Ach,* my dear, if only you'd heard the stories she wrote! When my family was deported and she rescued me and hid me in the attic of her parent's home, she'd spend hours up there reading them to me. Sometimes she even managed to make me laugh. And believe me, there was little to laugh about in those days."

"Did her parents know you were in the attic?"

"I'm not certain. I think Frau Lanzberg suspected, but she never gave me away. Even after the bombings in 1942 she managed to leave a little extra food for Ina. I'm sure it was for me. She was a good woman and Ina took after her. It was not their fault things were the way they were. People lived in constant fear of being denounced, even by their own children."

Tia Bella placed her hands on the wheels of her chair and turned it and looked out over the lake. "Sometimes, I watch the snowflakes piling up on the railings of my balcony and think: that's how we were, six million snowflakes, each a unique crystal, swept into a mass of lost identity at the stroke of a madman's pen."

"Oh my God! Nana wasn't a Nazi at all, was she?" Luna asked.

"Ina? A Nazi? Whatever gave you that idea? In 1943 the Allies were bombing Sollin every night. They knew high-ranking Nazis lived there. When Ina said we had to leave, I was afraid. I'd gotten used to the attic. Strange how the human body adapts and the mind finds comfort even in the strangest of circumstances. But Ina was determined we must leave. She said we'd go to Schloss Heil and join the resistance movement which Baron von Heil was a part of. Now that Eli was gone, she had nothing left to live for."

"Eli Wolf? Ephraim Wolf's twin? What did he have to do with all this?" "Everything." Tia Bella sighed. "Let me go back to the third of November of 1936..."

And so it was...

1936 — 1938

Schloss Heil, Bavaria, Germany, 1936

Each year on the third of November, Karina Lanzberg, her elder brother Rainer and her parents made the trip from Munich to Schloss Heil, the medieval castle on the shores of the Tegernsee belonging to Baron von Heil — a distant cousin of Frau Lanzberg — to celebrate the feast of Saint Hubertus and the opening of the hunting season.

And this year, Karina was excited. She'd just turned fifteen and for the first time, she would be allowed dinning with the grown-ups under the gothic arches at the oak dining table that sat twenty-six guests — a fact that Frau Lanzberg was eager to remind her of — and dressed with the finest porcelain and crystal and silverware. Mama had ordered her first silk dirndl from Lanz in Salzburg. The baron would pronounce a prayer to Saint Hubertus for a good hunting season and the wild boar head would be presented to him on a silver platter by two liveried servants. If she was lucky, she and Bella, her best friend whom she'd brought along, might even be allowed to toast with a glass of *sekt.*

It was almost three in the afternoon when the girls captured their first excited glimpses of the Schloss turrets shimmering in the autumn sunlight. Rainer sat next to them in the back seat, pretending to be sleep. He was in a bad mood because *Vater* made him change out of his brown Hitler Youth uniform, and obliged him to wear his moleskin loden jacket and trousers.

"Look ! That's the Baron, Cousin Heini, shaking hands with his old friend Aaron Wolf. And that's his wife, the Baroness, Cousin Fabrizia. She's Italian. They say she was born in a Palazzo even larger and finer than Schloss Heil itself. And those are the Wolf twins and cousin Florian," Karina pointed. "You'll love them all, Bella," she said, waving to the three boys punching one another's arms playfully on the lower steps.

The car came to a standstill. Karina opened the door and she and Bella tripped up the steps behind her parents while Rainer trailed sulkily in the rear.

"*Wilkommen!*" The Baron met them half way down the steps. "My goodness, my little Ina, you've become quite a young lady since I last saw you. Should I call you Karina now? You look so grown up!" He exclaimed kissing her on both cheeks. "And this must be your friend, Bella. Welcome to Schloss Heil, young lady. We're so glad you could come.

They said their hellos, then the Baroness led the way into the Great hall. It was just as Karina remembered; logs blazing in the medieval stone fire place, suits of armor and spears and paintings on the walls. Florian took her hand and she smiled at him. *Lieber* Florian, so kind and so sweet and so gentle.

Ephraim and Rainer had struck up a conversation, and Eli brought up the rear, his dark wavy hair tumbling over his forehead.

The girls were used to having *Kafee und kuchen* in the afternoon as was the custom among the bourgeoisie, but when the guests assembled in the Grand Salon for tea, Earl Gray was being served in fine china cups, custom-made in England. The girls left the grown-ups and stood near the door. Bella nibbled a slice of fruit cake.

"It's delicious," she said. "How many servants do you think they have?"

"I don't know. But lots. Do you think I look okay?" Karina tugged at the waistband of her new tweed suit and wriggled.

"You look great. Did you practice walking in those high heels?"

"Yes, but did you see when I almost tripped on the stairs coming down?" She giggled. "That's not surprising. They'll take a while to get used to. I'm sure I'd never manage to wear anything like that."

"Rubbish. Of course you will."

The shoes had been a point of contention between Karina and her mother. After much haggling, Hilde Lanzberg gave way and allowed Karina to wear a much coveted pair of tiny kitten heels. Her first pair. She felt very grown up. Bella wore flat brogues.

"I've never seen your mother look so beautiful," Bella remarked.

"It's true," Karina said, proudly. Hilde Lanzberg was unrecognizable in her silk tea gown, one of two new dresses confectioned by Frau Schwab, the dressmaker, and the three- tiered pearl necklace that she'd received as a wedding gift when she'd married *Vater* twenty years ago back in 1914. Poor *Mutti*. The wedding happened days before the Archeduke Ferdinand of Austria was murdered by a Serb Nationalist, an act that triggered the Great War, and *Vater* was obliged to go and fight. That's how he'd lost his left arm.

The third lady seated on the couch by the fire sipping tea with her mother and the Baroness, was *Mme.* de Lourriel, the Russian wife of the tall Swiss banker who stood in the middle of the room with the Baron and Mr. Wolf discussing the weather and the shooting program for the following day. The Lourriels came every year all the way from Fribourg, Switzerland, where Cousin Heini, Aaron Wolf and he had studied together at the University and had become friends.

"Boo!"

"Oh!" Karina jumped. The tea spilled. Laughing eyes under heavy brows met hers. Karina's cheeks suffused and her heart jolted.

"Sorry. I didn't mean to frighten you. Here, give me that." Eli Wolf grabbed the cup and placed it on an antique to his right, then pulled a handkerchief from his breast pocket. He frowned at the stains on the front of Karina's new blouse. "Perhaps you should try and wipe it."

"It doesn't matter," she muttered. The stains were on her breast. Her face burned with embarrassment. Aside from her father and brother, she'd never been this close to a man. She dabbed ineffectively and pulled her jacket closed.

"Can I help?" Eli made a gesture. "No!" She pushed his hand aside.

"You look different. Really grown up," he said tilting his head.

"Not really. Bella and I turned fifteen last week, so we're allowed to dine with you all this year. This is my friend Bella, by the way. Bella this is Eli."

"Hello. Pleased to meet you." He smiled, a frank and genuine smile that reached the soul. Karina returned the handkerchief.

"Don't worry about the blouse. No one will notice and I'll wash it for you tonight in the basin in our room," Bella whispered.

"Thanks." She looked up.

Eli was nineteen. He was slim and matt-skinned and not as tall as her brother Rainer. His hair was dark and unruly. His eyes sparkled with fun and he had a crooked smile. Karina crossed her hands demurely as the nuns had taught her and tried not to feel nervous.

"Shall I get you more tea?" Eli asked.

"No thanks," she grimaced. "I didn't really like it." "What about you?" He turned to Bella.

"No thanks. I think I'll go upstairs and read for a bit. Is that alright?" "Of course. You must feel free to do whatever you like, Bella."

"Are you going to go and read too or shall we go and explore this place?" Eli asked.

Karina peered across the room at the grown-ups. Should she tell someone she was leaving the room? They were all deep in conversation. Even Rainer, by the window looking out over the lawn rolling down towards the lake, seemed preoccupied talking to Ephraim. That was surprising. These days, Rainer had turned odious and never deigned to talk to anyone since he'd joined his band of Hitler thugs two years ago. Little Florian von Heil was busy too handing out a plate of cakes to the guests.

"Well?" Eli's right brow rose. "Are you on for the tour?" "Alright."

He opened the door and they slipped out into the Great Hall. Karina loved the scent of pine cones burning among the logs under the von Heil coat of arms; a shield and an eagle, a three-pronged coronet and two fleur de lyse and a motto inscribed in Latin.

"What does it mean?" Karina asked pointing upwards. "To the truth I stay loyal."

They stood silent for several seconds among the sea of scrolls and swirls on the antique rug and peered up at the gallery and ornate arches and gold leaf finishing. IT took the eighteenth century Italian artists three years to finish the work.

Propped against the walls were suits of armor belonging to von Heil's ancestors dating back to the second crusade. A seventeenth century tapestry took up most of the far wall.

"Impressive, don't you think?" Eli remarked.

"Yes. It is. I wonder what it must feel like to live in a place like this."

"Gloomy, I imagine. I prefer modern architecture. I just got back from New York. You should see some of the skyscrapers."

"You went all the way to America?" Karina said in awe. "Yeah."

"Did you like it? What was it like?"

"I loved it. It's another world out there. People are open and fun and life is free. There are wonderful artists, museums, galleries, clubs, musical shows on Broadway and jazz and—" He raised his palms and laughed. "It's just amazing."

"What's Jazz?" Karina frowned.

"It's a new kind of music. They play it a lot in Paris too. The Black US service men introduced it to the French at the end of the Great war."

"I've never heard of it."

"No. You wouldn't have here," Eli said dryly. "*Herr* Hitler doesn't approve." "Well, it sounds terribly exciting," she murmured. "I wish I could go."

"Maybe someday you will." "Maybe."

They smiled at one another.

"Come on. Let's investigate the dining room." Eli grinned.

They crossed the hall and Eli opened the door, then grabbed her forearm.

"Sshhhh." He placed a finger over his lips and pointed to the butler dressed in a tail coat and stiff starched white tie, his chest puffed out like a robin and two servants measuring the distance of the silverware and the plates with a ruler. "Good Lord. What a *palava*. Give me a diner in New York any day," he whispered.

Karina had no idea what a diner was, but Eli's way of saying things made her want to laugh. Several minutes went by before the servants left via the side door.

"The coast is clear. Come on. Let's see where they've seated us."

They moved down the table, peering between flower arrangements, candelabras and two silver epergnes at the place cards.

I found you. Your next to Franczeska von Holstein. My God, what a cow." Eli said. "What a horrid thing to say. You don't even know her."

"Oh, but I do. They sat me next to her at a dinner in Munich once. She has breasts like her namesake and breath to match. She ate three helpings of *palatshcinken* for pudding. She'll bore you stiff."

"Eli ! You shouldn't say things like that," Karina giggled. "By the way, I've found you too. You're next to *Mme*. de Lourriel," Karina pointed.

"Oh." Eli's face dropped.

"What's wrong? She's awfully nice."

"Of course she is. But—look why don't we do this?" Eli said leaning forward and switching the cards. "This way, we'll be next to one another."

"You can't do that, it's not allowed."

"I just did. And now you're seated between me and Florian. He's a good kid. He won't bore you. And neither will I, I hope."

A noise on the other side of the baize door had them scuttling back out from where they came. Eli shoved Karina through the door and closed it silently behind them.

"Oof! that was close."

"You're dreadful," Karina giggled. "What'll they say when they see you've changed the cards? We could get into big trouble."

"Rubbish. They'll be far too busy to notice and too polite to mention it even if they did.

Noblesse Oblige and all that."

They headed back towards the salon. The door was open but the room was empty.

"Oh gosh, they've all gone up to change!" Karina exclaimed. "I'd better go too." She hurried towards the grand staircase.

"See you later, Funny Face." Eli grinned and waved as she ran up the stairs.

Munich, Germany, 1938

On October 19th, Karina turned seventeen and her mother ordered Trude, the cook, to prepare a special meal. She invited their friends Jutta and Georg Brandt and their teenage children, Getrude and Hans to the birthday dinner. Karina had invited Bella, even though Rainer was there, resplendent in the shiny jack boots and a black uniform he paraded like a peacock in front of the mirror, admiring himself. He left the Hitler Youth movement and joined the SS six months prior and already he'd been promoted. At times, Karina had the impression that her mother and father were afraid to contest when he spewed his demagogic ideology at the dinner table. Only she confronted him.

That night was no different. Rainer held the floor expounding his views regarding the Olympic Games that had taken place in Berlin. Young Hans Brandt, dressed in his brown Hitler Youth uniform — now mandatory for all boys from the ages of ten to eighteen — listened to him, shiny eyed.

Rainer moved on from the Olympics to the subject of Jews, and Karina bristled. She sent Bella an apologetic glance. How rude of him to mention a touchy subject when they had a Jewish guest.

"Why do you hate the Jews?" Karina burst out, handing Gertrude the schnitzel platter. "What have they ever done to you?"

"I would have thought it was obvious to anyone with a brain," Rainer retorted. "The Jews undermine our society. Our economy is suffering because of their greed. They have tainted blood and are not pure Germans. That's why the Nüremberg Laws were created. To separate the wheat from the chaff and make sure we have a pure Aryan society."

"What utter rubbish!" Karina exclaimed.

The table went silent. Bella sat with he hands folded in her lap. All eyes were on Karina. Gertrude Brandt stared at her, full of wonder, and fifteen-year-old Hans looked belligerent and glanced at Rainer. The adults exchanged horrified looks across *reh* stew and noodles.

"Well it is rubbish," Karina insisted, ignoring their reaction. "Take people like the Wolfs. Or Bella here. They're all Jewish and what have they ever done to undermine our economy?"

"They deal in degenerate art, warping people's minds and filling them with perverted Jewish propaganda," Rainer hissed.

"What about Nazi propaganda? What could be more perverted than that?" Karina threw back, clutching her fork.

"Karina! That's quite enough. You're boring our guests." Her mother exclaimed.

Rainer laid the serving spoon down on the platter. He turned towards his sister's eyes, then raise his right hand and slapped her hard across the cheek.

Karina gasped. Her hand flew to her face and her eyes filled. "Rainer!" Frau Lanzberg jumped up from the table, horrified.

"Karina go to your room." *Vater* said. "Elsa sit down, please. We are at dinner."

"She should be properly punished for insulting the Führer," Karina heard her brother say as she ran from the dining room and up the stairs, followed by Bella.

"I have to say, if she was my daughter I would lay my belt across her bottom and make sure she got a good hiding for saying such things," Georg Brandt agreed.

"Absolutely right, my dear. She could get into serious trouble if she continues to air those sort of views," Hilde Brandt agreed,

The last thing Karina overheard before slamming her bedroom door was Jutta Brandt's squeaky staccato. "A woman's place is in the home, looking after her husband and breeding Aryan children, not flaunting her views as though she was a man."

Two weeks later, the Lanzbergs left Munich for their yearly visit to Schloss Heil. Rainer has refused to join them. He had a party meeting. Plus, he'd refused to consort with Jews. Karina wanted to remind him that last year he'd spent the entire weekend closeted up with Ephraim Wolf. But she remained silent. Rainer was increasingly unpredictable. At times, it she felt sad that he'd distanced himself from her and her parents. He came in and out of the house when he felt lit it, and treated their home like a hotel. He gave orders to Mama and even *Vater* seemed afraid to contradict him. The two hadn't spoken since the slap. When she'd tried to address the subject with her mother the following day, Elsa Lanzberg had cut her off abruptly. *Vater* refused to be drawn into the conversation.

In the back of the car Karina stared out the window. Her parents commented endlessly on the glories of autumnal colors, the wonderful state of the roads since the Führer came to power and the beauty of the *Bayerische Wald* — the Bavarian forest. Would Eli be at Schloss Heil? Last year he'd called her Funny Face and taught her some English. There was something warm and endearing and vibrant about him, as though he'd encapsulated the world's energy and had been made invincible. Just thinking about him made her smile.

The Wolfs and the Lanzbergs moved in different circles. The former lived in a luxurious villa in Borghausen built by Aaron Wolf's father and his aristocratic French wife in the 1890's. The Wolfs frequented high society and intellectuals, whereas the good burgers, Rudolph and Elsa Lanzberg, moved in a more traditional, upper middle-class world where little altered from generation to generation. Ladies wore loden hats with feathers and met for *kaffee und kuchen* at *Käfer*, exchanged recipes and went to church each Sunday. Contrary to the Wolf family home, which Eli and his father bought modern art and furniture for as well as antiques, the Lanzberg family home in Sollin oozed stiff couches, Biedermaeir sideboards and heavy carved oak chairs, plumped with *Omama's* hand embroidered cushions.

The car headed along the shores of the Tegernsee and past pretty villages, white-washed houses with dark wooden beams and thatched roofs and men in *leder hosen* raking the leaves and tending to their gardens.

Soon they veered off the main road. Again, Karina's thoughts turned to Eli. He must be twenty now. And she was only seventeen. What would a handsome, witty, wealthy young man like him see in a silly and insignificant girl like her when he had beauties in Paris and New York running after him?

The car came to a standstill in the courtyard. A glistening burgundy Horch stood parked to the left of the great doors. Her heart beat faster. They went through the usual greetings on the front steps. Florian looked quite grown up this year too. He was wearing a prelist's robe and had entered the seminary. Mutti and the Baroness entered the Schloss arm in arm.

"What a car!" Her father exclaimed examining the Horch.

"Oh that! It belongs to Eli. Very smart, isn't it? Here. Come over and take a look. He won't mind. In fact, he's offered to take us for a spin in it during his stay."

Karina held her breath. He was hereafter all. She watched her father and the Baron walk over to admire the car. It was ridiculous to feel panic.

"Hello Funny Face."

She spun around. Eli stood in the doorway. Their eyes lock. He moved towards her. Their hands meet and he grabbed her left arm.

"Let's go for a walk," he said. "I want to show you something." "But what if they look for me?"

"Tell them you went to see the swans."

They walked sedately through the grounds, past the rose garden and the English shrubbery designed by the Baron's grandmother, and headed on towards the lake. They walked side by side. Karina's pulse raced. Was she dreaming? When they reached the path and were out of sight of the Schloss, Eli slipped her hand in his and naturally, as though they'd been doing it all their lives, they ran, skidding and sliding on the fallen leaves. Eli laughed and caught her. Karina squealed. She slipped and they tumbled laughing into each other's arms and into love, a place where time and politics did not exist.

Down by the lake, a breeze picked up and the leaves swirled. Golden light and clear translucent water lapped the pebbles rippling gently towards them. Eli slipped an arm around Karina's shoulders and they walked in silence.

When they reached the boat house, Eli took her hand once more and led her up a slight incline towards the thousand-year oak tree where they'd played as children. It was here the Baron's ancestors had gathered to swear allegiance, before departing on the second crusade to Jerusalem.

"Remember this place?" He said

"Of course. Ephraim got stung by a wasp here and Rainer was kind for once and didn't make fun of him. He even ran to get Schwester Carla back at the Schloss."

Eli removed his tweed jacket and spread it open next to the giant trunk.

"Sit down Funny Face." He gave her his hand. "Now wait just one second."

Karina curled her legs up under her and waited agog while Eli disappeared behind the tree trunk. He reappeared seconds later holding a large square box tied with brown ribbon.

"Happy birthday Funny Face." He placed the box on her lap.

"Oh my Goodness! *Dankeschön,*" she murmured in awe. "What is it?" "Open it up and see."

Eli dropped down on the jacket next to her. His closeness made her nervous and she fumbled with the ribbon.

"Here, I'll help you.

Eli's deftly untied the ribbon. His fingers were long and elegant. An artist's hands. He lifted the lid off the box and Karina's heart raced, too afraid to touch it.

"Go on," Eli urged.

His scent left her dizzy. Slowly, she removed a layer of tissue paper. Under it was a dust bag about 40 cm wide. Eli leaned forward and pulled it upright, untied the strings and pulled out a beautiful caramel colored hand bag.

"There," he said proudly, removing the box from her lap and placing the purse there instead. "It's a handmade *Sac à Dépèches* made by Hermès, the best *sellier* in Paris, on the Faubourg Saint-Honoré. They're all the rage there."

"And you brought it all the way from there for me?" She whispered, eyes brimming. "Yes. For you

Funny Face. Here, I'll show you how to open it." Eli turned the purse towards him and undid the metal clasps that secured the flap of the purse and opened it. "Go on," he grinned. "Look inside."

Karina bit her lip and dipped her hand inside the fine, rich scented leather. The tips of her fingers touched something soft and silky. She lifted it up and a silk *carré* unfolded, in glorious colors.

"You like it?"

"Oh Eli, I love it, all of it! They're the most beautiful gifts anyone has ever given me. Thank you," she whispered, gulping back tears.

"Don't cry, Funny Face. I thought you'd be happy, "he said, pulling a handkerchief out of his pant pocket and wiping her cheek.

"I *am* happy. I'm so happy I could burst. Oh Eli—"

The *Sac à Dépèches* and scarf squished against her chest as Eli folded his arms around her and their lips met.

Her first kiss. Karina felt the touch of Eli's tongue and the taste of his lips. She knew then she would never love anyone as she loved him.

After several seconds Eli drew back. "I mustn't do this."

"Why not?" She whispered, touching his cheek bewildered as his eyes turned suddenly dark.

"I've dreamed of nothing but you for a year," he said. Drawing abruptly away he leaned his head back against the trunk of the oak."

"But what is it, Eli? I don't understand.

"Because it's wrong. You're still very young, but more importantly, in today's Germany, you and I are going against their damned laws!" He exclaimed bitterly.

"What do you mean?" Karina sat up straighter.

"Since the Nuremberg laws were passed, it's illegal for you to marry a Jew." "But that's ridiculous! They can't tell us who we're going to marry."

"Oh can't they just? Of course they can. Just like they can kick Jews out of the Civil Service, and professors from universities and burn books by Jewish authors. Papa says that the only reason they haven't closed our gallery yet is because his relations go way to the top and because our mother was French, so we're not considered to be fully Jewish. Still, that didn't stop a creep in jack boots from coming around the other day with an order to take down the flag that always flew above the villa. He said either we took it down, or father would be arrested."

Karina reached over and took his hand in hers. "Eli. I don't care what they say, we can't allow them to dictate out future. Surely we could leave Germany?"

"Father's looking into it. Last time I was in America, I was in contact with high ranking officials from the State Department to see if we could still get visas. But it isn't easy. It'll take a few months before we know the outcome."

He reached out and drew her back into his arms. Karina lay her head on his chest and caressed the *Sac à Dépèches*. The sun sank into the lake and the scent of burning leaves from a bonfire close by blended with that of the man she loved. She could hear his heartbeat under the soft wool of his sweater and basked in the strength of his arms. Eli. Her Eli. Karina closed her eyes and sighed. This is all she wanted. All she'd ever want.

For the rest of her life.

Schloss Heil, Bavaria, Germany, 1938

Eli closed the trunk of the Horch 850 and looked towards the fresh-faced young man in the black habit standing at the top of the steps of the Schloss entrance.

"That's the lot," he said, wiping his hands on his handkerchief and mounting the steps.

"I doubt they'll look for Jewish owned paintings in a castle on the Tegernsee under the noses of Nazi's who themselves are stashing art in monasteries," Florian said.

"We are so grateful to you and the Baron."

"It is the least we can do when our countrymen are behaving like savages," Florian responded.

"Is it true that you are going to a seminary in Switzerland?"

"Maybe. In Fribourg. But not right away. You remember the Lourriels? "Of course."

"Oncle Jean is acquiring a property for the Ordine Divina di Roma. It's all terribly hush hush," he murmured. "I may have to do a couple of trips back and forth. I promised I'd take as much of your father's cash with me as I can when I go. My habit has its uses."

"You mustn't put yourself in danger, Florian. It's a huge risk. You know what will happen if they should catch you."

"Don't worry. It's all very kosher."

"That's a good one, coming from a fervent Roman Catholic," Eli laughed.

"What I meant was, *Vater* is arranging my trips with Cardinal von Anim in an official car. Two Swiss Guards are coming from the Vatican to accompany us. Father said to tell Uncle Aaron to send only English pounds and gold coins as Reich marks are worthless abroad. We could do it in several stages. He doesn't want him to go by the bank either, just in case."

"Thank you. I'll pass the message on." Eli said, serious once more. "Would you be sad if you ever had to leaving Germany, definitively, Florian?"

"I must go where the good Lord sends me," he smiled. "I'd tell you to stay for dinner and a chat but it's time you got going. Father gave the servants the day off but they'll be back soon. It would be best if they didn't see you."

"I'm off then, but there's something I need to ask you." Eli pulled up the collar of his loden jacket and moved closer.

"What's that?"

"It must remain a secret between us, okay?"
"Scouts honor."

"Karina and I are getting married."

"Golly. Are you serious?" Florian goggled.

"Of course I am. But obviously, we can't go about it in the usual manner. Do you know a priest who can be trusted who would be willing to perform the ceremony?"

Florian's brows meet in a straight line across the bridge of his nose, making him appear older than his sixteen years.

"I do."

"Really?" Eli looked at him in anticipation.

"I haven't told father yet because he's so worried about what's happening politically, and I didn't want to add to his concerns, but I took my final vows last month."

"You mean you're a full-fledged priest and you can marry us?"

"That's right. But how will you get the necessary papers? You know that a marriage between—" Florian cut off.

"An Aryan and Jew," Eli supplied. "I know. It isn't allowed. Don't worry about papers I'm arranging them. In fact, I should have them by tomorrow night."

"Then bring Karina out here to Schloss Heil. We'll have to watch out for the servants. Several of the younger members of the staff have joined the Hitler Youth and are fanatical Nazis, but Lucio, the estate manager and his wife Constanza who came from my mother's estates in Puglia, can be trusted. In fact, they can act as witnesses and keep watch for us while I conduct the ceremony in the chapel. "*And*," he added with a mischievous grin, "I'll arrange for you to spend the night in the hunting pavilion by the lake. It's very romantic."

"Don't joke Florian, this is serious."

"You're damn right it's serious! It's the first marriage ceremony I'm to perform!" "Ha! Make sure u get it right."

"I promise."

"Thanks!" Eli exclaimed, playfully punching him in the shoulder.

"Shhhhh." Florian raised his right hand abruptly and cocked his ear. "It's the servants returning. Leave via the West Gates, then drive along the lake until you reach the main road. It'll be safer."

Eli leapt over the car door and dropped into the driving seat. He switched the key in the ignition and revved up the engine. Pulling his goggles over his eyes with one hand, he crammed on his leather helmet with the other, then slipped on his driving gloves. "*Auf wiedersehn* Flo. We are deeply grateful for all your family is doing for ours as am I on a personal level."

"It's nothing." Florian cleared his throat and flushed.

Eli pressed his right foot on the clutch and placed his hand on the gear shift. "She's a beauty," Florian said, stroking the burgundy paintwork.

"She's yours whenever you want to take her for a spin. How about tomorrow after the ceremony when I'll be otherwise engaged? He grinned. He waved and changed gears. The tires crunched on the carpet of leaves on the earth-beaten track heading right towards the lake. He was pleased today's mission had gone according to plan. Baron von Heil and his father's strategy had worked brilliantly. No one, not even his brother Ephraim, would suspect that the bulk of the Wolf Gallery collection was now safely stowed in the von Heil's secret cellar and the paintings at present gracing the walls of both the Biennerstarsse Gallery and Aaron Wolf's private collection in the villa in the Herzhogpark, brilliantly executed fakes.

The cool autumn air and the gold and russet forest glimmering in the afternoon sun were glorious, and the scent of burning leaves from a bonfire nearby reminded him of the carefree happy times spent here; laughter and roast sausages and mulled wine shared after a day's hunting. But the burnt leaves triggered other images too: the shouts of fanatics as they threw books onto the bonfires of ignorance and prejudice.

Eli slowed and drank it all in. Two swans and a cygnet glided across the blue waters of the lake. A bugle sounded in the distance. A picture-perfect hunting season was about to begin. He thought back to when he'd first become conscious of Karina. At fourteen, even with her pigtails and knee socks she was already breathtaking. And they'd fallen in love, oblivious of the dark clouds gathering over Germany. Was he right to marry her? God knows he'd tried his best to persuade her. Even last week, as the sat in the Englische Garten, he'd taken one last stand…

~

"You're still only seventeen. We'd need your parents' permission for us to marry," he reasoned. "And they'll never let you now that it's illegal. There's no way around this, Karina."

She shifted closer to him on the wooden bench and dropped her head on his right shoulder. "Why does it have to be this way, Eli? It's so unfair," she sighed. "Why do people have to hate one another just because they hold different beliefs?"

"I don't know." He glanced up and down the paths of the Englische Garten before slipping his arm around her shoulder and drawing her close. "I love you Karina. I will never love anyone else, but I don't want to cause you harm."

"How could you possibly cause me harm?" She exclaimed, raising her face to his. "Just being here with me now could put you in danger."

"I don't care."

"I'm not certain if that's brave or foolish," he smiled. "You know as well as I do that in 1938, it's unheard of for a well-brought up girl from a good Munich family like yours, to marry a Jew."

"I told you. I don't care. I love you. That's all that matters. Arrange it Eli! Bribe someone to alter my birth certificate if you have to. Whatever. They'll never know the difference. They won't even care."

He gazed into her eyes, tempted.

"What about your parents? They'd never forgive us. And there's Rainer. He's moving up the ranks of the SS like Jack up the beanstalk. What would he say if he so much as suspected his sister was marrying a Jew? I'm certain he didn't come to Schloss Heil this year because we were invited."

"So what?" She shrugged. "Who gives a damn about Rainer. He hates me anyway. He's a jealous, stupid ignorant misogynist. He likes uniforms and pomp and being a part of something bigger. I don't even think he understands what it's all about."

"If we have to flee Germany, it would mean giving up your entire life as you've known it until now. Are you sure you could live with that?"

"If they want to disown me, then that's their problem. I love you, Eli. I want to be your wife and bear your children."

Eli cupped her face tenderly between his palms. Her hands slipped around his waist. "Are you one hundred percent certain you won't regret this?"

"Two hundred percent certain. In fact, I've never been *so* sure of anything and I never will be again. Please, Eli darling. You're the only man I'll ever love. Just find a way for us to marry as soon as it can be arranged. And now stop talking and kiss me."

~

Once on the main road, Eli headed north in the direction of Munich. He wished he'd been born in different times when he could have married Karina openly in a church or a synagogue or simply a registry office. But it was too dangerous. Since June, the criminal police had arrested people indiscriminately. Papa had tried to get visas for the US through influential friends in the New York art world, but neither the United States nor several other countries, would alter their immigration policies to allow German Jews to relocate.

Up ahead, a convoy of military vehicles moved at a snail's pace. He slowed. Several recruits seated in the back of one of the military trucks waved and whistled, leaning out the sides of the vehicle below the tarpaulin to admire the Horch 850 as she overtook them. If another war really was just around the corner as so many predicted, would he be expected to fight? Right Jews were banned from the armed forces, but no doubt that would alter if Germany actually went to war. They'd need more canon fodder, surely? Would he be obliged to fight for a country that had disowned him and wanted to crush and rid themselves of all he stood for?

The car drove smoothly on the newly paved road. The only good thing to be said about the Führer was that infrastructure had greatly improved since he'd come to power. He checked his watch. Papa was waiting for him at home. In an-hour-and-a-half he'd be able to tell him that all had gone smoothly. Then, once the gallery closed for the night, he'd go find Ben in the framing room below the stairs and receive an update on the paper-work for his marriage papers.

Eli smiled. Things were not so bad after all. And tomorrow a new life would begin.

Munich, Germany, 1938

It was 8pm by the time Eli walked quickly down the Briennerstrasse and stopped in the doorway of the building across the street to Wolf Kunsthandel AG, the gallery established by his Great-Grandfather Julius Aaron Wolf, in 1902.

After glancing left and right, Eli crossed the street and slipped around to the side entrance. Two soft knocks, followed by a second's silence, then two more. The heavy metal door with the peep hole that his father had installed last year, creaked open and Ben Kleinmann, who'd worked for the Wolfs since his grandfather's death, beckoned him inside.

The basement smelled of turpentine and oil paint coming from the restauration studio. Ben shuffled ahead of him until they reached the frame room and Eli closes the door behind them.

"So. Did you manage it?" He asked, moving towards the table where several sheets of paper were spread out.

"*Natürlich*," Ben replied. "Don't I manage everything in this place? Not that I'm not appreciated," he grumbled. "Are you sure you know what you're doing, Elias?"

"I am sure, Ben. She's a wonderful girl."

The old man sniffed. The bald patch where he'd removed his yamulke glistened under the light bulb as he peered through round glasses at his handiwork. "It's not for me to be advising you, I stopped doing that a long time ago," he muttered continuing to shake his head, "but you should tell your father about this, Eli. You're betraying the family by marrying this little *chiksa*."

"She's not a little chiksa," Eli bristled. "If you met her, you'd love her, Ben."

"Love is blind but the neighbors ain't," Ben grunted and rolled his eyes. "It's sheer foolhardiness, if you ask me. In times like these, we must stick together, not marry out of the faith. Have you thought properly of the consequences of what you're doing? Your children will not be Jewish. They'll be hated and despised, neither one or the other."

"That's old-fashioned nonsense," Eli scoffed. "This Nazi stuff is just a passing phase. Soon it will be over and children like ours will be the future. Surely you must see that mixing faiths is what'll build a better world where none of this matters any longer?"

"*Ach mein Gott*, to think that I should live to hear such words spoken from the lips of a Wolf. Your grandfather must be turning in his grave." Ben shook his head once more and sat at the wooden table where he lifted a gilt frame. "Here. Take a look.

Eli scanned the birth certificate. "It's brilliant, Ben. No one will ever know it's been tampered with. Did you manage to get the special license?"

"Didn't I just tell you I resolve everything? I talked to Avi Stein. He has long fingers that reach into many pies."

"So he knows." Eli looked up from the document that would render his marriage to Karina legal.

"Of course he knows. Did you think this could be managed without help? *We* know whom to trust. That's because we are loyal to each other. Listen to what I am telling you, my boy. You'll be cutting yourself off from the community. The fact that Avi knows doesn't matter. He's a good man who can keep his mouth shut. But what of the others? Are you aware the girl's brother is with the Waffen SS?" "Yes."

"You'll be like Daniel stepping into the Lion's den."

"Well," Eli grinned, "he looked after himself pretty well, didn't he?"

"May the good Lord will look after you too, my boy. There are bad times coming, Eli. Much worse than anything we can imagine. I read history. I know."

"Then we'll have to face it as best we can, won't we?"

"*Ach*, it's useless talking to you, young folk." Ben threw up his hands, placed his yamulke back on his bald skull and started preying.

Schloss Heil, Bavaria, Germany, 1938

Surely no woman ever looked lovelier, dressed as she was in a pale silk dirndl, her hair glistening like the gold leaf framing the ancient fresques of the baroque chapel reflected in the glow of candle light in Schloss Heil chapel?

"To love and to cherish, for richer or poorer, in sickness and in health, until death do thee part."

"I need the ring," Florian whispered.

"The ring? Oh, yes of course, the ring," Eli flushed. He sent Karina an apologetic glance and fumbled in the right-hand pocket of his swede *trachten* jacket.

Karina smothered a giggle. How typical of her darling to get carried away. She was tempted to reach up and pass her fingers through his hair and tell him not to fret. Instead, she lowered her eyes and bit her lip as he handed Florian the ring.

"Repeat after me," Florian said. "With this ring I thee wed."

How many vows were spoken, how many promises of a love and a life to be shared had these sacred walls witnessed? Was it wrong of her not to mind that only Bella was present and her family weren't there to share her joy? All that mattered to her at this moment was the man next to her, the man she loved and whom she'd spend the rest of her life with. Surely God will forgive her breaking the law in the name of love?

"I do." Karina's voice broke and her fingers trembled as the ring slid onto her finger.

She and Eli, husband and wife. The dream she'd dreamed in her young girls' rosebud bedroom was finally true. Now they could live happily ever after.

"Congratulations." Florian shook Eli's hand. Karina reached up and kissed him on the cheek. "Thank you Florian. That was beautiful."

"Are you sure? I was afraid I might forget some of the text."

"Even if you had, it wouldn't have mattered, would it, Eli?" she said squeezing his hand. "Perfect! You'd think he'd been doing it for years," Eli teased. "You'll make a great priest, Florian."

"Shut up and come along with me. You must sign the registry, then I'll take you go to the hunting pavilion. And don't either of you talk too loudly, okay?"

"We won't."

"What about Lucio, shouldn't we thank him and say goodbye? It was very loyal and kind of him and his wife to be our witnesses," Karina said.

Florian turned suddenly serious.

"Better not. I'll tell him for you. I'd rather he kept watch outside just in case anyone turns up who shouldn't."

He led them through the back of the chapel via the vestry. Once outside, they headed down a small path. The leaves crunched under their feet. Karina giggled. Eli placed his arm possessively around her waist as they headed through the *Klein Wald* towards the hunting pavilion nestled at the foot of the trees by the lake.

"Here's the key," Florian said, stopping before the low, gothic shaped double-paneled door. "I'll leave you now and be back just before dawn."

"Thanks, Florian. You're a *Mensch*."

"I'll take that as a compliment. Good luck you two," he says gruffly. Karina watched Florian's flowing habit disappear back up the path.

"I hope he's made the right decision and that he'll be happy as a priest," she murmured, folding her hands tightly as Eli unlocked the heavy oak door. He turned on the threshold. She hesitated.

"Is something wrong?" he asked. "No, no, I'm fine."

"You're not afraid, are you?" Karina shook her head.

Eli stroked her cheek tenderly and kissed her. "It'll be fine, you'll see."

"I know. Just carry me over the threshold. For luck," she whispered, looping her fingers around his neck.

Eli scooped her up into his arms, their lips met, then gazing deep into her eyes he carried her up the staircase.

Through the mullioned windows of the hunting Pavilion, the lake lay motionless, a mirrored tray emerging from under a cape of rising mist.

"I could lie here forever," Karina whispered, nuzzling her cheek further up Eli's chest, her head snuggled in the nook of his neck.

"We shall lie as we are now for the rest of our lives," he said.

"Promise?" She stroked his arm, letting her fingers travel to the crook of his elbow. "Promise." He kissed her, then pulled his watch off the nightstand. "It's 5am already.

We'd better get ready. Florian will be back soon."

"I don't want to go," Karina pouted. "I think I'll stop time and stay here forever. Hold me tight Eli, this place is freezing."

"If things were different I'd be taking you on our honeymoon to Paris or Rome," he sighed, pulling the covers up over her.

"It doesn't matter. We're together, aren't we?"

"Yes, but I hate that we must go our separate ways and pretend." "It's only for now. Soon we'll be together all the time."

"You're right, *Liebling*," he leaned across and dropped a kiss on her right breast. "Come on Funny Face. Rise and shine. It'll take us an hour or more to get you home and safely inside the house before the servants or your parents wake. I need to show up at gallery before ten, if I'm to avoid suspicion. Ben knows about us and he won't rat on me, but the others mustn't know.

Ben's so negative about the future, though. He's convinced things will get worse," he said, pulling her close.

"Is your father trying to get the visas for America?"

"He is. It's not looking great. But we'll find an answer. Let's not think about all that now."

A smacking kiss. A giggle.

"I want to begin all over again."

"Eliii!" she squealed, wriggling in his arms.

"What's wrong with wanting to make love to my own wife?"

"Eli, darling, I hope we live to a hundred and wake up like this for the rest of our lives." "That's what you say now, but years from now you'll be sick of me," he teased, arms

looped about her rib cage.

Karina let her toe travel up and down his inner calf. How natural it felt to be intimate. How right… the two of them, lost to the world, skin to skin, heartbeat to heartbeat. How silly she'd been to fear. But weren't all young girls anxious before their wedding night?

A knock on the paneled oak door. "That must be Florian."

"Get up you two. The servants will be up and about soon. I'll wait for you downstairs." "We won't be long," Eli said, dropping a last lingering kiss on Karina's lips.

Minutes later, they tiptoed hand in hand down the wooden staircase and entered the gun room. Rifles and all manner of hunting weapons hung on the walls and in glass cases. Florian was perched, feet dangling, on a narrow table backed against a wall.

"I thought you were never coming," he complained munching a *salz stangl*. "The car is at the back entrance. Are you hungry? I brought *brötchens* and cheese and a thermos of hot coffee," he said, pointing to the basket next to him.

"Actually, I am a little hungry," Karina murmured, her cheeks flushed. "And I could eat an ox!" Eli exclaimed.

"That's not surprising. I suppose you've been at it like rabbits," Florian teased. "Florian, you're a priest now. You can't say things like that!"

"Why not?" He grinned. "Because you can't."

"She's right. Priests are supposed to be holier than thou and preach the perils of the sins of the flesh, not encourage them. Are you sure you've chosen the right vocation, old chap?" Eli retrieved the thermos from the basket and poured steaming coffee into three plastic beakers.

"That's rubbish! I'm going to be a modern priest, not a stodgy moralistic old grump" Florian declared, "I'll be a priest who knows about real life. It doesn't make any sense otherwise."

"I'm sure you'll be a wonderful priest, Flo," Karina said. Reaching up she pecked his cheek. "Thank you for all you've done for us."

"It's nothing," he answered gruffly.

Steam twirled upwards like the smoke from Aladdin's lamp. Karina listened to the boy's banter. She wished it could last forever. But they were all growing up fast. Life, with its twists and turns and hard choices, stretched out before them like an open road. Where would their steps lead them? For she and Eli, the choice was easy now that they'd begun their journey. They would walk the road of life together, side by side, wherever the road led them.

She gazed at her handsome husband. How lucky she was, how blessed to love and be loved by him. They were one now and nothing could keep them apart, not her parents nor Hitler. A cold draft of air made her shiver. She took a sip of coffee, then laid her beaker down and reached for Eli's hand.

"What's wrong, *Liebling*?" he frowned.

"Nothing." She squeezed his fingers tight. Eli slipping his arm around her and drew her close.

"I something the matter?" he whispered.

"No. It's nothing. Just—" She shook her head and smiled and turned her face up to receive a kiss.

"You'd better be off now," Florian said, wiping the crumbs off his habit. "Let's go."

Minutes later, the newlyweds sat in the Horch.

"Here, let me cover you." Eli retrieved a plaid rug from the back seat and tucked it carefully over Karina's knees, then he leaned out the car window.

Thank you again for everything, Flo. We shall never forget what you've done for us."

"It's my pleasure. God speed to you both."

Eli let the car descend the slope in neutral. Karina slipped her hand in his and watched the swans on the lake take flight as the sun rose over the water. The eight-cylinder engine of which Eli was so proud picked up speed. For now, they'd have to fake it and pretend to their parents; go on with their lives as if nothing had changed. But in a few days, they'd be back for Saint Hubertus. Then they'd make plans. Maybe even manage to sneak away and make love.

Surely nothing could ever be more perfect than this?

Florian placed his hands in his pockets and watched as the rear lights descended among the trees. The fingers in his right pocket touched metal. He withdrew a bulky unusual key.

"Damn!" he muttered. "Eli, wait!" He ran down the hill waving the key frantically and tripping on the hem of his habit. But the car picked up speed and he gave up, panting for breath.

"Damn," he repeated.

Florian dangled the rusty key, then shrugged and slipped it back inside the right trouser pocket under his habit. Never mind. There was no big rush. The paintings were in safe keeping in the hidden cellars built by his ancestor during the Bavarian War of

Succession. It was a secret passed down from one Baron to the next. Only he, *Vater* and now Eli knew about it. As for the key itself, he'd pop by the Wolf villa and give it to him. He was due to go to Munich in a few days' time anyway.

Munich, Germany, 1938

Eli sat across from his father at the desk in the library of the Wolf villa, a room rife with tension after the terrible events that had taken place two days before. Little by little news was trickling back: Nazi mobs throughout Germany and Austria had waged a night of terror against the Jewish population.

"It's estimated that more than 1,000 shops and synagogues have been destroyed. They're talking of 30,000 arrests and God only knows how many killed," Aaron muttered. "They're calling it *Kristallnacht* — Night of Broken Glass. The Goldsteins have packed up and left, and Avi Levine was last seen being clubbed over the head by a Gestapo thug. We must get you and Ephraim out of here as fast as we can. Heini von Heil is seeing ways of getting the money to Switzerland. Your idea regarding the painting was a good one. It's become too dangerous to stay now. We've been lucky that both the Gallery and this house were spared. But for how long?" Aaron dragged his hand through his hair and looked up at the portrait of his grandfather above the fireplace. "My mother's parents escaped the pogroms in Odessa in 1859 and my father's family those of 1871. And now it's happening all over again."

"Then if we have to, let's pack up and go while there's still time. Forget the American visas. We'll drive to the Swiss border at St. Margerethen. It's only a few hours. You're' right, it's too risky to stay here now. And there's something I must tell you," Eli hesitated. Papa looked worn and sad and absent. But Karina was on her way here and there wasn't a moment to lose. "Have you seen Ephraim?" Aaron asked.

"No. Not for several days. But I doubt anything's happened to him," Eli muttered, his face turning dark.

Aaron rose "Eli, start removing some of the paintings in the hall and in the dining room and pile them against the wall. Make it look as if we were removing them to store them."

"But they're fakes. Who cares?" "Just do as I say."

"Papa, I need to speak to you now—" Eli insisted. "Afterwards. Do as I say first."

Eli hesitated. He turned impatiently on his heel and stepped into the hall. "Shmuel. Help me remove the pictures form the walls," he muttered, lifting a Mönsch off its hook next to the library door.

Silently Eli and Shmuel — the elderly butler who'd came as a footman in Aaron's grandfather's time, removed the pictures one by one and stacked them against the wall at the foot of the Rodin."

A grumbling sound grew louder and louder.

"What's that?" Shmuel stood still and cocked an ear. A Renoir lay cradled in his arms like a baby.

Eli bounded into the dining room and peered out the window. "*Lieber Gott*! There's an SS staff car stopping outside and a truck," he shouted. "They've come, Papa. What are we going to do?" He cried, running back into the hall.

Aaron stood silent. He adjusted his waistcoat and straightened his tie.

"Run Eli. Go out the back and get to Schloss Heil as fast as you can. I am ready for them," he said.

Loud banging echoed on the front door. "I won't leave you, Papa. It's too late anyway. They're surrounding the house. And I can't leave Karina."

"Karina?" Aaron's head shot up. "My wife."

"*Mein Gott*. Where is she?" "Upstairs. I was trying to tell you."

The banging increased. The door trembled. Shouts.

Aaron grabbed Eli's shoulder. "Go my son. Take Karina and go." "No. I won't leave you."

Aaron Wolf closed his eyes for a split second, then he turned. "Let them in, Shmuel. There's no use trying to stop them. They'll simply destroy everything if we do."

Schmuel stepped up to the door and opened it and was roughly pushed aside. SS men swarmed inside the hall.

"*Rein! Schnell* Get them before they try to flee."

An officer marched in followed by several armed men. Aaron stepped forward. "Good morning,

Rainer. There is no need for haste. No one is going anywhere.

Rainer Lanzberg halted and his eyes flickered. He pointed his riding crop at a stack of paintings propped against the wall.

"What are these pictures doing piled up like that?" He threw. "And address me properly. I'm *Oberst strumfüher* Lanzberg to the likes of you."

"They paintings are being readied to go to my Gallery in the Brienerstrasse in order to be catalogued for the Reich," Aaron replied.

"Interesting," Rainer smirked.

"My goodness, Rainer, what's all this about," Eli said, stepping forward. Rainer stared at him showing no sign of recognition.

"The two of you will accompany my men. We must clarify this situation. Take these two back to HQ while we search the rest of the house," he ordered his subordinate.

"Herr Oberst, look what I've found up here?" A man from the gallery called.

All eyes turned to the top of the stairs. An SS trooper held Karina by her upper arm "Leave her alone," Eli cried, lunging towards the stairs.

"Stop him," Rainer barked.

Two SS men grabbed Eli from the back as he ran up the stairs. A third raised the butt of his rifle and knocked him out. A scream tore from the gallery as he fell bleeding to the ground.

Rainer took the stairs two at a time.

"You can dispose, Helmut. I'll take it from here," he told the underling. "Go make sure those two are properly taken care of."

"*Jawohl, Herr Oberst.* Heil Hitler." The man's right arm jutted out and he cliqued his heels.

"Heil Hitler."

The man in the black uniform descended the stairs shouting orders as Rainer pulled Karina back by the neck in a vice-like grip.

"One word of this and they die, understood?"

She nodded. Rainer was capable of anything. They were pushing Aaron through the front door and dragging Eli out by his heels. She heard the thud as his head bumped on the step. Blood trailed like a brush stroke of red paint across the marble floor.

"Please, Rainer, please don't' do this," she begged.

"Shut up!" Rainer spin around, gripping her by the hair so hard her eyes watered. Her head reeled from the slap that followed. "What are you doing here?"

"Eli is my husband," she said, her cut lip swelling.

Rainer's grip loosened. He turned deathly pale. Karina grabbed his arm. He shook her hand away.

"You married a Jew?"

"It's not like that. It's Eli. He's your friend, Rainer. You've known him all your life. Please. You must see that it's different. I love him."

Judensow! I should have you deported, you filthy bitch." He slapped her hard on the other cheek. Karina gasped. He kicked her hard in the shin. She fell to her knees.

"Please, Rainer, please don't harm him." "Get up," he ordered.

Slowly Karina stumbled to he feet.

"One word of this to anyone, including Mama and Papa and I'll have his balls cut off and sown into his fowl Jewish neck and he'll never fuck you again, understood? Now come and get your stuff. Normally, understood? Do exactly as I tell you."

Rainer shoved her down the corridor. "Which room is it?"

Karina pointed trembling to the door on her left. "Get your things. Hurry."

He marched her inside the bedroom. The room, filled earlier with love, hope and love expectation, had turned dark. The silk negligée she'd bought for her wedding night lay on the bed next to her half-unpacked.

"Hurry! *Schnell!*" Rainer's voice cracked like a whip. Eli's discarded his Burberry raincoat lay on the armchair. Karina grabbed it and tugged it on. The sleeves covered her hands. The *Sac à Dépèches* stood on the chest of drawers where she'd placed it earlier. Shouts in the corridor... Rainer stepped outside the room and Karina rushed to the chest of drawers. She grabbed Eli's gold lighter and money clip, a small picture of Eli and the Romeo & Julieta cigar he'd carried in his pocket for several days but never smoked, and stuffed them inside the purse.

Rainer returned. Karina lifted the silk scarf. Her fingers shook as she folded it diagonally and placed it over her head trying to buy time. But for what?

A last glance at the room that was to be her love nest for a lifetime... Rainer pushed her out the door and shouted over the banister.

"Act normal," he hissed as they descended the stairs.

Her legs shook. She could barely walk. She hid her face behind the silk scarf and lowered her head.

"Should we take her in for questioning too, Herr Oberst?" Someone asked.

"No. I'm letting her go. She's just the hired help here to teach the Jews some proper manners," he guffawed.

The men laughed and cracked a few lewd jokes.

In the hall, Karina pulled her arm from Rainer's grip. She bent down and touched the bloodstains shining like rubies under the crystal chandelier. She pulled a handkerchief from Eli's pocket and wiped the blood.

"Stop that," Rainer hissed and dragged her to her feet. She tried to shake him off.

"Don't even think about it."

The sound of motors disappeared up the street. Shmuel was carrying paintings down the steps. Blood trickled from the old man's temple.

Karina's shoulders shook. Rainer pinched her arm so hard she cried out.

"Dry up bitch, and move. And make sure you go straight home or you'll be next." He twisted her flesh between his thumb and index, then he prodded her hard between the kidneys with his riding crop.

"Get the fuck out of here, *judensow*, before I change my mind."

Chapter 41

Tia Bella's voice died in the restaurant turned silent around a table littered with coffee, cake and heartbreak.

Luna reached out her hand. Tia Bella clasped it.

"Nobody knew where Eli and Aaron Wolf had been taken," Tia Bella continued. "They simply disappeared. Ina was desperate. Rainer blackmailed her, forcing her to go with him to fine Nazi homes decked out in furs and jewels. She did as she was told. She had no choice. Anything for Eli to be spared. The more her despair grew, the more Rainer taunted her. Then, she caught the eye of his boss, *Obersturmführer* Helmut Volker. Ina said she would rather die than sleep with him. But I told her do it. To do it for Eli's sake. Maybe there was a chance. Maybe he knew something."

"So, that explains the newspaper clipping." Luna mumbled.

"I don't believe Helmut was an evil man, just a man caught up in the events of his time like so many others. People portray Germans as monsters when most of them were simply trying to get on with their lives. In the end, it was Helmut who found out that Eli and his father had been gassed in Dachau.

"Ina aged overnight. Her face lost its dimples. But if anything, her grief and her courage rendered her more beautiful. It was late 1943 by then and that's when we fled to Schloss Heil. It was quite an escape. Ina stole some National Socialist Women's League uniforms to disguise us in. Strange the silly thing one remembers… my skirt was too big and we had to roll the top up about my waist.

"It was the first time I'd come down from the attic in nearly three years. The devastation and rubble shocked me. I saw rats scrounging as we walked to the nearest bus station. I was never more frightened of the rats than the soldiers.

"There were uniformed SS and Gestapo on the bus. Ina and I sat in separate seats. We pretended not to know each other. The *Hauptbanhoff* — the main station — crawled with soldiers armed with rifles and Alsatian dogs trained to sniff out Jews. But we got passed them and took a train to the Tegernsee. There, Baron von Heil's chauffeur picked us up at the station and drove us to Schloss Heil.

Once there, they passed me off as the secretary. What a lovely woman the Baroness, Fabrizia was. She taught me to crochet and read Dante in Italian. That's how I picked up the language which helped me later on when I went to Colombia and had to learn Spanish.

"The Baron was actively involved helping the resistance since Eli and Aaron's arrest. And now Ina became involved as well. Then, after the White Rose movement was exposed and Sophie and Hans Scholl, her brother, were shot in cold blood after a kangaroo trial that lasted only a few minutes, things became tricky and they had to be more careful. Still, no one suspected a man of the Baron's stature, living as he did in a Schloss on the Tegernsee surrounded by Nazi high-hedeans.

"Did you ever discover why Rainer descended on the Wolfs that day?" Luna asked.

"He went there to steal the art, but when Ina told him she'd married Eli she signed Eli's death sentence. They took them to Gestapo headquarters and we never heard of them since.

"So much of what I've just told you happened in between. Then, in summer of 1944, the war was going badly. I still don't know why Rainer became suspicious of the Baron. One day he arrived at Schloss Heil and declared them all to be traitors of the Third Reich." Tia Bella paused. "It was so awful," she whispered, her eyes moist. "He rounded up the family in the hall: the Baron, the Baroness and her father. He shot them one by one in cold blood. The Baron fell next to the piano. The Baroness threw herself on top of him and collapsed in his arms. Father Florian's grandfather — Marchese di Copertania — stood straight and looked Rainer in the eye. I'll never forget his expression. Ina and I were hiding behind the arches in the gallery above the Great Hall and we saw it all. Of course Rainer found us. I have no idea why we were spared — if being sent to that hell-hole that was Belsen — can be considered spared. Perhaps even Rainer could not bring himself to shoot his own sister." Tia Bella's hand shook as she raised the water glass and sipped.

"Belsen was everything it was described to be and worse. I've no need to go into details. There is enough footage and testimonies and I don't like going back there."

"I understand," Luna murmured.

"Do you?" Tia Bella looked up. "People say that, but it would be impossible for anyone who hadn't lived what we went through to begin to understand. Not just the physical and psychological horror, but coming to terms with the fact that one lot of human beings could do such things to another. Animals do not commit genocide. They kill to survive. Only humans are predators. Therefore, genocide is doubly horrifying because it pertains to the mind and man's dark side."

Tia Bella's words lingered. *Dark side*… The words repeated in Luna's head. "Was it in Belsen Nana met Carolina Orlowska?" Luna asked.

"Yes. She was in the same hut as us. She was beautiful as was Ina." Tia Bella's face sagged. "I was not beautiful."

"Did it matter?"

"No. It saved me. If you were plain, you only had a number tattooed on your arm and not *nur fur offiziere* as they did."

"Oh my God! For officers only… So that's why Rachel acted as she did."

"Yes. The beautiful girls were singled out to be the officer's whores. They found them some nice clothes and accessories. That's how Ina held on to the *Sac à Dépèches*. The men lined up outside a special hut. Each was allowed half-an-hour. It killed Carolina in the end. Ina was more resistant, though she too was gravely weakened by it. If it hadn't been for Henry, I think she would have died too.

"Those last days of 1945 before the liberation came, were the worst," Tia Bella said. "There were no more pine needles to cook and I can't describe the stench. I'd turned 20 the week before and I remember thinking that in a few hours I'd be just another corpse that they'd walk over. Our bellies were empty and we itched all over, but not even the flees bothered us any longer. In a way, they'd become our friends. They reminded us that we had bodies and were still alive. Ina didn't get the typhus and she never lost hope. I was too sick to think. I just wanted to be back home with Mama and Papa again. I didn't know if they were dead or alive. Only later did I learn they were all gone.

"But the worst of all were the guards, girls like us with hopes and dreams who were now less than human. I'll never forget that girlish laughter and those cackles that echoed as those young women picked their way among protruding ankles and elbows, pulling shoes off feet that yesterday walked. I remember a bracelet ripped from a dangling arm; an arm that I hoped had once embraced. They tore the rags from the corpses with complete indifference. The most dreaded of them all was Ludmilla. She was a pretty blond with innocent eyes and the mind of a devil. One day she plucked a cap from a lolling head and placed it on her own at a suggestive angle. Then she posed, arms akimbo, her right foot poised on the rib cage of its previous owner. She was popular among her peers. The day before she'd pulled a girl out of the barracks and tied her to a young man's corpse to make them look like lovers, then set fire to them to a chorus of screams and jeers and putrefied smoke.

"But then in April things began to change. The guards looked worried and scared. Some of them left. And then one day, I heard a rumble, like distant thunder getting louder and louder and closer. An old man stumbled towards our hut waving his arms. Noise burst out. People shouted to one another and ran towards the gates. *Oh mein Gott*," Tia Bella whispered, "Those gates with *Arbeit Macht Frei* written above them were open at last!"

"And the guards?" Luna asked. "Did they catch them?"

"They were fleeing, running towards the forest and the trees. They didn't matter any longer. Everybody cheered. Those who could still stand up were waving. Weeping. Men and women flanked the path. Some climbed onto the sides of the armored tanks moving like mammoths into the heart of this valley of death.

"I crawled back inside the hut. "Ina," I cried, shaking her arm. *"Something strange is going on outside. People are running everywhere. Come on. Get up. The* gates are open."

"We helped one another and struggled to the door. Then a tank rolled up. A soldier spoke into a loudspeaker. They were translating his words simultaneously.

"It's the British. The British have come to liberate us," someone said.

"Pinch me," Ina said. And I pinched her arm hard so we both knew it was true and we were alive. Then the convoy of tanks slowed. Two helmeted soldiers in khaki uniforms jumped down from the second one that had stopped a few feet away from our hut. One of them saw the bodies piled a few feet away and gagged. The other walked towards us. I was terrified. Urine coursed down my inner thighs. I feared for Ina. Would he do to her what the others had?

"The soldier stopped a few paces away. "That was her first encounter with Henry, an American officer on loan to the 11th British Armored Division who was in the second tank that entered the camp. He looked like something out of a dream.

"What's your name?" He asked Karina.

"Ina," she answered. Then she gasped and her legs gave way and she crumpled to the floor.

"After, they'd shipped us to a camp in Norway. It was there the Allies began enquiring about a Karina Lanzberg, the sister of a high-ranking Nazi SS officer they believed was hiding in Belsen."

"They thought she was a Nazi?" Luna asked.

"Yes. After all, she'd been seen in the highest circles and Rainer had disappeared." "And that's when she became Carolina?"

"People knew her as Ina. I'd kept the few things Carolina had managed to hide after she died. There was a locket with her name inside. When they offered us the option of resettling in Colombia I said we should do it. Leave the past behind and get a new life. And that's how we ended up in Bogotà."

"But what about Henry? Did he look for her?"

"There was such confusion at the liberation, there was no way of keeping track. It was only years later in New York that they met at a dinner party by chance, or, as I prefer to believe, by synchronicity. I think he was the only man Ina could have married after all she'd been through. She trusted him, you see. And only he knew the truth."

"So that's why she never re-opened the *Sac à Dépèches*," Luna, said.

"That's right. She put it in a glass case to be treasured but not touched. She knew if she did, she'd keep seeking Eli's spirit and stare at the cigar that she'd managed to grab off the dressing table and slip inside her purse on the day of the arrest while Rainer's back was turned."

The tragedy and pain expressed in Tia Bella's words rocked the Baur au Lac restaurant as the past reached back through a telescope in reverse.

Tears trickled down Luna's cheeks.

Several minutes passed. Then Tia Bella spoke.

"There is no point in dwelling on sadness, but there is a point in remembering what triggered it. It frightens me to see politicians adopting similar language to what stoked the fires of evil back then. I know the world has changed, but people haven't. And what frightens me the most is when I recognize that gleam of fanaticism in their eyes, and the same expression on their faces as in the 1930s. I think to myself: don't they read history?

"And then I hear it... the rumble... that voice beyond the wind growling, stirring inside the belly of the beast, and I fear all we've built since those dark days could be swept away as easily as it was before, and the world return to being a place of darkness and evil as we experienced then. It takes only a few to turn the tide. People vote for their personal agenda, not the common good. True democracy elects officials with the capacities to represent and defend real issues, not demagogues risen to power on the whim of popular emotion."

Chapter 42

He didn't like it. Not one little bit. Dr. Frankel said travelling was out of the question.

The suitcase stood half-packed on the luggage rack and cigarette butts vied for room in the ashtray on the nightstand. It was a cruel twist. How was he to speak to Florian now? The main thing was to get Florian on his side. In truth, Florian knew little about events that had taken place in and after 1938. He'd recalled it was shortly after Eli and Papa's arrest that he'd disappeared. At the time, no one had mentioned where Florian went and there was little contact between Ephraim and Baron von Heil after Papa's disappearance. It was easy to put two and two together. How small the world was. And getting smaller. He knew Florian had never liked him much, but that at their age, such trifling details were insignificant. What mattered was the fact that Florian was the only person still alive who could vouch for him.

Ephraim took a long drag to calm his nerves. Carl hadn't called back.

"*Irgend was stimmt nicht*," he muttered. Something didn't feel right. He'd experienced this same sensation in 1944 the day after an Allied bomb hit the house next door and he'd finally escaped Munich and headed West towards the French border. The old bullet wound in his left arm bothered him at times. But it had been a small price to pay. Even now, the eyes of the young Belgian guard who crumpled to the ground as he'd pulled the blade out of the side of his neck and wiped it on a dock leaf, lingered. He shuddered. Was there retribution? Were souls returning to haunt him? He didn't believe in all that mumbo jumbo, but still. It was uncanny at times how uncomfortable and clear these visions had become…

~

He regretted telling Rainer what he'd seen that day at the station in Tegernsee. He'd meant to please him. But since returning from Schloss Heil three days later, Rainer had changed and no amount of wheedling could persuade him to tell Ephraim exactly what had happened there.

In fact, Rainer barely spoke. As news from the front worsened, the sex that he'd enjoyed those sexual games that ensured Ephraim's hold on him — no longer did the trick. Dresden was rubble; Köln, and the entire Ruhr valley a dump, and German industry was brought to its knees. But still the Führer insisted they fight on. According to Rainer, even Speer had handed in his resignation.

The Allied forces were rolling in from the North, the Russians from the East and between them, the Americans and the Brits had most of the Western front from Arras down to the South covered. It was only a matter of days now. And for Ephraim, there was a choice to be made.

Rainer hadn't appeared for several days. Food was scarce and Frau Schenker had left to the country to her niece. At least they had hens left and two cows. Ephraim peered at the two SS uniforms hanging in the cupboard. He took them out and laid them on the bed. What if Rainer had been captured? There was no knowing what could happen now. He slipped his hand inside the right pocket of the black dress uniform: a key, a receipt and at the bottom, something metal.

Rainer's signet ring. He'd said he'd lost it shortly after he returned that night from Schloss Heil. Ephraim frowned. Rainer's noble connections were distant, but he set great store by them. Why pretend he'd lost it?

Ephraim studied the ring closely, then slipped it on his left pinky. It fit perfectly. It was a bulky piece, but Ephraim knew why. Rainer had every eventuality covered.

He'd waited another night in the cellar while the RAF bombed the city. He must get out. Now. Before it was too late.

The next morning he'd climbed the stairs. Some water remained in the bucket in the kitchen and he carried up the narrow stairs to his room. The streets were deserted. Could he risk going up to the attic? He must know what was going on.

Carefully, Ephraim pulled down the trap door and climbed up beneath the roof. The antenna he'd installed a year earlier was still in place undetected. Ephraim kneeled on a dusty cushion and played with the buttons of the radio that he'd purloined form the Villa. It worked. He played until he caught the right frequency and could hear the Free French radio broadcasting from London crouched among Frau Schenke's old carpets. The end was near. God only knew where Rainer was. He pulled the antenna off the roof and hid it with the radio behind a pile of broken furniture, then descended once more to the landing.

In the room, he paused and studied the uniforms again. He and Rainer were of similar build although the German was taller. Ephraim went to the basin. He lifted the bucket next to it and tipped in a sparse amount of water. First he washed, then shaved with what remained. He used the last trickle in the bucket to quench his thirst then put on a clean undershirt and drew on the black uniform pants. He buttoned the braces to the waist, then pulled on a clean shirt and heaved the braces over his shoulders. The starched buttonholes were stiff as he fixed the swastika cuff links. Carefully, he knotted the tie, then pulled on the jacket. Lastly came the jackboots. Rainer had the new pair on and these were worn in and comfortable. He thought of his papers hidden inside the heel of his shoe. Depending on events, he might need them to prove who he was. If the Nazis caught him with is old passport, he was dead meat. But if he made it into Allied territory, it could be his salvation.

Ephraim stood in front of the mirror. He did the goosestep. He looked good. He looked Aryan.

He reached for the battered leather case from on top of the armoire. He placed it on the bed. One by one he packed the remainder of his clothes: a grey suit and shirt, the shoes with his documents hidden inside, socks, and the Bavarian jackets and *leder hosen* that he'd adopted these past two years to blend in with the population costumes and disguises to guarantee his escape.

At last he was ready. He glanced at Rainer's ring on his right hand, then at the small bed where he and Rainer had shared their passion. Love. Hatred. Connivance and treachery. At the end of the day their relationship was Shakespearean. Yet it had survived in the face of the impossible: a Jew and a Nazi. What could be harder to define than what they felt for one another? He didn't trust Rainer. Rainer didn't trust him. Was that the paradox? That despite everything, neither of them existed fully outside the other?

Ephraim picked up the suitcase. A last glance about the room, then he closed the door behind him. The stairs creaked as he descended. Mitzy, Frau Schenker's Siamese cat whom he was supposed to feed, scuttled past him in the hall and whined at the front door. Ephraim unlocked it and placed his hand on the handle. He opened it slowly and peeked out. The street was empty. The house next door had been reduced to rubble a week earlier. He shuddered. Why them and not him?

The cat slipped between his legs and out the door. He watched it climb onto a pile of debris, sniffing, searching for food.

Where was Rainer now? On the run, or facing a firing squad?

He stepped out onto the stoop and for the first time in years, he prayed. Only God knew what awaited him.

~

Ephraim pulled himself up and switched on the TV. It kept him from thinking and worrying. The Russians had interfered with the election? What next, he wondered. The world was increasingly mad. How did the new president imagine he'd govern if he quarrelled with his intelligence team?

That cohesion, that tight-knit camaraderie between the Gestapo and the SS and informants among the population, and the gradual dissemination of distrust was what had given the Nazis strength. This man obviously had a lot to learn if he thought running a government was on a par with running a private business. Still, he seemed strong and determined and tough times needed tough measures. At times, Ephraim wondered if he'd live long enough to see him govern. January seemed like a long way off. Not that it mattered anyway. Politics were all the same. What concerned him was his family fortune. The rest were minor details.

A flash of anger coupled with regret.

The wooden floorboards creaked under Mrs. Katz weight as she trundled down the corridor with his medicine and the tray.

"You've burned the toast again, Mrs. Katz. How often do I have to tell you I like it golden brown, not charred? It makes the apartment smell" Ephraim grumbled.

"I'll get you some more, Mr. Wolf." Mrs. Katz removed the silver toast rack and scuttled back down the passage to the kitchen.

Ephraim reached for his teacup. In the last few days, so much of the past had surfaced. In fact, it seemed clearer than what he'd eaten for lunch the day before.

"Here's fresh toast, Mr. Wolf. I hope it's alright this time."

He jolted and peered at the toast rack. It smelled like the toast of his childhood. He selected a slice and reached shakily for the silver butter dish. It was the wrong butter knife. Why hadn't she given him the mother of pearl one?

"Stupid woman," he muttered under his breath. The phone rang.

The strident ring continued.

"*Um Gottes will*, pick up Mrs. Katz. Can't you hear the damned phone ringing?" He croaked.

"I'm just getting there, Sir."

Ephraim shook his head and stared at the toast. That better be Carl on the line. "It's for you, Mr. Wolf."

"Who is it?" "Carl, Sir."

"Ah! Good. Give it to me." He laid down his napkin and reached for the receiver.

Chapter 43

Carl, Nikolaj and Hubert sat opposite Father Florian on the leather sofas in the library at the Angel House.

Carl was excited. What must it feel like to talk to someone you hadn't seen for three- quarters of a century?

Several rings resounded. Carl placed his hand over the phone and smiled at Father Florian. He was grateful to the priest for receiving him so promptly. "I have a surprise for you," he said.

"Oh?" Father Florian looked taken aback. "What do you mean?" "Someone you haven't spoken to in a while."

"Who are you talking about?"

"My Great-Uncle Ephraim, your childhood friend back in Germany." Carl said triumphantly.

"Ephraim?" Father Florian's face turned livid.

"Yes." Carl nodded. "Hi, Uncle Ephraim, I have someone here who wants to speak to you. Here," he said grinning and handing Father Florian the phone. "He's on the line."

"But—" Father Florian shook his head. Reluctantly he accepted the phone. Carl was disappointed. Father Florian's reaction was not what he'd expected. He'd been certain both he and Uncle Ephraim would be delighted to be reunited again after all these years. Maybe he'd been wrong?

"Hello? Hello? Who is it?" Silence.

"Hello?" Ephraim repeated. "Who is it? Damn it, speak!" "Florian von Heil."

"Florian. *Mein Gott!* After all these years."

What a godsend. Carl had come through after all.

"This is so unexpected. A gift from God." Ephraim exclaimed. "Or a poisoned chalice from hell."

Ephraim frowned. This was not the way a conversation with Florian was meant to go. "I don't know what you mean. This is an extraordinary coincidence," Ephraim said.

"Is it? When was anything ever anything but a well-thought out calculation where you're concerned?"

"Ah Florian, Florian. Let's not dwell on the past. Life has been good to us and set us once more on each other's paths." Ephraim scrambled to keep the conversation going. "I'm so glad my great-nephew has brought us back together."

"And is there a reason for that?"

"Carl is in Fribourg, thanks to you and our old friends the de Lourriels. At last we will recover what is rightfully ours. And you, Florian, can vouch for my family."

"Vouch for you? I'd vouch for the souls of your father and for Eli, but never for you." "I don't understand. What do you mean? They're dead and gone and any family fortune they may have left behind is mine!" He hissed.

"Then use it to pay the devil when you enter the gates of hell. It's too late for you, Ephraim. *Adieu."*

The phone went dead but Florian's words still resonated. Ephraim stared at it lying like a stunned rat in his palm.

It's too late for you.

What did he mean by "too late"?

Ephraim's hand shook. He felt suddenly sick and dizzy. It was all going too fast. This was not how it was supposed to pan out.

Ephraim blinked. His fingers shook so badly he could barely reach the packet of cigarettes in the breast pocket of his pajama top. He stared at the cold hard toast and pulled out a fag. It hung between his right index and middle finger. He inserted it with difficulty between his parched lips. Eli swam before him; his father's haggard face as he was hauled by two SS men to the truck on that dreadful day that had sealed all their fates. Rainer had said "just a scare." Eli's unconscious body, his head bumping down the steps of their home and being dragged and thrown like a sack of cement inside the truck… And the sound of the truck's engine, that sound that had haunted him for years as he'd watched it turn the corner at the end of the street through the rearview window of Rainer's staff car. He'd wrestled with doubt. He'd wanted so badly to believe. He'd told himself over and over it would work out as planned, and that in the end they'd thank him… Did Florian know? He stared at the Chagall before him on the wall. It had taken him nearly eighty years to get it back but he still felt empty-handed.

After Papa and Eli's arrest, he'd had no choice but to become a chameleon. He'd gone from charming *Bürgelicher* gentleman to Nazi party sympathizer, dropping a word in the ear of the right official about any Jewish family he knew was hidden someplace in the hopes of discovering Papa and Eli's whereabouts. Bayreuth and the Opera. Rainer loved the Baroque plotting and the politics between love and power.

Rainer played cat and mouse. He'd used the Chagall to taunt him. He was cunning. He must've sensed there was more to the painting of which Ephraim happened to be fond of.

The lighter shook. Ephraim flicked it. Once. Twice.

The war. Things had gotten worse and Hitler's hatred of Jews increased to complete fanaticism. Only Rainer's protection had saved him from being denounced and deported. He'd dyed his hair even blonder. Thank God for his mother's blue eyes. Eli could never have gotten away with it. Some nights he'd retched over the toilet bowel in the bathroom of the tiny apartment he'd rented in the Dachau Strasse — a name that later would haunt him. At times, he justified his actions and achieved some level of satisfaction knowing Rainer had chosen *him*. He was the favored one. But it was never long before the sick horror of what he'd done gripped him again. The drugs helped. For a few hours, the pills Rainer procured for him helped to ease his conscience. Rainer. The pills. The Chagall. They were all a part of the game; a waiting game; a game of subtle menaces and subtle threats delivered with a thin-lipped smile and cold blue eyes, eyes that turned icier as the years passed.

It's too late for you.

Yes he'd done things. Bad things. Things he preferred not to remember. Like the time he'd discovered where the Blum's were hidden. If only he'd turned the corner and pretended not to see Levi, hat pulled down over his eyes, crossing the street on that spring morning. But he had. And it was impossible to lie to Rainer. He could read him like a picture book.

For years, he'd justified what followed and swept it from his mind. He had to. He'd acted to survive. It was each man for himself. The Blums had an impressive art collection. Almost as impressive as theirs. If he hadn't said the word, someone else would have. They would have been caught in the end anyway. He was persuaded of that. For nigh on eighty years, he'd convinced himself that he'd acted out of necessity. At times, he'd even forgotten, until he found that chilling cartoon in the back of the Chagall.

He thought of the switchblade; flipping it open and slicing the back of the frame. It was all worth it, he hadn't lost his touch. He'd flicked that blade with the same ease and elegance he'd used in the past, the same way he lit his fags, the same way he disposed of a body; as easily as he had a cigarette butt, and with utmost discretion. His father and Eli's arrest was not his fault, but theirs. They'd brought it upon themselves. If only they'd trusted him. If only they'd told him where they'd hidden the money and what the code was.

It's too late for you.

Chapter 44

"I will not, I cannot condone!" The elderly priest's words echoed like shots through the library. His face was livid. What had Uncle Ephraim said to cause this reaction?

Carl stood next to him holding the phone, which he hung up so abruptly seconds earlier. He exchanged a questioning glance with Nikolaj and Hubert, seated opposite Father Florina's armchair on the leather couch, uncertain what to do. In the end, he sat down on a chair to the right of Father Florian, enveloped in shadows, as the afternoon turned to dusk, and waited.

Something had gone terribly wrong. But what?

At last, Father Florian cleared his throat and looked up. "Could one of you turn the lights on, please?"

Nikolaj jumped up and switched the chandelier on. Tomes of leather-bound books came to life. Father Florina's bed stood in the corner. On the nightstand was an oxygen mask and a tray of pills.

"Would you like some water?" Carl ventured. "Yes, please."

Carl rose and fetched the glass and handed it to him carefully. The old man's hands shook. His fingers were ice cold.

Carl glanced at Nikolaj and Hubert once more. Neither dared break the silence. Father Florian sipped, then cleared his throat.

"I am sad for what has occurred here today, but I am sorry, young man," he said turning to Carl. "You do not deserve to be caught up in the trials and tribulations of the past. *Hélas*, there is no escape. Each of us must face the truth at some point in our lives. There is a day of reckoning for each of us, and today is Ephraim's."

"Excuse me, I'm afraid I don't understand," Carl murmured.

"I know," Father Florian nodded. And sadly, it is my duty to enlighten you. Sit down please, and bear with me while I take you back to a day long ago, a day I would rather not remember; a day that God and not I, must be the judge of…

~

The lights in Hans, the keeper's cottage, were on as Florian's beetle chugged through the gates and up the wooded driveway and came to a halt before the steps leading up to the oak doors of the Schloss.

His hand shook as he withdrew the key out of the ignition. He sat several minutes in darkness. But there was not time to waste. He must go.

Inside the Great Hall, candelabras cast shadows on the oriental rug and the Gothic arches and a fire roared in the massive stone hearth. How could everything — the baroque paintings, stag heads, coats of arms and spears — look the same when Eli and Aaron were likely cast in some awful cell, or worse, at Gestapo headquarters? There were increasing rumors of torture. Executions. Nobody knew what happened to those who disappeared and few returned to tell the tale. Nobody spoke of it. People preferred to remain silent, pretend that nothing had changed and that life continued in the same comfortable vein that it always had.

Benedict the butler entered the hall via a baize door.

"Good evening *Herr* Florian." The stooped old man helped him remove his laden overcoat.

"*Danke*, Benedict. *Wo ist Vater*?" He asked. "*Herr* Baron is in his study, *Herr* Florian."

Hoisting the hem of his habit, Florian mounted the stairs two at a time, then hurried down the gallery, past his Ancestor's portraits and suits of armor and towards his father's study in the turret at the end of the East wing. He stopped before the oak-paneled door to catch his breath. How often has he stood here preparing to tell his father something he'd rather not? Often. But never anything as bad as this.

He knocked. "*Kommen sie rein.*"

Florian turned the handle and stepped inside the hexagonal turret. Bookcases lined the walls from floor to ceiling; trophies, knick-knacks and foreign treasures brought home by the Baron and generations of ancestors vied for space on the crammed shelves. A fire crackled in the grate and the damask curtains were drawn.

The Baron looked up from behind the desk on the far side of the room, and laid down his pen, his fine hands etched in the aureole of the desk lamp.

"Come in my son," he smiled and capped his fountain pen. "What brings you back to Heil so quickly? I thought you were staying in Munich with the Wolfs for a few days."

Florian opened his mouth to speak but no words come out.

Baron von Heil frowned. "Is something the matter Florian? You look dreadful. He rose and came out from behind the desk. "Come and sit by the fire."

Florian stood in the center of the turret. He stared at his father, then dropped onto the leather couch next to the hearth and peered into the flames. His hands shook. His throat ached.

"Something terrible has happened," he whispered at last. "*Was ist passiert?* Tell me."

"It was awful," Florian muttered as he took the cigarette his father tended him. "I was approaching the Wolf's villa to give Eli the key to the cellar. I forgot to give it to him the other day after we stashed the paintings in the hidden cellar.

"Go on,"

"I'd just turned onto the street when a Gestapo car and a truck full of SS men pulled up outside their house and men poured out the back. A staff car halted a little further down the street. I could distinguish two men in the back. After a minute or so, an officer got out and headed up to the Wolf's front door. He looked familiar. There were SS men running around everywhere. I didn't know what to do, so I hid among the trees inside the gates of the villa on the opposite side of the street. A few minutes — maybe ten or so later — the front door flew open again and SS men came out of the house." Florian shook his head and swallowed. "*Vater*, they were pushing Aaron down the steps and dragging poor Eli by his ankles as if he was a corpse. His head was banging on the steps. I don't know if he was alive or dead."

"*Mein Gott!*" The Baron stood straight as a rod, his fist clenched, his face livid.

"They pushed them into the truck. Once it drove off, I hurried down the street, but stayed in the shadows. I wanted to see who was in the office's car on the curb—" he broke off, unable to continue.

"Go on."

"*Vater*, you will not believe who was inside—"

"Ephraim?"

"How can you possibly know that?" Florian stared at his father in horror.

"My sources tell me he is carrying on a liaison with Rainer Lanzberg, the rising star in the SS," he said bitterly.

"But how can that be? *Vater* I must tell you something. Karina and Eli were married only last week, here in the chapel."

"Married? How so? Who performed the ceremony?"

"I did."

"I see." Baron von Heil remained silent for several seconds. "So you took your final vows after all.

"Yes, *Vater*. I was going to tell you, but with so much going on, I didn't have the chance.

Nonno and Mama acted as witness. I'm sorry. But I had to do it."

"Never mind. You were probably right. All that matters now is that we find a way to rescue Eli and Aaron and discover where Karina is and make sure that she's safe. I'll make some calls immediately and see what I can find out. Meanwhile, we must carry on as if nothing has happened. Nothing. Is that understood? You won't do them any good by talking about it. Quite the opposite. We must also make sure Aaron's wishes are carried out. He and I have discussed what to do if something like this happened. He made it clear to me that his primary concern was for Eli and the collection. At least the pictures are safe and hidden in the cellars. They're impregnable. Perhaps Eli forgetting the key with you was meant to be."

"Who gives a damn about the paintings, *Vater*? Surely it's them we should be concerned about?"

"Florian, my boy. It will not help either Aaron or Eli if we rush in like bulls in a china shop. These are tricky times. By acting rashly or too hastily, we would merely close doors that need to remain open if we are to help them and not put ourselves uselessly at risk. This must be done in a subtle manner. Up until now, I have kept all doors — even to those sympathizers of the present regime — open, for precisely that purpose. I will make enquiries. In the meantime, you must leave at once for Switzerland with Aaron's cash and gold. We must shift the pictures in to the inner sanctum of the hidden cellar. Only you, Aaron, Eli and I know of its existence. And *Nonno* and Old Lucio of course."

"Are you certain Lucio is trustworthy? I've never understood why you and he are so close."

"Our families go back a long way. In fact, it's said that we're related and that his grandfather was the bastard son of my Great-Grandfather Umberto di Copertania. Nonno sent him from his estates in Puglia when your mother and I married. Lucio's father had problems at the turn of the century when the Mafia became powerful. That was the reason your grandfather sent him here. His own brother was sent to America where he has apparently become successful. Lucio's son was sent there at fourteen to join him. I believe he's become successful too. You will take his address with you when you go to Switzerland in case. You never know, we made need those contacts in the future."

"Yes. Fine," Florian said impatiently. "But Eli and Uncle Aaron will be freed, won't they, father?' Florian looked his father straight in the eye. The Baron remained silent. He picked up a hunting knife from among the art books on the low-slung coffee table, passed his right index over the sharp blade, then then laid it carefully back down in the same spot.

"In these dark times I can guarantee nothing, but I give you my solemn promise. I will move heaven and earth and everything in my power to do so," he said at last. "Now listen carefully, Florian. I will arrange for you to travel to Switzerland with Cardinal von Armin. Officially, he is going to accompany the acquisition of the Château d'Hauterive, the property that Jean de Lourriel has found for the *Verba Divina di Roma*. It will be a seminary for young priests like you, and you will go as part of his retinue."

"Very well. But you'll make sure Karina is safe won't you *Vater*? She may not even know about Eli's arrest. There was no sign of her there when I left."

"If Rainer Lanzberg gets a whiff of his sister's marriage, then he will either kill her or use it to blackmail her. They are pitiless, Florian. And possessed. They believe themselves to be the master race. All complete folly," the Baron exclaimed bitterly. "Each day I ask myself how it is possible such things can be taking place in the land that gave birth to Schiller and Goethe."

"And now go my son and prepare." "Must I?" Florian pleaded.

"Trust me," the Baron replied. "It is for the best."

Florian rose and nodded. There was nothing else to do but obey. The Baron gripped Florian's shoulder and led him to the door. "Tell *Nonno* I need to speak to him at once."

"Yes, *Vater*."

"And remember, Florian. You descend from men of honor. You are a German, not a Nazi."

~

"Forgive me," Father Florian muttered. "I had no choice."

Carl nodded. He rose, brushed the tears from his cheeks and descended the stairs in silence. It was dark outside and the wind blew. Somewhere an owl hooted. Tree trunks stood etched like gibbets — their bare branches protruding like gallows. Shadows resembling dangling bodies with lolling heads and their tongues hanging out.

And Eli's cartoon face grinning like a carnival mask.

Chapter 45

Up until recently, destiny and fate were peripheral concepts for Carl. He considered himself a man of reason, of thought. A Cartesian.

I think, therefore I am.

But he'd thought and believed he *was*… . And today he'd discovered he was *not*. His hard drive was stacked with wrong information. Reality was no more real than the warped imagination that created it, a convenient *assemblage* of testimonies, picked, then fermented in time-tested barrels; matured and packaged in fine bottles, selected and labeled, tasted and approved; poured into long stemmed crystal and accepted as a fine vintage.

Ephraim was a lie. He'd poured a lifetime of fine vintage lies into his small boy's ears. And Carl had drunk from that cup down to the last drop, never questioning the content, setting aside incoherences, never admitting the bottle might be corked or the bouquet tainted. He never questioned when details altered in the stories Uncle Ephraim repeated; it was so long ago, how could he possibly remember everything? Carl's father was more sanguine and skeptical of the old European uncle with his quirks and mannerisms who turned up his nose at them, yet had made Carl his protégé. All the more reason for him to feel protective of his uncle; he too knew what it felt like to be misunderstood.

For a moment during that afternoon's revelations, Carl had hated Father Florian for twirling his swizzle stick of truths and taking the fizz and sparkle out of his flute of beliefs. What did it matter anyway? Then all at once, the priest's voice penetrated the jumble inside his brain. His shield dropped and the words stabbed. Each syllable plunged the dagger of betrayal deeper and deeper until his heart lay open and exposed, a gaping wound; his spirit shrunk, his soul a squashed pile of corroded scrap metal.

It was over; the Machiavellian twists and turns of Ephraim's warped imagination lay like smashed smithereens; fragments of exhumed mummies turned to dust at the first breath of air exuding the trapped putrid gases of truth, a poisoned atmosphere that ensured the quick demise of meddlers, fool enough to turn a deaf ear to the clamoring gods…

Carl's existence lay in tatters. He'd accused Carolina, rubbed Luna's nose in what he'd believed to be her adoptive mother's crimes, and had jumped to conclusions, never verifying or questioning his source. He too had conformed to outdated standards. He too had bowed to the dictates of appearances. But hers were real and his were props. He loathed himself for having given up his dreams, rejecting who he was at heart, refusing his sexual orientation and pretending to despise the very people he wanted to espouse. Was he just like Ephraim? A false witness, a coward? A traitor?

Carl rose from the bed. If Aaron's spirit was present as Luna suggested, would he forgive him? He moved shakily over to the window. He opened it and leaned on the icy sill. He must breath. Flesh out the anger, inhale cold, clean night air. Would it help cleanse his soul?

Christmas lights sparkled in the street. Bells called the faithful to prayer. What had Aaron felt like being a Jew among so many Catholics? Did a generation wanting to shed the carnage of four years of hopelessness and senseless killing, care about such things? Perhaps the rule of law, philosophy, cheese fondue and white wine shared with friends at the Café du Gothard where Nikolaj had insisted on taking him to dinner the night before, was all that mattered. None of them, least of all Aaron, could have imagined he'd spawn a son who'd betray him or that tragedy born of evil would reach out and touch his descendant in this very room in years to come.

Snowflakes piled on the copper gutters like the shame accumulating inside him. How had he been so quick to turn judge and jury and condemn? Where had the liberal values he so prided himself upon disappeared to? He'd let venom and mistrust blind him. He'd scraped the coat of varnish that separated civilized men from brutes and let prejudice and bigotry seep into his psyche like termites into ancient beams. The ease with which he'd toppled frightened him. How easily one event and one voice could sway the tide, stoke the fears and whip up waves of righteous indignation, sowing the seeds of mistrust that justified the unjustifiable and sweeping aside civil liberties, all the while forgetting to look back. The radical beliefs spreading their tentacles out across the planet once more endangered rights conquered at great cost. Lately, words hushed for over half a century were echoing once more, like the bark of wild dogs, from the depths of forgotten forests.

Carl closed the window. He wished he didn't have to, but he must go home. He must face the devil in his lair. He must try and listen, attempt to understand what it meant to be gay in a world where a gesture between two men construed to be degenerate could get you labeled with a pink triangle imprisoned without trial, tortured and murdered. He and his generation and those that came after him had forgotten that a century earlier, the world was a different place. Surely he must fight to make sure those unalienable rights remained exactly that: unalienable?

Carl picked up his roll-on and placed it on Aaron's bed. He'd go back. He'd clean up the mess. He'd defend Aaron's honor. He understood it was not Uncle Ephraim's relationship with Rainer which Father Florian deplored, but his betrayal; the collaborator, the kapo. Uncle Ephraim was a war criminal who'd committed crimes against humanity. That was what was on trial here.

Carl's fingers shook as he removed a bath towel from the wooden towel horse and trod down the creaking corridor to the old fashioned, white tiled bathroom. He doubted it looked any different to when Aaron last showered here. He lay the towel down carefully on a chair and looked at the tub. What was Aaron thinking about when he last stepped inside it? A girl? His future? What he'd do once he finished his degree and returned to Munich and took over the family business?

Carl glanced up at the rusty shower-head then turned on the taps and waited for the water to heat. Steam gathered. Rivulets ran down the tile walls. Carl stood beside the tub. He coughed and spluttered. All at once, the white air seeping from the ceiling turned to gas and panic rose. Screams filled his ears. Nails clawed the tiles then slithered down among naked bodies, terror filled eyes and despair. Carl gasped.

He could see the face of the bored SS guard pumping the gas through the pipes. He tried to reach the slippery taps. His fingers trembled and he couldn't twist them.

At last he managed to turn them off and sat trembling on the edge of the tub. Had they pumped enough gas to kill Aaron and Eli quickly? He'd read of cases where, in their haste to get the job done and in the interest of economy, the Nazis turned the taps off too soon and threw the bodies into the ovens still alive.

He couldn't stop shaking. He leaned over the toilet bowl and retched as he had behind the shed in Dachau. Then, clutching the basin, he rose. It was time to leave all this behind. He leaned across the tub once more and turned the water back on harder this time. Carefully he stepped inside the tub and grabbed a bar of soap and scrubbed and scrubbed. He scrubbed himself until his skin hurt. He must cleanse himself of the ghosts wrenching him from the present.

Carl stepped out of the shower. He dried himself. The face staring at him from mirror was one he'd not seen for many years. Was he back, at last?

He needed a shave. He must pack. He must get to the station and catch a train to Zurich then a flight out to New York tonight.

Father Florian was right. The day of reckoning was upon them. It was time to go home back to himself.

Chapter 46

The keys squeaked in the lock. He'd meant to call a locksmith weeks ago, but with all that was going on, he'd forgotten. Carl pushed harder. Finally, the lock gave way and the door of Uncle Ephraim's apartment opened. Maybe it just needed oiling. Either way, he'd have to see about it.

The apartment was pitch black and smelled of charred toast. Uncle Ephraim must be sleeping for the place was silent. Perhaps he'd told Mrs. Katz he planned to stay in bed and not to leave the lights on before she'd left. He could be stingy about things like electricity. Old habits die hard?

He switched on the hall light and removed his coat. Ever since leaving Fribourg, he'd thought about how he would confront his great-uncle. Would he have the nerve? Could he stand up to evil when confronted with it face to face? What would it be like to see him through a different lens?

Carl switched on the corridor light as well and headed towards the bedroom. He needed light. Bright light. A torch to pinpoint the filth left hiding in the corners.

He opened the door of the bedroom softly. He tip-toed over to the bed. It was empty. He turned and hurried back towards the living room, worried. It too was in darkness.

Something wasn't right. Carl switched on more lights. The living room chandeliers blazed. Mrs. Katz must've cleaned the crystals.

"Uncle Ephraim?" Silence.

The room was freezing. The curtains fluttered. He hurried over and closed the window. A scratching sound. He recognized the needle on the old gramophone. The cat ran between his legs meowing.

Carl flicked on the nearest lamp. The old man was asleep in his wheelchair. Or was he? Carl rushed towards the figure propped in the chair, head tilted against the tapestried cushion.

"Oh Jesus." He grabbed Ephraim's pulse. Nothing. He listened, but no breath came. "Uncle Ephraim, wake up."

Uncle Ephraim's face looked strangely calm and more peaceful than he'd ever seen it. The features were smooth and the lines on his forehead and around his eyes had disappeared. The tension was gone.

Carl knew at once that Uncle Ephraim was dead. A heart attack?

Carl frowned. There were traces of powder on Ephraim's thin greyish lips. He peered closer and experienced a pounding inside his chest like a heard of buffalo surging towards water. He crouched and steadied himself on the arm of the wheelchair, his face close to Uncle

Ephraim's whose hands drooped on the cashmere throw. A signet ring lay in its folds. Carl reached for it. The top was loose. Inside the gold cavity were traces of powder. He sniffed.

"Oh my God," he muttered. "Oh my God..."

Still holding the ring, he slipped to his knees. Tears choked him. Where had he gotten the poison to commit suicide? Anguish, anger. Carl laid his head in his great-uncle's lap and stared through his tears at the ring clutched in his right palm. Would the remains of the powder be enough to send him over to the other side too?

He tried to breathe. His asthma spray was in his coat pocket. He struggled to his feet. He must remove the ring and all traces from Uncle Ephraim's lips. No one must know about this. The needle on the gramophone scratched. It was driving him mad. He raised it and clutching the ring in his left fist, Carl placed the needle back on the record.

Maria Callas' voice filled the room. Only Callas, Uncle Ephraim insisted, only Callas...

Carl dropped slowly to his knees on the Persian rug next to the gramophone in the same spot he'd sat when La Callas' voice had conquered him one bright spring morning, long ago. He lifted the record cover and stared into the tragic eyes, the cat-like sixties black eyeliner of the woman whose soul had conquered his; as it had when he was seven years-old. The purity and enchantment of her voice helped him breathe.

… *O mio Babbino Caro.*

He reached for Uncle Ephraim's hand. A cold hand. The hand that had conducted the symphony of his life until now. It was better so. But he would miss him. Lies… truths… It didn't matter anymore.

… *O Dio vorei morir.* His shoulders shook. It was all over.

Chapter 47

"Luna... Luna wake up."

Tia Bella's voiced reached her, and the pile of used syringes strewn among the rumpled sheets, faded. Luna opened her eyes. She'd fallen asleep on the couch in Tia Bella's suite at the Baur au Lac. In the past 48 hours, Nana had gone from Carolina Orlowska the Countess, to Karina Lanzberg the Nazi, to Ina the brave resistant. It was a long road to travel in such a short time span.

"I'm sorry. I fell asleep." She struggled up.

"You were screaming, dear child. Are you alright?"

"I'm sorry I disturbed you. I must have had a nightmare. It happens all the time." "Do you remember the dream?"

Tia Bella switched on the lamp and sat next to her and took her hands in hers. Her soft warm palms brought tears to Luna's eyes. She shook her head.

"Yes and no. It's always the same one. The words of an album. I've heard it since I was little. Jeff played it one day and I asked him what it was and he told me it was *The Dark Side of the Moon* by Pink Floyd. That was the first time we—" She cut off. "Never mind." Luna rubbed her eyes and sat up.

"Dreams are significant, Luna. They are the insight into our soul. Tell me about it."

"It's muddled. In the dream, I'm running from someone who wants to catch me. And the tunes from *The Dark Side of the Moon* repeat louder and louder in my head. It happens when I'm awake sometimes too. But then it goes away — sometimes for months. And then one day, boom! It's back, haunting me again. I don't know why, but I have the impression that maybe the dream is related to my mother — whoever she was. Sometimes I hear a woman calling my name and I think it might be her."

Tia Bella's arms folded around her. She hesitated. "Luna, try not to be upset by what I'm about to tell you." "Tell me what?"

"Charlotte — Ina's daughter — was your real mother."

The words resonated like cymbals in a symphony; a bugle call, a medieval town crier shouting an announcement: *The King is dead. Long live the King.* Charlotte — a ghost, a refuted spirit — cut off from their lives like an amputated limb. A gangrene-filled memory pitched into oblivion.

"Charlotte was my mother? But why did Nana never speak about her? It was as if she'd never existed. Surely she couldn't have been so awful that she'd deny her own daughter?"

"They were too alike. They never got along and once Charlotte fell into drugs, that was it. Henry buried himself in his work and Ina buried Charlotte as she had her past. Then one day the phone rang. It was the Miami Dade Police Department saying they had a little girl with Ina's phone number inside the child's jacket pocket."

"Me?" Luna whispered. "Yes."

"What happened to Charlotte?" Her voice sounded monotone.

"She'd overdosed on heroine and died. Ina became obsessed. She thought if you knew the truth, sooner or later you would follow in Charlotte's footsteps. She was determined to protect you. She was so afraid for you. Afraid the fragile shell of security she built around herself could shatter. All she'd lived through left her scarred to a degree that was impossible to repair. She wanted your life to be perfect — a fairy tale — and that's what she replaced reality with."

"And what about my father? Where was he in all this?"

"They never found out who he was. I don't believe they tried. Carolina and Henry adopted you legally in case there was ever any claim."

"And was there ever?"

"No, my dear. It's quite likely he never knew Charlotte was pregnant. By that stage she was far gone."

Words caught in her throat. Luna rose and moved close to the window. The Christmas lights in the trees in the hotel gardens flickered on and off. A hailstorm of images showered. Luna running as fast as her little legs could carry her; a gramophone; a woman's voice; arms folded around her and holding her close.

Tia Bella and Luna talked until midnight. Things Luna never understood lined up like cherries on a slot machine. Would knowing who her mother was change her life? Could she come to terms with a mother who'd gone off the beaten track? What was she to do now?

"… what lies before you is an opportunity," Tia Bella said. "A chance to start over, to discover who you are and be yourself. It's time to let go of the past. Let go of Ina's *Sac à Dépèches* full of useless regrets. They are hers, not yours. Get yourself a new purse and a new laptop to write those books you told me about. It's time to go down your own road. It's never too late to start over. I'll tell you little secret," Tia Bella continued. "Stop living chronologically. By that I mean, stop splitting life into sections according to age and status. Don't deprive yourself of the wonderful adventure which constitutes the whole. Learn to live anachronistically."

"Anachronistically?" Luna murmured." I don't think I know that word."

"Likely not, since I invented it. Or maybe someone else did. It doesn't matter. It's about living in the past, present and future all at once. Play, rewind and fast-forward together in sync. Will this moment we are experiencing be any less real to you in ten years time? Align yourself in the *whole,* my dearest Luna. Feel. Listen. Hear the Universe and defy chronology as we know it. Delve into oneness, a space that is not parceled up in lots according to age, rank, color or beliefs but rather, the sum of all parts."

Luna reached for a box of matches. She lit one and held it to the wick of a candle in a silver holder on the coffee table next to the couch. The flame flickered, like her, it was uncertain whether it would stay alight and shine, or go out. Tia Bella seemed so certain of her words. She sat down next to her on the couch. Tia Bella reached out and took her hand in hers. Could she ever let go the past and build a life in the now? She wouldn't know where to begin.

Strains of a piano echoed. Likely there was a pianist in the restaurant. "Do you hear that?" She asked.

Tia Bella tilted her head and listened. "Yes, I believe I hear what you hear," she nodded. "That was Nana's favorite song," Luna whispered.

"I remember. Eli played it on the piano in the Great Hall at Schloss Heil that last Saint Hubertus."

"*Look for the Silver Lining*. Isn't that a cliché?"

"We should give clichés more credit," Tia Bella smiled. "Silver linings are definitely worth the time it takes to find them."

Chapter 48

It was over. Uncle Ephraim was gone but the shadows remained.

Carl replaced the needle on the vinyl record and sat on the tapestried cushions of the window seat in the Brooklyn apartment and let Maria Callas transport him back to the Borghausen Park villa; an island in the midst of the 1930s darkness, the timeless universe of Uncle Ephraim's dreams where Carl had roamed, setting the bar to match a non-existent set of standards and by so doing renouncing his own chance of happiness. Had he bartered his soul? Was he a 21st century Faust? Or a boy caught in a snowdrift where past and present avalanched into an amalgam of ownerless images, like bits of fruit swirling in the blender of collective consciousness.

And now it was over and there was only he, Carl — who he was trying so hard to reconnect with after all these years — and Ephraim's ghost to vent his feelings to. He peered through the open doors into the dining room. The cat leaped off the wheelchair and scuttled across the rug. Mrs. Katz had left the table laid; the silver toast rack, the black cherry jam, and on the wall above the sideboard hung *The Girl in The Red Dress Under the Moon* that Uncle Ephraim must have brought it out of the bedroom and returned to the same position it had occupied in his childhood. Yet, like so much in Uncle Ephraim's life, it too, was a brilliantly executed fake.

And then there was Rainer Lanzberg who'd likely died comfortably in his bed years ago. What karma had connected those two in a Third Reich swept by bigotry and fanaticism? Which of them was more wicked? Rainer the Nazi for losing all sense of humanity and adhering to the dictates of the time? Or Ephraim who'd betrayed his own and condemned others to save his skin and fulfill the wishes of a blackmailer whom he'd wanted to believe would save them? Would Rainer have stuck to his bargain and merely questioned Eli and Aaron and let them go if Karina and Eli's marriage hadn't jeopardized his existence? It was easy to sit here and be judge and jury. Was Father Florian's version of the story real or were more layers waiting to be stripped to uncover more light, more dark, more hidden love and betrayal?

Forgiveness.

Forget *them.* What about him, Carl? Would he ever forgive himself and come to terms for living in a fool's paradise? In the aftermath, it was all so obvious, so clear — the final piece of sky in the puzzle that connected the entire picture. Had Luna felt the same way when she saw the newspaper clipping? They'd both experienced parallel time-lines running side by side until the signal altered and the tracks changed and the trains crashed head-on; carriages of lies derailed and an eighty-year-old-passenger named *Truth* catapulted from a moth-eaten velvet seat to explode among them.

Little by little the street returned: holiday decorations, lights, a woman wrapped in an ethnic poncho, hair streaming from a red woolen beanie and weighed down with shopping bags bursting with gifts. Where would he spend the holidays? Mrs. Katz asked him that this morning. Poor woman. She seemed lost without old Ephraim's haranguing. He must give her a bonus. She deserved it.

Carl rose. It was time to go. He glanced at his Smartphone. Two messages: one from Luna and the other from Rick Marchese — the man he hoped to hand Luna's affairs over to.

Carl took a last look at the lost world he'd stepped inside years before, soon to be dismantled piece by piece, boxed and left to gather dust in a storage unit or peddled in a flea market. The ghosts, the scents, the treasures and the dreams and the familiar scent of belonging he'd experienced each time he'd entered this space, would be gone forever. Could he leave it all behind and step into the future?

He stepped into the hall and opened the armoire. Uncle Ephraim's cashmere coat and silk scarf hung there. He hesitated, then slipped his own coat on. He touched the silver nob of the cane in the umbrella stand, then pulled open the front door. It creaked as it had the first time Uncle Ephraim opened it drew him in.

Carl turned. Uncle Ephraim was reaching for the toast. He looked up. He waved. Carl slammed the door shut and shivered.

Chapter 49

"How was Maria when you arrived?" Luna asked. "About as warm as January in Spitsbergen, Norway." Carl replied. "I told her the incident in Nana's closet was a misunderstanding." "I guess she didn't buy it."

"Never mind. She'll get over it. Are you still one hundred percent sure you want to quit,

Carl?"

"I have to."

"I know. But I wish you'd stay. But listen, that's not why I called. I have news." "Shoot." Carl said.

Despite its prestigious location and modern architectural design, Rick Marchese's corner office looking out over Central Park retained the same sense of intimacy as did Henry's study; bookshelves, a bronze Remington statuette serving as a paper weight on a pile of documents on the left of Rick's long glass desk, and several fine paintings on the walls.

Carl and Rick sat across from one another. Except for some gray at the temples and a few facial lines, Rick hadn't changed. And as always, he'd taken time out of his busy schedule at short notice to receive Carl, and seemed genuinely pleased.

Carl remained silent and gave his former college pal time for his words to sink in. He'd made the right choice when choosing Rick to manage Luna's affairs.

In truth, Rick represented everything Carl wished he was: successful and charismatic; a man who wore his good looks and self-confidence with ease like an old cashmere sweater with no self-consciousness or pretension.

Carl had never understood why a popular man like Rick with his good grades, his sports trophies and following of debutantes had bothered to befriend an outsider like him. In college, like every other area of his life, Carl made few friends. But although they weren't close, he and Rick stayed in touch. Once every two or three years they lunched together at the Harvard Club; Rick hopping from one success to another, while Carl remained stuck in the spot he'd allotted himself on the periphery of the Hampton's and Uncle Ephraim's worlds, a place he liked to think he mattered. How foolish of him to believe he could get by like a blinkered horse, with no lateral vision.

But in the end, it boiled down to this: if he was

to have any chance rebuilding his life, he needed time away to think out the next step. Since Uncle Ephraim's suicide, he'd realized he must break with the past. And the future beckoned, brighter than it ever had. He and Gunnar exchanged several messages now. He had no idea how it would end but he was ready to live whatever they were destined to share.

He turned his attention back to Rick. Rick wasn't a blue blood either. He was third generation Italian. He had come to Harvard Law after a stint in the Marines, was elected president of the Debate Club and after graduating went on to create a successful law firm and hedge fund that had put him on the Forbes list. He'd sold it at the right time and now had a family office. At 39, Rick had it made. He managed business ventures favoring climate change, advocating human rights and other causes. He'd make a good consigliere. Henry would approve. In fact, there was something in Rick's manner that reminded him of his late boss. He hoped he'd accept to take on the task.

Rick Marchese sat across from Carl on the leather couch and digested the amazing story his old college friend had just poured out. It explained a lot. It filled in the blanks he'd never understood about Carl Wolf. Now he knew why Carl had not pursued a brilliant career and chosen instead to take care of the Hampton family's affairs. At the time, it had struck him as strange that someone so talented would opt for something with so little challenge.

He'd also wondered why Carl denied being gay. But he'd accepted his friend, hoping one day he'd come to terms with the man he sensed lived in deep conflict beneath the urbane surface. Now he knew.

The story read like a novel; a past that had reached out and affected so many lives. Would votes and decisions taken today determine the destiny of his own great-grandchildren some day? Right now, Rick footloose and fancy-free and planned to remain so. But *Nonna*, his Italian grandmother, complained at breakfast every morning that she was destined to die without great-grandchildren.

"So what's your plan?" He asked at last.

"I'm not sure. Take some time off, I guess. Rethink my life. Live. Which is why I'd like your office to take over the Hampton Trust and Luna's affairs. Will you do it?"

Rick hesitated. He was up to his eyeballs working eighty-hour weeks right now, but Carl looked at the end of his tether. How could he refuse? Plus, the story Carl told intrigued him.

"Will you pick up the ball for me, Rick? At least for now?" Carl insisted. "Sure. I'll do it."

"Thanks. I knew I could count on you." "I'll need all the files though."

"Most of them are still in Henry Hampton's study."

The phone on Rick's desk vibrated. He rose. "Excuse me, I need to take that." He stepped across the room and picked up.

"Manny. How are you? Really? Go ahead."

Carl watched Rick jot something down on a pad. Already he felt a weight off his shoulders.

Rick hung up and turned.

"This is fucking amazing," he said. "Remember you sent me a receipt for a Chagall that belonged to Henry Hampton and asked if I could research art dealers in Buenos Aires?"

"Of course I remember. Why? Did you find something?"

"Well, Manny Alonso's colleagues in Buenos Aires have just identified a Reinaldo Monteflecha. He's an elderly private art collector who lives as a recluse in an upscale residential neighborhood of Palermo in a villa he bought shortly after WWII. Seems he has a bunch of blond-blue-eyed bodyguards surrounding the place. He was closely tied to the Military junta and before that with the Peron government. Nobody knows where he came from but it doesn't take a rocket scientist to figure that out. Plus, here's the kicker," Rick paused.

"Yes?" Carl sat up straighter.

"Reinaldo and Rainer are pretty similar names, right? Monte, in Spanish translates to *berg* in German and *flecha* translates to arrow in Spanish and in German is *lanz.* Reinaldo Monteflecha equals Rainer Lanzberg."

"Holy shit! The motherfucker's still alive?" "And kicking."

"So, how do we get to him?" Carl jumped up. "Arrest him? An international arrest- warrant? There's no prescription for war crimes, is there?" Carl's excitement grew.

"No. But it's not that easy. He's covered his tracks and according to Manny, he has friends in high places. We'll have to find a way of getting to him. He has a private secretary, a guy called Claus von Stossberg who's of German descent. Manny's figuring out a strategy.

Apparently, aside from his closest circle, he doesn't let anyone inside the villa, and he's not one hundred percent trustworthy. It'll be tough. He's pretty impregnable."

"Why not just advise the authorities and have him arrested?" Carl exclaimed. "It's too risky."

"Why?"

"You can be sure he has a contingency plan figured out. They need a good excuse to get inside his villa."

"Okay," Carl nodded. "But even if they got in, what then?" "Manny has friends in Buenos Aires."

"What do you mean?"

"Friends whose ancestors were given a one-way ticket to Auschwitz. They'd be only too happy to lend a hand."

Carl rose and paced the office, clenching and unclenching his fists. He needed to get the bastard and have his day in court and avenge Aaron and Eli, Karina and even Uncle Ephraim.

"I have to go down there at once. I have to look this motherfucker in the eye and see him go down," he said pacing the office. "He tortured and murdered my family and God only knows how many others, Rick. He ruined our lives, he corrupted my great-uncle and destroyed us. He's responsible for some of the worst crimes in history and I want to be there when the truth hits that Nazi fuck between the eyeballs. Maybe there is a God after all. I'm going down there."

"Ok. But are you sure you want to do this, Carl? You said you were ready to let go of the past and move on with your life. Why not let Manny's people deal with it?"

"I can't," Carl shook his head. His hands felt hot and dry, his head feverish. "I must go, Rick. For Aaron, for Eli for Uncle Ephraim and all the others. Luna told me he even shot the priest's father, Baron von Heil, and his wife and father-in-law too. He even sent his own sister to Belsen." He shook his head and flopped back down on the couch. "No way am I missing out on seeing him in handcuffs if it's the last thing I do. After that, I'll start looking for closure. But not until I've seen justice done."

Chapter 50

Buenos Aires.

The Villa Solina, Rainer Lanzberg — alias Reinaldo Monteflecha's — luxurious home, sat in the heart of the upscale Buenos Aires district of Palermo. He'd bought it in the early 1950s for two reasons: one it was built in the German style popular in Argentina at the turn of the century and therefore reminded him of his family home in Sollin — the Munich neighborhood where he grew up and that he'd named the villa after — and secondly, the garden's lush vegetation ensured the privacy that he required. Except for his private secretary, Claus von Strossberg, the son of an old friend, he trusted no one. The Jews were still on the hunt for Nazis and he did not intend to end up tried for war crimes by some kangaroo court; a second Nuremberg, with *stücke* — things — as the Jews were named in the camps, condemning him from the front row.

Rainer reached Argentina in late 1945 and had made Buenos Aires his home. Which — considering the alternative — was not so bad. As the years went by he even considered it to be a blessing. Europe was in chaos. Soon Aryans would be a minority. The continent's misguided post-war governments should be ashamed. First, it was the Common Market. Then that turned into the European Union, which allowed all sorts of riff-raff to come and go freely between countries. How different things would have been had Germany won the War. Europe would have thrived — even dominated — the world under the aegis of Berlin. Proper values would have been instilled from the start. The British would have understood and at some point, an accord would have been struck and a man like Moseley elected as Prime minister. There would have been no silly nonsense, no syndicates, no communists, no French intellectuals, no Jews and anarchists sowing dissidence in the minds of the populace. In Rainer's view, the equipment from Auschwitz and the other camps could have been shipped directly to Africa and the Middle East and been put to good use. At the end of the day it was necessary to recognize that the only solution to the problems affecting world order was The Final Solution. How else could you ensure the world remained an Aryan society as God had intended?

Sadly, none of these dreams had materialized and Rainer was obliged to stay alert in the face of the enemy. In the days of the Peron government and the Military Junta, things were easier. A blind eye was turned. But now, Argentina was like the rest of the planet, run by foreigners and Jews. Even women. The entire world had turned into a Zionist complot. Hitler knew that. The old guard here had known it too. But they were dead for the most part and the younger generation was contaminated by globalization, the internet and God knows what other diabolical inventions the Zionists had come up with to dominate the world.

The salon of the Villa Solina was a large and somber room with heavy, dark wood furniture upholstered in faded velvet and brocade that had seen better days and looked out over the well-tended gardens. Centuries-old trees blocked out spying eyes from the balconies of the high-rise buildings that had popped up in the neighborhood over the past years. At first Rainer had opposed their construction, then he'd realized that they offered him an extra shield of anonymity and protection and had withdrawn his objections from city hall. Now the villa remained an island, shrouded by trees and hedges amid an ocean of concrete, marble and double-glazed glass.

"*Buenos dias*, Colonel."

"Ah. Claus. *Guten Morgen*. On time, as usual, I see." Rainer glanced at his wrist watch then rose stiffly from the heavy Biedermaier armchair and stood erect to greet the middle-aged man entering the room carrying a briefcase. His private secretary was one of the few men he allowed into his inner sanctum. Claus was of German descent. A man of few words, he kept his views to himself. But Rainer knew that his heart was in the right place. His family had all been good Nazis. Some had remained in Germany after the war, integrating into society without much trouble. Others had fled in a hurry and come to South America where they owned large tracts of land and made a new life.

"What have we today?" Rainer asked. Several slow steps led him to his desk in the far corner of the room. Exercise. That was the secret. And diet. Despite his ninety-six years, Rainer woke at 6am, showered and dressed alone, ate breakfast at 7am sharp in the lugubrious dining room swathed in read damask, and at 9am the trainer arrived to take him through a ritual of callisthenic exercises selected from a Third Reich book of physical movements that he'd discovered in a stall in the flea market in San Telmo, one Sunday morning many years ago, before he'd retreated into the lost world of the Villa Solina.

Rainer had known but one weakness during his long life; a weakness that could have cost him his life. In the early post war years relegating the past to the nether regions of his brain proved easy, but lately it crept up on him unawares, seeping through cracks of his memory, a pernicious enemy increasingly hard to track. There were days when he woke with blood on the marble floor and the horror of discovering his sister at the top of the stairs in the Wolf villa on the day he'd arrested Eli and Aaron. His action was easily justifiable. After all, he'd had no choice. It was he or them. Still, that horrible scream from the landing still rang in his head and the shock he'd sustained when Eli dash towards the stairs and he'd understood the truth about those two still haunted him. Again and again he'd relived that terrifying moment when his life hung in the balance. But God had intervened. Eli was intercepted by a storm trooper and hit hard across the temple with the butt of a rifle. Who knows what might have been Rainer's fate have the SS found out that it was *Oberst Sturmführer* Lanzberg's sister up there. He still experienced the rush of indescribable relief as Eli crumpled to the floor and blood oozed like crimson paint onto the black and white lozenges of the marble hall floor. It had taken him only two seconds to pull himself together and climb the stairs two at a time before the men realized anything was amiss. One word and his future — maybe even his life — would have been over. He'd stood behind Karina and pinched her so hard she nearly fainted. The sergeant had looked from one to the other. He'd frowned. Karina trembled. Seconds of tense silence followed. Then he'd commmanded the man to go back down to the hall and hurried dwon the stairs shouting out orders while Karina stared at him in disbelief.

At times he'd experienced a moment's regret for being obliged to keep Ephi — his one weakness — dangling. But he'd soon learned to stifle such feelings and erected a barrier between himself and the past. Still, at times he woke up in a cold sweat, suspicious: of the maid, of the gardeners trimming the trees, the dog walkers in the *Barrio* and ten years ago he'd imported two German shepherds trained by a special unit of the Bavarian police for drug enforcement, to protect the property at all times. You could never be too careful. You never knew what spies might be lurking in the bushes.

"As I mentioned last week, life is increasingly expensive," Claus was saying as he approaching the desk.

"Ah! Money. Probably the Jews are upping the interest rates and causing inflation as usual. They've been at it since Septimus Severus."

"It's the cost of living that's risen, Colonel."

"I know what you'll say next," Rainer sighed. "Another painting that must go?" "I'm afraid we don't have a choice," the secretary murmured.

"Which one had you in mind?"

Claus von Stossberg eyed his boss across the desk. His impeccably combed white hair was parted in a straight line to the left of his widow's peak and his razor never erred. The starched shirt collar stood erect and his tie was perfectly knotted. There was no room for slovenliness in the Colonel's world. He watched as the old man placed his silver nob skull-

and-cross bones cane against the desk then lowered himself slowly into the hard-backed chair.

Claus sat opposite and opened his briefcase. His fingers fumbled with the clasp. He would have given much not to be in the position he now found himself, but it was too late and he'd had been offered no choice.

"Well?"

"I've heard through the usual grapevine that there's a collector in the market for a Breughel."

"I see."

Claus wet his lips as his boss' eyes travelled to the wall next to the fireplace to the painting he'd squirreled out of Germany together with several others, including a Chagall that was sold to an American several years earlier. The sale, with the addition of brokering art for other Nazis who, like Lanzberg, had come to South America through the Vatican route and changed their names, had kept the boat afloat nicely up until now.

Claus watched the Colonel fight an inner battle. He loved the little Dutch figures skating on a lake that reminded him of his childhood trips to the Austrian mountains and his own prowess—which he'd mention to Claus several times —on the ice.

"Is there nothing else we could sell?" He enquired.
"Not of that caliber, I'm afraid," Claus said.

"What would it fetch?"

"Fifteen million dollars, I believe."

"Fifteen million dollars? *Mein Gott"* Rainer said,

taken aback. "I suppose it's a Jew?" "I don't think so. His name is Löwen."

"Ah! A good German name."

"Like your favorite Löwenbraü bier, *Colonel*," Claus said, allowing himself a rare touch of humor.

"True. True. In fact, it is almost time for my *Schoppe*."

Each day and at noon the butler served the Colonel a chilled beer in his stein beer mug. He barely sipped it these days. His digestion was not at its best. But Claus knew the sight of the beer mug took the old man back to pleasant afternoons spent in the Café Heck off Munich's Odeon Platz and lunches at the Osteria Bavaria, the Führer's favorite *Stamm* — local with his fellow officers.

"Are you sure there's really no other choice than to sell?"

"Not unless we downgrade your standard of living, or sold the villa," Claus said. "*Nein*! That is *ausgeschlossen*,"

Claus watched the Colonel drum the desk with his right index.

"I will die here, not in some paltry apartment with God only knows who for neighbors."

"Then I'm afraid—" Claus cut off and waited.

"*Verdammt noch mahl.* I hate to let it go but if that's the only choice, then so be it. That painting's given me much pleasure over the years. But I suppose like everything and everyone in life, there's a time to say goodbye."

"Yes, Colonel. There's just one little detail I should mention." "What's that?"

"The buyer wishes to inspect the painting and meet you first."

"*Warum*? Why would he want to do that for? Usually all contact is made through our intermediaries. I don't understand."

"I'm not certain why. It appears Herr Löwe always deals directly with the owner of any artwork he acquires. Perhaps he's an eccentric."

"Perhaps," Rainer mused. "Or perhaps he's just nosey. I'm not sure I can agree to such a condition."

"Then there's nothing more to be said. Apparently, this is the one condition that he never backs down from. It's a deal breaker." Claus replaced the papers he brought back in his briefcase and snapped it shut. He watched the Colonel hesitate and gave him space to think.

Having conditions imposed upon him went against the grain. Was he being overly cautious? The buyer was a German after all. He'd known some Löwen's in Sollin when he was young. They'd lived not far from his parent's home destroyed in the bombings in late '44. His mother and father and his golden retriever, Titus were killed. He should never have left the dog there. The animal's death still caused him pain.

"Very well," he said at last. "Where is this Herr Löwen?" "He's staying at the Alvear Palace."

"At least he knows what hotel to choose. Perhaps it's a good omen," he muttered. "When does he wish to come here?"

"Tomorrow morning, Colonel."

"Very well. If you insist."

"I'll transmit the message," Claus nodded.

Rainer rose. Now that he'd taken the decision to part with the Breughel it was clear he did not wish to dwell on the matter. He watched the old man rise slowly from behind the desk and stand for several moments by the open window. He did not allow air conditioning in the house.

Clause hurried forward and moved to open the French windows. All was going according to plan.

"It's a beautiful day," Rainer remarked stopping in his tracks. "It's spring, soon the heat will be here, Colonel."

"Yes. So it will."

Rainer lifted the monocle that hung on a ribbon around his neck and peered through the window at the cherry blossom. Back home, the *Bayerische wald* — his beloved Bavarian forest

must be russet and gold or covered in snow. If he closed his eyes he could smell the bonfires and winter just around the corner. Beyond the Villa's walls he detected the sound of traffic. Children's laughter filtered from the playground of the building to the left of the property. The noise irritated him.

"Colonel?"

Rainer turned back from the window. He leaned on his cane and steadied himself. He was still six foot two in his stiocking soles. He had not shrunk with age and his dark navy blazer fell as immaculately from his shoulders today as the black jacket of his SS uniform had years ago.

He glanced at the flat gold watch. Eli's watch. He'd worn it on his left wrist ever since he'd found it in Eli's belongings at Gestapo HQ later, on the day of the arrest. It kept good time.

"Where is Ramon with my beer?" He asked.

"He's about to serve it for you on the terrace, Colonel."

"*Sehr gut.* You will join me for lunch, Claus," Rainer ordered. "With pleasure, Colonel."

Rainer pulled back his shoulders and took a few slow steps towards the French door. He did not take a last look at the Breughel as he passed the fireplace. It had to go. That was that. He'd already eliminated it from his universe as he did most unpleasant matters. The thing was decided. *Schluss fertig.*

It was time to move on.

Chapter 51

Four days after his meeting with Rick in New York, Carl sat nervously in the back of the limo as it pulled up at the gatehouse of the Villa Sollina, hidden by lush vegetation in the upmarket Buenos Aires neighborhood of Palermo. The driver — an armed SWAT team officer

let his window down. He said a pleasant *buenos dias* and stated his business to the tall, blond, blue-eyed guard who grunted and peered suspiciously inside the vehicle for his passport. Carl's pulse quickened as he handed over the fake German document: Helmut Löwen from Frankfurt. The guard inspected it and phoned through to the house. Carl closed his eyes behind his Ray Ban sunglasses and prayed. Getting him inside the villa was an essential part of the arrest plan. Was his German good enough to carry off the role of Helmut Löwen, the art buyer? It had to be. At least for the few minutes it required Manny, the authorities and the police team waiting around the block to surround the Villa.

It must have been no more than a few seconds, but Carl's shirt was wet by the time the guard handed the passport back and waved them through the gates. As the car moved sedately into the drive, Eli and Aaron flashed before him. How long must a few seconds seem when you're being tortured?

The limo circled a fountain and drew up at the front door of a German style villa — an architectural style that, per Manny, was favored in South America at the turn of the last century. Lucky for Rainer Lanzberg, there were even mullioned windows and the semblance of a turret.

Carl took a deep breath and stepped out of the vehicle. Two men in dark suits stood by the door and a butler ushered him inside the foyer. There, a gray-haired man in a blazer and tie greeted him.

"Herr Löwen, welcome to the Villa Sollina. I am Claus von Stossberg, Herr Motnefelcha's private secretary. If you would kindly step this way?"

The two men shook hands. Carl noted a slight dampness of the palm. It was no wonder. The man was the mole on the inside who'd been "persuaded" to give up his boss.

Carl took in every detail of the foyer, the tropical plants, the fine Persian rugs, the paintings hanging on the dark wood paneled walls. The house was lugubriously elegant.

Claus von Stossberg stopped before a large door. Carl swallowed as he gave it a perfunctory knock, then opened it and stepped aside for him to enter.

"Herr Löwen," he announced.

Standing under the chandelier, with the sun at his back flooding the room and his right hand elegantly placed on the marble mantle of a fin de siècle fireplace, stood a tall, slim elderly man in a grey suit and tie with smooth white hair parted on the left and a monocle hanging on a ribbon around his neck. He raised it with his left hand as Carl entered.

"Ah! Herr Löwen, kommen sie rein." The erect figure moved slowly towards him. "How do you do, *wilkommen* to my modest abode."

"*Dankeshön*." Carl mustered every ounce of fortitude. It hadn't occurred to him that he'd be obliged to touch the hand of Aaron and Eli's murderer and Uncle Ephraim's lover. But there was no escape. A shiver ran through him as their hands met in a firm handshake.

Rainer Lanzberg indicated an armchair next to a small antique table covered in war decorations and other memorabilia, and invited him to sit. Carl sat on the stiff tapestried chair and watched his host — whose eyesight was evidently poor — feel his way to the armchair on the table's other side. A door at the far end of the room opened and a uniformed maid and butler entered with silver salvers. Carl watched von Stossberg leave the room. In a few minutes it would all be over, but for now it felt as though the curtain had risen and the first act of a play was about to begin. He accepted a coffee and ordered his hand to remain steady as he took an *alfajora* — caramel dulce de leche — sandwiched between two small crumbling cookies. If he ate, he'd throw up.

Rainer lowered himself with difficulty into the chair on the opposite side of the glass table and propped his can next to him.

"Did you have a good journey?" He asked in German

"*Ja, danke*. You speak such excellent German, Senor Monteflecha," he added, "I'm impressed."

"*Dankeshcön*. My mother's family was of German extraction. We were taught the language as children. I used to read a lot in German too, but alas, macular degeneration prevents me from doing so these days."

"I'm sorry. It must be a trial not to be able to appreciate your exquisite painting collection." Was it him carrying on this conversation, Carl wondered.

"It is, it is indeed," Rainer sighed. "Mercifully I am blessed with an excellent memory, or so my doctor tells me."

"Indeed?"

"*Ja*, but the truth is, Herr Löwen, I am no more a young man and time is catching up with me."

"How aptly put," Carl murmured. He took a sip of coffee. It tasted as bitter as his feelings.

Rainer made an elegant gesture with his left hand. "Nowadays I must content myself with memories. But you are here on business and I don't want to hold you up. A young man like yourself has better things to do in Buenos Aires than make conversation with an old man like me," he laughed. "Behold your Breughel," he said pointing above the fireplace. Please, inspect it as much as you like."

"Danke." Carl rose. As he did so, a ray of sunshine caught the signet ring on Rainer's pinky. Carl stood taught as a tightly strung bow. Surely it was identical to the one in Uncle Ephraim's lap, the one containing the poison that had killed him? His hand slipped inside his pocket and he pressed Manny's number. It rang once and he switched off, his eyes fixed on the old man. He tried to picture him and Ephraim as the two boys at Schloss Heil Father Florian had described.

He stepped towards the fireplace and pretended to inspect the painting. Was it a painting from his great-grandfather's collection or was it one of old Ben's fakes?

"Do you like it?" Rainer asked. "I shall be sad to see it go, but alas, the times require it." "It's impressive," Carl murmured. Where the heck was Manny and everyone else? How

long could he control himself?

"And tell me about Germany these days. It is many years since I've been back. I imagine it has changed a lot since my time," he sighed.

Carl spun around. Was the nostalgia not the final provocation? Where the fuck were they all? He glanced at the window. Had something gone array?

"You seem distracted, Herr Löwen." Rainer said.

"I'm imagining the painting in my villa in Munich, in Borghausen Park actually. That must bring back memories, *Oberst Sturmführer* Lanzberg," he cried. "Perhaps we could begin with the day you smashed your friend and my great uncle Eli Wolf's skull and arrested his father. The day you sent them to be tortured at Gestapo headquarters, then deported and murdered. The same day you robbed this very painting from their walls and you betrayed your false promise to Ephraim. Is that still clear in your mind?"

Rainer remained motionless.

"Ephraim," he murmured at last. "So you lot finally found me. I should have shipped him off with the others that day but I had too soft a heart."

"You mean too hard a dick, you bastard! You didn't arrest him or get rid of him because you were afraid that if you did, he'd rat on you and that you'd end up in an oven with your balls sown in your neck as you threatened Eli," Carl hissed.

"What did you come here for, should I say *Herr* Wolf?" To whine? It's thanks to me you're great Uncle stayed alive you unappreciative little *judesheisse.*

Carl shook. He wanted to throttle the man, but would not give in. He would see justice done.

A noise in the garden. A shout.

"So, you thought you'd get the better of me," he said. His hand shot out under the table. A flash of metal.

Carl lunged forward.

"Don't touch me you filthy Jew." He dragged his hand away. The door burst open. Rainer lifted his right hand.

"The Führer gave me this for such an occasion," he said pointing a Mauser pistol at Carl. He and Rainer's eyes locked.

"No!"

A voice from the door shouted.

A shot resounded. Something burned inside Carl's chest. His left side went numb. He grasped at Rainer's right hand.

Carl's last vision as he slumped across the desk was Rainer Lanzberg placing the pistol inside his mouth.

Chapter 52

Luna got off the phone with Rick Marchese and stared numbly past the tray of tea and scones on the coffee table in Tia Bella's suite. Carl. Dead. A bullet wedged deep in his heart. Carl, shot with a Mauser pistol, a collector's item; a gift from Hitler to the monster who'd pulled the trigger: the man who'd altered the course of all their destinies.

"Is something the matter?" Tia Bella asked.

"The arrest didn't go according to plan. Rainer shot Carl, then put the pistol in his own mouth and pulled the trigger."

"*Mein Gott!*" Tia Bella paled.

"I can't believe it. I talked to him three days ago. He was happy. He was going to Buenos Aires then to Oslo. He'd come to terms with the past and his own identity. He was ready to live, at last. What devastating irony is at work? What evil force has the power to ruin your and Nana and Eli and Aaron Wolf and the von Heil's lives and survive long enough to take Carl's as well? I don't understand what peculiar brand of paranoia causes a human being to act like this towards another because of his race, color, or beliefs."

"It's as if I'm seeing that night at Schloss Heil when Rainer murdered the Baron and his family all over again," Tia Bella whispered.

"It's horrible. All these years later and still the tumor festers. When will it end? Carl went there to seek closure. What a price to pay for demanding justice."

"Indeed. It is uncanny Rainer should have survived long enough to commit one last wicked act. But in a way, he was offered the chance."

"What do you mean?" Luna frowned and dropped in the armchair opposite. "Carl was simply acting as a means to capture Rainer, then hand him over to the authorities."

"But he and the others who participated in the operation did not respect the rules." "What do you mean? They were afraid Rainer would slip through their fingers."

"My dear child, how far would a ninety-six-year-old man in hiding have gotten? Even if he'd escaped they would have caught up with him quickly enough and charged him. The rule of law is what separates a democracy from a dictatorship, fascist or otherwise. It's possible Rainer would still have shot himself and not have gone on trial, that would have been unsatisfying to Carl and all of us seeking vindication. But sending out a posse and taking justice into their own hands only perpetuated more violence."

Luna was too upset to respond.

"I'm sorry to leave you Tia, but I have to go," she said, rising. "I must get back to the Angel House tonight and pack and fly home tomorrow. Maybe there's something I can still do for poor Carl."

"Go darling. But promise me you'll be back soon."

"Of course." Luna came and crouched next to the couch and took Tia Bella's hand in hers. For several seconds, they remained silent, each wrapped in their thoughts. Then she kissed the old lady's cheek and rose. "Carl's death makes me so mad," she said. "It brings home all that's happening in America. We fought a war against Hitler and fascism. Millions died to preserve our freedoms. We can't allow the rising tide of evil to go unchallenged in our own back yard."

Three hours later Luna was back at the Angel House seated with Rose, Lizzie and Sylvie around the kitchen table. The warmth and the wine, the Christmas candles on the wreath under the cherub chandelier and the friendship reminded her of Carl's holiday plans and all he'd never know.

"What about Father Florian?" She asked.

"He's staying upstairs tonight. He was deeply affected after your call. I told Nikolaj and Hubert and they're are on their way over. *Pauvre Carl*," Rose said, shaking her head. "I only met him on the day he came to see you and then with Nikolaj and Hubert to talk to Father Florian but he seemed a nice, sensitive man," she sighed, pouring the wine. "I'll prepare the fondue. It'll do us good to eat."

"It seems unbelievable, an old *merde* like that could still shoot someone. You'd think he'd have repented or someone would have gotten him by now," Sylvie remarked.

"I guess he went on believing his truth. He never saw the evil in what he'd done," Lizzie said.

"But couldn't Carl have grabbed the gun from him?" Sylvie insisted. "Likely he was so surprised he didn't react," Luna said.

"Or maybe he didn't think the gun was loaded," Lizzie added.

"What's even sadder is he'd finally come to terms with who he really and was and was about to get a life. He met a guy on the plane coming over here. They'd arranged to meet in Oslo for the holidays. It was the first time he'd escaped his Great-Uncle Ephraim's clutches and had a chance at real happiness." A sob caught in Luna's throat.

"And does the guy he met on the plane know that Carl died?" Lizzie asked.

"Maybe not. But his number must be on Carl's phone. I'll see about it and advise him when I'm back in New York."

"It'll be strange here without you. What time are you leaving tomorrow morning?" Rose asked.

"I have to check. My flight leaves sometime around noon."

"That story about the Wolf Collection still being hidden in the Schloss cellar is incredible," Lizzie said.

"I'm glad I was able to tell Carl about it. I must see Father Florian tomorrow before I go," Luna said. "Carl and I discussed the Schloss Heil Refugee center for the arts in our last conversation. It should be Carl's legacy, a step in the direction of a more integrated world."

It was 10pm by the time Luna said her goodbyes. Lizzie and she shared a tearful hug.

"*Oh la la*! I almost forgot," Sylvie exclaimed, plunging her hand inside her pink tote. "I have a gift for you."

"*Vraiment?* You shouldn't have. You already gave me the purple purse."

"It's nothing. I know you have everything, but I just thought..." Sylvie's voice trailed and she flushed as she handed Luna a package.

"May I?" Lizzie and Rose crowded around and Luna unwrapped the box and opened it. Inside was a collection of bright colored nail varnish.

"For your new life," Sylvie said gruffly.

"I love it! *Merci,*" Luna hugged her. She'd never ventured beyond a French manicurc. Maybc shc should dare to try something different?

It was time to go upstairs and pack. She kissed Nikolaj on the cheek and straightened his tie. "There," she said. "I've wanted to do that from the moment I met you."

Hubert hugged her. "It's been a *plaisir* meeting you, Luna. Promise us you'll be back soon? And don't worry. We'll take care of everything and make sure Carl's legacy is properly looked after. In fact, we're going to Munich tomorrow for the day to meet with the Schloss Heil lawyers."

"Thank you for everything," Luna said. "None of this has been easy for any of us and you've been wonderful. It's strange how we've all come together, it's as though their spirits wanted us to reunite," she said, pointing upwards. Imagine what it meant for Carl to stay in your home and sleep in the room his great grandfather did. And isn't is amazing Father Florian and Tia Bella's lives are crossing once more after all these years? He said he's going to visit her in Zurich the minute he's better. Or maybe she could come here to the Angel House?" Luna turned to Rose.

"Avec plaisir. I'll come up to the loft tomorrow morning and we can have breakfast together," she said in an aside.

Luna nodded.

"Thank you all for everything. And *à bientôt*!"

Upstairs in the loft Luna stood in the dark. Through the window a crescent moon sat like a cardboard cutout above the gnarled branches of the chestnut tree. The Chagall lay etched in the shadows on the couch where she'd left it. She'd return it to Father Florian tomorrow. Strange how she felt no regret, as though now its job was done she no longer needed proof of Nana's presence; her spirit was with her and always would be, wherever she went.

Her last night in the loft. Luna switched on the lamps and recalled the relief she'd experienced the first time she'd entered it. Was her time at the Angel House over or was there more to come? She glanced at her laptop on the table. The words had zipped from her fingers here as never before. It was a thought…

Early next morning Luna rose and packed her belongings in her roll on. She hadn't advised Maria of her return. She'd be upset with her of course, but it couldn't be helped. So many emotions in such a short time span could not be processed without a transition period, however brief. And she'd decided to give herself one: a few hours back home alone before picking up the reigns of her life.

At seven thirty the next morning, Rose, wearing a bright Indian scarf around her neck, stood before the door with a tray of fresh croissants, steaming coffee, and clotted cream and a pot of the homemade black-cherry jam Luna'd become addicted to in the past days.

"I'm taking two jars back with me in my luggage," Luna said. "You've done so much for me since I arrived here Rose. I don't know how I'll ever pay you back."

"It is not a debt, Luna. *C'est un plaisir*. You know you're welcome to come back and stay for as long as you like," she said, placing the tray on the ottoman. "Have you had time to think of what you're going to do? Once you're back in New York?" She asked, sitting next to the Chagall on the couch.

"Not really. Right now, I'm still coming to terms with the shock of Carl's death. I have to meet with the guy he named to replace him. I guess there will be a lot to take care of."

"And Christmas?"

"Honestly? I haven't the faintest idea."

"*Bon*. But make a plan. It can be a lonely time of year on your own." "Right now it's one day at a time."

Rose poured more coffee then got up. "Just a moment," she said, returning to the door. She opened it and stepped out, then reentered carrying a large square orange box.

"Oh my God!" Luna's hands flew to her mouth and she gasped. "*You* bought it!" "*Oui*. I kept it in custody for you."

Rose laid the Hermès box down on the coffee table next to the breakfast tray. "Open it," she said.

Luna's pulse leaped. Her first Birkin was back in her possession. She lifted the lid of the box the same way she had the first time, filled with expectation. As she withdrew the Birkin from the dust bag, her life since age sixteen flashed before her; a detailed synopsis of feelings, events and emotions.

She touched the handles and closed her eyes. She couldn't go back.

Taking a deep breath, she turned to Rose. "It's yours now," she said. "You bought it fair and square."

"*Mais non!* It is a dream purse and I've always wanted one but I only bought it to keep for you. You can buy it back *pas de problème*."

"Rose, I want you to have it. It's done its time with me. Tia Bella's right. I must buy a new purse and fill it with new memories—my memories. The memories *I* chose."

"Are you *certaine*?" Rose said doubtfully.

"One hundred and fifty percent. In fact, I'll pay you back and give it to you as a gift, how's that?"

"*Tu es folle*?" Rose laughed. "I'd never accept that."

"We'll discuss it later. In the meantime, the Birkin stays right here with you where it belongs." Luna plopped the purse in Rose's lap. "And now I'd better take my bag downstairs and return the Chagall Father Florian. I booked a car to the airport by the way, to give me more time before I leave."

Fifteen minutes later Luna knocked on the library door.

"Entrez."

Father Florian lay propped up in bed next to the bookcases. He waved as she entered the room.

"*Bonjour.*"

"*Bonjour, ma chère*. How lovely to see you even in the face of more sadness. Come here and sit next to me." Father Florian beckoned her over to the chair next to the bed.

"I brought the Chagall back," she said. Where should I put it?"

"Ah... Yes. The Chagall. Father Florian went silent. Luna waited. He seemed deep in thought.

"Should I prop it against the wall over there, perhaps" She said. "*Non.*"

Luna held the painting and shifted from one foot to the other. There were things to discuss and the car would be here soon. She couldn't linger too long.

"Bring it over here," Father Florian said at last.

Luna approached the bed. Father Florian reached for the picture. He stared at it several seconds, then handed it back to her. "It's yours. You were given a fake, but now you'll have the real one."

"But—"

"No *arguments*!" Father Florian lifted his right hand. "Now. Sit down and let me enjoy your company for a few minutes. I told you they found the key of the cellar I Eli's jacket pocket in the closet, didn't I?"

"Yes, you did. And the pictures were all there. It's amazing. I'm so glad I was able to tell Carl."

"So am I."

"He wanted the collection to be housed at Schloss Heil in your arts center for refugees, and in our last call we agreed the Banque Lourriel account would finance it. I'm sure Eli and Aaron would have wanted the money to help such a great project, aren't you?"

"Bless you both. Yes, Aaron and Eli would have liked that. It's a drop in the ocean, but maybe it will inspire others to follow suit."

Father Florian sat up straighter and reached on the nightstand for a small plastic bag. "The lawyers sent me this," he said.

"What is it?"

"There rest of the things that were in Eli's pocket. Here, take a look."

Luna sat on the chair beside the bed and pulled out the contents of the bag: a dried up candy, a gold lighter with the initials EW and a receipt. She unfolded it. It looked like an order from Hermès. Had Eli ordered another purse?" She frowned. "May I keep this?" She asked.

"If you like. It is very strange to see Eli's things again. And Bella. Dearest Bella. As soon as I'm well enough, I'll go to Zurich. We have a lifetime to catch up."

In the car Luna turned and looked out the rear window and waved back at Rose standing on the front steps. An aura of winter sunlight bathed The Angel House; haven preserved from the world, a place of passage, for body mind and soul.

She waved until the car turned out the gates and drove into the lane and Rose was no more than a speck and the château and the park a glistening frosted Christmas card.

She'd ended up here while in search of Nana's past. She was leaving to step into her own future.

Chapter 53

Luna had chosen Sunday to return to the Penthouse, a time she was certain Maria and Juan would be at church, then lunching at their nephews. She hadn't announced her arrival. She wanted time alone, something she'd never experienced in all the years she'd lived here.

The first thing that struck her as she stepped out the elevator and into the foyer was the baccarat vase filled with Nana's rigid roses and the patch on the wall where the fake Chagall used to hang.

Nothing had altered. But she had.

Luna slipped off her jacket and laid her case down on the marble floor, unzipped it and pulled out a plastic shopping bag from among folded jeans and sweaters, and withdrew the real Chagall. She rose and carried *The Girl in the Red Dress Under the*

Moon over to the glass console and eased it onto the hook on the wall above. She stood back and tilted her head. old Ben and Levi at the Wolf Gallery in the Briennerstrasse had done their job down to the last detail; even the wires on the back of the frames of the real and the fake Chagall matched, and the painting hung to perfection.

Here, in the brightly lit foyer, the subtle differences between Chagall's and old Ben's brushstrokes were visible. The depth of color in the carmine pigment of the girl's dress, the trance-like expression of the violinist and the dazed eyes of the flying goat went from two to three-dimensional. She'd spent hours in this spot searching for a crutch, a banister on which to lean as she mounted the spinning platform of Countess Carolina's carousel of dreams, her ticket, a scrap of scribbled paper and a withered cigar, her bags packed with doubts and false hope. But the organ ground to a halt. The girls in white dresses and pink satin sashes wore sackcloth and their hair was shorn. Men in black uniforms and women in silver fox stoles carrying fine leather purses filled with secrets pushed them through the fairground gates under wrought iron letters: *Arbeit Macht Frei.*

"Welcome to the real world," Luna said.

The girl in the red dress smiled. Of course she'd smiled. There was no room left for fakeness left in her life either.

Luna didn't tarry. The Chagall — hidden under a bushel of secrets for nigh on a century — was not an antenna any longer, but an exquisite work of art. Now it could go back to doing what it did best: inspire the eye of the beholder.

Leaving the case half-open before the elevator, Luna moved down the corridor and entered the kitchen. The General yawned in his basket, then padded over to greet her. She crouched down and stroked him behind the ears and smiled at the refrigerator door plastered with postcards of Colombia and Maria and Juan's family held in place with tropical fruit magnets. Would Maria throw a fit if she grabbed a snack? To hell with that! It was her home, damn it! Surely she could eat, drink and sleep whenever she wanted?

But could she? Would Nana's ghost backed by Maria haunt her every step from now on? No way. She'd flown this cuckoo's nest. She'd bought groceries. She'd made coffee and fixed her own salad the way *she* wanted it. She'd eaten with stainless steel not silver. She'd munched crêpes and drunk mulled wine at stands in Fribourg market. She'd laughed and cried and said 'fuck'. And more, much more than this — as old blue eyes sang — she'd done it *her* way.

She couldn't go back. But she was back. So, how was she going to go forward?

Luna opened the cupboard doors. How ridiculous did it get? She didn't know where the snacks were kept in her own kitchen. After some rummaging, she came across a box: *A nutritious blend of wholesome organic whole grain cookies.*

"Come on, boy, we're out of here," she told the General.

In the passage, she looked from left to right debating whether to head to Nana's room or Henry's study. She'd had a flash of inspiration on the plane. She knew now what purpose Nana's designer wardrobe should fulfill. She'd create an organization for women who'd fallen on bad times, seeking to reinstate themselves in the workplace. She'd outfit them appropriately for high- end interviews, boost their self-esteem and help them land the job.

She glanced at her watch. She had a few hours still before Maria and Juan's return.

She headed towards Henry's study with the General in tow. At the door, she stopped and opened the packet of cookies. She removed one and took a bite. Crumbs fell on the polished marble floor. The General sniffed and licked them up. Maria wouldn't notice.

She opened the door. Bright daylight penetrated the French windows leading out to the terrace. Luna switched the lamps on anyway and leaned against the door jamb. Cigar smoke lingered. Cluttered books and magazines. Hunting prints. Henry's sailing trophies stood exactly as they had since he'd moved here in the 1950s. Henry Hampton III was buried six feet under in Arlington Cemetery but his presence dominated the room. Was she ready to clear the decks?

Luna noticed Henry's old briefcase standing upright on the desk. She stepped across the room and picked up a note lying next to it:

Luna, I left Henry's personal briefcase for you to go through yourself. Call me when you get back.

Carl

Tears sprung to her eyes. She sat down with a bang in the swivel chair. Just how unfair was it Carl had suffered the fate of his ancestors at the hands of the same executioner's Mauser?

The note shook in her hand. Raw, unadulterated anger crumbled between her fingers. She opened her palm. This was not the way the cookie should have crumbled.

Was she at risk of taking a bullet in the chest too? It was time to clean the barrel of the Gatlin; clear out the two hundred cartridges of memories ready to pierce her heart and start afresh.

Luna wiped her hands, then her eyes. Surely she'd wiped them more during these weeks than her entire life, but that did not include the first four years with Charlotte of which she remembered nothing.

It was two in the afternoon. Too early for a drink. But what the hell? She needed one. Luna stepped over to the wet bar and filled a glass with ice and poured herself a vodka tonic, then sat down once more at the desk. She took a long sip and let it take effect before pressing her thumbs on the rickety brass locks of the briefcase. It took two tries before they gave, wearily, as though they too were tired.

She pulled up the lid. Papers, Henry's passport, a gold Dunhill cigarette lighter and a pack of Marlboros. So, Henry smoked behind Nana's back?

The thought of him hastily taking a puff before getting inside the elevator made her smile. Darling Henry. How she missed him. But no. She'd promised herself she wouldn't go there.

She spread the rest of the items in the briefcase out on the desk: a pair of worn leather gloves, his membership to the Yale Club — she must cancel that — a couple of envelopes with receipts for Susan to send to accounting, a paper knife and a small blood stone tucked in the corner at the bottom of the lid pocket. Luna held it up. Had he kept it there for good luck?

At the bottom of the briefcase a large photo frame lay face-down. She pulled it out and turned it over. A girl with a sad smile and big eyes stared back at her…

~

… *Me me me And you you you*

God only knows it's not what we would choose to do…

Hair, long blond strands falling from the gurney almost to the ground… Blue uniforms and a big white ball shining through the shattered window.

… *I'll see you on the dark side of the moon.*

~

There was still much for her to understand. But all in good time.

Luna stood by the window holding the frame and stared into Charlotte's eyes. She raised the photo to her lips. "Goodbye," she whispered.

Her mother had chosen to walk on the dark side. But from now on, Luna planned to walk on the bright side of a moon that shed light and showed the way.

Luna stood Charlotte's photograph on the lowboy next to the French door leading to the terrace. The need for neediness was gone. It was three weeks since she'd opened the *Sac à Dépèches* and left for Europe in search of Nana. Officially, it took twenty-one years to go from birth to adulthood. Had she fast tracked the process in twenty-one days? She wouldn't rush into anything or take major decisions before she was ready; there were still tears to be shed before plunging headlong into the present.

Henry's cardigan lay folded on the chair next to the window. Luna slipped it on, opened the French doors and stepped out onto the terrace. Would the sky be as blue and the sun shine as liberally once the new administration took office? Or would rising political temperatures cloud the horizon?

Luna looked up. High above, two planes like silver bullets intersected leaving a St. Andrews cross in their wake. Was she ready to fly that high and that far? She stepped up to the balustrade and peered over. Three floors below a man with earphones swayed back and forth on the scaffolding as he cleaned the windows. He looked up and smiled. She smiled back. He took the earphones off and turned up the volume: *living la vida loca…*

Her phone rang. Luna turned. At the door, she looked back. The planes were gone and the trails remained. She let the phone ring and watched the trails merge into a question mark.

A sign? Luna stepped back inside.

It was early days and living *la vida loca* was not up there on her agenda… yet.

She glanced at the ringing phone. Rick Marchese's name flashed on the screensaver. It was time to take the call.

THE END

FIONA HOOD-STEWART is the author of several bestselling novels, including *The Journey Home* and *The Stolen Years*, translated into thirty languages. She has studied and lived in many parts of the world. Today she lives and writes in Switzerland.

Printed in Poland
by Amazon Fulfillment
Poland Sp. z o.o., Wrocław